STEEL TREAD

More tales of the Astra Militarum from Black Library

VOLPONE GLORY
A novel by Nick Kyme

KRIEG
A novel by Steve Lyons

CADIA STANDS
A novel by Justin D Hill

CADIAN HONOUR
A novel by Justin D Hill

TRAITOR ROCK
A novel by Justin D Hill

HONOURBOUND
A novel by Rachel Harrison

THE LAST CHANCERS: ARMAGEDDON SAINT
A novel by Gav Thorpe

SHADOWSWORD
A novel by Guy Haley

BANEBLADE
A novel by Guy Haley

IRON RESOLVE
A novella by Steve Lyons

STEEL DAEMON
A novella by Ian St. Martin

YARRICK
An omnibus edition of the novels *Imperial Creed, The Pyres
of Armageddon,* the novella *Chains of Golgotha* and several
short stories by David Annandale

GAUNT'S GHOSTS: THE FOUNDING
An omnibus edition of the novels *First and Only, Ghostmaker*
and *Necropolis* by Dan Abnett

STEEL TREAD
AN ASTRA MILITARUM NOVEL

ANDY CLARK

BLACK LIBRARY

A BLACK LIBRARY PUBLICATION

First published in 2021.
This edition published in Great Britain in 2022 by
Black Library, Games Workshop Ltd., Willow Road,
Nottingham, NG7 2WS, UK.

Represented by: Games Workshop Limited – Irish branch,
Unit 3, Lower Liffey Street, Dublin 1,
D01 K199, Ireland.

10 9 8 7 6 5 4 3 2

Produced by Games Workshop in Nottingham.
Cover illustration by Manuel Castañón.

See Black Library on the internet at

blacklibrary.com

Find out more about Games Workshop
and the worlds of Warhammer at

games-workshop.com

Printed and bound by CPI Group (UK) Ltd, Croydon, CR0 4YY

---

*Dedicated to my fellow retail staff of Games Workshop Reading during the
glory days! If you were there, you know, and you're all legends…*

For more than a hundred centuries the Emperor has sat immobile on the Golden Throne of Earth. He is the Master of Mankind. By the might of His inexhaustible armies a million worlds stand against the dark.

Yet, He is a rotting carcass, the Carrion Lord of the Imperium held in life by marvels from the Dark Age of Technology and the thousand souls sacrificed each day so that His may continue to burn.

To be a man in such times is to be one amongst untold billions. It is to live in the cruellest and most bloody regime imaginable. It is to suffer an eternity of carnage and slaughter. It is to have cries of anguish and sorrow drowned by the thirsting laughter of dark gods.

This is a dark and terrible era where you will find little comfort or hope. Forget the power of technology and science. Forget the promise of progress and advancement. Forget any notion of common humanity or compassion.

There is no peace amongst the stars, for in the grim darkness of the far future, there is only war.

PROLOGUE

Hadeya Etsul gritted her teeth behind her rebreather mask as smoke and heat haze danced about her. Gunfire poured down on her tank from the walls of the ravine, bullets rattling against the hull like driven hail. Fear and panic fought to master her, but Etsul thrust them to the back of her mind. She had her duties. Death would have to wait.

'The Emperor protects,' she told herself, then bit back a yelp as *Oathkeeper* rang like a struck bell. The Leman Russ tilted with the force of impact before settling back on the steel coils of its suspension.

'Damage report.' Commander Masenwe's voice was calm, projected over the vox from his bucket seat above and behind Etsul's gunnery station as little more than a static-laced whisper through her headset.

'Keep your mind on what's before you.'

It had been a favourite saying of her mother's, one of many

Etsul still heard as clearly as though the woman stood behind her. Normally that sensation of connection made her feel by turns comforted or forlorn. Here, now, it brought the creeping sensation that her mother's shade lurked close by. The idea was incongruous, a nonsense, yet it sank its teeth in and wouldn't let go. Etsul felt the icy touch of imagined breath upon her nape and pictured her mother waiting to welcome her through the veil.

The hair rose on Etsul's neck and her skin prickled. She shook her head and spat a curse into the plastek muzzle of her rebreather.

'Throne alive, pull yourself together,' she breathed.

'Vesko, damage report?' Commander Masenwe repeated. This time his words came to Etsul more clearly. She shot a glance through smoke and firelight, to where Yvgan Vesko occupied the driver's station. Like her, the big man sat on a fold-out seat of plasteel and flakfoam. Sweat slicked his bald pate. Drops had gathered in his eyebrows and Etsul watched them clinging to hair, defying gravity.

'Hit to right flank armour, directed explosive, but she's holding, sir,' said Vesko. She saw his jaw move behind his rebreather as his mouth formed the words, but with the tank's power plant roaring and enemy fire hammering the hull, she heard them only through the yox headset clamped over her ears.

'*Oathkeeper* wouldn't let us down,' Masenwe replied. 'Maintain combat speed and stay close on Commander Lethwan's tail. Only two hundred yards to the end of the canyon, then we'll make the Emperor proud!'

Masenwe's calm did not reassure Etsul. Heat washed over her as though she stood too near an open furnace door. Smoke coiled about her, alarmingly thick and dark. She could taste it, overpowering her mask, worming in. Etsul's chest hitched, and she stifled a coughing fit.

Their loader, Osk, was supposed to be extinguishing the fire in the bowels of the tank, but he hadn't spoken for what felt like hours.

Etsul wanted to look back and check on him.

Fear of what might meet her eyes held her rigid at her station.

Today is the day we die.

The thought startled Etsul. It felt alien, an intrusion. She screwed her eyes tight shut and felt sweat trickle over the scrunched-up lids. She grubbed it away with the back of one fist then opened them again on firelight and smoke. The tank shuddered as it bulled along the canyon's rubble-strewn floor. Etsul had to look back, to see what had become of Osk, to check whether the fire was about to ignite her tank suit or touch off their shell magazine.

She didn't.

Couldn't.

'Etsul, target one-hundred-twenty yards ahead, fifty degrees right, elevation twenty degrees, confirm?'

Masenwe's voice broke her paralysis. Etsul applied herself to her instruments, checking *Oathkeeper's* glowing auspex screen then pressing her eyes to the rubberised viewing scope. The tank jolted, mashing her face hard against the hot metal and plastek. She hissed with pain. Eyes watering, she tried to focus on the juddering blur before her. She caught snatches of dark ferrocrete rushing past to either side, canyon walls studded with the dark hollows of windows like eyes. Watercolour smudges of green showed where Croatoas' verdant undergrowth was reclaiming the ruins. Above the ravine was a strip of open sky turned bruise purple and umber by twilight. All around were the enemy, too many to count, too swift to focus on. Etsul made out humanoid silhouettes. Their outlines were distorted. Spurs and deformations rendered them nightmarish. Her one fixed point was Commander Lethwan's tank, *Restitution in Blood*, just ahead of them. Unlike *Oathkeeper*, *Restitution* had side sponsons. The terrain was so close they struck sparks from out-thrust chunks of rubble as the tank charged for the canyon's end.

'Gunnery Sergeant Etsul, do you have the target?' snapped Masenwe. She blinked, gasped, tried again. Still, she couldn't focus. The harder Etsul tried, the more sluggish her thoughts became.

'I… Commander, I don't…'

Restitution in Blood transformed from a speeding tank to an expanding fireball.

Vesko yelled through the vox and tried to rein *Oathkeeper* in. Leman Russ battle tanks might not be the fastest vehicles, but they could stop quickly and were almost balletic when manoeuvring. Yet in his eagerness to escape the trap, Vesko had left too narrow a gap, and the collision came regardless.

Etsul's head hit metal.

She sprawled between her seat and Vesko's, fire-heat raking her flesh.

Then came a violent cacophony. Rapid metallic clangs, the wasp-whine of ricochets, a sound like tenderisers thudding against meat in her father's abattoir back on Tsegoh. Something hot and wet splashed her face.

Etsul felt boneless, weak as a fever victim. She tried to stand. She pressed her palms to the hot metal of the deck and sought to push herself upright but could not. Etsul slumped and turned to see Osk's limp form sprawled amidst the flames filling *Oathkeeper*'s belly. Fire danced gleefully over his corpse.

Etsul dragged her eyes away. Beside her, Vesko leant against a stowage box. His gaze was unfocused. Blood drizzled from a cut on his scalp.

Etsul forced her head up, feeling as though she were deep underwater. And truly, she realised, her face was wet, but the liquid felt too warm to be the ocean. Commander Masenwe was slumped in his chair, limbs dangling like a doll's, blood running in rivulets down his arms and drizzling onto Etsul from his crooked fingers. The turret was a ragged mess of bullet holes. So was her commander.

A detached part of Etsul's mind noted that it would have taken an autocannon, or something even heavier, to inflict that sort of damage on a Leman Russ. She pictured hordes of mutants closing in around *Oathkeeper*, preparing to peel the machine open and drag her and Vesko out like morsels of meat scooped from a ruptured shellfish.

'We have to get out of here,' she croaked. Realising her mistake, she activated her vox-mic. 'Vesko, we have to get out of here! Can you drive?'

Etsul shook him by the shoulder until he looked up. She felt a spark of relief at the recognition in his eyes.

'Vesko, we need to go! Now!'

He nodded with renewed purpose, bending over his station while Etsul tried to calm her breath and turned to her own. As gunnery sergeant, she was the Leman Russ' second-in-command. Masenwe's burden now lay upon her shoulders. He had left her in charge of a burning tank, trapped prow-deep in wreckage and surrounded by foes.

'Worry what is, let the rest go,' Etsul told herself.

Another of her mother's sayings. They just had to clear

the ravine before the fire consumed them. If they could manage that then maybe they could bail out and escape the enemy.

Somehow.

Etsul grabbed her controls, only to snatch her hands back as searing heat tore up her arms. She looked at her palms. They were scorched raw. It didn't seem possible that the fire could have heated the metal of the tank's interior to such a degree without consuming her and Vesko both.

Today is the day we die.

This time it was a whisper in her ear, the breath of a gheist.

Etsul turned to face Vesko and saw he was shouting. His eyes bulged with fear.

She tried to issue her orders, but it was as though her rebreather had melted to her flesh. She couldn't speak through its cloying mass. Blood pattered down, a carmine baptism of her short-lived command. Flames licked about Etsul, dancing over her clothes, her skin. The enemy were right outside the tank. She saw them in her mind's eye, pressed against the white-hot plasteel of the hull, flesh sizzling, fat spitting like meat on a griddle as they heaved inwards from every side.

Oathkeeper gave a terrible groan, a submersible gone too deep. Etsul cast about for escape. She saw nothing but flames and smoke. She imagined the venerable tank's machine-spirit straining to resist the mass of bubbling flesh squeezing ever tighter.

'I know you'll make us proud...' came her mother's voice from deep within the inferno.

Oathkeeper's hull gave way.

Hadeya Etsul screamed.

* * *

She jolted awake with a grunt. One hand was halfway to the laspistol at her hip before she remembered where she was. She felt the reassuring solidity of the restraint throne into which she was belted, heard the basso roar of the Valkyrie's engines as it soared over the Mandriga Delta. Etsul's redeployment orders were a hard knot of folded parchment stuffed into her breast pocket. She didn't need to check them to recall what they said. She'd read and reread them enough times, but they never relayed anything different, no matter what she might wish.

She was to report to Mandriga command. She was to take command of her own tank. She was to do so effective immediately.

Etsul eased back, clenching and unclenching her hands unconsciously. Her palms still tingled as though they'd just been burned, yet the layers of synthskin looked fresh and unhurt.

Her seat was one of five on the rear wall of the troop bay. Five more faced it. Only a handful of the thrones were occupied, by Etsul and a few other officers of the Astra Militarum. Besides them, a pair of troopers manned door guns that jutted from the Valkyrie's open flanks. Their flak coats billowed in the wind. Their helm visors glinted in the bruised light of Croatoas' sun.

She tried to gauge if anyone had noticed her discomfort. Being consolidated into a Cadian regiment was daunting enough without making a poor first impression.

The two gunners had their backs to her. They watched the skies, and the ruins and mangrove swamps that rolled past below. One of the passengers, a Geskan judging by his neck tattoos, was snoring. The other two were awake. Etsul could see by his violet-tinged irises that one was Cadian born.

He had a shock of close-cropped white hair and a captain's insignia on his uniform. His eyes lingered on her then flicked away in apparent disinterest.

The other passenger's cyan uniform and elaborate brocade marked him as hailing from the Maesmoch Clanguard. His skin and eyes were even darker than her own. Where Etsul buzz-cut her hair to stubble, the Maesmochan wore his in elaborate braids. He offered her a sympathetic smile and tapped his vox headset. She took his meaning and keyed her own, allowing him to speak to her over the howl of the gunship's engines.

'Lieutenant Horathio Aswold, Maesmoch Seven-Seventieth,' he said, then winced. 'Cadian Forty-Ninth, sorry. I am not used to that yet.'

'Lieutenant Hadeya Etsul,' she replied. 'You're consolidating too?'

'By the grace of the Emperor I have that honour.'

'You're still wearing your old uniform.'

He glanced down at himself then grinned at her.

'Sentimental, I know, but I'm giving it one last outing. I have commanded three different tanks in the colours of my home world, and that begs a little commemoration. Let the Emperor witness me in the uniform one last time. Let Him know that as a Maesmochan I was glorious.'

Etsul chuckled despite herself. She had left her own Tsegohan fatigues in the barracks back at Helbor, folded crisply despite the bloodstains that had ruined them. Presumably, they had been incinerated by now.

Her faint smile died.

Something of her thoughts must have shown on her face. Aswold's expression grew serious.

'Hadeya Etsul, was it? I heard about that business in Yarroe Canyon. How did you get your tank out of that ambush?'

'The canyon, yes,' said Etsul, grimacing as she stilled her hands mid-clench. 'We fought our way out.'

Aswold watched her expectantly. When she did not continue, he held up his hands.

'My apologies, lieutenant. You can take the lad out of the family commune, but never the reverse it seems. I am too used to everyone's business being mine and vice versa. But for what it is worth, I think what you did was heroic. Commander dead, squadron cut to pieces, a hundred or so heretics raining death on your position and you still got your tank out of there!'

Etsul was surprised to see that spark light his eyes again.

'It has been a week of debriefings, medicae tents, prayers and miserable farewells,' she said, trying to keep the bitterness from her voice. 'The squadron got cut to pieces, and we made it out with our tail between our legs.'

'You extracted a valuable war engine from an impossible situation, and scored four armour kills into the bargain, from what I read,' Aswold countered.

'I lost Commander Masenwe.'

'He was dear to you?'

'He was my commander, and I trusted him,' Etsul replied sharply. Aswold's expression became grave, the mask of youthful excitement set aside.

'I read the after-action report on Yarroe Canyon just last night,' he said. Seeing her brows draw down, he held up a forestalling hand. 'Not just you, I inloaded every file I had clearance for on the commanders of Eleventh Company. I am a thorough man. I like to know who I am fighting alongside.'

Etsul felt a stab of concern. She had been too busy even to consider that she now had clearance to do such a thing.

She realised that Aswold was still speaking.

'You did well, Lieutenant Etsul, though you hardly need my validation. You have the Emperor's, and that is all any of us needs. I am glad to fight alongside you.'

Etsul's hands twitched. She made a point not to inspect her tingling palms.

She was saved from finding a reply by a squawk of static. A brass-chased human skull was set above the door to the cockpit, its eye sockets home to lumen bulbs and jaws stuffed with a vox-grille. Etsul had assumed when she boarded that the relic was the remains of some favoured pilot.

'Two minutes to Mandriga command,' the co-pilot's voice blared through the vox-grille. *'Secure and brace. Prepare for combat landing, this is a potential hot zone. The Emperor protects.'*

'The Emperor protects,' echoed Etsul automatically, making the sign of the aquila. Aswold and the Cadian captain did likewise, and all three held on to their restraint straps as the Valkyrie's engines screamed. The aircraft banked, affording Etsul a view of fortifications and trenches amidst the marshes below. People swarmed around the site. Olive-green tents formed neat rows across what had once been an industrial lot. Armoured vehicles rumbled along a crumbling transitway raised on thick ferrocrete columns. Imperial banners flew from smokestacks above vine-choked rockcrete ruins.

Duty waited for her below.

She was a Cadian now.

Etsul felt her chest tighten. There'd been no time to drill with her new regiment, no time for cultural reorientation or command induction. She hadn't even sworn fresh oaths, for Throne's sakes!

I know you'll make us proud.

Her palms tingled. Hadeya Etsul squared her shoulders and scowled in silent agreement.

ACT ONE

JOTUNN

CHAPTER ONE

THE LINE

The Salamander was a light armoured vehicle, often employed for scouting purposes, or to ferry officers around hostile warzones. As with so many enduring Imperial technologies, its design leaned upon rugged simplicity. Salamanders were built for speed and resilience.

They were not, reflected Etsul, made for comfort.

She was crammed onto the Salamander's open-topped fighting platform along with the tattooed Geskan, Lieutenant Aswold, three Cadian infantry officers and all their kitbags. Adding to the press were the Salamander's commander, its gunner and a robed Munitorum adept. He had introduced himself as Umboldt while herding them aboard their transport back at Mandriga command. He had not spoken since, and clung to a grab rail with an intensity that bespoke either annoyance or fear.

Aswold had made some attempts at conversation, but Etsul fended them away. She hung on near the rear of the vehicle's troop bay, and fell back upon a calming technique Commander Masenwe had taught his crew.

'Widen your focus,' he had always said. 'Observe the world around you. Anchor yourself in its details. Tally patterns or coloured objects, it sometimes helps. It's no bad thing to glue your eyes to your targeter, but be sure to look up at the wider battle once in a while.'

Etsul started with the sky. It looked bruised today, blue and amber swirling like milk stirred into recaff. She counted five distinct rafts of cloud coiling across the heavens. They diffused the light of Croatoas' star and made it possible to look skyward without risking a poisonous glimpse of the Rift.

Unwilling to look long upon that void-borne wound, she hastily turned her attention to the landscape. The Salamander rumbled along a raised transitway, which must once have carried macro haulers between industrial complexes. It was held high on ferrocrete pillars. Beneath, all was mud, stream and thicket.

The transitway had not escaped unharmed. Lianas thicker than Etsul's forearm had grown over the road's saviour rails. Plants had sunk their roots into ferrocrete, prising it apart. She counted several blackened patches where flamer teams had burned the rapacious growth, and even the freshest bore signs of the flora of Croatoas returning with obscene vigour.

Other vehicles used the roadway. Several Taurox transports rumbled past, and Etsul saw the caduceus of the medicae blazoned on them. A squadron of quad-wheeled Geskan scout bikes overtook them and roared into the distance.

'Those warquads are fine vehicles for traversing troublesome terrain,' commented Aswold. 'One assumes this stretch of the front will be just as troublesome as where we've come from.'

Etsul grunted in response. A roadblock appeared ahead, all sandbag redoubts and emplaced heavy stubbers. Cadian soldiers manned it, alert despite the lack of obvious threats.

Raised barriers allowed traffic through the blockade. Their Salamander joined a queue of vehicles being checked by a pair of Guardsmen with data-slates. Servo-skulls buzzed overhead, playing auspex lenses across waiting vehicles and their passengers. Speakers on fold-out legs blared prayers over the chug of their portable generatoria.

The Salamander reached the front of the queue. Umboldt exchanged words with a Cadian gate guard. He tapped his data-slate, she hers, then she waved them on.

'Impressive organisation,' Aswold said. 'Keeping track of every vehicle moving along this roadway, even in an active warzone. Maintaining a data-schedule for them all. Cadians do things properly.'

'It isn't just data-keeping they have a reputation for, Aswold,' Etsul replied.

She turned away and craned out over the Salamander's left track. The wind whipped around her, bringing the smells of swampland, salt water and smoke, and underneath them a sinister sweetness she knew well. It was the smell of death borne on the winds of war.

Resuming her exercise, Etsul looked down upon the swamplands. Below the nodding fronds of guasa trees were Cadian and Geskan soldiers, knee-deep in mud, slogging their way through a half-built line of flakboard trenches with arms full of supplies. Etsul grimaced. Her home planet, Tsegoh, was a damp agri-world with high-yield protein farms clinging to ridges of land jutting into its oceans. She knew how the wet got into everything, how the mud clung, and how disease would burn through the workforce like wildfire.

Etsul was perversely pleased to find that, even after Yarroe Canyon, she still longed for the confines of a tank over the dubious freedoms of the footslogger.

The Salamander slowed. Etsul gripped her grab rail and adjusted the heavy kitbag on her shoulder with a grimace.

'I believe this is our exit,' said Aswold. The Salamander plunged down an off-ramp, descending into more overgrown industrial ruins. As fronds and boughs whipped past, Etsul breathed deeply. She had been lulled by the rhythm of the journey, the temporary release from responsibility that came with being a passenger. Now the spell was broken. Giving up on her calming ritual, she ran through the names of her crew, muttering them to herself like a mantra. It didn't do to forget such things, and repetition was the ally of memory, as they taught in basic training.

Rhus Vaslav, gunner, sergeant, Cadian.

Isaac Trieve, driver, Brethian.

Erika Moretzin, loader, Cadian.

Nix Chalenboor, sponson gunner, Dakturian.

Garret Verro, sponson gunner, Cadian.

And then there was the tank itself, *Steel Tread*, an Agamemnor-pattern Leman Russ Demolisher. According to her briefing slate the vehicle had seen centuries of warfare. *Oathkeeper*, by comparison, had been practically new, rolled off the forge lines barely three years ago. Its machine-spirit had been fierce and eager.

Etsul wondered what sort of spirit inhabited an ancient war engine like *Steel Tread*. She had worked with older tanks before. One had struck her as wise and protective, but others had tended towards bestial savagery, steeped in centuries of spilt blood.

Etsul would have liked to go over the vehicle's specifications again. Many systems were unfamiliar. Crammed in as she was, though, and unsure of how soon they might stop, she didn't dare unsling her bag to rummage for her data-slate. She sighed and rolled her shoulders as best she could. There were entire inloads of Cadian strategic procedures and battle-field jargon she'd barely had time to absorb.

Etsul resigned herself to learning on the job. At least she knew her way around the inside of a tank well enough.

The transitway reached ground level. It carried them on through thickets and between tidal estuaries, then abruptly into an industrial belt. Buildings soared skyward, hollowed by war. Their flanks slumped amidst vomited spills of brick-work. Empty windows stared down upon her. Pipes wider than the Salamander ran alongside the roadway and formed rusting arches under which they passed. Nests of thorned vines and plants with vibrant red flower spikes grew every-where, boiling up from within ruined buildings like guts from an opened belly.

Etsul saw bullet holes and shell craters.

Clouds of biting insects thrummed through the air, thick as mist.

The smell of putrefaction grew stronger.

'Was not always like this,' murmured Aswold. 'Croatoas used to be a bustling industrial world. Tens of billions of good, Emperor-fearing folk.'

Etsul knew this. Even the densest soldier of the Coronal Crusade had some knowledge of the planet for which they fought.

'It was the darkness that changed things, after the Rift opened,' she said. 'Something dreadful happened to the people, the cities...'

'Not to mention the plant life, the weather, and whatever else you care to note,' Aswold agreed.

'And then we came, the Coronal Crusade, here to reclaim Croatoas as the God-Emperor willed.'

'So the Commissariat and the priests tell us,' replied Aswold, careful to keep his voice low.

Etsul glanced a sharp question his way. Aswold shrugged.

'Better to go to war in His name and thus find purpose, than to sit becalmed in the void wondering where the tides of the immaterium have hurled you and what has become of the Emperor's realm, no?'

'I don't need anyone to tell me why I should kill heretics,' said Etsul. 'Hate is reason enough.'

Aswold gave her an appraising look. 'I might say, hatred and faith, one informing the other.'

Now it was Etsul's turn to shrug. 'Either is better than fear.'

Their conversation was broken by thunder. She jumped and reached again for her sidearm. Those around her ducked instinctively, except Umboldt.

'Mobile Imperial artillery engaging in speculative suppression,' he shouted, straining to be heard over the booms rolling from all around. As they crossed a junction, Etsul spied a trio of Basilisks, their long barrels elevated, their crews hastening to load fresh shells. The muzzle of the nearest gun spat fire, rocking the vehicle back on its treads. Then the Salamander was past, and forging on towards the gap of daylight at the end of the processional.

'Is there a battle in progress?' Aswold asked. 'Should we be ready for combat?'

'There are frequent attacks. The heretics dash themselves against the Mandriga Line like wild beasts,' sneered Umboldt. 'Fear not. You shan't have to fight them today.'

'None of *us* is afraid of a fight, quill-pusher,' replied Aswold. Umboldt scowled. One corner of Etsul's mouth quirked in a half-smile.

The Salamander left the shadow of the ruins. The transit-way became a rutted dirt road. The tank banged and lurched as it passed over plasteel plates laid down, Etsul presumed, to prevent the route from being churned to a mire. Islands of foliage rose to either side amidst broad streams and a network of trenches and bunkers. Imperial Guard soldiery were everywhere, packing the trenches, running messages or out on patrol. The Salamander passed communication dugouts and mortar pits veiled by screens of flakboard and cameleo-line. Etsul saw towers for artillery spotters jutting proud of the marshes. Here and there squatted platforms mounting anti-aircraft cannons.

'We're close,' she said to Aswold.

'Have you thought the thoughts that needed thinking?' he asked her. The words had the cadence of a saying.

She eyed him.

He returned his bright and guileless smile.

'As it happens, I have, despite your chatter.'

'Forgive me,' he said. 'If words earned the Emperor's grace, I would be a saint by now.'

'Some words do,' she said.

'Rarely my chatter, Hadeya,' he replied, and Etsul snorted a laugh.

'Are those turrets ahead?' she asked, pointing. As the shapes resolved, Aswold's smile broadened.

'I believe those are our tanks.'

She saw he was right. There were Leman Russ battle tanks of various patterns dotted amongst the trenches, painted Cadian green. On each was displayed a stylised hammer design, haloed in flame. Etsul's eye had been fooled by the redoubts of packed earth and flakboard around each vehicle. These weren't gun turrets. Rather, the tanks had been dug in so that they could serve as such.

'If they've emplaced our tanks, then the tides of war must move sluggishly here,' she said.

Beyond the tanks and trenches sprawled a half-drowned no-man's-land of rubble, greenery and the remains of drowned roadways littered with wreckage. Smoke rose in the distance, tattering into the wind. Etsul thought of the Basilisks and their 'speculative suppressing fire'. She hoped those dark plumes marked fresh enemy dead.

The Salamander wheeled off the road and came to a halt. Its power plant cut out, leaving Etsul's ears ringing. This tinnitus slowly gave way to the sounds of the front line: murmured conversations; shouts, and barked orders, and prayer; the rumble of engines; the crackle of cook-fires and the tinny squawk of voices through vox-sets. Artillery fire thumped in the distance. She smelled meat cooking and the funk of hundreds of unwashed bodies. Stronger than ever was the sweet tang of death. It crept from the swamps, and no amount of fortifications could hold it back.

Umboldt flourished his data-slate.

'Officers of the Astra Militarum, please confirm your belonging to the following regiments. Cadian Eight-Hundred and Thirty-Second Heavy Infantry. Cadian Forty-Ninth Armoured. Geskan Forty-Third Light Infa–'

'No one calls us that,' rasped the Geskan.

'What?'

'We're the Trenchrunners. They're the Dauntless Eight Thirty-Two, and they're the Hammers.'

'Whatever nicknames the common soldiery bandy about

is of no interest to the Departmento Munitorum,' sniffed Umboldt, words as clipped as cogitator keystrokes. 'You will all confirm at this time that you belong to or are being transferred to one of the regiments aforementioned.'

'I believe we can all confirm that, yes?' asked Aswold. There were murmurs of assent. The Geskan bristled and spat off the side of the tank.

Umboldt stared expectantly.

'Throne's sake. Yes,' snarled the Geskan.

Umboldt nodded in satisfaction and tapped at his dataslate.

The device chimed.

'Oh, data-spirit of knowledge, we offer you this day our thanks for your continued guidance and thrice-blessed autopedantry,' he intoned solemnly, before returning his gaze to the gathered soldiers.

'This is section one-three-one of the Mandriga Defence Line,' Umboldt told them, the reverence of a moment before replaced by disdain. 'You should already be fully briefed with regard to joining your assigned combat units and immediate commencement of front-line command duties. Any questions should be addressed to your platoon commanders in the first instance, or to regimental section officers in the case that such personnel are indisposed. May the Emperor bless your endeavours.'

Etsul was first to climb down from the Salamander and into the connecting trench behind it. She took a few paces, enjoying the simple feeling of comparative space. She was tempted to throw her kitbag onto the duckboard floor and stretch out the knotted muscles of her back. However, she had spotted a small group of soldiers waiting nearby, watching the officers dismount. At the sight, another of Masenwe's lessons came back to her.

'You can't be merely human in front of your troops. You keep that for when it's just you and the Emperor. Rest of the time we're the strongest, the toughest, the ones who don't get tired or sad or afraid. They need it from us, and it's the only way to earn their respect.'

Etsul kept her kitbag on her shoulder.

'This will be our reception committee,' muttered Aswold.

'You're still not dressed for it,' she noted.

'You would prefer that I had attempted to change in the back of a moving Salamander?'

Etsul snorted.

'They will get used to me soon enough,' Aswold said. 'Besides, it will do these Cadians good to remember they are not the only worthy soldiers in the Imperial Guard.'

Etsul smiled. Her expression curdled, however, as realisation dawned on her. Soldiers saluted their new officers and, one by one, offered to lead them to their stations.

All except her.

Umboldt had her name on his precious data-slate, so there surely couldn't be any mistake. Etsul looked around for the adept, willing to endure his impatient scorn in order to make absolutely sure she was in the right place. He had already hopped from the Salamander and vanished. Etsul grimaced. She'd find no aid there.

She had expected Sergeant Vaslav to meet her, had counted on a few minutes alone with him to get oriented before she met the rest of the crew. From the scant notes on her data-slate Etsul knew him to be a veteran Cadian who had fought for his world long before it was destroyed. He didn't seem the sort to be late.

Etsul scanned around until she spotted Russ turrets jutting above the trenches. She frowned and squared her shoulders, willing away tiredness, hunger and travel-sore aches. If Vaslav was delayed Etsul wasn't about to wait around for him. She would just have to find her tank the hard way.

'No sign of your gunner?' asked Aswold. Etsul started, realising that he must have noted her predicament and lingered. His own second-in-command stood to one side, wearing a guarded expression.

'Sergeant, do you know where I can find *Steel Tread*?'

Aswold's gunner cleared her throat.

'Absolutely, sir. Follow the trench that way along the back of this section. She's the last tank before the lookout tower. If you pass that, you're into one-three-two and you've gone too far. Oh, and keep your head down, sir. Snipers, you know…'

'Thank you, sergeant,' Etsul said. She spared a glance for Aswold, whose eyebrows were raised, then turned and set off along the trench. She did as the sergeant suggested, staying low between the flakboard walls. She was still several hundred yards back from no-man's-land here, but complacency was dangerous. The enemy could be out there, sights ghosting across the front lines, seeking targets worth a bullet.

I'm not getting shot before I find out what in the Emperor's name is going on here, she thought. There was a chance she was about to walk into a crisis and be expected to aid people she had never met. And if there *was* no crisis, Etsul wasn't sure if that would be better or worse.

Tank crews spent countless hours crammed into a confined space together. They relied upon one another for survival just as much as their machines. If one of the crew failed in their duties, all suffered. The thought that her new crew might be this unreliable from the off was not encouraging.

Etsul passed artillery positions, then a side trench in which several wounded Cadians lay on stretchers, then another where a slight and wiry man in a tanker's uniform led a group of soldiers in prayer. The man looked up at her as she passed. Ice-blue eyes pierced her from under his wild, black brows.

It seemed they were not the first non-natives consolidated into this Cadian regiment. She would not be alone.

Etsul was spattered with mud by the time she found *Steel Tread*. She knew the vehicle even from a distance. The Demolisher's blocky silhouette and squat cannon were unmistakable. As she got closer, the tank's name resolved in curling Low Gothic letters stencilled along the turret's side. Next to it, someone with passable artistic talent had painted a horned helmet being crushed under a steel-shod boot.

Someone sat atop the tank, rendered in silhouette.

Clearly the risk of snipers had been overstated, or this person had a death wish. She saw it was a woman, heavily muscled and with her tank suit undone to the waist to reveal the olive vest below. Her right arm was a bulky mechanical augmetic. Her blonde hair was shaved short and her eyes glinted violet as she glanced Etsul's way.

Recognition passed over the woman's face. She rapped her mechanical fist against the hull, then slid off the tank and out of sight. Etsul rounded the corner and marched up the short ramp connecting the trench to the tank's emplacement. There was enough space between the makeshift ramparts and the tank itself to form a walled-off enclosure with *Steel Tread* at its heart.

Despite herself, Etsul felt a moment's pride at the sight of the Demolisher: *her* Demolisher. The vehicle looked well maintained. Its exterior stowage appeared in good order.

Steel Tread was bulkier than *Oathkeeper* had been, with

thicker armour and more firepower. Sponson-mounted heavy bolters offered anti-infantry point-defence. A tank-busting lascannon jutted from the vehicle's prow, while a pintle-mounted storm bolter on its turret sat above the Russ' main weapon. The fearsome Demolisher cannon's menace was somewhat undercut by the wire of drying laundry strung between a grab handle on the hull and a nearby lumen pole.

Two of the tank's crew were rising from fold-out stools either side of a table improvised from a munitions crate. Across it was scattered the paraphernalia of a card game.

One was male, Cadian by his eyes and with youthful features, dark skin and a close-cropped beard. The other was a woman, also young to Etsul's eyes. Her skin was a shade lighter than her companion's and her eyes were so dark they looked almost black. Her hair was longer than regulation, with metal beads braided into it, and her nose and ears were both pierced multiple times. Tattoos forested her knuckles and forearms. A stylised teardrop marked the skin beneath her right eye. Both tankers stood to attention, and Etsul was immediately struck by the hostility in the woman's glare.

The crewman with the augmetic arm ambled around the tank to join them at attention. To the vehicle's other side, Etsul saw an older man with a sergeant's insignia pulling himself to his feet. Her errant gunner, still in the process of waking up.

Vaslav dragged one hand over his narrow face as though to scrape away a rime of exhaustion. He was pale and scarred, with a shaved head and a pencil moustache. His violet eyes had bags beneath them. He wore an expression of thinly veiled annoyance.

Etsul took her time with the last few steps of her approach, giving herself a moment to consider what she was going to do. She could play the hard disciplinarian and shock them into shape, or the confident commander, ignoring the troubling details. She knew what Masenwe would have done. For that matter, she knew what *she* would do.

First impressions mattered.

'I am Hadeya Etsul, your new commander,' she said. Dropping her kitbag to free both hands, she made the sign of the aquila. Her crew returned the salute, though she noted the glaring woman's aquila was just sloppy enough to be disrespectful.

Etsul kept her gaze level and let the silence stretch. It had grown uncomfortable by the time Vaslav cleared his throat.

'Welcome to *Steel Tread*, sir. I'm Sergeant Vaslav, your gunner.' He gestured to each of the others as he introduced them.

'Loader Erika Moretzin,' he said. The big woman saluted smartly.

'Sponson Gunner Garret Verro.' The young man's salute was also crisp, and accompanied by a respectful, 'Sir, it's a pleasure, sir.'

'And you are Sponson Gunner Nix Chalenboor, yes?' asked Etsul. The woman with the gang tattoos wore an insouciant grin.

'Yeah,' she replied, and Etsul fancied she saw a challenging glint in the gunner's eye.

'My briefing did not suggest we were a stationary unit, sergeant,' said Etsul. Vaslav looked nonplussed.

'Stationary, sir?'

'We have a driver?' prompted Etsul.

'Ah,' said Vaslav, glancing about as though only just realising there was a crewman missing. 'Driver Trieve is leading prayers in a nearby trench, sir. Faith is our first weapon against the Archenemy, after all.'

Etsul said nothing.

'I told Trieve to return in time for your arrival but…' Vaslav continued, letting out a breath. 'But, well–'

'He's proper pious, him,' sneered Chalenboor.

'Speak when spoken to, Chalenboor,' snapped Vaslav.

'Yes, boss.'

'I was given to understand the discipline of Cadian regiments is second to none,' Etsul said. 'Instead, I find nobody waiting to meet me at my drop-off point, and now you tell me my driver is absent without my leave. I find myself underwhelmed.'

There was something sullen in Vaslav's continued silence.

'Yeah, so if–'

'Commander,' said Verro, cutting Chalenboor off, 'would you like to inspect *Steel Tread*? I can see to your belongings.'

'That would be good,' said Etsul, replying to Verro but keeping her eyes on Chalenboor. The young woman stared back.

'Local orientation would also help,' she said as Verro hefted her kitbag with a wince. 'Commissary, section command post, latrines, all that.'

'Of course, sir,' began Vaslav, then his gaze slid over her shoulder and set hard. Etsul turned. The man from the side trench with the sharp blue eyes was walking up the ramp.

Leading prayers. Isaac Trieve, I presume.

Trieve was, at least, better presented than his crewmates. His tank suit was crisp, his stride purposeful. Somehow, he had contrived to keep the mud off himself almost entirely. He held a prayer book in one hand and wore a machine-stamped aquila on a chain around his neck. His expression was unconcerned, bordering on smug. Etsul was struck by the sudden thought that Trieve's absence had been deliberate, that the man had engineered some distance between himself and his crewmates.

Trieve stood to attention and offered a sharp aquila salute.

'Commander Etsul, it is a privilege.'

'Is it? A pity, then, that you were not present when I arrived as you should have been.'

'Of course, sir. My apologies.' Trieve smiled, seemingly perversely pleased with the rebuke. 'I was detained by the divine spirit of the God-Emperor, for He moved me to a surfeit of piety that ran overlong. I'm sure you understand, sir. When He speaks to us, His will supersedes all others.'

Etsul shook her head.

'What I understand, Driver Trieve, is that when my crew musters, I expect you to be present and punctual. If you must make your peace with the God-Emperor afterwards, then He will have to be understanding. I stand between you and Him in the chain of command.'

At this borderline blasphemy, Trieve looked as though he'd taken a mouthful of something rotten. A flush crept up his neck. Etsul heard a sound behind her that might have been Chalenboor stifling a snort. She swung around to see an expression that was half guilty, half amused on the sponson gunner's face.

Verro still clutched her kitbag, expression pained.

Etsul looked to Vaslav. He was her second-in-command. He knew these soldiers far better than she. A good gunnery sergeant dealt with day-to-day discipline so that their commander could rise above such things as a figure of authority and respect. Vaslav just stared into the middle distance, hands clasped tightly behind his back, expression carefully unreadable.

'Let me be perfectly clear,' she said, raking them with her

gaze. 'This has not gone well. I am going to inspect *Steel Tread* then get some food, and once I have–'

A loud clearing of the throat caused Etsul to wheel about. A Cadian soldier stood at the bottom of the ramp, Ninth Army Group command insignia on her shoulder. She held a data-slate and had her helmet tucked under one arm.

'What?' barked Etsul.

'Apologies, lieutenant commander. Captain Brezyk requests your presence for a strategic briefing at Mandriga command.'

Etsul felt her shoulders sag. Tiredness, hunger, frustration and a painful longing for her old crewmates threatened to crack her composure. Instead, she took a deep breath, and then the proffered data-slate. It told her little more than the messenger.

'I have just come from Mandriga command,' Etsul bit out. 'I am engaged in inspecting my new tank and crew.'

'With respect, lieutenant commander, the captain was unambiguous.'

'Of course,' Etsul replied with a hard smile. She had been a soldier long enough to recognise a stress-test.

'Verro, get my belongings stowed,' she told the sponson gunner. 'The rest of you be ready for full inspection upon my return. And no more excursions.' She directed this last to Trieve, before turning and following the messenger back up the trench.

CHAPTER TWO

FIRST IMPRESSIONS

Garret Verro watched his new commander vanish around the corner, then let out a breath. Despite the events of the last few minutes, he felt a slow welling of relief. There were officers who would have invoked the Commissariat for what Commander Etsul had just witnessed.

At least she's not a petty tyrant, he thought.

'You were supposed to wake me at thirteen thirty,' snapped Sergeant Vaslav. Verro's relief was replaced by guilt. For all he knew, the sergeant was still going to catch it in the neck when Commander Etsul returned.

'I'm sorry, sir,' he said.

'Lost track of time, boss,' Chalenboor added, entirely unapologetic.

When Chalenboor had first joined the crew, she had told Verro that her early years had been spent as an underhive gang fighter on Dakturia, then later as a militia conscript hurled in as cannon fodder. She asserted that she had survived as much as any Cadian, and lost as much too by the time her regiment's few survivors were absorbed into the Coronal Crusade.

Vaslav turned his glare on their scattered card game.

'I can see how that could have happened. Verro, you at least should know Cadians don't gamble.'

'Just a friendly game, sir, no stakes but honour,' said Verro, glad now that he had talked Chalenboor out of placing wagers. Verro respected Vaslav, but when one of his dark moods took him, the sergeant could turn nasty. He'd been worse since Commander Holtz died. Or perhaps it was simply the months mired in salty ditchwater that had worn down Vaslav's nerves.

The sergeant spared a last glare for the scattered cards, then turned his scowl to Moretzin. The loader wore an expression as placid as the still waters of a Cadian moorland tarn. She held up her bare wrist.

'No chrono, sir,' she said. 'Smashed, remember? You were requisitioning me a new one.'

Vaslav's scowl deepened. He dragged his palm over his face again. It was a gesture Verro had come to know and dislike these past months. It made the sergeant look harassed, somehow, and terribly tired.

Evidently considering the exchange done with, Chalenboor prodded Verro in the ribs.

'Come on then, what's in that holdall? Way you're 'oldin' it, I reckon she's packed it with rocks.'

'Are you mad?' Verro asked.

'Not nickin', am I?' Chalenboor grinned. 'Just want to get a look-see, yeah? Can tell a lot 'bout someone from their stash.'

'You are not going to rummage through the commander's bloody kitbag!' hissed Verro.

'Duct-squirmer,' she shot at him, snatching for the holdall. 'Throne's sakes, Nix, I'm serious.'

'Chalenboor,' growled Vaslav.

'Boss,' she said, subsiding with another mischievous smile. Verro rolled his eyes.

Trieve had hastened forward, evidently intending to intercede should Chalenboor get hold of the bag. Now he stepped back with a scowl.

'You know that no other crew in this company behaves with such a lamentable lack of discipline, yes?' Trieve made no effort to keep the disgust from his voice. 'When I learned that I was to be consolidated into a Cadian regiment I was glad. How I must have displeased the God-Emperor, then, to be saddled with... *this*...'

Chalenboor rounded on the driver.

'Why don't you pray to Him for a transfer, yeah?' she sneered.

'My prayers are occupied with appeals that He might instil in you a sense of duty and civility,' replied Trieve stiffly. 'But then, one wonders if some miracles are beyond even Him.'

'Worry less 'bout my soul, and more about *Steel Tread*'s,' Chalenboor shot back. 'Driver's job, right? Or you going to let our Garret do your work for you again?'

Trieve bridled. Verro sighed. He had always had an enquiring mind, and as a child in Kasr Vark he had loitered around the repair shrines when not at study or drill-practice. Verro had picked up all manner of useful titbits in those days; since becoming a tanker in the wake of Cadia's fall he had only added to his knowledge. Commander Holtz had joked that Verro might have been a tech-priest in another life, with the way he was able to soothe the machine-spirit of *Steel Tread*.

Trieve, by comparison, took a hostile view of what he

called 'meddling in Martian apocrypha'. Verro thought it more likely that the driver didn't want to admit a humble sponson gunner had more of a way with their tank than he did.

'Enough, Nix,' Verro snapped. 'Haven't you done enough damage already today?'

'What you chattin' about?' she asked.

'You've already angered Commander Etsul, and she's not even stepped inside the tank,' he exclaimed. Chalenboor responded with a three-fingered Dakturian gesture that Verro knew was the equivalent of a shrug.

'She's got provin' to do yet. Ain't Holtz, you know?'

'God-Emperor rest him,' said Vaslav. Verro looked between them uncomfortably.

Brenner Holtz had been an officer worth fighting for in his glory days, but when Cadia broke so did he. The old man had become erratic since the beginning of the Croatoan campaign, veering between needless risks and virtual torpor. Moreover, Vaslav might have covered for him but Verro knew Holtz had become increasingly fond of the bottle.

Holtz's reputation, coupled with Vaslav's excuses, had kept consequences at bay. But stagnation on the Mandriga Line had done the old man no good. The official story was that Holtz had been shot by an enemy sniper as he moved from one trench to another.

Rumours persisted.

'Trieve's not wrong,' said Verro. 'Commander Etsul is in charge now, and we've a reputation for discipline to uphold.'

The sergeant's expression soured again.

'Being Cadian means more than obedience and faith, Whiteshield,' he snapped. Verro considered reminding the sergeant for the hundredth time that he hadn't been a

Whiteshield since Cadia's fall, then discarded the idea. It was not a trench worth dying in, as the saying went.

'Being Cadian means knowing the right cause and the right officer,' Vaslav continued.

'Sir,' said Verro, unsure how else to respond.

'It's realism, pragmatism, recognising value. It's knowing the Emperor only forgives those who earn His forgiveness.'

'Sir,' Verro repeated, aware now that he'd hit a nerve.

Trieve snorted.

'The God-Emperor sends His servants suffering and pain that we might prove our worthiness through glad endurance. So we teach on Brethia. If the Cadians were all they claimed to be, they would bear their hurts more gladly.'

The driver strode away towards *Steel Tread* without waiting for Vaslav to dismiss him. Verro looked to the sergeant, but Vaslav only glanced away, his expression brooding. Frustrated, Verro called after Trieve.

'Our planet broke beneath us and still we stayed true. Watch your tone talking about things you don't understand, Isaac.'

Acting as though he hadn't heard, Trieve clambered up the flank of the Demolisher and vanished into a hatch. Verro unclenched his teeth. He realised he was still clutching Commander Etsul's bag.

A hand landed on his shoulder. He found Chalenboor looking at him with genuine concern. The rough-edged humour was gone.

'Mate, you're proper shut down today, aren't you?'

Verro almost laughed.

'We're on the front line of a warzone fighting degenerate heretics with no sign of reinforcement or hope. Our old commander's dead and now our new one thinks we're a bunch of ill-disciplined rejects. Frankly, I'm not sure how far off her assessment is. And that's without even mentioning...' He shot a quick look upwards, unwilling to name the Rift aloud. 'Aren't *you* "shut down"?'

Verro realised he was gesticulating with one hand and brandishing the commander's bag with the other. Alarmed, he set it down in case he made matters worse by breaking Etsul's belongings.

'Listen, we're a crew in all the ways that matter, yeah?' Chalenboor assured him. 'Don't matter if we're Cadian or Dakturian or... whatever she is...'

'*She* is Tsegohan, which bears no comparison to being a Cadian,' grumbled Vaslav.

Chalenboor scowled, but before she and the sergeant could lay into one another again, Moretzin cleared her throat.

'Go on,' she said, rolling her augmetic shoulder with a whine of servos. 'Take a guess.'

Verro shot her a grateful smile.

'Moretzin, we were ordered to make ready for inspection,' said the sergeant. 'We don't have time for guessing games.'

'Commander will be gone a while yet,' said Moretzin, leaning back against *Steel Tread* with her arms folded. The augmetic whined and clicked, glinting in the wan daylight. Verro knew it coupled with cybernetic bracing that ran through Moretzin's shoulder and into her spine. He knew that it helped the loader heft massive Demolisher shells as efficiently as any carousel mechanism, and that he'd seen senior officers with lower-grade augmetics.

What neither he nor the rest of the crew knew was why Moretzin had such an incredible augmetic limb.

'Pirates,' said Chalenboor. 'Our Erika took up with pirates, yeah? First mate, wasn't she? Had that arm done so she could teach 'em all t'respect her captain's authority.'

Moretzin laughed softly and shook her head. Verro was surprised to see even the sergeant crack a smile.

'Well, that can't be right, Chalenboor. Otherwise, she'd have used it on you.'

'Not likely, boss,' the gunner scoffed. 'But I ain't arm-wrestlin' her again anytime soon.'

'All right, I think–' began Verro, but he was interrupted by the rising howl of a klaxon. Adrenaline shot through him. Air raid? Attack? They all looked to Vaslav. The sergeant held up a hand, gesturing *wait*.

As the klaxon's blare died, hubbub from all around spilled in to replace it. Verro heard shouted orders and booted feet beating against duckboards.

'General call to arms,' barked Vaslav. 'You know the drill.'

Verro took several steps towards the tank before remembering Commander Etsul's bag. He hastened back and heaved it onto his shoulder, already mentally plotting where he would stow her possessions for the commander's convenience. Chalenboor gathered up their cards and canteens. Moretzin easily hefted the crate back into its waiting stack, then began an inventory of the spare fuel barrels and cans lashed in the Demolisher's outer stowage.

'Sergeant, we're still two barrels down,' she called to Vaslav.

'How many times do I need to chase them about this?' he groaned. 'So noted, Moretzin. I'll procure them from reserves next time I see a Munitorum adept, even if I have to shake him warmly by the throat.'

'Thank you, sir,' said Moretzin, saluting. She vanished into *Steel Tread*.

None of them had said it out loud, but Verro suspected they were all wondering the same thing. After months of waiting, defence, attrition, the indignity of *Steel Tread* becoming a motionless gun emplacement... Were they finally going on the offensive?

Shedding the question, he set about stowing his new commander's gear. He rapped on one of the side hatches set into *Steel Tread*'s armoured flank. The hatch gave a muffled clank as its locking bolt was released from inside, then swung open. He clambered through, reassured as always by the tight confines and armoured bulk of the tank.

The interior was standard for a Leman Russ Demolisher of this pattern: commander's bucket seat up at turret level, benefitting from several vid screens and with a cupola position above that; driver's and gunner's stations to fore, small fold-out seats and rugged controls; his and Chalenboor's sponson stations set a little way back and to either side, each equipped with external vid-links and remote controls that let them sight, traverse and fire their weapons; ammunition storage, air-exchanger shrines and of course the main power plant taking up the back third of the tank's interior; stowage boxes, rebreather rack, emergency medicae shrine, arms locker and other minor necessities wherever they fitted. They had a little more space to move than some crews, as the Agamemnor pattern dispensed with an ammunition carousel in favour of manual loading by chain-sling and main force. Or in their case, Verro thought proudly, by Moretzin.

She was crouched by the ammunition, muttering perfunctory prayers as she checked over the Demolisher shells and made notes on a data-slate. Chalenboor was folded into her seat and testing her controls. Trieve sat at his driver's station and frowned intently as he fiddled with the settings for the internal vox, his rancour set aside for now. Verro didn't suppose he would ever bring himself to like the Brethian, but at least the man knew his business.

Verro had just finished stowing the commander's belongings and was beginning his own checks and prayers when the sergeant leaned down through the turret hatch.

'Best give everything a second check, ladies and gentlemen,' he said. 'We've got half a dozen field engineers and a pair of ogryns out here with orders to break down our redoubt. I think we all know what that means.'

Verro felt his heart beat faster. He exchanged a look with Chalenboor, saw his excitement and trepidation mirrored there.

The sergeant lowered himself into the gunner's seat and set to his own checks. As he did so, Verro heard him muttering.

'Not even a Cadian at the helm. Never even set foot on the training fields.'

'She's our commander all the same, sir.' Verro knew he risked the sergeant's ire, but he couldn't help himself.

'Not 'til she earns it, yeah?' said Chalenboor. For his part, Vaslav cast a dark look at the two of them, then bent to the task of checking his controls. Moretzin hadn't looked up during the exchange, carrying on with her tasks as though she hadn't heard. Trieve wore a small but unpleasant sneer.

Verro sighed. If the redoubt was coming down, then they would be going into battle soon enough. For better or worse, Hadeya Etsul would be their commander. Providing, of course, that she got back from Mandriga command before the order to advance came down the line. He'd have bet a canteen of good Uruski vintage that the sergeant was hoping she wouldn't.

Verro doubted the armoured company would leave without their new officers, however.

'Emperor, let her be up to this,' he breathed.

The truth was Garret Verro had no control over matters

either way. Such was life in the Astra Militarum. All he could do was see to the purity and wellbeing of his own systems, serve as a Cadian should, and beseech the Emperor that all would work out. He applied himself to his awakening rituals and systems checks. As he did so, quietly and privately he continued to pray.

CHAPTER THREE

ORDERS

Etsul disembarked the Taurox into the tightly controlled whirlwind of industry that was Mandriga command. She stepped down onto a ferrocrete square at least a mile across, surrounded by towering structures resembling man-made mountains. Behind her came a handful of other mid-ranking officers, rounded up from her part of the line.

It would be quite the time for the enemy to attack, while all the officers were parading about back here. But, then again, the Mandriga Line had held for many months and the defenders were well entrenched. If an assault did come, they could no doubt hold long enough for the command staff to get back into position.

Still. This was a risk that would have been considered. Evidently this meeting was important enough to merit pulling all the officers off the line at once.

Etsul wished she could discuss her thoughts with someone, but though she stood amidst a great mass of humanity she found herself alone. The only face she'd recognised aboard the Taurox had been the Geskan officer who'd spoiled for a fight with Adept Umboldt. She'd managed to drag from him that he was called Graves, and that he held the rank of barst-gan, which was the Geskan equivalent of lieutenant or possibly platoon leader. He'd been monosyllabic, however, and Etsul had taken the hint.

Fatigue dragged at her. The ache of back-and-forth transit felt like a hangover. Etsul had always found waiting to fight far more tiring than battle itself. She had never been sanguine when it came to uncertainties or delays. At least in battle you knew where you stood.

'Live what is,' she told herself, another of her mother's sayings.

The aide stepped down from the Taurox's cab.

'If you will follow me,' she said, striking out across the grey expanse. Etsul and her companions followed.

The buildings around them had once formed part of an industrial complex: the cog and skull of the Adeptus Mechanicus was much in evidence. The Cadians had transformed them, however. Each one had been shored up and fortified. Gun turrets and stablights pointed skyward from battlemented roofs. Slabs of armour had been bolted to the structures doughty enough to support them, while heaps of rubble showed where ailing buildings had been simply bulldozed. In their place rose prefabricated bastions emblazoned with Imperial aquilas. Etsul saw soldiers and menials swarming around them. Something had evidently dropped a stone into the pool. She wondered what.

The plaza bustled. Her group threaded between neat stacks of munitions and fuel, sand-bagged bunkers and tents whose guy ropes stretched to holes cut directly into the ferrocrete.

Columns of soldiers jogged past with lasguns shouldered. Robed officials swayed above the tumult on servo-litters. Sentinel walkers stalked here and there, the pilots manipulating their cargo-grapples to hoist laden metal pallets.

Elsewhere Etsul made out the ugly augmetics of a servitor. It lumbered closer, dragging a fuel pipe towards a Valkyrie gunship waiting on an improvised landing pad. There were others, too, aiding robed engineers with repairs. Etsul did her best to ignore the pallid flesh and glassy eyes. Servitors were rare on her home world, since the salt air degraded them too quickly. She hadn't seen the creatures up close until she had joined the Imperial Guard, and had never really got used to them.

Looking away from the mindless cyborgs she found herself instead a witness to true death. They were approaching one of the huge structures now, a heavily armoured shrineplex. Nearby, a commissar stood to attention. Beside her was a rank of Cadians with lasguns aimed. Backs to the shrineplex wall stood a miserable gaggle of blindfolded soldiers awaiting the Emperor's mercy.

'...and for the charges of dereliction of duty, and misappropriation of the blessed arms and armour which the God-Emperor has seen fit to bestow upon you, and...' The commissar's voice, amplified through a vox-speaker, rang over the hubbub. Yet even she was drowned out as a wing of Marauder bombers thundered overhead.

Etsul glanced up at the massive aircraft. She looked back down in time to see another huge servitor about to trample her. She leapt back, throwing out an arm to pull the aide back with her. The hulking cyborg thudded ponderously on, passing so close that Etsul was bathed in its unguent reek.

The servitor was a walking mound of muscle and servo-driven plasteel, its head jutting low between huge shoulders and hidden by a crimson hood. More red cloth draped its bulk and trailed the ground behind it, bells jingling on wire tassels. Behind the servitor came a procession of tech-priests. Etsul saw glowing eye-lenses, rubberised robes the colour of blood and mechanical tendrils. They were blaring binharic prayers over the engines of the vehicles rumbling in their wake. She gazed at the massive rocket racks of Manticore artillery tanks, then gaped as she saw the still-more-ominous shape of a Deathstrike missile launcher bringing up the rear. A single enormous missile occupied the tank's launch cradle. She imagined the carnage such a weapon could wreak amongst the foe.

'You might look where you're going! Throne knows you've enough eye-lenses under those hoods,' shouted the aide. One of the priests halted and leant on his cog-toothed axe. His face was a metal half-mask. His eyes glowed green.

'Factual: you were distracted by the proximity of combat aircraft and were thus the careless parties in this exchange. Advisory: exercise augmented caution as you traverse this staging area. Additional: my procession accompanies the divine ordnance furnished as gifts by the Omnissiah for the defence of this location, and will brook no interruption to our sacred duties.'

With that, the tech-priest turned away.

'Your name, priest?' the aide barked after him. 'I shall be reporting your carelessness to my superiors.'

'Magos-Fissilum Apetrus Hengh.' The priest's reply floated back over his shoulder. 'Permissive: engage in whatever emotionally compensatory acts of petulance will bring you optimised emotional equilibrium.'

Etsul exchanged a look with the scowling aide. Behind her, Barst-Gan Graves spat again. As the last artillery tank passed, the commissar was revealed, marching away through the crowds with her execution detail on her heels. In their wake, servitors heaped bodies for disposal and mopped up blood. Etsul shuddered as she imagined different faces beneath those pitiful blindfolds. She wouldn't let it come to that, not while she was their commander.

'What is all this for?' Etsul asked. 'I haven't seen this much activity in one place since the muster at Wyrmwech.'

'You'll have to wait for the briefing, lieutenant,' snapped the aide. 'I don't know how it's done in other regiments, but Cadians stand by protocol.' She set off again. Etsul winced and followed. She was neither a sergeant nor a Tsegohan any more. She couldn't allow herself these slips.

The aide led them below a gothic arch bristling with candles and censers. Banners hung above it, regimental standards surrounding the colours of the Ninth Army Group. Elite Kasrkin flanked the door, helm visors glinting, hotshot lasguns cradled across their chests.

The shrineplex had the chill and gloom of a holy place, but its sepulchral sobriety did little to curtail the industrious bustle. Soldiers, aides and robed adepts were everywhere, exuding purpose and energy.

Through one stone archway Etsul saw a chamber filled with cogitators and their operators. Another housed arrays of massive vox-sets, Cadians hunched before them scribbling notations and transmitting messages. Serfs in Ninth Group tabards hastened past bearing trays of food and drink, or armfuls of data-slates. Munitorum adepts, many accompanied by honour guards, shoved importantly through the press. Etsul saw more groups of field officers like her own, all hastening deeper into the building.

Another huge arch swept overhead, and they emerged into a flagstoned corridor that stretched away to right and left. Its high ceiling was vaulted and decorated with frescoes. One wall was dominated by stained-glass windows whose grandeur was only slightly dimmed by the flakboard panels bonded over them from outside. The crush of humanity was even greater here. Tired as she was, the noise and jostle and smell of unwashed bodies threatened to overwhelm Etsul. She wasn't helped by a corpulent priest who hovered low above the crowd in a suspensor-pulpit, bellowing fire and brimstone through vox-speakers.

The man thrummed low over Etsul's head, causing her and those around her to duck.

'...and in that time did those who were faithful to the God-Emperor welcome the coming of the holy fires, for though they burned their flesh so too did they grant righteous immolation unto the heretics who, in their wickedness, opposed His divine will. And amongst the unbelievers was the burning worst, and so the faithful did raise up their scalded hands in praise to the divine God-Emperor and they did offer Him great thanks for His gift of pain that in their...'

Straightening up, Etsul couldn't help scowling after the priest, tiredness and irritation taking momentary possession of her while the human tide resumed its flow. She gave a sudden start, then groaned as she turned to see her group were lost amidst the crowd.

Etsul craned her neck, trying to see over the mass of people. It was all she could do not to be swept away.

'Throne's sakes,' she cursed.

Unfamiliar faces whirled about her.

Voices blended in a dull roar.

Etsul entertained a momentary wish the flying priest would

come back her way, so that she could introduce *him* to a gift of pain.

Then, a flash of recognition amongst the crowd. Etsul lunged through a gap, sidestepped an indignant adept, and grabbed the man's arm. He spun in surprise, then beamed with recognition.

'Lieutenant Aswold,' she said.

'Lieutenant Etsul! Did you find your tank?' he asked.

'Eventually, just in time to get dragged back here and lose my group instead.'

'Come with us then, lieutenant,' said Aswold, pointing with his chin at another aide hovering nearby. 'You're Eleventh Company also, yes?'

Etsul forced her tired mind to recall the briefing details from her data-slate.

'Throne, yes, of course. Idiot.'

He raised an eyebrow.

'Me, not you,' she clarified.

'Not at all,' replied Aswold, his smile infuriatingly reassuring.

Etsul joined Aswold's group as they turned right down the corridor. She noticed more tanker uniforms amongst this group. She wondered how many of her new regiment had just heard her admit to getting lost. There were more than enough violet eyes amongst them. Etsul held herself erect and ignored their glances, instead looking Aswold up and down.

'Cadian fatigues at last, I see,' she said.

'One must embrace change or lie broken in its wake.' He smiled. 'Speaking of which, how many of your new crew already lie broken in yours?'

'Less than they deserve,' she replied. 'I take it they've a reputation?'

'Oh, nothing my lot have said out loud. But the Emperor speaks in the silences people leave.'

They passed through a cloud of incense that left everyone choking. When she could breathe again, Etsul asked after Aswold's own crew.

'I am embarrassed to admit they seem the picture of Cadian excellence, from the few minutes I was permitted amongst them,' he said. 'I feel that I must impress them, rather than the other way around.'

'I know what you mean, my lot notwithstanding.'

He shot her a searching look then made a small 'ah' sound of understanding.

'You will find the commander's seat becomes more comfortable by the day, and we will both earn the mantle of Cadian soon enough,' he said, low enough that only Etsul could hear.

'I'm sure,' she replied, arching an eyebrow. Aswold grimaced, registering his own patronising tone. She sighed and slapped him on the shoulder.

'I don't need a mentor, lieutenant,' she said, striving for a more friendly tone. 'I just need some sleep, and for my crew to stow their gear, and to stop feeling like a passenger in my own life. Emperor's grace, I just need to kill some heretics.'

They passed beneath another archway, graven with stylised warriors of the Adeptus Astartes that stood thirty feet tall. Beyond them was a broad cloister that had been transformed into a chamber by the addition of an armoured roof and plasteel support columns. Once, Etsul noted, plants had grown here. Now the grasses and flower beds were all trampled, and the trees were withering for want of natural light. The contrast with Croatoas' rampant jungles was stark.

At the cloister's heart an auto-pulpit had been erected. Atop it hunched a Mechanicus adept. His face was a cluster of swivelling eye-lenses. A forest of servo-arms emerged from his back, each tipped with quills or manipulator claws. He was flanked by a pair of lesser adepts bearing hoppers of folded parchment on their backs. This spooled over their shoulders and through the elaborate quill-mechanisms that replaced their lower jaws, which printed endless reams of script. As the parchment piled at his feet, so the spider-like adept gathered it up with inhuman speed and studied the words before tapping at an oversized data-slate.

The entire process resulted in the updating of an ornate vid screen erected before the pulpit. It was here that the aides led their groups, gathering in a press before the screen. As Etsul joined them she saw the signifiers of regiments, companies and platoons flickering over the display.

'There we are,' said Aswold.

'Briefing chamber, corridor forty-one – second corridor left, third door right, Eleventh Company briefing with Captain Brezyk,' Etsul read aloud from the screen. She remembered his name from her slate and wondered again what sort of commanding officer she served.

They saluted their aide, who returned the gesture then vanished into the crowd.

'On our own from here then,' said Aswold, scanning the cloister's edge. Etsul saw dozens of corridors leading off from it. Above each, numbers had been seared into the stone.

'Corridor forty-one,' said Etsul, pointing. They set off through the crush, doing their bit to trample what remained of the pallid grass. Other tankers came with them, evidently destined for the same briefing. She heard Aswold introducing himself and caught a few names in return: Amelia Askerov of *Brigand*; Daisuke Karch of *Orkgrinder*; Fitz Lothen of *Paragon's Pride*; Olgher Jorgens of *Ogre*.

Jorgens was a compact man with a smile as firm as his handshake.

'Welcome to the Hammers,' he said. 'I trust you've received the proper welcome?'

'Cordial and efficient,' replied Aswold with a genial smile. Etsul grimaced vaguely. Pleasantries could wait, she thought; first, she wanted to get back to her tank and get her crew in order.

'They might be polite on the parade ground, but they're killers all in the field,' commented First Lieutenant Askerov. She was slight and spare, Cadian-pale and with the insignia of first tank, Fourth Squadron on her shoulder. She had a fierce grin that Etsul warmed to at once.

By the time they found their briefing chamber, Etsul was thoroughly sick of Ecclesiarchal decoration. The space boasted the seemingly obligatory tapestries, candles, choral balconies and stifling censers. She ignored it all, focusing on the holotable that had been installed at the chamber's centre. A space had been cleared around it and fold-out canvas chairs set in rows there. Many were already occupied by people in the uniforms of Cadian tank commanders. By the table stood a figure Etsul recognised. Her heart sank.

Captain Brezyk's glance was no less dismissive now than it had been on the Valkyrie flight however many hours before.

Etsul hastened to her seat. As she and the others settled themselves, Brezyk gestured to a muscular man lingering at the door.

'First Sergeant Moss, if you would,' said Brezyk. Moss swung the door shut with a hollow boom, then moved amongst them with an armful of data-parchments. While the sergeant distributed these, Brezyk started speaking.

'Ladies, gentlemen, you have been briefed regarding your

transfer, but for the newcomers I will reiterate. You are now property of Eleventh Company of the Forty-Ninth Cadian Armoured Regiment. You are Hammers. You will live up to your name. For clarity, donning a Cadian uniform does not make you Cadian. Those of you who do not yet know what *does* make you Cadian, learn quickly. Inferiority of origin will not be accepted as an excuse for poor conduct.'

Etsul kept a scowl off her face with a conscious effort.

'I am Captain Brezyk. I command Eleven-Co, and as far as you are concerned, I speak with the authority of the God-Emperor Himself. Clear?'

'Yes, sir!' they barked.

Moss, passing, pressed a data-parchment into Etsul's hands. She glanced up at him, but his violet eyes had already moved on.

Brezyk's gaze raked them like a stablight.

'You will note the non-standard squadron size. The company will be operating four squadrons, increased to four tanks apiece. This ratio is to counteract the diluting effect of consolidated recruitment.'

Etsul couldn't stop her frown this time. The Astra Militarum routinely consolidated under-strength regiments, blending human soldiery from myriad worlds. Cultural barriers aside, it had always been her belief that forging such alloys made those regiments stronger.

There was no dilution here. They were not untrained youths dragging down a veteran force. They were survivors, warriors of countless battles and regiments – them coming together was strength, not weakness.

Brezyk was talking blithely on, running through squadron composition as though he hadn't just insulted a good third of the officers sat before him.

'…and Fourth Squadron comprises entirely Leman Russ Demolishers. Fourth Squadron officers, you report to First Lieutenant Askerov aboard *Brigand*. Now, some of you have served under me since before we invaded this grox-turd of a planet. I know you. I trust you. We have fought shoulder by shoulder for worthier worlds than this. For the rest of you, the Emperor in His beneficence has furnished you with an opportunity to prove that you belong in those uniforms.'

Brezyk paused in his address to stab at the holotable controls. Glowing lines flickered above the device, stubbornly refusing to resolve. The captain scowled, muttered something that could have been prayer or oath, then tried again.

The projection resolved into a holomap. It had been set to display vertically, as though the map were pasted to the wall behind it. Etsul saw the Mandriga Line glowing gold, a little way above the jagged coastline. It made for uncomfortable viewing. She hadn't realised how close their backs were to the wall.

The rest of the map showed a sprawling region of mangrove swamps, watercourses, lakes and ruined industrial sprawl, rising into drier uplands further north. Blue lines cut across it, indicating transitways still deemed navigable. The out-thrust foothills of mountains lined the top of the display.

Near the foot of the largest peak glowed a blood-red skull rune.

'Regimental consolidation and reinforcement has been the final step in the preparations for Operation Jotunn,' Brezyk continued. 'After extensive reconnaissance and no small loss of Cadian and Geskan lives, it has been determined the enemy's base of operations in this region is the former Temple of Saint Carthusas, amongst the foothills of Mount Auric.'

The red skull pulsed at these words. High Gothic script flickered to life above it.

'This is the nerve centre for those traitor elements that have harassed us ever since the retreat from Ruega. Moreover, it is the base of operations for our turncoat former comrades from the Four Hundred and Forty-Fifth Vostokh and the Six Hundred and Sixty-Fourth Lothor Armoured.'

Vengeful muttering passed like a breeze through the assembled officers.

'Spinebacks…'

'Leering Skulls…'

'Traitorous bastards.'

'My sentiments exactly,' barked Brezyk. 'That would make the temple target enough. Knocking it out allows us to regroup and push north-west to break the siege of Hive Joragh. How-ever, through psychic augury we have learned more. The site you see before you is believed to be the current stronghold of the so-called "heretic king" Baraghor.'

This drew oaths from the assembled officers.

'Quiet in the ranks,' rumbled First Sergeant Moss.

Baraghor the Butcher. Baraghor the Corruptor. The heretics' warlord had other, less complimentary names amongst the Imperial soldiery, but to his followers he was Baraghor the Divine, their king and unquestionable master.

'You have doubtless heard enough horror stories about this heretic,' said Brezyk. 'Would that we had as much hard intelligence as we did baseless rumour. No eyewitness has lived to provide credible report on his nature. The facts we do possess are these, and by the Throne they are enough. Baraghor is the figurehead and mastermind of the heretical war effort on mainland Croatoas. He is a traitor warlord and possible witch. He is also within striking distance, and as mortal as you or I. Strategos claim, however, that Baraghor himself appears unaware of this last point. They believe that if we offer him sufficient challenge, he will come forth in person to fight. Only through cult of personality do these heretics keep a leash on their treacherous followers. Operation Jotunn aims to push on Baraghor's position, tempt him to battle and secure his demise.'

Etsul thought again of Yarroe Canyon, and hoped that it would be as easy as Brezyk made it sound.

'With their master slain, the lesser heretic warlords will fall upon one another in the hopes of securing his vacant throne. While they are shooting one another, they will not be shooting us. And that, soldiers of the Emperor, is when Ninth Group will consolidate our strength sufficient to put our fist all the way down the enemy's traitorous throat. I do not overstate matters when I say that the outcome of this operation may secure victory in the entire South Peninsula theatre.'

Some of Brezyk's audience could not restrain themselves at this thought.

'Emperor be praised!'

'We shall be the instruments of His vengeance!'

'Slay the heretic filth!'

'I don't care how formidable he is, let's see what's left of their king after he takes a Demolisher shell to the face!'

This last came from First Lieutenant Askerov, and elicited a few grim chuckles. Etsul had the sense she would get on with her direct commanding officer, at least.

Brezyk and Moss let the oaths die away. When silence had returned, Brezyk began running through the mission briefing and operational codes, whose details took up the rest of the data-parchment. Etsul paid attention with half her mind as glowing arrows scored the map and runes flared to indicate company-level routes of advance, suspected enemy strengths, staging and regrouping points and so on.

The rest of her was back amidst the fires of Yarroe Canyon, feeling Commander Masenwe's blood splashing hot across her face. Silently, she vowed to him that she wouldn't waste her chance. Not a troubled crew, not legions of heretics, not the damned Dark Gods of scripture themselves would stay her hand.

Hatred and faith had already fuelled her. Now Etsul had the chance for vengeance, too.

'Thank you, God-Emperor,' she said, staring down at the parchment in her hands. 'That is plenty.'

CHAPTER FOUR

INTO THE DARK

Fire.

The tank was awash with fire.

Sweat, or maybe blood, stung her eyes and bleared her vision. Hissing with frustration she tried to wipe it away. Masenwe's ruined corpse screamed as it burned.

The enemy were outside, beating fists against the hull, making everything shake. Etsul felt the crush of them, the heaving mass of flesh and muscle and bulging eyes bunched around the tank like a fist. She felt the flames as though they leapt inside her chest. The agony was unbearable.

'Please,' she gasped, and embers spewed from her mouth. She felt the fire building inside her like a volcanic eruption. She heard the tank's hull groan as the pressure became insurmountable.

I know you'll make us proud.

* * *

Etsul jolted awake and banged her head on *Steel Tread*'s turret ring. The stab of pain chased away the last traces of the nightmare. She clenched and unclenched her tingling palms.

She'd fallen asleep in the commander's seat, she realised, immersed in the roar of the Demolisher's power plant. She smelled the tang of promethium fumes that no air-exchanger shrine could ever wholly remove, and felt the omnipresent vibration of an armoured vehicle in motion. *Oathkeeper* had shuddered a little quicker but rattled the stowage lockers a little less.

It was just another adjustment. For all the vehicle's unfamiliarity, being ensconced within a moving tank had been enough to lull Etsul's exhausted mind into sleep. She glanced at her wrist-chrono and found she'd been out for a handful of minutes.

It was worse than not sleeping at all, raindrops to the tongue of a castaway with an empty canteen. Her head was stuffed with wool. Her limbs felt heavy.

Most patterns of Leman Russ had two seats for their commanders, one in the cupola of the tank's turret and the other a little lower, placed above and behind the driver's and gunner's stations. The former existed to allow a commander to sit in the turret hatch, eyeballing the terrain or employing their vehicle's pintle-mounted weaponry.

Upon first entering *Steel Tread*, Etsul had been surprised to find the Agamemnor pattern's turret 'seat' was actually a pair of flakweave-and-plasteel stirrups that allowed one to stand proud of the turret from the waist upward.

To her relief, the lower commander's seat had proved more familiar in its design. That said, Etsul had to consciously stop herself from clambering on down to the gunner's station.

This seat placed her in full view of her crew and they of her, connected and exposed.

She rubbed thumb and forefinger briskly into her eyes then shot a look down at her new crew.

Isaac Trieve sat straight-backed at his controls, silhouetted by the glow of his vid screens. His shoulders twitched as he made slight adjustments to his steering levers. The driver radiated a sense of upright efficiency which made Sergeant Vaslav's slouch look as though someone had poured him into his seat.

Her sponson gunners would be sitting on their own small fold-out seats slightly behind and below her, Verro on the left, Chalenboor right. Loader Moretzin would be further back still near the power plant and ammunition stores. There was no subtle way to crane around and check on the three of them. Instead, she thumbed the activation rune on the vox-speaker set next to her seat. No headsets in this mark of tank, for all its advanced vid-feeds and data-outputs, just lean-in-and-talk units slaved to ear-beads.

'Crew, full sound-off and status,' she said, speaking loudly into the vox-pickup. There was a static-laden pause. Etsul was just wondering if she needed to speak louder when Vaslav replied. His voice was tinny in her ear-bead, but not so distorted that she couldn't detect his tone.

'Confirm, sir. Are you requesting crew-station readiness report?'

Etsul cursed silently. Embarrassment prickled her skin. Her groggy brain had provided the Tsegohan phrasing for her order, not the Cadian.

'Confirmed, sergeant.'

Another pause. Etsul scowled.

'Crew-station readiness report,' she snapped, thinking that

she and Vaslav would be having words when they had some
privacy.

'Driver Trieve, station green,' Trieve began. 'We're four point
three miles from waypoint tertius, sir, moved off Six a few
minutes ago and ahead-steady over marshy ground. We've
left the worst of the tidal terrain behind. *Steel Tread*'s feeling
a little sluggish, but by the God-Emperor's blessings she's
always like this until offered a proper challenge.'

'Loader Moretzin, station green,' Moretzin took up the
refrain. 'Confirming ammunition stores at forty-five shells
primary load, six power packs for lascannon and four reloads
for each sponson gun. Just to advise the commander that
we are down by two reserve fuel drums, which puts us at
two-thirds recommended operational reserve.'

'Moretzin, I already told you the matter's in hand,' Vaslav
cut in.

'See that it is, sergeant,' said Etsul. 'In future I expect to
be apprised of any operational deficiency before we're in
the field.'

'Sir, Cadian protocol is that the commander isn't to be
bothered with such matters unless they bear directly upon
immediate operations,' Vaslav replied.

'And do you believe our fuel reserves irrelevant to immediate operations, sergeant?'

'Provided they're replenished in good time, sir, I don't–'

'Assume until advised otherwise that I do,' she overrode
him. 'Tsegohans are trained that omissions can kill.'

'Very good, sir,' said Vaslav tonelessly. 'Gunner Vaslav, station
green. We're maintaining formation with Fourth Squadron,
hundred-foot regulation advance spacing and close visibility.
Cadian and Geskan infantry assets maintaining pace and dispersal. Still no live targets.'

'Sponson Gunner Verro, station amber,' said Verro from below. 'One vid screen spirit disquieted, but I'll minister to it at the next halt, sir. Otherwise, gun spirits roused and wrathful.'

'Sponson Gunner Chalenboor, station green,' said Chalenboor. 'Awake to all threats down 'ere, sir.'

'Maintain formation and speed, advise me of any change,' Etsul said, settling now into the Cadian form of command. 'The Emperor protects,' she added, and they chorused it back. She sighed wearily after taking her finger from the vox-key.

As she had a thousand times in this past week, Etsul found herself missing Masenwe. The commander had observed a tradition at the beginning of each new mission. It stemmed from the old Tsegohan custom of standing in the Emperor's sight to beseech good fortune upon commencing a voyage. She straightened in her seat at the thought. Cadians be damned, she would do this part as a Tsegohan. She owed Masenwe that much.

Etsul reached up to the turret wheel and spun it, releasing the locking bolts. Braving the unfamiliar stirrups, she pushed the hatch open and stood tall in the cupola. The cold of early evening hit her. She took a deep lungful of air. It stank of stagnant water, rotting vegetation and carrion. Even so, Etsul felt refreshed by it. Out here the roar of the tank was louder, accompanied by the clattering song of its tracks and the wet hiss of muddy ground churned beneath them. Still, *Steel Tread*'s clamour was almost lost amidst the greater thunder of the Imperial advance.

Dozens of tanks ploughed through the marshes, power plants snarling as they ground over tangled undergrowth and drowned ferrocrete. Those closest bore the heraldry of Fourth Squadron. Around the tanks came masses of Cadian infantry.

They slogged through the mire at double time with expressions of grim resolve, even where rancid muck rose to their thighs or bloated corpses bobbed about them. The luckiest troopers rode aboard Chimera and Taurox personnel carriers. Looking back Etsul could see the second wave following perhaps a mile behind. Mobile artillery dotted this second line: long-snouted Basilisks; Wyvern mortar-tanks; rakish Hydras with their flak-barrels tilted skyward.

The Imperial advance flowed around blackened trees and wreckage. They dominated the wilderness with numbers and determined human purpose. It stirred Etsul's heart to be part of such a vast undertaking.

Remembering her ritual, Etsul turned her eyes upward. The sky was bruised in shades of apricot and purple by the sinking sun, clouds straggling grey and gold across it.

'Almighty God-Emperor, we ask that you watch over our travails,' she prayed. 'As we venture from safety into peril, from harbour to open waves, we ask you to bless us with your benevolent protection, and lend us strength that we might return at last to safe harbour.' She thought for a moment, then added, 'And watch over the soul of Eli Masenwe, God-Emperor. He was one of your best.'

Etsul's breath hitched at the last word. She closed her eyes and gripped the edge of the cupola, breathing steadily until the tightness in her throat and chest eased. Saving it for when it was her and the God-Emperor, just as he'd taught her.

She let out her breath in a rush, blinking hard as she returned her gaze to the swamplands. It wouldn't be safe to look skyward much longer. Already the first stars speckled the firmament, and with them came the leprous glimmer of the Rift.

More stars glowed closer at hand, more welcome in nature.

Geskan scouts moved ahead of the main advance, their pillion riders driving guide-lances into the ground to mark paths that would take the weight of tanks. It was the lumen beacons set in each lance-butt Etsul saw now, paths of firefly lights.

She had seen enough waterlogged craters, bogs and snarls of wreckage since leaving the line to make her exceptionally grateful for the scouts. Here and there the ferrocrete bones of dead buildings jutted from the ooze. She saw the glint of human bone, too. Battle had cursed this region, sporadic but unceasing. It had left scars.

The gloom yielded no signs of the foe. She felt their presence, though, somewhere out there amidst the wrack and ruin.

The vox-bead in her ear squawked.

'Lieutenant Etsul, this is First Lieutenant Askerov, do you receive?'

Etsul almost thumbed a non-existent headset rune. Instead, she detached the vox-mic from its housing inside the turret, extending it on its thick wire and speaking into it.

'First lieutenant, sir, I receive.'

'Why are you top-hatch, Etsul?' asked the first lieutenant. *'Seen something?'*

Etsul glanced across to Askerov's tank, *Brigand*, plying the swamp a hundred feet to her right. As she watched, the Demolisher slammed into a splintered tree trunk and ploughed it under without breaking stride.

'Negative, sir, no eyes on,' replied Etsul. Static hissed expectantly. 'It's something my old commander used to do, sir. I've got periscope and vid-feeds inside *Steel Tread* but... I want to feel it without the tank to shield me, sir. I want to make it real.' She left out any mention of prayer beneath an open sky. She was enough the outsider already.

'*Sounds as though your old commander knew what he was about, lieutenant,*' said Askerov.

'He was one of the best, sir,' said Etsul with a surprised surge of gratitude.

'*Good, because I am too, and I only permit the best in my squadron. I expect you to live up to his reputation and to mine, Etsul.*'

'Yes, sir, I intend to.'

'*You've inherited a job of work from Commander Holtz, Etsul. That unit has… quirks. But you'll find none sturdier in a pinch, provided there's a strong hand at the tiller. Understand?*'

Etsul understood all too well. Askerov knew the crew of *Steel Tread*, and she would see Hadeya Etsul sink or swim along with them.

Etsul had always been a strong swimmer.

'Clear, sir,' she replied.

'*Smashing. Now, if you're done observing your ritual, lieutenant, button up, there's a good woman. The Spinebacks had some keen sharpshooters in their ranks, even if they have proven to be a gang of shiftless heretics. I'd prefer you didn't get your head shot off. Makes the job harder.*'

'We're acquainted, sir. I've heard what happened to my predecessor.'

'*Very good, lieutenant. Carry on.*'

'Yes, sir,' Etsul said and dropped back into *Steel Tread*, shutting the hatch with a firm clang.

Two hours later, darkness had settled like a shroud over the swamp. With it, the vid screens within *Steel Tread* had switched to grainy green night-sight and transformed the Geskan lumens to vivid emerald smears. First Lieutenant Askerov ran half-hourly vox checks. Each time Etsul gave the same answer.

'Status green. Nothing to report.'

Once, Lieutenant Aswold voxed through on a private chan-nel, enquiring as to how she was enjoying the swamps. She had smilingly told him to get off the damned vox unless it was urgent, and he had offered a wholly unrepentant apology.

There had been a few voxed exchanges between the crew as they went about their duties, but Etsul resisted the urge to join in. She was commander now. The rapport she had to build with these people was different to that she'd had with her previous comrades. Besides, she had no desire to micro-manage: against her expectations, her crew seemed perfectly capable of going about their duties with Cadian efficiency.

Etsul instead retrieved her data-slate from her stowage locker and set about reviewing protocol and operational orders. The tank's internal lumens were dim. Her tired eyes soon felt grainy straining to read the data-slate's green-on-black text. She persevered, bludgeoning her tired mind into absorbing everything, going back and starting her page again each time she realised she had stopped concentrating. She would not slip into Tsegohan command language again. Her gaze flicked to the vid screens every minute or so. Her ears were alert for the call to engage over the vox.

She was surprised when Chalenboor suddenly addressed her.

'So, what's the score, sir?'

'Score, Chalenboor?'

'Like, what's the op? The job, yeah? What's the Emperor expect?'

'Chalenboor,' Etsul said, 'you have your orders. Are you asking for further operational details?'

'Sir, Commander Holtz used to brief us in detail,' put in Verro, sounding faintly apologetic.

'You've been advised of our destination,' she said. 'You know why we're out here, and that the Emperor expects. Is that not enough for soldiers of Cadia?'

'Commander Holtz didn't believe so,' Vaslav replied.

Etsul drummed her fingers against the side of her seat, then opened a private channel to Vaslav.

'Speaking freely, sergeant, what is your opinion on the matter?'

'Speaking freely, I believe Commander Holtz was right. Soldiers who know a little more of what they're doing can set about their duties with greater precision and focus. Banishes the dread of the unknown, the old man used to say. I appreciate many regiments struggle with compartmentalisation of information, but Cadians can be trusted, sir.'

'Very well then,' said Etsul. She might have mentioned that Masenwe had in fact briefed his crew in detail for every operation, but she found herself unwilling to do so. Either she would sound as though she was justifying the credibility of Tsegohan regiments in response to Vaslav's disparagement, or else leave her crew wondering whether she didn't trust them as her old commander had trusted her.

Feeling their expectant silence, she took a breath and began.

'The goal of Operation Jotunn is to advance on Mount Auric and in so doing draw the enemy's supreme commander into the field, whereupon we will ensure his demise and hopefully destabilise the heretic command structure in this theatre.'

'Baraghor the daemon king,' spat Trieve.

'Baraghor the heretic warlord,' Etsul corrected. 'Don't let superstition lengthen his shadow, Trieve.'

'No, sir,' replied the driver, sounding unconvinced. Etsul pressed on.

'Our first objective is to reach waypoint sextus, which, if the advance continues on schedule, we will do at approximately oh two hundred hours. Sextus is located in the ruins of Fort Cowl. There we will dig in for a four-hour period while the lines redress. I intend for us to eat and sleep in shifts. Sergeant, take the opportunity to deal with our fuel shortfall.'

'Fort Cowl fell during the Axefall Push,' said Trieve. 'It's a place of ill-omen, sir.'

'Nonetheless, that is our objective,' she replied. 'The advance will recommence at oh six hundred, at which point we'll trek our way to waypoint quarturus in the Costmarus manufactorum sprawl. That'll be our consolidation point, before we push on further to the Orphide hab-belt.'

'That will put us a day's march from the foothills of Mount Auric,' said Vaslav.

'And then we get to turn that duct-squirmer Baraghor into a bloodstain, yeah?'

'I doubt we shall advance as far as Mount Auric,' mused Verro.

'Why so?' asked Etsul. She knew the answer, but wanted to see how sharp the lad on the sponson gun was.

'Each muster point is somewhere we can easily fortify,' said Verro. 'Besides which this is a combined advance. The footsloggers are setting the pace. If command wanted us to surprise the enemy we'd have been going in spearhead along the transitways, full-speed armour charge and hope to the Throne we got there before Baraghor could muster his response. Or, even more likely, in that case why wouldn't they just have called in the Imperial Navy to bomb his stronghold to rubble then rain Glory Boys onto the remains?'

'Just so, and doubtless command have their reasons for

ANDY CLARK

doing neither,' said Etsul. 'As you have established, Verro, there's no effort at surprise here. If I had to guess, group command don't want to spook the enemy into retreat.' She didn't voice the other possibility, that they didn't have sufficient air power or fast-assault assets left.

'Lure him out, but make him come to us while we're dug into one of those defensible muster points,' said Moretzin.

'Break 'im on the wall,' said Chalenboor.

'Knowing our luck, they'll hit us when we're as far between musters as they can,' commented Vaslav.

'It's the Geskans' job to see they don't, sergeant. We can trust them.' Etsul was annoyed with Vaslav for souring the mood, even if she didn't completely disagree.

'Heretics can have a go wherever they like, ain't going to matter,' spat Chalenboor. '*Tread*'s ready for them, aren't ya, girl?'

'She'll reap her toll,' agreed Verro.

'She'll need to, if we're going after Baraghor himself,' Vaslav persisted. 'It'll be like Kasr Kraf out there.'

'You are aware, sir, that there have been famous battles fought upon worlds other than Cadia?'

Etsul knew she should reprimand Trieve for impertinence to a superior officer, but leave it to Vaslav to make a reference only the Cadians would understand. Before she could intercede, First Lieutenant Askerov's voice crackled through her ear-bead.

'*Squadron to combat ready, Geskans report malfeasance ahead.*'

'Crew to high alert, rouse weapon spirits and stand to,' barked Etsul. Vaslav bent at once to his scope, Trieve to his instruments. A massive shell swung past, almost close enough to nudge Etsul's leg, held aloft by a rattling chain-sling and Loader Moretzin's augmetic strength. With her free hand, the

76

Cadian spun the wheel on the Demolisher cannon's breech. As it swung wide she rattled the shell forward into place.

She rapped her metal fist thrice against the hull, a signal audible over the Russ' power plant. Vaslav raised a clenched fist to acknowledge load-in, while Moretzin faded back. Etsul frowned at her grainy green vid screens as she sought some sign of the foe. The terrain was the same morass of swamp and ruin. There'd been no report of direct contact over the vox, nor any of the diabolical manifestations Etsul assumed would herald empyric malfeasance.

Her heart thumped at the base of her throat. She stared at her screens as though she could will them to reveal the enemy by intensity alone.

'Dead ahead,' barked Trieve. 'What in Throne's name is it?'

Etsul saw a strange mound emerging from the gloom ahead. It rose higher than the top of *Steel Tread*'s turret. Its silhouette was jumbled, but its shape reminded Etsul of the witch-burning pyres that had dominated the square of her home town every Ascension Day. Through the night-sight filters, smudged, green Geskan figures skirted around it aboard their quads. She could read their agitation in their body language. Their wide eyes glinted like green coins.

'It's bodies.'

As they drew level with the foreboding shape, Etsul realised Vaslav was right.

She saw an attenuated pyramid of corpses, all facing inward. They looked as though they had perished in the act of clambering atop one another. Rigor mortis had frozen some seemingly reaching for an unknown prize.

'Cause of death's no mystery,' Verro observed, sounding horrified. Long metal spikes burst from the corpses' backs,

ANDY CLARK

their torsos, their necks, as though the climbers had impaled themselves and their fellows alike with heedless abandon.

'How hard do you have to be shoved onto a spike to get impaled like that?' asked Moretzin.

Another metal spear, longer than the rest, rose from the top of the ghastly corpse-mound. Atop it was a warped sigil, a disc from which jutted a flowing protrusion. Two half-moon curves bisected it, one larger, one smaller, each curving away from the other. At the sight of it Etsul felt light-headed. Her skin crawled with sweat.

'Do not look at the sigil,' she snapped into the vox. Tearing her eyes away from the awful sight, she felt *Steel Tread* swerve. 'Driver! Trieve! Do not look at it!'

Trieve gave a start as though jolted awake. He wrenched his steering levers and brought the tank back on course. They passed the carrion mound scant feet to its right.

'Tell me those aren't Cadian soldiers,' said Vaslav.

'They aren't,' replied Verro. 'I got a good look at their uniforms as we passed, Emperor help me. Those were Vostokh.'

'Spinebacks? We just passed a bunch o' dead Spinebacks?' asked Chalenboor. 'What scragged 'em?'

'The God-Emperor gives us clear sight and we might trust its evidence,' intoned Trieve. 'You all know what you saw. It is cowardice to pretend otherwise.'

'The heretics did it to themselves,' said Verro. 'They just... clambered on top of one another and all... impaled themselves.'

'Why?' asked Chalenboor.

'It doesn't matter why,' snapped Etsul. 'The ways of heretics are insanity, and the less we understand the better. We are in enemy territory and we were ordered to high alert. Eyes on your screens and minds on the task.'

'Our armour is ignorance, our shield denial,' quoted Trieve. 'But sir, we should flagellate, that we might ward ourselves against this fell omen. We ought to offer of our pain to Him on the Throne.'

'Trieve, if you want to offer prayers for the Emperor's protection, I wholeheartedly endorse it. But now is not the time to halt our tank and engage in blood offerings. Maintain heading and combat effectiveness.'

'Sir–'

'No, Trieve,' Etsul ordered. 'This is not Brethia. We are Cadians, all of us, and we will act accordingly.'

Vaslav's shoulders stiffened as much as Trieve's. Etsul tried not to take his silence as mutinous.

If any of her crew offered prayers to the Emperor after their grisly encounter they did so privately, hidden from Etsul's hearing by the gruff bass of *Steel Tread*'s power plant. Yet as a second charnel pyramid loomed in the distance, and then a third, she muttered one of her own.

CHAPTER FIVE

CONTACT

By an hour after dawn, Etsul had sunk into an exhausted trance. She snapped back to wakefulness as the clipped tones of First Lieutenant Askerov filled her ear-bead.

'Squadron commanders, we're getting word of contact ahead. No corpse-piles this time, it's the real thing. They're hitting our skirmish screen hard.'

The muster at Fort Cowl had passed in an uninspiring jumble of overgrown ruins swallowed by darkness. There had at least been time for rations and brief sleep shifts. Etsul had taken on some fuel, which was more than could be said for *Steel Tread*. Thanks to a heavy hauler bogged down in a submerged trench, the logistical support train hadn't caught up to the front line by the time they had rolled out again. Thus, Vaslav's increasingly frustrating quest to fulfil the tank's logistical shortfall had come to naught.

Etsul had added this to the laundry list of lapses to discuss with him when the opportunity arose. She'd been rehearsing that conversation in her head when Askerov's call came through.

'Front line in our sector's been ordered forward to engage,' said Askerov. 'Captain Brezyk wants Third and Fourth squadrons on this. Plan is to hit the enemy hard and pull them into a stand-up fight, try to drag in more reinforcements. Captain didn't say as much, but it's my guess command want to escalate from this point. Feather in their caps if they can get the head heretic to throw in here and now, without a lot of fiddling about.'

'What's the plan, sir?' asked Lieutenant Jorgens of *Ogre*.

'Geskans are pinned down in a rubble field beyond a line of enemy-held bastions. Heretics ambushed them once they'd passed the structures, then surrounded them.'

'Someone's getting hauled up for not checking those towers properly,' commented Lieutenant Svekh, commander of *Consequences of Folly*.

'Geskan orders were to rune-mark possible strongpoints for aggressive probe by Cadian front lines, then bypass them in the interests of expediency,' said Askerov. 'All the same, Svekh, you're likely right. Third Squadron are to act as armoured spearhead for a column of Eight-Thirty-Two Chimeras. They'll flank out through sector three-four-one, circle around the bastions and relieve the Geskans before they get overwhelmed. For our part, we've got infantry support from every Eight-Thirty-Two platoon in this sector, and artillery from reserves.'

'Target, sir?' asked Etsul.

'Bastions, Etsul, and I should make it clear I expect nothing less than gratuitous property damage. Captain wants those towers reduced to rubble and the heretics thoroughly purged.'

'Yes, sir,' chorused Etsul, Jorgens and Svekh.

'Be advised, also, psykana division are prophesying empyric turbulence,' added Askerov.

'*Eclipse on its way in, sir?*' asked Jorgens.

'*You know witches, Jorgens, nothing's certain. But we've been asked to cascade the warning to all crews. Keep one eye on the skies through daylight hours, ladies and gentlemen, in case the Emperor seeks to test our mettle.*'

Etsul glanced at her vid-feeds. The dawn sky stretched like jaundice-yellow glass over the endless swamps. Sepia scuds of cloud stained it, edged with silver and coiling in patterns that seemed disinclined to obey the prevailing wind. She'd been on Croatoas long enough to recognise the signs of an impending eclipse storm. To her mind, the Rift had more to do with such unnatural phenomena than the Emperor.

'*You have your orders, squadron. Who are you?*'

The question threw Etsul. Jorgens and Svekh evidently knew what was expected of them as they both barked, '*Hammers!*'

'*And what do you do?*'

'*Crush heretics!*'

'*Smashing. Advance combat speed and make ready for a brawl. For Cadia and the Emperor.*' With that, Askerov cut the link and tactical data began to scroll over *Steel Tread*'s read-out displays. Jittery tension tried to crawl up from Etsul's gut. She recalled dark figures, close canyon walls, blood…

'Worry what is. Let the rest go,' she told herself. She had her tank, her crew and her orders. What more could the Emperor provide?

Etsul keyed the crew vox.

'Geskan forces engaging up ahead and getting the worst of it. The rune on your auspex maps shows a line of enemy-held fortifications cutting us off from them. Third Squadron are escorting armoured fists in a right hook through sector three-four-one to relieve the Trenchrunners. We're rolling up with the infantry to knock out those towers. Crew to high alert, rouse weapon spirits and stand to. Maintain advance speed, Driver Trieve.'

Around them, the ponderous Astra Militarum war machine dragged its feet from the mud. Infantry formations picked up their pace. Cadian soldiers, doubtless cold, wet, leech-bitten and fatigued, nonetheless broke into a jog at their officers' orders. Etsul shook her head in admiration. To right and left, *Brigand*, *Ogre* and *Consequences of Folly* accelerated to combat speed. Demolishers were not swift beasts, but all the same they pulled ahead. Black fumes snorted from their exhausts. Fans of muddy water and churned vegetation sprayed up behind their tracks.

'Trieve, maintain formation and pace,' Etsul ordered. 'All of you, keep your eyes peeled. Heretics have no honour. They won't hesitate to entrap us if they get the chance.'

Off to the left, Etsul saw the tanks of Third Squadron accelerating away on their own mission. They accompanied more than a dozen Chimeras packed with Cadian soldiers. She spotted Aswold's *Vexation's Cure* on the right flank of the formation. Etsul felt a pang of longing for the more familiar vehicles, and her old gunner's seat. She keyed her vox and selected Aswold's channel.

'Good hunting, Lieutenant Aswold,' she said.

'And to you, Lieutenant Etsul! Try not to knock those towers over on top of us, eh?'

'Have some faith, Horathio. The Emperor protects.'

'That he does, Hadeya.'

She cut the link with a tight smile.

'Terrain changing ahead, sir,' said Trieve.

Etsul took a moment to decipher the odd sight on her vid screens. It was a slope of ferrocrete, stretching across the line of their advance until it vanished in the haze of distance. It rose out of the waters like a shallow ramp, reminding her of nothing so much as one continental plate sliding under another during subduction. The impression was reinforced by broken fault lines and outcroppings of ferrocrete that showed where the artificial ground had broken under the stresses of being consumed by the natural.

'This was the foundation of the Signetine industrial belt,' voxed Vaslav, consulting a map-slate. 'Throne knows how it's subsided like this.'

'We'll have scouted the area as best we could, with boots on the ground and eyes in orbit. If it wasn't navigable, command wouldn't have sent us this way,' said Etsul. 'Ahead-steady, Trieve.'

Steel Tread shuddered and tilted as they followed the rest of the squadron up the ferrocrete slope, muddy water sluicing from their track skirts. Etsul felt her tank surge as it found better purchase on the solid surface.

'Relief for the 'sloggers,' commented Verro.

'Yeah, don't know about that,' replied Chalenboor. 'About as much cover as a macro-duct. Wouldn't want to be runnin' 'round out there in skivvies.'

'Focus, sponsons, eyes up for threats,' Etsul admonished them. She found herself agreeing with Chalenboor. The grey expanse was broken here and there by the tangled remains of industrial pipelines or a ragged fault line frothing with thorned creepers. Otherwise, there was little enough cover for the tanks, let alone infantry.

'Slope levels out one mile ahead,' said Trieve after a glance at his auspex screen. 'Reading structures approximately one mile further beyond that, as well as a major geological feature crossing through sector three-two-nine.'

'Looks to be the line of Transitway Twelve on the old maps,' said Vaslav.

'Contacts?' asked Etsul.

'Energy augury from the rough location of the Geskans' engagement, sir,' said Vaslav, switching his attention to another read-out. 'Blurs over the fortifications, though, can't make out specifics.'

Taut silence fell between the crew as their tank rumbled towards the light show of a battle in progress. Etsul watched her screens with feverish intensity. She probed the shadows of each fissure and ridge, seeking foes crouched in ambush.

As they reached the top of the slope, they found the ferro-crete had erupted into jagged spars like the splinters of a broken bone. The Demolishers ploughed through the obstructions, scattering rubble in their wake. Verro whistled softly over the vox at the sight before them.

The fortifications could be seen ahead. They were slab-sided, bristling with sentry guns and fire-slits, surrounded by a network of barricades. Stretching between them and the advancing Imperial forces was a wasteland of shattered ferro-crete. Broken pipes jutted from chasms, wide enough that *Steel Tread* could have driven into their maws. Mazes of chain-link fence sagged between rusty poles, weighed down by plant life. Here and there a gantry or crane still teetered, or else lay in a broken sprawl. Whatever catastrophe had rent this region, it had not spared Transitway 12. Its mountainous rubble formed a line of hillocks that coiled across the landscape and wound around one flank of the fortification line.

'Throne, that's a lot of hiding places,' breathed Etsul.

'Auspex readings resolving into major conflict beyond the fortification line,' said Vaslav, rather redundantly, Etsul thought. They could all see the distant maelstrom of gunfire and explosions.

'What about the status of the bastions themselves?' she asked.

'Confirming solid auspex returns from their position, significant energy signatures and life signs,' said Vaslav. There was no obvious sign of the foe amongst the defences, but then, if they had any sense, they were hunkered down and waiting for the loyalists to close the distance.

'Elsewhere?' she pressed.

'Sir, we're not a Baneblade. We have only the standard auspex suite,' replied the sergeant, sounding aggrieved. Etsul's instincts prickled. *Steel Tread* ground forward, lurching over rubble and across shatter holes. Stowage rattled, the crew's possessions shuddering within lockers and webbing-slings. Rebreather masks swayed and clinked together on their rack above Vaslav's head. The squadron pressed on across the ruin-field, Cadians toiling around them.

'Sergeant, sponsons, confirm we have range then commence suppression fire against the towers until other targets present,' ordered Etsul.

'Sir, lascannon and heavy bolters can comply. Main gun is still several thousand feet out of range.' Etsul cursed herself silently. She was in a Demolisher now, and they might as well drive up and tip the shells out of the top hatch for all the range their main gun possessed.

A voice broke into the short-range command channel. Its accent was Geskan, its tone panicked.

'*...again, we are pinned in place, sector three-four-six, enemy forces on all sides. They have us surrounded. Requesting immediate reinforcement, there's–*' The voice cut out.

'*Squadron, form up and accelerate into bombardment range,*' voxed Askerov. '*Third are less than two minutes out. Whatever the enemy have lurking in those forts, we need it looking at us not them.*'

Etsul could restrain herself no longer. She keyed a private channel to the first lieutenant.

'*Lieutenant Etsul?*'

'Sir, I think we're being drawn into an ambush.'

'*On what basis?*'

Etsul stared at the vox-unit, trying to work out if Askerov was testing her.

'Terrain. Flanking high ground. Enemy haven't engaged even though they must have us in heavy-weapons range by now. Vostokh regimental strategic preference is for heavy fire from high ground and with the rubble hills to our right… Sir, it's…' She bit down on the word 'obvious'. To her surprise, Askerov heard something quite different.

'*It's Yarroe Canyon all over again. Understandable, Etsul, but don't let past trauma colour your conduct.*'

'Sir–'

'*Your instincts are good. I encourage my officers to think for themselves. The likelihood had not escaped my notice, but right now our duty is to bring down those towers and we can't do it from all the way back here. Consider this a lesson in Cadian caution, Etsul. Keep your eyes peeled and stay on mission.*'

Etsul allowed herself a slow three-count after Askerov cut the link. Cadian caution. She wasn't sure whether to curse or laugh.

'Trieve, tighten up on *Brigand*,' she ordered. 'Bring us into main-gun range of the fortifications then get us hull down. Focus on guarding our right flank and let *Brigand* watch the left.'

'Yes, sir,' Trieve replied.

Steel Tread's power plant snarled as the tank accelerated across the broken ground. Etsul saw chain-link vanish under the treads as they burst through a decaying fence line. In her rear vid-feed she saw Cadians hastening through the gap, dashing from one outcropping of cover to the next.

The slit windows of the fortifications blossomed with muzzle flare. Deformed silhouettes rose above the parapets, hefting heavy guns and missile launchers into position. Projectiles roared down on trails of flame, bursting amongst the advancing Cadians. Bodies were tossed high.

In the same instant, Chalenboor sang out, 'Contact right, contact right!'

Etsul heard the whoop of the incoming shells even over the roar of the tank's power plant. She could have sworn she felt the visceral thump as they detonated amongst the Cadian ranks.

'Mortars on the ridge,' Vaslav reported. Explosions blossomed like hellish flowers across the ruin-field. Etsul saw a nearby command squad fall into cover behind a heap of rubble, banner held high, officer shouting into her voxman's handset until a mortar round landed in their midst. The Cadians dissolved in blood and flame. The handset spun through the air and out of vid-image, but Etsul was sure it bounced from *Steel Tread*'s hull.

'*Squadron, maintain advance,*' Askerov ordered through her ear-bead. There was no panic in the first lieutenant's voice, or else it was too well masked for Etsul to hear it. '*Stay on mission. Fire discipline, no chancy long-shots, conserve ammunition for stationary fire. Infantry can take care of themselves.*'

They were certainly trying to. On the vid screens, Etsul saw the nearest Cadian squads dive for cover then come up shooting. They gave the closest bastion a volley, fingers of lethal laser-light questing for fire-slits or raised heads above battlements. The squads' weapons teams set up their heavy bolters and autocannons, loaders slotting ammo feeds into place even as gunners' lips moved with rites of awakening. Etsul's attention was torn away as something hit the turret armour hard enough to ring it like a gong and dislodge stowage from the interior webbing.

'Mortar round, minimal damage,' reported Vaslav. More shells screamed down. Las-bolts flashed back and forth. A rocket glanced from their left track skirt. Etsul's heart was hammering. Her mouth was dry. She jumped at the feel of blood running down her face then hissed as she realised it was sweat. She reminded herself again that this wasn't Yarroe, then silently cursed that their main gun was still, somehow, out of range.

The bastion's automated guns were firing now, heavy bolters raining shells on the Cadian soldiers.

'Let me give the bastards some back, sir,' snarled Chalenboor.

'Negative, wait until we're stationary,' replied Etsul, wishing she could tell them to let fly with everything they had.

'Sir, we're not juvies, we can shoot straight on the roll.'

'Doubtless, Gunner Chalenboor, but you have your orders,' snapped Etsul.

'Sir.' Chalenboor made the word a slur.

The Cadians were falling behind them now, dug in and trading fire with both the enemy in their fortifications and the invisible foes up on the ridge. Etsul winced as explosives rained down on the loyalist positions. The fortress line loomed ahead, and now she saw dark figures moving behind the barricades about the towers' feet. She was about to vox a warning to Askerov when Vaslav called out.

'Main gun in range!'

'Halt in cover, acquire targets and fire at will,' Etsul barked. Now, at last, she would see what this new tank of hers could do.

Steel Tread jounced as Trieve swung them down into a shallow crater, and Verro felt a little safer as the driver put a slab of ferrocrete between them and the ridge. Verro hung on to the grab rail beside his station, riding the motion with practised ease. His restraint belt caught him about the waist as the Demolisher lurched to a halt and the power plant's bellow slackened off. In the comparative lull, he imagined he heard small-arms fire plinking from the hull.

He recognised the eye of the storm and braced in readiness.

'Main gun, target acquired,' called the sergeant. A rune lit up on Verro's targeter. A blocky, gargoyle-encrusted tower rising right at the heart of the defence line. Its gun-slits flickered with muzzle flare. It looked indomitable, a stone-and-steel wave cresting high to crash down upon all before it.

'Main gun firing!'

Verro let his mouth hang open; to do otherwise was to risk the overpressure from the Demolisher cannon blowing his eardrums out like bloody little frag-charges.

The cannon fired, all seventy-something tons of tank bucking with the recoil. The huge shell left the barrel in a blast of propellant. It crossed the distance to the enemy-held fortification and detonated like the fury of the God-Emperor unleashed. On his vid screen, Verro saw the ferocious fireball, saw the tower shudder so hard that it looked as though it were attempting to rip up its foundations and flee. Ferrocrete and bodies tumbled through the air. The tower's battlement jerked as though someone had given it a hard shove, then collapsed forward into the catastrophic wound torn in the floors below it. A landslide of rubble poured down the tower's front and Verro grinned to see heretic corpses amongst it.

Filtration shrines whirred to life, dragging fyceline fumes from the air.

The engine revved as Trieve nudged them back into position.

The commander, still keyed into the internal vox, breathed a heartfelt, '*Bloody Throne...*'

'That's the stuff, old girl,' muttered Verro, patting the tank's hull with pride.

'Main gun, reload,' Etsul ordered, clearly remembering herself. 'Sponsons, there's heretics at the barricades. Purge them. Sergeant, get that lascannon firing.' The orders brought Verro back to himself. It had been so long since they'd seen any real action, he'd forgotten how mesmerising it could be watching the Demolisher cannon do its work.

'Targeter green, weapon spirit wrathful,' he said, deftly working the controls of his sponson gun. More target runes flared red on his display and he saw that Spinebacks troopers were indeed moving at the barricades. Verro had seen to the issue with his vid screen while they had been halted overnight, and now had a nice, clear view. Probably he ought to have slept more, but he couldn't stand working with suboptimal equipment.

'Emperor, I beseech thee, guide my aim,' Verro prayed, hurrying through the third psalm of armaments as his autoloaders cycled. 'Oh, wrathful weapon spirit, spend this day your fury upon the heretic foe.'

He hit his firing runes and the heavy bolter flared to life. Sat virtually nose to the hull as he was, Verro dimly heard the weapon's thunder and felt the barest ghost of its recoil.

There was an art to remote-operating a sponson gun, guiding it through a vid screen and a targeter while you sat perpendicular to the direction you were firing. Verro had taken some time to get the knack, but when Nix joined the crew she had taken to it like a natural.

Their bolt-shells roared away on trains of fire. Some hit the barricades, blasting massive rents in them. Others impacted living flesh. Those caused geysers of blood and bone to erupt, and sent dismembered limbs spinning skyward. Verro watched his ammo-runes, retrained his aim, kept firing.

Moretzin moved past, a dark shape in his peripheral vision. She had a new shell in the chain hoist and was swinging it forward, supporting its massive weight with her augmetic arm.

'She was a cyber-gladiator for uphive toffs,' he voxed to Chalenboor. 'Mashed up muties and sump rats like you for entertainment.'

Chalenboor made a rude sound through the vox, then whooped as she scored a particularly visceral hit.

'Mashed up muties? Relatives of yours, yeah?' she replied conversationally.

'My mother was a captain in the Kasr Varg garrison and received the Order Crimson for valorous conduct,' he replied with mock affront.

To his right, Moretzin had the breech open. With the economy of motions oft repeated, she swung the shell into place and spun the hatch closed. She clanged her metal fist against the hull a foot from the sergeant's head thrice.

Loaded and ready.

Furious blooms of fire showed where the other tanks of Fourth Squadron had loosed their own shells into the defence line, but none had nailed their shot like *Steel Tread*. Sergeant Vaslav was a lot of things, Verro thought, but a poor shot was not one of them.

The tank jerked as something exploded against its hull. Verro's ear was practised enough to pick out armour-piercing impacts.

'Direct contact right,' reported Chalenboor. 'They've got rocket-lobbers on the ridge, big enough to give us trouble. Engaging.'

'Negative, Chalenboor,' the commander replied. 'Focus forward. Let the infantry worry about the ridge.'

'No wonder she got her last tank shot up, yeah?' hissed Chalenboor on Verro's local channel.

'We start splitting fire, the trench rats will be over their barricades and into our tracks before you know it,' Verro replied.

'They'll be storming over the barricades if someone on the ridge scrags us with a lucky shot, that's for sure.'

'Main gun, traverse forty degrees right, depress ten, acquire target,' ordered the commander, her words overriding their conversation.

'Yes, sir,' replied the sergeant, then, 'Main gun firing.'

Verro opened his mouth. *Steel Tread* bucked. Their shell gouged a massive crater in another enemy-held tower, and it toppled sideways like a poleaxed drunk to bury a bunker and several barricades.

'Praise the Emperor!' cried Trieve.

'Fine shot, sergeant,' said Commander Etsul as Moretzin rattled forward with a fresh shell.

'Thank you, sir,' said the sergeant, and his tone doused Verro's delight. To the commander, it no doubt sounded businesslike, but Verro had known Sergeant Vaslav long enough to hear the acid dislike there. He was surprised at the surge of frustration he felt in that moment. They had all loved Holtz, whether he deserved it or not, but the old man was gone and they had a new commander. He knew Nix took time to warm to authority figures, if she ever did, but he wished that Vaslav could just set aside his dislike for Etsul and get on with the job.

He viciously twisted his controls, traversed his heavy bolter in its mount and sent a stream of rounds punching into the enemy.

To their left, two Demolisher shells hit the last enemy

tower in quick succession. The second plunged through the breach made by the first and the tower blew apart in an apocalyptic rain of debris.

'Dreg me, must have hit a magazine!' shouted Chalenboor. Hunks of rubble the size of Tauroxes were crashing down around them. Verro thumped his console with renewed elation at the sight. Trieve was hunched forward, doubtless offering prayers of thanks. Commander Etsul's voice cut through their celebrations.

'Steady at your posts. Hold fire and redress on the barricades. Sergeant, main gun left ten degrees, depress forty. Everyone ready to fire on my mark.'

'Sir?' asked the sergeant. 'Enemy are shell-shocked. I don't know how it works in lighter marks of Russ, but–'

'Sergeant, we don't have time for you to question orders. Shut up and do your duty.'

Verro flinched. On his screen, he saw *Ogre* surging forward from its firing position, Lieutenant Jorgens clearly sharing Vaslav's opinion that the enemy were as good as beaten.

A ferocious string of explosions marched along the rubble ridge and turned their vid-feeds white. The shock wave from the artillery barrage shook *Steel Tread* on its tracks, even from hundreds of yards away.

A volley of bundled krak grenades sailed from behind the barricades to detonate beneath *Ogre*'s tracks. Verro was dimly aware of metal shapes spewing from under the tank's armour skirts, but took long moments to grasp that they were severed track links. *Ogre* slewed and ground to a halt, side-on to the foe.

In the same instant came a cacophony of howls so deafening as to be audible even through tank armour. Far from teetering and breaking, the Spinebacks burst from cover and charged headlong at the Cadian tanks. It was the first time in many months Verro had seen any of the formerly loyal Vostokh infantry up close.

His mind rebelled at the sight.

He saw rebreather hoods fused like flesh to skulls, lumpen bodies splitting their grey uniforms where they had bulged in mutant profusion, bone spurs and quills growing from backs and limbs. The howls poured from the distended jaws of the most hideously mutated foes, whose mouths yawned like fanged cannon barrels. That was as much as his conscious mind could absorb, but later Verro's nightmares would be troubled by bulging yellow eyes behind grubby lenses, by red wet maws, maggot-pale scarified flesh and grotesque piercings. Many of the heretics clutched lasguns or trench clubs, but others carried bundles of krak grenades lashed to what looked like meathooks. If just one of those charges found its way into their tracks it could mean death. Commander Etsul's voice cut through the madness, cold and hard as iron.

'All guns, fire!'

Training took over. Verro's jaw dropped open even as his thumbs depressed his firing runes. *Steel Tread* rocked. Caught point-blank by the Demolisher's fusillade, the charging foe came apart as though they'd run headlong into an industrial grinder.

The commander had seen the counter-attack coming, he realised. She had good instincts. Verro hunched forward over his controls and concentrated on culling the foe.

'You don't get to catch me unprepared again, you vermin,' snarled Etsul.

She had to admit her respect for the Demolisher was increasing. As her tank's main armament reduced the foe's front ranks to vapour, she forgave the gun its paucity of range. Still, her knuckles were clenched, and her teeth gritted hard enough to grind.

'Good work, Lieutenant Etsul!' barked Askerov in her ear. 'Squadron, keep the heretics away from Ogre. Jorgens, status report?'

'Holed right flank, tread's a wreck. Pietov and Deiso are injured, and… I think Masra's dead, sir.' Jorgens' voice was groggy.

'Hold on, lieutenant, support is on its way,' urged Askerov.

Brigand's main gun spat another shell into the charging traitors. More Spinebacks were slain, yet still more charged heedless through the flames and screamed as they came. Etsul had the awful impression that not one of the enemy soldiers felt fear. Instead, their expressions spoke of bestial elation. Bolt-shells burst some like bloody blisters, yet their comrades ran on and seemed to exult in the visceral sprays that drenched them. More and more foes poured over the barricade, and as the tide swelled Etsul realised that their charge would hit home. At this rate, Jorgens and his crew would be overrun.

'Driver Trieve, wheel to address. Gunners, do what you can.'

Steel Tread's blazing guns culled more heretics. Still there were too many, their momentum too great. Amongst the press Etsul made out a larger figure, a traitor horribly stretched and swollen with mutant muscle. It thrust a path through its fellows, its shoulders crested by bone spines, its arms ending in thick metal hooks that looked as though they would rip the armour plates right off Ogre's hull. A lascannon blast skimmed over the monster's shoulder. Bolt-shells detonated around it, slaying the traitors to either side but leaving their champion miraculously untouched. It appeared to have the luck of the Dark Gods themselves.

'No, I don't think so,' said Etsul. Leaving her crew to work, she threw open the turret hatch.

Smoke fouled the air. The stench of burned flesh and ordure was choking. The screams and the roar of gunfire were deafening. Bracing her feet firmly in the turret-stirrups, Etsul thumped the arming rune on her pintle storm bolter and swung it to bear.

'Holy bolter, be bellicose in thy wrath,' she prayed, then squeezed the triggers. Her gun barrels spat flame and the massive mutant stumbled as she riddled it with bolts. They detonated in rapid succession, blowing the beast to bloody gobbets twenty yards from *Ogre*'s flank. The crowd behind it barely missed a step, swarming over its corpse, while yet more heretics spilled through the ruins of the bastions to the north. Etsul had a grim premonition that it wasn't just *Ogre* about to be overwhelmed.

She wouldn't run. She would honour Masenwe's sacrifice with her own.

'*Hold the line!*' Askerov was shouting. '*Hold the line!*'

Etsul kept shooting. She knocked down a heretic aiming his grenade launcher at *Ogre*'s rent flank. She cut the legs from under a screaming mutant who brandished a bladed steel icon. She blew the head from a scar-faced horror.

The enemy surged closer.

Suddenly a rain of las-bolts joined the fire of the Demolishers. Blasts of plasma burned through the air. Bolt-shells blew heretics from their feet and took off their heads. Etsul blinked as she realised the fusillade was hitting the heretics from both front and back. Askerov had taken to her own turret and now Etsul looked across at her senior officer. Their eyes met, and they grinned fiercely at the shared realisation.

The infantry had caught up. Better yet, the fight beyond

the towers had been won. The heretics were trapped between hammer and anvil.

Etsul saw hulking shapes moving amidst the smoke, the tanks of Third Squadron emerging like deep-sea leviathans and pouring fire into their trammelled foes. Engines roared as Geskan Aquilus warquads sped around the tanks, their pillion riders snapping off las-shots to fell one heretic after another.

Cadian infantry sprinted into position alongside Fourth Squadron. They dropped into firing crouches and peppered the enemy with shots. Etsul worried the two loyalist forces would threaten one another with their crossfire, yet both regiments knew their work well. The Cadians aimed low, scything shots into legs and bellies, minimising the chances of stray rounds. The Geskans flowed out around the traitor flanks, their camo-cloaked infantry moving like wraiths to take up firing positions amidst the rubble.

It was over with remarkable suddenness, considering the desperate bloodshed that had come before. The last Spine-backs were gunned down with ruthless efficiency. Then there were only loyalist forces, bloodied but unbowed, blinking at each other across a field of corpses.

'Victory,' said First Lieutenant Askerov in Etsul's ear. 'Praise the Emperor, we have victory.'

It took some time before the advance could recommence. Etsul had heard tell of Imperial military formations who could fight on tirelessly, moving swift as the wind and dog-ging their enemies relentlessly. The soldiery of the Militarum Tempestus were apparently capable of such feats, as suppos-edly were the legendary Space Marines. Privately Etsul had long wondered if the Adeptus Astartes were more folklore than fact, a hopeful tale told to bolster flagging human spirits.

Whatever the case, she and her fellow Cadians were not Space Marines, and the Astra Militarum could not react so swiftly to changing circumstances. The lines of advance needed to be redressed. Emergency repairs and medicae attention took time. So it was that Askerov ordered her squadron to dig in amidst the rubble of the bastions they had laid low, then gave them an hour's comparative peace. Etsul ordered her crew to check over *Steel Tread*, to tally ammunition and fuel reserves, and then to eat and rehydrate.

For herself, she clambered out of her tank and took a short walk through the devastation to stretch her muscles. The post-battle adrenaline comedown left her shaking slightly. Her lamentable lack of sleep made her limbs and brain feel leaden. She needed a little time away from the crew to process her impressions of them in action, and she wanted to show Vaslav that she trusted him in command, whether it was true or not.

Sensible to the danger of an active combat zone she went only a short way, rolling the kinks out of her neck before crouching in the lee of a heap of rubble and staring off at nothing.

'I'm told you fought well.'

She looked up and offered Aswold a wan smile as he picked his way over the rubble and squatted next to her. His fine new Cadian fatigues were rumpled and sweat stained, and there were dark shadows under his eyes.

'It seems you did the same,' she said. He shrugged, keeping his attention on the medicae teams picking their way over the battlefield. Each time they found another wounded soldier they would raise a crimson flag that brought orderlies and servitors hastening to their position. Some were borne away on stretchers, while others less fortunate were covered with shrouds and heaped for collection.

'I must have done something right,' he said, his tone dubious. 'They're making me first lieutenant.'

She looked at him sharply.

'Clarson?'

'First Lieutenant Clarson's tank caught a Spinebacks rocket. Brewed up before anyone could get out.'

Brewed up. Soldier's slang for a tank turning into a raging inferno from within, the crew trapped inside, screaming as they burned. Etsul clenched and unclenched her palms.

'Damn,' she said at last.

'Hmm,' agreed Aswold, his face a mask of uncertainty that looked ill-fitting after the confidence he'd exhibited in the scant few days she'd known him. Etsul pulled a small metal flask from a pouch on her tank suit and unscrewed its cap. She held the flask aloft.

'First Lieutenant Pavol Clarson, may the Emperor look kindly upon your soul and guide you safe to harbour,' she said, then took a swig. She offered the flask to Aswold. He took it.

'Unusual prayer,' he said then drank. She couldn't help but smile a little at his watering eyes and stifled cough. 'First Lieutenant Clarson,' he wheezed, and handed her back the flask.

'Medoch,' she said as she stowed her flask again. 'Tsegohan captains take flasks of it out on hunting voyages. They toast the lost back to home-harbour when someone goes overboard, or gets taken by an iguados. Tsegohan regiments adopted the custom, Emperor knows how many generations back. It matters to us, to be toasted on our last voyage.'

'There are worse traditions. On my home world, the death

of a warrior has different periods of mourning depending on how long they were in service. You could end up spending months in mourning for some moribund great-uncle you had never met, but who somehow drank their way through a decade of service.'

They both chuckled, but the spark of levity dwindled quickly. Silence breathed between them.

'So. First lieutenant now,' she observed.

'First lieutenant,' he replied glumly. 'And down to three tanks.'

'Same here,' she said. A Trojan recovery vehicle had arrived, enginseers fussing around the mauled *Ogre* before it was hauled away for repair behind the lines.

'This wasn't the stand-up brawl command wanted,' said Aswold. 'According to Captain Brezyk the line's encountered three more opportunist ambush parties like this one, all focused across a ten-mile stretch of the front, and all fought like daemons. We're the only ones who wiped ours out, though. The other enemy forces retreated north.'

'Looking to thin our ranks, test our strength?' Etsul suggested.

'Who understands heretics?' Aswold replied with a shrug. 'Word is we're progressing as planned once we've got the front line straightened out. Just waiting for second-line infantry reserves to move up and bolster the Eight-Thirty-Second, then it's on to the Costmarus industrial sprawl.'

'I don't trust any of this, Horathio,' she said. 'The Spinebacks... What's *happened* to them?' Nearby, servitors were throwing heretic bodies onto piles, while a Ministorum priest with a swan-necked golden flamer kept the pyres smouldering. There was scant to recognise as human about anything here.

'*Heresy* happened to them,' he replied. 'But I know what you mean. They're like animals. Still, someone's still in charge on their side of the fence, and still cunning enough to lay four simultaneous ambushes.' He stood and she followed him up, placing both hands on the small of her back and stretching until it clicked.

'Watch out for yourself, first lieutenant,' she said.

'You too, lieutenant,' he said. 'I've no desire to observe your toasting custom for you. Throne knows my throat couldn't handle two doses of that paint stripper!' He flashed her his usual smile, but as she walked back to her tank Etsul thought it had looked a little hollow.

For herself, and despite everything, Etsul felt oddly triumphant. She had prepared herself for the worst – for her crew to fail her and her them, for another disaster to set her sailing into the God-Emperor's harbour on her last voyage.

And yet her crew had performed well. Her tank had weathered the storm. Both, under her supervision. Because of it, even. As *Steel Tread* loomed ahead of her, Etsul allowed herself a private smile that even the poisoned clouds of the impending eclipse storm and the fields of dead could not sour.

CHAPTER SIX

WAYPOINT QUARTURUS

Etsul ground her knuckles into eyes raw with exhaustion. She took a dim view of combat stimms, but she knew she would have to resort to them soon. They were less compromising than unconsciousness. She'd managed to catch a catnap when she returned to her tank, but it wasn't the same as a solid eight hours on a real pallet.

She refocused on her vid-feeds. An hour ago, the Costmarus industrial sprawl had been a dark presence on the horizon, ominous as a tidal wave. Now it had resolved into ragged silhouettes. Smokestacks stretched for the unnaturally coiling clouds. Huge buildings hulked like wounded animals. Etsul could see the telltale flicker of explosions and muzzle flare amongst them.

She hoped the Geskan reconnaissance platoons that had pushed ahead were giving as good as they got.

Steel Tread's feeds showed the might of the Astra Militarum pressing forward around her. The terrain had transitioned from swamp-with-ruined-urban-outcroppings to ruined-urban-landscape-dotted-with-swamp a dozen miles back. Command had taken the opportunity to accelerate the offensive.

'*Looks as though the Geskans are having a sore time of it, no?*' asked Aswold over their private channel.

'Looks to me like they got overeager, and we have to pull their backsides out of the ripfish pool,' Etsul replied.

'*Probably not their fault. Command want their stand-up fight. I'm guessing they flung the Geskans into the grinder in hopes of keeping the enemy pinned.*'

'As though the animals we fought this morning need an excuse for violence.'

'*They do seem indecently keen for the fight. So much for digging in around waypoint quarturus. And I was so looking forward to a few hours shut-eye.*'

On Etsul's screens, flights of Imperial gunships screamed towards the industrial sprawl. Distant fires leapt.

'I just want to get on with it,' she sighed. 'Honestly, I hope Baraghor *is* here so we can kill the bastard, then get some sleep.'

Aswold laughed. '*Typical heretic, so inconsiderate.*'

Before Etsul could reply, a crisp chime sounded through her ear-bead.

'Got to go,' she said.

'*The Emperor protects.*'

Etsul switched frequencies and said, 'Lieutenant Etsul reporting, sir.'

'*Excellent, that's everyone,*' replied Askerov, voice crisp as the creases in a parade-ground uniform. '*We're half an hour out from the engagement zone. This is your brief in detail. Reconnaissance in force suggests a significant heretic presence deployed to hold the Costmarus sprawl and further enemy reinforcements moving down from the north. Strategos estimate a high probability*'

*Baraghor is among them, though there have been... irregulari-
ties... that are making it impossible to be certain.'*

Etsul felt gooseflesh prickle her skin. She knew a euphemism
for witchery when she heard one.

*'We're to operate on the assumption our primary target is present.
Be advised, we're only authorised for airborne or artillery support as a last resort. Command want Baraghor eyeballed and the
kill confirmed by ground troops, which won't happen if we just
reduce his probable location to a glowing crater. That means the
job falls to the Hammers, while the Eight-Thirty-Two mop up.
Standard urban conflict supporting deployment, but the muster
command is "hammer blow". Repeat, "hammer blow". Rouse your
locator beacons and keep them choral – if someone gets eyes on
the arch-heretic, Captain Brezyk wants us ready to re-form on the
roll and get the job done.'*

Standard urban conflict supporting deployment was a long-
winded way of saying command were breaking their tank
squadrons up, then attaching them temporarily to the 832nd's
infantry platoons. Etsul was glad. Urban terrain was a nightmare for tanks, with its poor sight lines and ample cover for
infantry to get close with track-busting weaponry. No one
worth their seat wanted to roll into a cityfight without footsloggers on their flanks and rear.

*'An additional note. Geskans are reporting more of those charnel
heaps scattered through the combat zone. Enemy have dug blood-
channels between them to link one to the next, presumably in a mis-
guided attempt to fashion some manner of macabre water feature.
Word from the psykana is they've no other apparent purpose. They
detect no inherent witchery around the heaps. All the same, orders
are to keep your distance, or to bulldoze the bloody things if you
can't. Oh, and be sure to get your prayers in before we roll on the
sprawl. Let us garner what assistance we can from the God-Emperor.'*

Etsul shuddered at the reminder of the charnel heaps. The very thought of them made her skin crawl.

'Tactical inloads and deployment data to follow. Go with the Emperor, Fourth Squadron, and good hunting.'

The vox-link cut out. Etsul sat in silence for a moment, thinking.

To her right, lines of green runeform scrolled across a black tactical screen. While she waited for the inload to complete, Etsul tuned in with half an ear to the crew vox.

'…and in their suffering, they proved their faith. Do none of you appreciate that it is those already dead who are most fortunate?' Trieve was saying.

'Throne's sakes, Trieve, give it a rest,' groaned Verro. 'I'm already way past my expected fifteen-hour lifespan. As long as the God-Emperor keeps doling out the hours, I'll keep taking them. I can do a damn sight more to repay Him on this side of the veil!'

'Committing borderline tech-heresy is hardly repayment, Whiteshield.'

'I get to call him that, Trieve, not you,' snapped Vaslav. 'You keep your eyes on the terrain and your Brethian mouth shut.'

'I'll prove my faith by stickin' some bolt-shells in Baraghor's mutie friggin' face,' Chalenboor opined.

'You think he's a mutant?' asked Verro. 'There's all kinds of stories, that he's a mutant, or a monster or a witch.'

'King o' these freaks? Bet a week's stimms he's a mutant! Probably got a bunch of tentacles where his–'

'It doesn't matter what Baraghor *is*,' Etsul cut in. 'He is our primary target. Anything else is irrelevant.'

'Commander's right. Cadians know heretics are nothing special. Their beliefs are madness. Baraghor is just another grubby little lunatic who took the coward's way out, and we're going to kill him.'

The vox quieted after Vaslav's pronouncement. Etsul was pleased the sergeant had done his job for once, but she mistrusted the intensity with which he had spoken.

Runes blinked on her tactical screen, signalling inload complete.

> *11 Platoon 2nd / 3rd / 4th squadrons dividing, attach to 832nd infantry platoons…[stop]*

> *Maintain formation with assigned platoon, command authority temporarily reassigned to platoon officers…[stop]*

> *Rally to squadron command tank in event of muster command 'hammer blow'…[stop]*

> *Individual assignments follow…[stop]*

> *Waypoints and individual tactical objectives follow…[stop]*

> *Duty is its own reward. Zeal is its own excuse…[stop]*

'Be advised, squadron is adopting standard urban conflict supporting deployment,' Etsul voxed to her crew. 'I'm auto-linking tactical inloads to your stations and patching you into the squadron-level command channel for the duration.'

Her screen chattered again.

> *Assignment 4th Company, 6th Platoon…[stop]*

> *Assignment temporary commanding officer Captain Fynn… [stop]*

> *Tactical objectives: advance through Acetos refinery district / proceed and secure Teuchrius macro-warehouse / proceed and secure Seryph Bridge / hold line on north bank of Verivan Canal. Waypoint inload to follow…[stop]*

A flurry of runes pulsed on the auspex.

'Our assigned platoon is three miles west along the line, sir,' said Vaslav. 'Puts us out near that flank.'

'Driver Trieve,' said Etsul.

'Yes, sir,' he replied. *Steel Tread* wallowed then lurched as Trieve swung the vehicle about and made for their assigned platoon.

A flurry of impacts rang against *Steel Tread*'s hull. The tank was halfway along a processional, rusted processing vats looming to either side. Etsul was keenly aware of the alleys between the vats, thrown into gloom by the pipes and fronded lianas that formed a ceiling overhead. She saw figures moving through the gloom, but relaxed and let out a breath as they resolved into soldiers of Sixth Platoon.

Artillery shells whooped overhead. Fireballs blossomed above the ruins. Ahead, a rubble barricade blocked the far end of the processional, studded with improvised flakboard screens. Half-seen figures moved behind them, firing sporadically upon the advancing Cadians.

'Do the heretics have anything troublesome that you can see, sergeant?' asked Etsul.

'Looks like small-arms only, sir,' Vaslav replied, then, 'No, wait, lascannon, they have a lascannon!' Etsul's heart jumped into her mouth as a crimson beam leapt towards them.

'Close enough to blister the paintwork,' commented Verro.

'Main gun, depress ten degrees, acquire target and fire,' said Etsul, voice steady.

'Main gun firing.'

She parted her lips against the overpressure and watched as the shot blew a rent in the barricade. Moretzin's chain-sling rattled past Etsul's knee as the loader did her work. Etsul's knuckles relaxed.

'Blessed fine shot, gunner,' exclaimed Captain Fynn over the vox. *'Appreciate your removing another obstacle for us, lieutenant. The Emperor smiles!'*

'Just keep the heretics off our skirts, captain, and I'll consider us even,' she replied.

'Hah, just so,' he said. *'Hold back now if you would, I'll send our Chimeras through first to secure the junction. You roll up with the rearguard, eh?'*

'By your order, sir,' said Etsul.

Cadians dashed forward. Squads crouched in cover, loosing volleys to cover those advancing. Heretics returned fire, their sharpshooters loosing rounds from gantries and upper floors. The Cadians, in turn, poured shots into each sniper's position as they were revealed. Etsul felt grim satisfaction as corpses fell from blasted vantage points.

Seeing they were outgunned, the last handful of Spinebacks abandoned their barricade and charged headlong into the Cadians' guns.

'It's like they want to die,' commented Verro, sounding disgusted.

'More like they're stimmers,' said Moretzin.

'How so?' asked Etsul. It was Chalenboor who answered.

'It's like they ain't got it in 'em to run, like they're revvin' on the noise and violence and that. Like they need it.'

'You think they're taking combat drugs?' she asked.

'That, or something worse, sir,' Moretzin answered.

'Heretics,' said Vaslav, clearly feeling that was explanation enough.

A pair of Cadian Chimeras nosed through the ruined barricade in single file. Their small turrets swivelled, multi-lasers spitting light. Etsul saw Captain Fynn and his command squad leading the platoon up behind them.

Hulking figures burst from a side street and ran at the Chimeras. Their bulk marked them out as ogryns, but disfigured by the marks of heresy. Their torsos were bare, heavily pierced and scarified, and they bore the stigma of mutation. Each carried a long silver lance, incongruously elegant weapons for the meaty fists of the abhumans.

The Cadians let fly. First one then another of the ogryns went down in sprays of gore. The last drove his lance point first into the flank of a Chimera. Etsul winced, but instead of plunging deep into the tank, the lance's tip exploded with a flash. The ogryn reeled back and turned, dropping the spent weapon. A heavy bolter shell took his head off.

'Well. That was oddly underwhelming,' Verro commented dryly.

Frowning, Etsul voxed Fynn.

'Captain, damage report? Did they cause harm we can't see?'

'Not much, lieutenant. Shaped charge, just enough to blow a small hole in the outer hull and dislodge a plug of spalling. Couple of shrapnel casualties in the troop bay, that's all.'

'Ritual significance, perhaps? Truly the way of the heretic is that of the lost and unclean fool,' said Trieve. He gunned the Demolisher's engine and rolled them through the barricade.

'Thank the Throne for that,' exclaimed Verro. 'Imagine if they gave those monsters something that could really hurt a tank.'

'Consider them a threat nonetheless,' said Etsul as she frowned over data inloads. 'I'm seeing reports of those creatures all along the front line. They've holed a number of our armoured fighting vehicles. There's casualties reported. You all know what loose shrapnel does when it bounces about inside a tank. Might as well fire bullets through the top hatch.'

Her words had a sobering effect.

Fynn's voice came through the vox again.

'Tenth and Eighteenth platoons have pushed up through the

processing shrines and are securing the macro-warehouse. Twenty-First and Twenty-Sixth have fortified the counting house opposite Seryph Bridge and are holding for support. We need to pick up the pace, or this sector's going to stall.'

'Air support, sir?' asked Etsul.

'Nought, lieutenant,' he replied, a jouncing in his voice suggesting he was running. *'Aeronautica have squadrons aloft but they're all committed to ground attack ops in sectors seven-one-one and one-two. Throne alone knows where their Marauders have got to. No, job's all ours and the Emperor expects.'*

'Yes, sir. We won't disappoint Him.'

The loyalists pushed ahead with renewed urgency, meeting each ambush and snipers' nest with murderous firepower. *Steel Tread* claimed fresh kills with each exchange. Etsul felt a little stab of satisfaction each time. At the next intersection they were forced to skirt one of the enemy's ritual corpse-mounds. Etsul found herself watching the corpses closely, as though waiting for them to twitch to life and attack. She reproached herself for her superstitious fears, but still kept an eye on the mound until it was out of sight.

They rounded a corner and beheld the macro-warehouse. It was an architectural leviathan, its partly collapsed roof decorated with huge stone cherubim and saintly statues brandishing metal swords. The structure's walls were cratered, and statues had toppled from alcoves to shatter on the ground below. Heretic graffiti was everywhere.

Wrecks and bodies were scattered around the structure's cavernous southern entrance.

'Auspex shows heavy fighting near the northern end,' reported Vaslav.

The southern arch gave onto a vast interior space that made

Etsul think of cathedrums. Ferrocrete aisles ran between miles of conveyor belts and processing hubs where servitors hung rotting from their alcoves. Towering storage racks had toppled, spilling containers to form artificial hillocks. Damaged gantries climbed towards the distant ceiling. To Etsul's surprise she saw figures clambering up there, the flash of gunshots. She made a mental note not to unbutton the top hatch unless she had to.

'Engagement zone one hundred feet and closing,' said Vaslav. Etsul checked the feeds and saw fire leaping beyond the next mount of containers.

'Crew station readiness report,' she ordered. Everything came back green. She considered saying something more, a bit of inspirational oratory. In the end she settled for, 'Let's make the Emperor proud.'

They rounded the treacherous hillock of mangled containers, each larger than *Steel Tread*. Cadians fanned out to either side. Ahead lay the northern arch of the macro-warehouse, and beyond it the span of Seryph Bridge. Between them and the arch was an expanse of open ground where conveyor belts had been torn out and gantries snapped like severed threads. Pinned down on the near side of this space were the Tenth and 16th infantry platoons, crouched in pitiful cover. Etsul saw a couple of tanks among their number: a Fifth Company vehicle she didn't recognise and a burning hulk. The thought of Aswold flashed through her mind, chased by that of Askerov.

'Worry what is, let the rest go,' she murmured.

On the opposite side of no-man's-land, hull down behind a formidable barricade, were traitor tanks. Etsul scowled. The clean lines of once loyal Leman Russ were buried beneath bio-organic extrusions and metal spikes. Heraldry had been daubed over with colours that clashed so violently they hurt her eyes. Draconic maws snarled around cannon barrels. Long silver tubes coiled like serpents about each tank, cresting above their turrets in fans of war-horns.

'Partial match for Lothor Six-Sixty-Four Armoured,' Vaslav reported. 'Vehicles are too... debased... for definite ident.'

'Throne, that sound!' gasped Captain Fynn.

Etsul heard it, even through the tank's hull and the roar of their power plant: a cacophony of jarring notes at once atonal and weirdly melodic. It made her skin feel tight and hot. Saliva flooded her mouth, forcing her to breathe hard through her nose as she tried not to vomit. On the feeds, many Cadians had stopped firing and were staring slack-jawed, or else doubled over in puddles of vomit. Others fought on. Between the scant cover, the awful din and the return fire of the traitor tanks, though, their advance had stalled. Bodies strewed no-man's-land where squads had attempted to bridge the gap.

'Witchery,' Etsul snarled. 'Driver Trieve, your prayers please. All guns, focus fire on their turrets. Let's do what we can to silence them.'

Trieve rolled them up behind the toppled wreck of a Sentinel combat walker. As he drove, he prayed in the strident peal of a born zealot.

'Oh Emperor! See your faithful servants as they do battle in your name! See your faithful servants as they suffer, and as they bleed, and as they make offering of their pain unto your blessed being! Witness, oh Emperor, our sufferings and in them we beseech thee to see our piety, our purity, our resolve! Lend us but the merest portion of thy might, oh great God-Emperor, that though we might be all unworthy in our mortal flesh, still we might do thy work upon this mortal stage.'

As Trieve's oratory filled the vox, Etsul's gorge settled. She shook her head, feeling her thoughts clear. Evidently the driver's prayers were steadying her crew, as their fire bit home into the foe. Bolt-shells ripped through silver horns. A lascannon beam punched through the turret of a mutated Leman Russ, killing its main gun in a belch of smoke. A Demolisher shell blew a chunk out of the barricade.

The foe maintained their own fusillade in return. Etsul hissed as a shell skipped off their hull. A second hit home with a deafening bang that caused the lumens to flicker. Demolisher shells rattled in their rack. Verro cursed wordlessly over the vox.

'Damage report,' barked Etsul.

'Tank round to our mantlet,' reported Vaslav. 'Hit but didn't breach. Emperor's watching over us.'

'How long for, though?' breathed Etsul, scanning her screens urgently.

Her vox-bead chimed, the sound giving way to Askerov's voice, warped by static.

'Fourth Squadron, be advised, psykana operatives are warning of empyric build-up. Seems those corpse-piles might be more than just decorative flourishes after all. Eyes open for malfeasance.'

Etsul felt a chill at the words, but kept her attention on the troubles at hand.

Moretzin had halted halfway to the breech, bracing a shell in its sling. Now she rattled it forward and slammed it home, rapping her fist thrice against the hull. *Steel Tread* bucked as Vaslav took his shot and blew apart the turret on an enemy Russ. As the smoke cleared, the remaining enemy tanks were still there, still firing.

A squad of Cadians broke from cover and pelted out across no-man's-land. A deformed turret wheeled towards them.

Its Punisher cannon howled to life. Ten loyal soldiers of the Emperor were chopped into bloody meat before they'd made it a dozen paces.

Etsul ground her teeth. The bridge was in sight, but they couldn't reach it. The heretics were dug in so well even a Demolisher cannon wasn't going to dislodge them, while charging the barricade would just get them killed. Any moment the foe might outflank the loyalist position or push troops up through the macro-warehouse to catch them from behind.

'Captain Fynn, we *have* to break their line,' she voxed. 'There's a handful of them for Throne's sakes.'

'We're doing all we… hnggg… all we can…' panted the captain. *'If you can't…. can't… dislodge them with that… guh… gun I don't know… Suggestions are… hn… welcome.'*

'Options,' Etsul snapped at her crew.

'Call up support? Get a platoon into their flank?' suggested Vaslav.

'Rear line is half a mile behind us, and the Twenty-First and Twenty-Sixth are pinned down at the bridge,' replied Etsul.

'Massed charge, martyrdom or glory,' suggested Trieve with unseemly eagerness.

'No. Keep praying.'

'Chuck a shell into that arch, hivequake 'em,' said Chalenboor.

'Best suggestion yet, if I understand you correctly, Chalenboor, but if we bring that arch down, we're not getting through either. The Twenty-First and Twenty-Sixth are on their own,' said Etsul. She thumped her fist against the hull in frustration.

'Sir, could we use that?' Verro brought up a targeting rune, drawing Etsul's eye to a spot several hundred feet to the left of the enemy barricade. A stack of armoured containers had toppled against the wall and left a spiderweb of fractures. Daylight shone around naked lengths of structural rebar.

'You're suggesting we put a shot into that weak point and open a second route of egress on the enemy's flank?'

'Yes, sir. We hit the weak spot, blast a breach, then get through and hit them from the side before they can turn to address. We could kill a couple of their machines before they had us in their sights, and if the Cadians attack from the front at the same time...'

Etsul almost dismissed the idea out of hand. It was risky to the point of foolishness. What if they brought the wall down on themselves? What if they rolled out into the open and got blown to bits? What if there were enemies they couldn't see, waiting behind that wall? Then she looked at the writhing Cadian soldiery, barely able to shoot straight.

'Captain Fynn, permission to try something risky?' she voxed.

'*Granted... Throne knows we... yes, anything,*' he replied. The wailing came through the vox and drove needles into Etsul's ears.

'Be ready to hit them with everything as soon as I give the word, sir.'

Etsul switched back to her crew channel and issued her orders.

'Trieve, get us into position thirty feet from the weak spot. The moment you see a big enough gap, you ram through then wheel to address. Sergeant Vaslav, Loader Moretzin, our lives are in your hands. The moment we blast a breach, reload main gun and be ready to lay on enemy armour targets. Moretzin, can you get us reloaded that fast on the move?'

'Yes, sir,' replied Moretzin.

'Sure, Moretzin? That's a damned swift reload with a chain-sling.'

'Yes, sir,' repeated the loader. There was no additional inflection in her words. She might have been agreeing to wait in line at the commissary. There was nothing more to say.

Etsul sat in her command seat and waited, heart thumping, as Trieve pulled them back and skirted around the back of the container hillock. She felt trapped, as though regretting too late the decision to climb aboard a dangerous ride.

At last, they were in position. Etsul prayed silently. No doubt their retreat from the line had been marked. She just had to hope none of the heretics figured out what they were doing before they did it.

She took a long, slow breath and gripped a grab rail.

'Main gun, fire.'

Steel Tread lurched with recoil.

The Demolisher shell hit home with a tremendous burst of light and sound, obscuring smoke spewing out in all directions from the impact.

Trieve gunned the engine and charged the breach on blind faith.

Shrapnel clanged from the hull. Smoke shrouded the vid-feeds. They plunged into it, still accelerating.

Moretzin's sling rattled forward, suicidally fast. Etsul flinched at the thought of the shell slipping loose in the confines of the tank. At least it would be a quicker death than some. The loader got one hand to the wheel of the breech but didn't spin it. Her augmetic arm locked in place, cradling the fat mass of the shell.

Steel Tread hit something with enough force to rock Etsul forward in her seat.

'Throne!' she hissed, and then they were through. Hazy daylight strobed the vid-feeds. The breech wheel spun and the shell rattled home.

Clang clang clang! The signal rapped against the hull.

On Etsul's auspex she saw the hard returns of enemy armoured vehicles, within engagement range, flank-on. She felt Trieve haul *Tread* hard about, leaning on the surprising grace of the Leman Russ for all it was worth. They tilted. Etsul held her breath.

The turret rotated even as Moretzin ducked clear of the breech's recoil.

'All guns, fire!' Fear and adrenaline made Etsul shout. 'Captain Fynn, attack!'

Steel Tread let fly.

The dust was still clearing as the lascannon beam strobed through it, sparkling with particulates, stabbing into the flank of the enemy Punisher. The tank deformed from within as its power plant went up. Its top hatch rocketed skywards. Flames belched from its ruptured hull.

Vaslav's Demolisher shot was nothing short of sublime. The shell skimmed mere inches over the sloped rear hull plates of the Punisher and slammed into the side of the next enemy tank along. The ferocious explosion tore the machine open and flipped it sideways. Something else beyond it exploded in turn with a satisfying *whump*.

'Have some o' that!' howled Chalenboor.

'Know the Emperor's wrath!' cried Trieve at the same time.

Something hit them from above like a sledgehammer.

'Is that incoming fire?' snapped Etsul. 'Damage report someone!'

Another impact followed, then another. The lumens died then flickered back to life. Half the vid-feeds cut out. The rest filled with dust. The power plant gave a strangled roar then cut out too.

The silence was cavernous and awful.

'What the bloody Throne was that?' asked Vaslav. It took Etsul's stunned mind a moment to process why he sounded wrong. In the ear-ringing quiet, she could hear her sergeant without the vox.

Verro peered hard at his remaining vid-feeds then hissed in frustration.

'Rubble. Cadia's blood, I think we dislodged one of those statues from its alcove. It's come down right on top of us.'

'Can we wriggle out, yeah?' asked Chalenboor. Trieve gave a mirthless laugh.

'The air-exchanger shrines are choked. *Tread*'s machine-spirit just got beaten over the head with a stone cudgel. How long shall she languish in her blessed sufferings?'

'Check hatches and get me a damage report,' barked Etsul. 'How's our motive force?'

'Reserve battery casket is enlivened,' replied Trieve. 'Even locked in sublime agonies, the tank retains two hours' motive force.'

'Yeah, can't open my hatch,' called Chalenboor.

'I've got mine a few inches open, but there's a damned great chunk of rock in the way,' said Verro, clanging metal against stone as though to prove it.

Etsul didn't bother to correct the gunners' lack of a 'sir'. They had bigger fish on the line right now.

Etsul recognised her mind was wandering as shock tried to smother her. She fought the feeling, bit the inside of her cheek. Pain brought focus. Hoisting herself upward, she tried the top hatch but found it buckled slightly inward. The release ring wouldn't turn all the way.

'No go here,' she reported.

'Damage is light, considering,' reported Vaslav. 'We've lost some vid-feeds, and it looks like most of what we had lashed to the outer hull is a write-off. Armour's held though, nothing we can't beat out with a lump hammer.'

Throne alive, how tough is this tank? thought Etsul, grateful and amazed. Even a standard Russ might well have been crushed under that rubble fall. They were pinned, half buried and trapped, but by the Emperor they were alive.

Her relief faded as she checked her remaining feeds and saw a traitor tank lumbering around the burning wrecks of its comrades. Its lascannon swung their way. Its turret gun depressed, lining up a killing shot. Etsul clenched her teeth.

Explosions rocked the enemy machine and it yawed off course before shuddering to a halt. Cadian soldiers spilled past it, the Fifth Company Leman Russ leading them out of the macro-warehouse. Etsul breathed a sigh of relief, then vox-hailed the tank.

'Hammers, this is Lieutenant Etsul of *Steel Tread*. Do you have time to haul us out of this trap?' she voxed.

'*Sorry, Steel Tread*,' came the response, a man's voice with a nasal accent. '*This is Lieutenant Brogva of* Lion Rampant. *Captain Fynn's ordered us forward to the bridge without delay. You already got your share of the glory! We'll get this done, then be back to drag you clear.*'

'Don't be too long about it, lieutenant, we've only got two hours of motive force,' Etsul replied.

'*Watch us work*, Tread. *We'll be with you in less than half that.*'

'Good hunting, and Throne's sakes don't forget we're back here,' said Etsul, and cut the connection.

Quiet descended upon them, congealing until it filled the tank. The plan had been foolhardy, its execution glorious. Somehow, thought Etsul, that only made the ignominy of its conclusion worse.

'Perhaps it is the continual blasphemy and unworthiness

of this crew that has brought us to this pass?' opined Trieve, shattering the silence with the tact of a drunk at a funeral.

'I've got a gun, yeah? I can *actually* shoot him,' Chalenboor suggested.

'Folly is the first resort of the fool,' retorted Trieve.

'Yeah, think we all know whose *folly* we've been stuck with, don't we?'

'Nix, shut up.' This from Verro and Vaslav both at once.

'Hold your nerve,' Etsul said, trying to reassert control before she lost it entirely. 'Shut your mouths and stand by your stations. Emperor's vessel, are you Cadians or penal legionnaires? Attend the remaining vid-feeds. If we can do no more than watch as our comrades secure the bridge then we will do that much, and–'

'Sir.' Vaslav's voice was a croak.

'Sergeant?' she snapped.

'Front-right vid-feed, sir,' he breathed. She looked, and felt fear grip her anew.

There was the bridge, all towering arches and fluttering banners over the fern-choked floodwaters of the canal. There were the Cadians, several platoons' worth of soldiers advancing with banners flying and armoured vehicles in their midst. And there, barring their passage like a monster from the darkest Imperial scripture, was a towering bipedal war engine. Looming over the loyalist soldiery, the engine boasted a hunched and armoured carapace, jutting exhaust stacks, tattered pennants and a telltale tilting shield emblazoned with an obscene device.

A Heretic Knight.

Etsul had only ever seen such super-heavy walkers once before, advancing into the breach during the siege of Jaegoh. Those had been distant, a trio of loyalist war engines with fluttering pennants and silver-and-blue panoply. Even at a great remove, and knowing they were on her side, the size and fury of the Knights had scared her as much as it inspired.

This machine was infinitely worse.

It might have stood fifty feet tall, had it raised itself to its full height. Instead, it stooped forward like a beast. Its armour was pearlescent white edged with shimmering silver. This only served to highlight the wet muscle and exposed tendons stretched across its spiked hull. Where its arms should have supported cannons or blades, they instead tapered to gleaming metal points, like impossibly huge needles. Its feet were the same, their points driven into the ground so that it balanced on them in a way that didn't look possible for something so big.

The armoured plates of the Knight's helm were splayed open, each hauled painfully back by lengths of hooked chain. They exposed a wet mass of flesh and eyes, drooling maws and shuddering cilia. It took Etsul a moment to realise she was emitting a low moan of horror.

The traitor Knight swung a dreadful pin-limb in a scything arc. Cadian soldiers were torn apart at its passing. A Chimera flipped off the side of the bridge trailing flame. The thing threw back its head and screamed, and it took everything Etsul had not to slip from her seat and cower.

It waded into the Cadians. Blood and bodies fountained. Weapons fire flashed from a shield of lurid green energy that shimmered about it. The Knight stamped and stabbed, now tottering on two spear-feet, now falling forward to skitter on all four blade-points. Each time it ripped one of its limbs skyward again, trails of gore spattered in its wake.

'What is it?' Chalenboor's voice was little more than a

whisper, but it was enough to drag Etsul from her reverie. She fumbled, hit the vox-rune on the third try, tore her eyes from the vid-feed.

'First Lieutenant Askerov… anyone who can hear this… there is a super-heavy enemy asset engaging on Seryph Bridge. It's a Knight, but it's like nothing I've ever seen. First Lieutenant Askerov, First Lieutenant Aswold, Captain Brezyk, anyone… please acknowledge.'

'Throne, *now* what?'

Etsul forced her eyes back to the feed, not liking the fear in Verro's voice. The Knight had waded deep into the Imperial lines, but the Cadians were fighting back with the desperation of cornered prey. Beyond them, rolling up the line of the canal from deeper in the Costmarus sprawl came a thick bank of mauve fog. It moved fast, swallowing up the ruined buildings, smothering everything.

'It's travelling against the wind,' said Vaslav.

The fog rolled over the battle on the bridge and surged hungrily up the banks towards *Steel Tread*.

When the vox squawked, everyone in the tank jumped.

'*Hammer blow, repeat, hammer blow,*' barked First Lieutenant Askerov. '*Visual confirmation of Baraghor in sector seven-five-three. Repeat, visual on primary. Be advised, Geskans report the target is Heretic Astartes, and is engaged in some manner of heathen ritual. We've got a crimson-class maledictum warning from the psykana. Maintain your prayers!*'

'Sir, we can't rally, we're pinned under rubble,' Etsul replied, fighting to keep her voice level. 'There is an enemy super-heavy engaging in this sector, sir, and there's some kind of fog rolling over the advance.'

'*Confirm, we have fog at this location also, visibility poor. Possibly some by-product of whatever the primary… it…*'

Askerov's transmission cut out, only to be replaced by the desperate voice of Captain Fynn.

'The fog! Throne alive, stay out of the fog! Don't breathe it! Don't bre–' He was cut off, but the vox stayed open, muffled indistinguishable sounds and static filling the inside of the tank.

'Sir, what's happening?' Verro's voice wavered, and Etsul found herself wondering how old he actually was under all that grime. She shook her head slowly. Fynn's vox-mic was still transmitting. She heard running footsteps and screams. Next came howls, and gibbering, and the crack of bone. Weapons discharged and she saw them light the fog from within.

Vaslav reached out with a shaking hand and worked the vox-control slaved to his station.

'…vapour everywhere. How's it getting in? Sergeant? Patch that hole someone, patch…'

'…fall back! They've gone mad! What…'

'…ere's the captain? Where's the captain? Where's…'

'…is coming off the corpse piles! Repeat, if anyone ca…'

'Praise the Dark Prince! Praise him with your flesh! Praise him with your pain!'

A horrible certainty gripped Etsul.

'Can we pressurise this vehicle?' she asked.

'What does that matter?' asked Vaslav, his tone so bitter that it gave her pause. 'Didn't you hear? Heretic Astartes. Cadia's Bane. We're done.'

The fog rolled closer with indecent eagerness, an avalanche of hungry clouds intent on swallowing them whole.

'For the Emperor's sakes, someone tell me, *can we pressurise this tank?*' barked Etsul.

'If we're buttoned up, sir, then by the Emperor's grace we can,' said Trieve.

'Sir, I can't...' She heard frantic scuffling from Verro's station, the rasp of metal on stone.

She remembered his side hatch, pushed part-way open. In Etsul's mind's eye she saw the mauve fog flooding into the tank through the open hatch, saw it engulfing them all. Horror would follow.

'Verro, get that hatch shut *now!*' she barked.

'I can't, sir, it won't bloody–'

Something big moved below Etsul. There was a loud rasp then a firm clang.

'Closed,' said Moretzin.

'Pressurising now,' said Trieve, fingers dancing over the runes at his station. '*Steel Tread* is old, sir. Her blessed flagellation may have torn a seal or compromised a weld.'

'The Emperor protects,' said Etsul, unsure if she was reassuring her crew or herself.

There came a series of dull clunks and clicks from all around them, followed by a slow groan. Etsul swallowed hard and moved her jaw until her ears popped. She glanced at the buckled hatch above her.

'Integrity?' she asked. The fog was almost on them.

'Amber...' said Trieve. Etsul's stomach lurched.

'What's wrong?' she asked.

'I don't know, sir... Something...'

Frantic scuffling from below.

'Here!' cried Chalenboor. 'Crack in the weld. Sealin' it!'

Etsul craned around to look as the sponson gunner wrenched open a hazard locker and pulled out a canister of sealing unguent. Muttering prayers, Chalenboor ripped the tab from the canister and shook it.

The fog rolled over them, smothering and silent. The vid-feeds turned to mauve gloom.

'Nix!' hissed Verro, frantic. Chalenboor pushed the blessed nozzle against the cracked weld even as the first mauve tendrils quested through it. She depressed the applicator rune and the unguent squirted out to fill the tiny gap. It set at once, with a sizzling sound. Moretzin grabbed Chalenboor under her arms and hauled the wiry gunner back, away from the faint puff of mauve gas that had invaded their sanctum.

'Runes green,' called Trieve.

Etsul exhaled slowly. Verro let out a breath he'd been holding. Vaslav closed his eyes. Chalenboor disentangled herself from Moretzin while Trieve checked his instruments, then rechecked them. Silence reigned for long, thudding heartbeats before Etsul said, 'Bloody well done, Gunner Chalenboor.'

'Now what, sir?' asked Moretzin.

'Vaslav, get me an auspex fix on the Renegade Knight. Everyone else, stay quiet. If the Emperor is with us, it won't know we're here.'

'We can't just sit here until our air runs out, sir,' protested Trieve. 'The arch-heretic is at hand! Our duty is clear!'

'You want to get out there an' give us a push, dregger?' hissed Chalenboor.

'You'd have to get the hatches open first,' Verro pointed out. 'And it's not like we could do that now even if we wanted to. We're stuck!'

Fighting to steady her breathing, Etsul tried to hail Askerov. No response. She tried again. Nothing. She cycled the vox, sending out hails to her squadmates, to Aswold, to anyone whose frequency she knew. Some channels opened onto static or screaming, others to the awful sounds of crunching gristle and saliva.

Whatever happened, it happened to everyone, she thought.

Baraghor is here all right, and he's beaten us. Whatever witchery he's unleashed, it's rolled over the attack and… Throne alive, what if it is everyone? What if this is everywhere?

She took her shaking hand away from the vox-panel. She wanted to try Aswold's frequency again, but was terrified of what she would hear if she got through.

She swallowed with a dry click, closed her eyes and willed away hysteria.

Chalenboor's hiss brought her back to herself with a jolt.

'Anyone else see that, yeah?'

'What?' asked Trieve. 'I do not–'

'There!'

Now Etsul saw them, ghostly shapes resolving from the murk. Spinebacks, and with them a band of their mutant ogryns. They were walking untouched through the mauve fog, and their leader was pointing straight at the mound of rubble that had trapped *Steel Tread*.

ACT TWO

THE HUNT

CHAPTER SEVEN

CHOICES

'Be silent,' hissed Etsul. 'Quiet the vox. Sergeant, issue rebreathers.'

She felt like a prey animal, cornered in its burrow. She glanced about at her crew. They were all staring fixedly at the vid-feeds. Vaslav showed no signs of obeying her order. Rather than risk speaking again, she reached down with one booted foot and gave him a firm shove.

The sergeant spun with an expression of such sudden fury that Etsul almost recoiled. Instead, she matched his scowl and nodded pointedly at the enviro-hazard rack above his station. She could see the objection in his eyes. What use were rebreathers against sorcery?

Etsul motioned again. Expression thunderous, Vaslav wrenched the rebreathers from their rack and thrust them at the crew. Etsul's he all but threw at her. She held his gaze until he looked away and turned back to his station.

Etsul pulled the mask's strap over her head, clipped its

bottle to a loop on her tank suit, checked the oxygen flow and muttered the appropriate prayer.

'Spirit of the rebreather, giver of life, thank you for the breath in my lungs, may your seals hold true and the Emperor smile upon you.'

All this she did automatically, but her mind was on Vaslav and his reaction to Askerov's words. She had said Heretic Astartes. Adeptus Astartes, the God-Emperor's angels, His will made manifest on the galaxy... turned traitor? Etsul's mind reeled at the implications. Denial sought to assert itself.

The sergeant didn't seem to have any doubts, that was for sure.

Etsul's hand crept to her sidearm.

On the monitors, the Spinebacks leader gestured again. His followers spread out, some forming a perimeter while others approached *Steel Tread*. The two ogryns lumbered with them. They seemed to grow to fill the vid-feeds, each hefting a silver lance.

Those weapons the crew had mocked earlier now set a panic in her throat. Their seeming failure to deal noteworthy damage to the other tanks had been a preamble to Baraghor's killing fog, a point of ingress for his witchery.

New figures burst from the murk. Etsul got a glimpse of Cadian heraldry and thought for an instant that salvation was at hand. Yet the uniforms were torn and darkly stained. Their owners sprinted towards the heretics without thought for cover discipline. A few scrambled on all fours, like beasts. Their flesh was livid and gouged with crimson runnels, torn by what looked like bite marks. One had half his face hanging off in a wagging flap of skin.

The Cadians' eyes bulged in their sockets, purple cysts about to burst. Black whorls radiated out from them as though the Guardsmen had been tattooed by an artistic madman.

All this Etsul saw in the space between one heartbeat and the next. Then the heretics' guns rippled. Tainted Cadians fell. Some lay thrashing or crawled onward, until they were shot again.

The ogryns showed no signs of having noticed the exchange. Etsul watched their lances until the weapons were too close to remain in shot.

'If you got a plan, *sir*, time's runnin' out,' whispered Chalenboor acidly through her rebreather.

Etsul's mind thrashed like an animal trapped in a sack.

Fight?

They couldn't disembark to do so – and even if they could, it was doubtful the rebreathers would help. What if the fog was absorbed through the skin? What if you couldn't stop witchery simply by breathing clean air? Her crew could perhaps wait for the enemy to bust holes in the hull, then fire out through the gaps until the fog took them. But the spalling from two lance-blasts would wreak havoc. Whatever resistance they put up would be pitiful.

Attempting to escape on foot posed the same issues: no way out, and no safe air to breathe.

That left trying to reawaken *Steel Tread*, which Trieve had said wasn't possible. The driver might be an insufferable fanatic with a borderline flagellation fetish, but over the last few days she'd come to trust his abilities. If he said the tank's intakes were smothered then she believed him, and *Tread* would choke on its own fumes long before it somehow shouldered its way free of the rubble. Operating the guns on casket power would drain their motive force all too soon and leave them helpless.

Besides, either way would make a lot of noise. Her gaze strayed in the direction of the bridge, lost in the fog.

Etsul forced herself to focus on one nightmare at a time.

There came a dull creak from outside the hull, then a rasp of stone against metal. The sound came from directly above Etsul's head, making her flinch down in her seat and unclasp her holster. Another clang, louder this time, from near the tank's haunches. She looked at her crew, who returned her questioning stare.

An impact on the side of the hull. Etsul's heart leapt into her mouth as she waited for the bang, the wild ricochets of spalling inside the tank, the flesh and blood-mist torn from the crew she'd led into this trap...

Instead, there was another grating sound then a crunch like stone on stone. *Steel Tread* settled a little lighter on its springs.

'They're digging us out!' hissed Verro.

'Why?' asked Chalenboor.

'Fun?' suggested Moretzin. 'Interrogation? Torture? Clear a hatch, pull us out and...' She made a grizzly wet noise suggestive of violence.

'Or maybe they think we're all dead in here, and they're going to take trophies,' growled Vaslav.

Today is the day we die.

Etsul swatted the thought like a fly. She did not know who else was gone, and she would not die in such damned ignorance.

She felt the Tsegohan flask in its pouch and realised there would be no one to toast her last voyage. Throne, the only person she'd told about that custom wasn't even one of her own crew. She wondered where Aswold was in this catastrophe.

'Trieve,' she whispered. 'How much rubble would they need to shift for *Tread* to break out?'

He leaned aside so she could see his controls. One of the indicator bulbs for the air-exchanger shrines was flickering between red and amber.

'More than they have, sir, but this is a doughty machine and faithful. Even choking, she may have the strength to wrench free if they relieve a little more of her burden. In our sufferings are we strongest.'

'What are we waiting for then?' asked Verro, then belatedly added, 'Sir.'

'We get one chance at this,' said Etsul. 'I'm not going before the Golden Throne and telling the God-Emperor we died because someone lost their nerve.' If Vaslav felt her eyes on him at that moment, he didn't show it.

Chalenboor muttered something Etsul didn't catch.

Another thump. Another clang. Harsh laughter muffled by the hull. A vid-feed cleared as another sizeable chunk of rubble was heaved aside. That must be enough for the heretics to wrench open a hatch, she thought. She didn't dare leave it longer… did she?

Trieve gestured again. The amber bulb had turned green.

One of three shrines clear.

Etsul willed *Steel Tread*'s machine-spirit not to let them down.

'Ready at your stations,' she ordered. Another thud from outside. Something clanged hard against the dented turret hatch.

'Now!'

Trieve roused the power plant. It coughed once, twice, then roared like a dragon. Verro's sponson bolter thumped. Blood splashed over vid-feeds. *Steel Tread* strained. Its tracks creaked. Its hull groaned.

'Come on… come on…'

On the feeds, Etsul saw an ogryn heft its lance and draw it back.

'Throne, come *on!*' she shouted, rocking forward in her seat as she urged the tank to free itself.

Rubble clattered and spilled. *Steel Tread* moved. Chalenboor's gun roared to life and the ogryn was punched off his feet by a barrage of shells.

Heretics spun in shock as the tank charged them down. They vanished under *Tread*'s tracks, crushed to bloody pulp as the Demolisher burst from its rubble tomb and roared into the fog.

'Orders, sir?' asked Trieve over the vox.

Etsul had this one moment to decide their course. Could this really be Yarroe Canyon all over again? Askerov's last order had been to rally what force they could and try to kill Baraghor... but she knew duty, and she knew folly. Whatever chance there had been of slaying the heretic leader was gone. They couldn't be the only loyalist crew left, and whatever strength remained of their attack force, it fell to officers like her to preserve it. Her duty now was to get her tank and her crew out of the engagement zone, then to get on the vox and determine a rally point. She wouldn't martyr them for nothing.

'Sergeant, plot me a course west out of Costmarus sprawl, shortest route.'

'Sir? Shouldn't we form up on the first lieutenant?' This from Verro. She ignored it, but Vaslav didn't.

'Why? To what end? Heretic Astartes! They were the death of my world, the bane of Cadia, and you think we can do anything to stop them here?'

'Sergeant, if you've a true Cadian bone in your body, pull yourself together. The Emperor has entrusted us with the lives of this crew and this tank, and we are going to preserve them. Plot me a route!'

Vaslav didn't reply, but to Etsul's immense relief a series of runic waypoints blinked to life on the auspex.

Steel Tread turned in the roadway and began to accelerate. Suddenly it rocked on its springs as something huge slammed into the ground scant feet from the hull. In the feeds, Etsul saw a tapering column of silver, streaked with gore, driven point first into the ferrocrete.

'Throne!' she gasped.

The titanic lance soared skyward again, vanishing through the murk. Trieve swerved across the roadway, grinding rubble and corpses as he went. *Steel Tread* shuddered with what Etsul realised were monstrous footfalls.

'Throne o' the sump-rottin' sainted Emperor!' Chalenboor was screaming.

'A daemon! A daemon is come!' cried Trieve.

The silver needle stabbed down again. Trieve wrenched at his control levers. The Knight's limb barely clipped *Steel Tread* yet still it was enough to deafen them with the metal-on-metal scream, and to leave a dent in the hull mere inches from Etsul's head. Bulbs lit up red across instrument panels. Sparks erupted somewhere below her. Verro cried out. Stowage and shells rattled madly.

'Get us clear!' shouted Etsul. Trieve needed no urging. He gunned the tank's power plant, hammered his control levers and stomped his pedals. *Steel Tread* executed a tight turn one way, lurched forward, swung back the other and ploughed through a mound of corpses that loomed from the fog. Carrion figures bounced across the tank's hull like rag dolls, their limbs and rictus grins filling the vid-feeds. The icon at the heart of the heap vanished under the tank's tracks.

Then *Steel Tread* was clear and accelerating along the processional. Blinded by fog, Trieve drove with reckless speed, praying aloud all the while for the Emperor to bless them with a clear path. At any moment, that monstrous pillar of sharpened silver could punch down through the hull and pinion the tank like an insect. Etsul held her breath.

It didn't come.

Somewhere behind them, she heard the Knight's soul-curdling roar, yet even as it howled so it receded. Still, Etsul didn't believe it until the sounds of the rampaging war engine had faded completely into the muffling fog.

At last, she slumped back in her command seat with a gasp of relief, and listened to the roar of the power plant mingle with the sick thudding of her heart.

Hours had passed and night was casting its shroud across the land by the time they stopped. The threatened eclipse storm still hadn't arrived, though Etsul had felt pre-shocks judder through her as the grim afternoon withered away to evening. Like a building migraine, the longer it held off, the worse it would be when it finally hit.

It was just more weight below the waterline, as they said on Tsegoh.

Steel Tread sat dormant in a jungle clearing. Within it the crew huddled in a cocoon of mutual shock. Etsul had ordered all non-essential systems powered down and their locator beacon rendered quiescent. They had ploughed a wide enough trail through the undergrowth as it was; no need to provide pursuers with any more signs of their presence.

It would have helped, perhaps, to get outside, cut some fronds and lay rudimentary camouflage over their tank. Yet Etsul wasn't letting anyone open a hatch until they had to.

Bad enough that they'd had to dispense with their rebreathers once the oxygen ran out.

Logically, she knew they had left the fog behind miles back. Certainly it hadn't been visible since they escaped the outskirts of the sprawl. But they knew nothing about the dark powers Baraghor had unleashed. It would be little use escaping their doom only to let their guard down, step outside and discover the corruption had somehow clung to their hull. Etsul told herself she was being prudent, but it became harder to ignore her crew's discontent by the minute.

They wouldn't be able to sit in here forever, she knew that. The pressurisation system could only stay on so long lest it drained their dwindling fuel reserve. Moreover, *Tread* had taken a furious pummelling. Verro had already asked twice to be allowed outside to inspect the damage. She didn't think she could deny him a third time.

The fug of sweat and tension was so thick inside the tank it was as though Baraghor's miasma had found its way in after all. Vaslav hunched over the vox-unit, staring fixedly at the dials as he scanned frequency after frequency. He hadn't spoken to anyone since their escape, closing in upon himself like folded parchment. Static hissed in choppy monotone. Verro had opined that the tank's primary vox-antenna had taken a hit when the Knight clipped them but, of course, until he was allowed outside neither he nor Trieve could confirm it. Without an enginseer on hand, there was slim chance of repairing it even if they did.

Moretzin was propped against the warm metal of the power plant, snoring softly. Verro sat, back to his station, mechanically chewing a ration block as though he'd been assigned the task as penance. Chalenboor stared at her monitors and scanned the darkened jungle fretfully like she could actually see anything out there without lumens or night-sight filters.

Etsul felt the tension simmering within her tank, resentments and despair forming convection currents within its pressurised vessel. She couldn't focus on them. Exhaustion left her little energy to do more than slither deeper into a self-recriminatory spiral.

She had got them clear, tank intact, crew alive. But she had run again, a coward in the God-Emperor's sight. Worse, the longer they spent without contact, the more Etsul's hope withered that other loyalist forces had survived.

It was Trieve who broke the fragile peace. He set aside the primer over which he had been silently praying, then turned in his seat to survey them all like a turret gun tracking targets.

'Perhaps when one of true faith warns of omens in future, you will find it within yourselves to master your arrogance and listen?' Trieve addressed the crew. 'There again, perhaps our travails are the Emperor's will, and our shared punishment for that very sin.'

'Yeah? Well maybe if you'd got clear and not dropped half a buildin' on us, we'd have been able to get stuck in.' Chalenboor offered him her dismissive three-fingered gesture.

Trieve's sneer dripped self-satisfaction. Even Etsul found herself wanting to punch him.

'What would you know?' he crowed. 'Faithless hive trash. I didn't hear your protests when we turned tail and fled.'

The chewed end of Verro's ration block flew across the confined space and hit Trieve in the eye. The driver recoiled, spluttering with indignation. Chalenboor cackled loud enough to startle Moretzin awake.

'Shut your mouth,' spat Verro.

'How dare you?' Trieve's voice had risen to a strangled

screech. 'You, who tamper with the secrets of the Omnissiah. It was you that corrupted the tank's machine-spirit with your... tech-heresy!'

'Oh, pull the aquila out of your arse, Trieve,' said Verro.

Trieve snarled and half rose from his seat.

'Try it, duct-squirmer,' said Chalenboor. Her hand dropped to the knife at her belt.

'For Throne's sakes, all of you, stop this,' snapped Etsul. She glanced in Vaslav's direction, but he was wholly absent, just a hunched shape limned by the glow of the vox-dials.

'Oh yeah, hide behind the new boss, Isaac – lick her boots 'n' see where it gets you,' jeered Chalenboor.

'I beseech the God-Emperor to forgive the laxity this crew has shown in tolerating your filthy tongue,' spat Trieve.

Furious, Etsul made to clamber down from her seat. If it took the issuing of punishment details to whip this crew into line, then it was past time she started doling them out.

'Enough.' Moretzin didn't raise her voice, but it filled up the close space of the tank. They all looked at her, except for Vaslav. 'Commander told you to stop. Want to wind up getting lashes? Stop acting like some pack of underhive killers. We were trained better.'

'Got a problem with gangers now, yeah?'

'I've got a problem with idiots who–'

'Commander,' said Vaslav, interrupting Moretzin's retort. 'It's patchy, but I've got a signal.'

CHAPTER EIGHT

THE SIGNAL

The crew huddled around Vaslav's station. The argument of moments before was, if not forgotten, at least thrust aside for now.

Vaslav hunched over his station, tweaking dials as he tried to boost the signal. Etsul craned forward, frustration urging her to shove Vaslav aside and take a turn at the dials. Words flitted from the emitters like ghosts through a barrage of static.

'...ration Jotu... ompromised. Catastrophic malefic event... Costmarus indust... sprawl at approxim... sixteen fifty hours... triggered by primary target, visually... onfirmed... site and assailed... ments of Forty-Ninth Cadian Arm... Geskan Forty-Third Light Inf... ighty per cent casua... Primary target lost... assault group broken, survivors scatt... established rally points... be considered compromised. New rall... coordinates Imper... Victus... egnum... Repeat, Imperatu... ictus Reg... N... This message... repeat... authority stamp Command... VanKalder, Cad... Forty-Ninth Armo... Operation Jotunn com...'

Vaslav hissed with frustration as the signal slipped like a fish from a line and was gone. He worked the dials with increasing impatience, then sat back and thumped a fist against his station.

The crew looked at one another then at Etsul. She imagined her expression was as conflicted in that moment as theirs.

'Eighty per cent casualties, did you hear that?' Trieve's voice was soft with shock or reverence, Etsul couldn't tell which.

'But we're not the only ones left,' said Verro. 'There're survivors. There's a rally point.'

'If it isn't a trap,' growled Vaslav. 'If they've broken our codes...'

'Then we would be riding into a trap,' said Etsul, pulling a folded sheet of plastek parchment from a pocket of her tank suit. She smoothed out the briefing document she had received what felt like a year ago at Mandriga command and scanned swiftly down it. She stabbed a finger at the codes transcribed there.

'Imperatus... Victus... Regnum... That's sector eleven-six-seven, but what was the last element? Did anyone hear? Was it Nox or Noctus?'

Silence.

'It *could* have been Noctus?' offered Verro.

Etsul balled her fist, crinkling the parchment, then shoved it back in her pocket.

'It's enough to be going on with. The first three elements get us close.'

'Sir, how much variance is there between Nox and Noctus on those codes?' asked Moretzin.

'Could be as much as five miles,' admitted Etsul. 'But if we don't find them at the first point we try then we search from there.'

'If we're not overrun by foes, and if the codes aren't compromised,' muttered Vaslav.

'Boss, not shuttin' you down or nothin', but how's that worse than we already are?' Chalenboor asked the sergeant. 'What else you want to do, turn round and go back to the sprawl? Chance runnin' south through swamps in a battle tank without them Geskans pickin' us out a safe route? No disrespect, but we'd be dead or sunk pretty quick.'

'In such an hour faith is strength, and despair but mortal frailty,' opined Trieve.

'Moretzin, what do you think?' asked Vaslav. The loader's augmetics whined softly with her shrug.

'As I've already clarified, this is not a democracy,' said Etsul. 'The transmission we have received carries official authentication codes and constitutes a direct order from our regimental commander. Emperor willing, that means he made it out of that disaster alive. Our duty is to follow his orders.'

There was silence as they digested this. Etsul felt suddenly as though she were balanced at an apex, and that the moment could tip either way. But the message offered hope, however slender. She could use that to hold her crew together. It was time to give them a shove before they slid back into infighting and morale collapsed altogether.

'Depressurise and disembark. Trieve, full inspection. Unpack the auto-awning, I don't want you pulling the cowl plate on the power plant only for the eclipse storm to break and drown our engine. Moretzin, stocktake. We've fired plenty of rounds and Throne knows we were low enough on fuel even before all this. Verro, Chalenboor, take lascarbines from the arms locker and patrol the perimeter. Stay in visual, I don't want anyone picked off if we get visitors. If you haven't already, all of you rehydrate and take a ration block.'

'What about stimms, sir?' asked Verro.

Etsul paused. None of them had slept worth a damn for the best part of two days. Their edge was blunted. Exhaustion wouldn't help frayed nerves. There again, being hyped on combat stimms wouldn't ease their tempers either.

Yet there was no time for rest. Emperor alone knew how they'd avoided the enemy for as long as they had, but Etsul wouldn't see her tank caught at bay while its crew slumbered. Masenwe would have asked her what other options they had, trusting that she would spot one if it were there.

The commander had trusted her judgement. Etsul thought that perhaps it was time she started to do so as well.

'Single dose each, that's it. We'll take rack time at the rendezvous. Coordinates aren't more than a day's ride away.'

Chalenboor scowled, cracked her knuckles, opened her mouth to speak. Etsul did not let her.

'We have all just been through rough waters. We've seen and heard things that have tested not just our courage, but our sanity also. I do not blame any of you for being tired, frightened and on edge. But we are a crew, and all we can rely on is one another. If any of you are planning to undermine that bond at a time like this then you can get out and walk to the rendezvous. The enemy are out there, not in here, understood? The next insubordinate will be digging and chem-washing our latrine pits for the next month. Dismissed.'

The crew busied themselves at once, yet all hesitated to break the tank's seal by opening a hatch. Vaslav had bent over his station's vox-controls again and was frowning mightily as though hoping to dissuade anyone from troubling him.

Etsul was not about to let him off so easily.

'Sergeant Vaslav, meet me outside in ten minutes. Bring a chem-lantern and our chart-parchments.'

When, a minute later, Trieve reported that internal pressure had been normalised, Etsul took a firm grip of the turret wheel, spun it decisively and clambered out.

She did not, thankfully, lose her mind to heretical sorcery. So, there was that at least.

The air was fresh and cool. It felt to Etsul like plunging into clear water after the sweat-thick fug of the tank. She smelled rich soil mingled with rotting vegetation, and something that reminded her of the greenhouses of her parents' agri-plex. She heard insectile chittering, distant whooping calls, the susurrus of stirring undergrowth. It might have been pleasant if not for the biting insects that closed in on her, and the constant risk of gun-wielding heretics bursting from the undergrowth.

For the next few minutes, Etsul busied herself overseeing the crew as they emerged cautiously from the tank. She helped Trieve deploy the telescopic poles of the auto-awning. She held a stablight for Moretzin while the loader inspected the crushed remains of fuel barrels whose contents had long since drained away. She noted a flattish rock a little way from the tank where she could spread the charts for her conversation with Vaslav.

Throughout, Etsul felt pulses of unnatural gravity pushing and pulling at her. Some of them seemed to thump through her body like an invasive heartbeat. Others made her ears pop, or her centre of balance waver. Each pulse made the jungle echo to distant shrieks and howls, and caused foliage to rustle so loudly that Verro and Chalenboor halted and raised their lascarbines towards the treeline. Etsul exchanged an uneasy glance with Verro as he passed her, seeing her thoughts reflected in his eyes. The eclipse storm was almost upon them, an unnatural onslaught of fluctuating gravity and unnatural weather that would play havoc with machine-spirits and put them all in even more peril.

Etsul sighed and leaned against *Steel Tread*'s flank. The tank's paint was scorched, its hull scored and dented. Yet for all the punishment it had taken, the venerable vehicle was still going strong. She patted the tank, *her* tank, and whispered to its machine-spirit.

'Thank you for getting us out of there alive. I'm going to ask a lot more of you yet. I pray you keep and aid us.'

Vaslav emerged from the tank dead on the ten-minute mark. Under one arm he carried several rolled charts. In his other hand was a shuttered chem-lantern. His expression was that of a man going to battle. Etsul motioned towards the rock, and they walked to it in silence. Her heartbeat was heavy in her chest.

She reminded herself that she had held his rank only a week earlier, and she knew its duties. Confrontation was part of command.

Vaslav spread the charts out on the rock, weighting their edges to prevent gravity pulses from fluttering them into the air.

'Have you assessed an optimal route, sergeant?' asked Etsul.

'For what good it will do us,' he said, stabbing a finger at the chart. 'This is us. We've got precious little intelligence of anything beyond our original route of advance, so my recommendation is to hold to it while we're navigating this guasa jungle. Where the trees grow this thick, the land has to be dry and firm enough to accommodate them. If we stick to the jungle, we avoid the swamps, you see?'

Etsul nodded, gestured for him to continue.

'We follow the advance route north out of the Mandriga Delta until we reach the Orphide hab-belt. Should be there just before dawn. Of course, if we've avoided the enemy that long it'll be a miracle.'

'Or we may have encountered more loyalists and joined forces,' countered Etsul.

'We were already out on the flank, sir,' pressed Vaslav. 'We ran west out of the sprawl, away from friendlies. Can't see us factoring in anyone's consolidation efforts all the way out here.'

'Even still.'

Vaslav gave a non-committal grunt then continued.

'Our best route on from the Orphide belt is the old silo road that exits sector eight-three-one and cuts through the Vervas chem-yards. If we're lucky then some of the macro-hauler transitways will still be in a condition to take *Tread*'s weight.'

His finger moved across the map. Etsul followed it, quietly relieved that the sergeant had at least showed diligence in his wayfinding. The route didn't necessarily look the safest, but it was expedient. She would have suggested it herself, in his position.

'From the yards, if we're somehow *still* alive, then Transitway Eight-Sixteen takes us through the Rhoes warehousing hub,' Vaslav pressed on. 'It's a straight shot from there to our approximate rally point, which I should note puts us amongst the foothills of Mount Auric and uncomfortably close to the enemy stronghold.'

'We have more immediate problems to worry about,' said Etsul. 'I've not had Moretzin's tally yet, but we expended plenty of ammunition in Costmarus. It's also patently clear our fuel reserves won't take us all the way to the rendez-vous.'

'Throne, I *know*,' snapped Vaslav. 'If the bloody reserve

tankers had caught up as they were supposed to it wouldn't be a problem! But by all means, pin it to my chest, like Moretzin couldn't have sorted this out back on the line.'

'I don't seek to lay blame, sergeant. My point is that we need to look out for refuelling opportunities as a matter of urgency. There is a Munitorum depot marked here amongst the Orphide belt, so I suggest we try there first. If we are unsuccessful then we'll need to be ready to syphon from any abandoned vehicles we find amongst the chem-yards or on Transitway Eight-Sixteen.'

'All right. Yes. Agreed,' he replied, his tone waspish. 'But you didn't need my input to decide any of this. You're the commander, not me.'

If the sergeant wanted to get to the point, Etsul thought, then she was glad to oblige.

'Gunnery Sergeant Vaslav, I require your input not just in this, but in all matters of operational detail and discipline. Frankly, your efforts have been almost entirely lacking.'

Etsul had wanted to maintain a positive tone but here, now, after all that had happened, she could no longer hold herself back. The wave broke through her and she was carried along like flotsam.

'You're consistently apathetic, bordering on downright neglectful. The fuel problem? That's just a symptom. Throne almighty, man, where were you when I arrived? Sleeping! Where are you each time the crew question me? Might as well be the same! Vaslav, you are poisonous to morale. I thought you'd lost your mind in the sprawl, ranting about Cadia's Bane. The one saving grace of your conduct is that I've barely had time to worry about my own reaction to all that, because I've been too focused on watching you in case you collapsed completely!'

Vaslav opened his mouth to speak. Etsul held up a warning finger, trembling with the effort of keeping her voice level.

'You are an excellent shot and a good sensorman, but even if that was all that I required of you we would *still* be having this conversation. You are part of this crew, *my* crew, and you are failing us dismally. We need you.'

'What we need is a commander worthy of Holtz,' Vaslav growled. 'Holtz as he was before.'

'Before?'

'Before Cadia. Before we lost the fight that mattered.'

Etsul slapped a hand down on the maps between them.

'This fight matters. Here and now.'

'Does it? The old man didn't believe that. He told me once, near the end, that he thought we were just living out the death throes of our species. This world is a spasm, a mind-less constriction. A hundred Croatoas wouldn't be worth one Cadia.'

'Sergeant, you stray dangerously close to heresy. I advise you to–'

'To what, *sir*? Even if the old man was talking through a bottle, even if this poxy planet does matter, we're *losing*. They have Cadia's Bane leading them, and what do we have? The likes of you.'

If he had thought to shock or wound Etsul with his words, Vaslav missed his mark. Instead, she felt a strange sort of relief. Here it was at last. He had no accusations to level that she hadn't already aimed at herself and disproved. Etsul could honestly say that Commander Masenwe would have approved of everything she had done. She required no fur-ther validation.

'Yarroe Canyon. Because you think I ran then, and now you see me doing it again.' To her surprise, Vaslav looked momentarily nonplussed. Then his face coloured with fresh anger.

'I'm not an idiot. I understand duty, and I don't mistake it for cowardice.'

'Then what?' asked Etsul, wrong-footed.

'You aren't Cadian. Not where it matters. The Munitorum think they can scrape up the dregs of the galaxy, stuff them into Cadian fatigues and like a miracle from the Emperor they'll have made new Cadians. As though that makes up for never having trained in the Whiteshields. As though that's a fair trade for having walked the ramparts of Kasr Helg, or fought off Archenemy raids day on day, year on year. The planet died, and Cadian blood spills every day. Our regiments bleed away like a gutshot trench raider. And then we get watered down with the likes of you and Trieve. Gates of Cadia, I'll bet you didn't even go through the training programme to bring you up to standard, did you?'

Etsul couldn't keep the shock off her face. It quickly gave way to honest outrage. She felt as if the sergeant had torn off a mask, and what she saw underneath was uglier than any Spineback.

'It's a question of us and them, is it, sergeant? Or rather, us and you? Go back to your own regiment?' Her words dripped scorn. Vaslav stared at her bullishly, without even the good grace to look ashamed. Etsul jabbed a finger at the darkened jungle.

'*Out there.* The enemy are out there, Vaslav. I'll keep saying it until you hear me. They sold their souls. They submitted to their fears. They gave up and made monsters of themselves. The traitors, the mutants – Emperor save us, the Heretic Astartes. We're not in our death throes. We're in the fight of our lives and every single loyal human needs to give their all, not give in to cowardice.'

His lips tightened into a bloodless line. She pressed on before he could rally.

'I was nervous about being transferred to a Cadian regiment. Yes, I'll admit it. Wasn't sure I'd live up to the reputation, no matter what my old commander thought of me. But Vaslav, I mean this sincerely, if you, and your excuses, and your... bigotry... If they're all the Cadians have left to offer, then I was sold a poor deal. You're *scared*, aren't you? Scared of change, scared of the honest fight, scared that soldiers like Trieve and Chalenboor and yes, even a meagre Tsegohan like me will disprove this myth of Cadian exceptionalism you're clinging to.'

'I don't–' he began. She overrode him, biting out her words.

'I don't serve Cadia or its memory, sergeant. I serve the God-Emperor and so do you. You will meet His expectations of what it means to be a soldier of the Imperial Guard. You will meet mine.'

Vaslav's throat worked. A vein pulsed at his temple. He looked like he was choking on his anger. Expression thunderous, he turned his back and stalked away towards *Steel Tread*. Etsul breathed hard as she fought to calm herself, to accommodate her disgust at Vaslav's attitude.

Pulses of errant gravity rippled through the clearing, heralds of the storm to come. Etsul felt them snatching at the fabric of her tank suit, felt herself momentarily lighter, then heavier, as though she stood on the deck of a ship in rolling seas. Her centre of balance yawed. Etsul put a hand to the rock for support. Thunder boomed overhead, one peal rolling into the next. Lightning bolts rocketed through the sky, following the tortured contours of the clouds, describing actinic spirals that rendered the sky momentarily nightmarish. Drops of warm rain began to fall, coming down in unnatural spiral patterns and stinking of ash and blood.

Etsul gazed skyward, Rift-be-damned, and felt a chill run through her.

'Emperor save us,' she murmured. 'The eclipse storm is on us.'

Verro squinted at his wrist-chrono. He could barely see the display in the shuttered half-light of Trieve's chem-lantern, but thought they'd been outside for about half an hour. He, Chalenboor and Moretzin huddled together under the auto-awning while hot rain drummed its twitching canvas. Trieve was sealing up the engine cowling. The commander was scowling at her data-slate as though it had personally offended her. The sergeant had clambered back into the tank some minutes ago with a face like murder. Verro didn't know what had passed between the two officers, but he could guess.

His guts churned with worry. There again, he told himself, that might just be nausea triggered by the gravity pulses of the eclipse storm fooling his inner ear.

Verro had been through four of these things now, and they never got any less unpleasant. As he understood it, Croatoas hadn't suffered them before the Rift opened. He still didn't understand why an eclipse should play havoc with gravity, or weather patterns, or why it would make the rain stink like copper and vomit.

What really unsettled him, though, was how a world without a moon could suffer eclipses at all.

He jumped, shaken from his reverie by a blast of ball lightning. It fell amidst the trees somewhere to the north. Flames leapt from its impact. Verro fervently made the sign of the aquila, muttering a prayer for protection. They had suffered all the misfortune they could stand. More would break them.

Trieve muttered a final prayer under his breath and locked

the cowl back in place. The commander looked up, stashing her data-slate.

'Reports?' she asked. She'd been caught in the downpour, and her tank suit was stained bile-yellow where the rain had touched it.

'The power plant did not make it through unscathed, sir,' said Trieve. '*Steel Tread*'s flagellation may please the God-Emperor, but it will slow our progress somewhat. Gunner Chalenboor's station has also suffered damage and I would not recommend traversing the gun lest we vex its machine-spirit.'

'Dreggin' great,' muttered Nix.

'Fuel's low, sir,' said Moretzin. 'We've got twenty-eight rounds left for the main gun, one-third charge on the las. Verro's bolter is down to three magazines. Chalenboor has two left.'

Verro considered making a crack about fire-discipline. He read the mood and refrained.

'Unfortunate, but myself and the sergeant have discussed contingencies,' said the commander.

Verro shot a glance at Chalenboor. She raised her eyebrows in answer.

'On the plus side, at least a Leman Russ engine will run on almost any form of fuel,' the commander continued. 'Our route will take us through the Orphide belt, then to Transit-way Eight-Sixteen via the Vervas chem-yards and then on to the rally point. I project our arrival around this time tomorrow.'

Verro heard the sound of a great many problems and perils being glazed over.

'We need to get moving right away,' the commander said. 'We will maintain lumen discipline, but we need whatever speed *Tread* will give us. There's no hiding a Demolisher, so our best hope lies in the cover of this storm and making the run as fast as we can. Driver Trieve, are you up to the challenge?'

'Emperor willing, sir,' he replied, and Verro was surprised to hear the pride in the driver's voice.

'Good enough for me,' said the commander. 'All of you, maintain a sharp lookout. Engage only on my order. We're not about to get bogged down in escalating fights we can't win, understand? Trust me when I tell you that there *will* be an accounting for Costmarus. I know something about vengeance. It keeps. Meantime, duty comes first. The Emperor protects.'

'The Emperor protects,' they replied, then they all made for the hatches.

Back aboard, Verro was surprised when *Steel Tread*'s power plant rumbled gamely to life. He was more surprised still that first one hour passed, then another, in nothing more than a steady haze of filthy rain and overgrown backroads. The ground climbed steadily, but the Demolisher lumbered onwards, seemingly undaunted by their adversity. Verro wished he could have said the same for the crew.

The jungle pressed close, undergrowth whipping across the vid-feeds and reducing visibility. At any moment, Verro expected enemy fire to blaze out at them. Somehow each minute that crawled past without contact made the waiting worse. Gravity waves pushed and pulled at him, the tank's hull no protection from such fundamental forces. Nausea kept threatening with every stomach-rolling pulse. They set the sensors sputtering and caused everything in the tank to rattle. The rain grew so heavy that it streaked the few feeds not choked with vegetation.

And yet, part of him would still rather be out there than in here.

The silence over the vox was as toxic as the arguments had been before. Verro felt as though the tank were stuffed with dry tinder, waiting only for someone to light a match.

Even with the rain outside, he wished he was anywhere but trapped in this box with people who hated each other. Chalenboor kept shooting dark looks up at the commander when she thought she was unobserved.

Verro had known Chalenboor long enough to understand the way she thought, and what she was capable of if she set her mind to something. He promised himself he would keep an eye on his friend and talk her down from anything unwise. It had taken Holtz a while to earn her respect too, after all, but once he had she'd been loyal to a fault. Some gang-culture thing, Verro supposed.

He found himself ashamed of the way the crew had behaved these last few days. He had realised in some detached way that they'd let things slip while languishing on the line, but he had assumed that once they were back in the fight with a cause to unite them, they would gel again. Verro couldn't remember the sergeant being this hostile towards Chalenboor, or even the frankly unlikeable Trieve, when they'd replaced Markov and Tesga. He briefly made the sign of the aquila over his chest at the thought of comrades lost.

Verro felt genuinely sympathetic to their new commander. She didn't even realise that she'd 'tipped the balance'. There were now as many non-Cadians as Cadians on the crew, and he guessed that the sergeant feared they had lost something in the transition.

He glanced back at Moretzin where she crouched by the power plant. If he'd hoped to gauge her thoughts, he was disappointed. Her expression remained unreadable.

The tank wallowed to starboard, and Verro feared some monumental grav-pulse might have pulled their tracks right off the ground. He relaxed as he realised they were merely following the road in a switchback turn.

'Auspex signals,' reported the sergeant. Verro twitched, then inwardly cursed the stimms for making him so jumpy.

'Elaborate, sergeant,' said the commander.

'Hang on,' snapped the sergeant, then, 'Trying... confirm! Imperial beacons. I'm reading them at extreme range of auspex cover, but looks like multiple contacts moving in concert.'

Verro's breath left him in a rush. They weren't alone out here, and it wasn't the heretics about to descend on them.

'Friendlies,' he voxed to Chalenboor.

'Yeah, and maybe one of them'll take charge, eh?' she voxed back, puncturing his mood.

'Should we hail them, sir?' asked Trieve. 'Awaken our choral beacon or divert to intercept their course?'

'Wait,' said Vaslav, his tone urgent.

'Sergeant?' prompted the commander.

'Another contact, entering range from due south,' he said. 'Throne, it's big, and moving fast... No Imperial designator...'

Verro turned cold. He could no longer blame the thump of his heart on stimms or storm.

'Sergeant, are you seeing this?' asked the commander.

'Mercy of the Gates,' Vaslav swore over the vox. 'That's...'

'Has to be. Super-heavy scale.'

'Oh, Throne... It's right on top of them.'

'Damn it, damn it!'

'Should we–'

'Absolutely not, what help would we be?'

Verro had no auspex screen. He could see nothing but his smeared vid-feeds and was in a torment of frustration as he listened to their fractured exchange.

Chalenboor lost patience before he did.

'What's goin' on out there?'

When she replied, the commander sounded drained, like something vital had been leeched from her.

'All Imperial contacts eliminated. Enemy super-heavy contact is... holding position at their last location. They're gone, Chalenboor.'

'It's hunting us,' said the sergeant.

'What is?' asked Verro, as though a charade of ignorance might hold the monster at bay.

'Can't see us though, can it, sir? Got no beacon lit!' Chalenboor insisted.

'You assume that such abominations obey the Emperor's natural laws,' said Trieve dolefully. Verro thought of that last, eager howl as they had lost the Knight amidst the whirling purple fog. A memory of home grazed his mind, of the predatory skarligs that prowled the wetlands in search of smaller prey. He recalled the dog-sized vermin stalking their victims through the marshes, stoking the hunted beasts' panic and fear, goading them to flight in the hope they would lead them back to their nests.

'Quiet, all of you,' snapped the commander. 'We don't know any more than we just witnessed. Wild speculation helps no one. Trieve, keep us on our heading and for Throne's sakes keep the pace up. Sergeant, focus on the auspex, warn me if you see that contact coming our way. Verro, Chalenboor, Moretzin, watch the feeds. We hold our course and pray that the Emperor protects.'

Verro did as he was ordered, staring at his vid-feeds with fevered intensity and praying silently. Yet as he did, he heard again the sergeant's words, the grim certainty in them.

'It's hunting us...'

CHAPTER NINE

LOYALTIES

To Verro, the night felt never-ending. Rain hit the hull like bullets. Spiral lightning exploded again and again, until the jungle strobed with harsh white blasts and inky shadows. Spheres of energy fell like artillery shells.

Steel Tread toiled up craggy hillsides and plunged through sheer cuttings. Fronds lashed wet vid-lenses, the grainy images making Verro's eyes ache. He feared the heretics could virtually walk up to the tank and slap krak-charges on the tracks without him seeing them. Coupled with the labouring pitch of the power plant, and the fear of the monstrous auspex ghost, he felt like he was living a drawn-out nightmare.

Once, a cannonade of lightning blasts illuminated deformed renegade tanks crossing a bare ridgeline to their east. The sighting prompted a heart-stopping half hour before they could trust the foe had missed them in the storm.

Towards dawn, the sergeant called out that he had sighted

the super-heavy auspex signature again, still due south, lurking at the far edge of sensor range.

Verro began to suspect the monster wanted them to know it was there, that it was toying with them. He scolded himself for paranoia, but without conviction.

By the time weak daylight seeped over the horizon he was almost pathetically grateful. Yet sunrise didn't help. Verro had known intellectually they were in the grip of a full-blown malefic eclipse, but to see Croatoas' star so corrupted did nothing for his mood. A corona of jaundiced gold danced about the churning mass of darkness obscuring it. Its light spread over the jungle like a stain. The canopy thrashed, battered by rain and by grav-pulses that dropped the bottom out of Verro's gut each time they hit.

'It's like an eye,' said Moretzin, breaking the long silence. 'Like there's something terrible up there looking down on us.'

'The only one looking down upon us is the God-Emperor, and His divine countenance was never so unclean,' Trieve replied.

Silence crowded back in following this brief exchange. Minutes limped past like wounded on their way to a medicae station. They rumbled on, moving steadily downhill. Verro sank into guilty reverie, wondering belatedly about acquaintances on other tank crews, whether they had survived Costmarus sprawl. He jumped as Trieve spoke again over the vox.

'Jungle fringe dead ahead, sir. Orphide hab-belt should be just beyond.'

'Auspex is a mess,' replied the commander. 'Sergeant Vaslav, are you having any more luck than me?'

Verro felt the quiet stretch out. Static rippled in time to the grav-pulses.

'Sergeant?' prompted the commander. Verro sensed the

brittle peace within *Steel Tread* straining. He was relieved when the sergeant replied, sounding like a man startled from sleep.

'Can't see anything on my screen, sir. With the full eclipse, though, I'd not expect to. Could be a platoon of the bastards out there and we'd not know it.'

'Keep trying,' urged the commander. 'We work with what the Emperor gives us. Trieve, can you locate the Munitorum depot?'

'I shall pray to Him on the Throne for the clarity to prevail, sir,' replied Trieve.

As the jungle petered out, Verro's grainy vid-feeds showed him a suggestion of what lay ahead. He wished they hadn't. Crumbling hab-blocks loomed through the spiralling rain, lit weirdly by the twitching light of the eclipsed star. They were so damaged that they looked to Verro like a mouthful of broken teeth. Some had toppled against their neighbours or collapsed into rubble mountains. Even at a distance, he could make out heretic graffiti, the unclean symbol he'd seen jutting from ritual corpse heaps, crude human figures engaged in improbable acts of debauchery.

The roadway joined a raised transitway like a tributary flowing into a larger river. Trieve guided them along it, still heading downhill as they approached the habs. The road was littered with burned-out wrecks, both civilian and military. Gaping holes had been blasted in its surface. Trieve gave them a wide berth, thinking no doubt how easily *Steel Tread* might plunge through the weakened surface.

'No plant life,' observed the commander. Verro saw she was right. It was as though, in leaving the jungle, they had crossed some invisible boundary. Here there was only rusting metal, broken ferrocrete and blackened bones.

'Sir, should we stop?' he suggested. 'Try to syphon fuel from the wrecks?'

'Negative, Verro. We're too exposed out here. Besides, look at them, most are burned out. We'd find no fuel there.'

'No, sir, I see that, apologies,' he replied, feeling faintly foolish for missing such an obvious detail himself.

'Whatever happened here, it wasn't recent,' said the commander.

'Perhaps by the Emperor's grace the entire area is dead, a city-sized mausoleum,' suggested Trieve. He didn't sound convinced. Mired in unease, Verro returned his gaze to his vid-feeds. The line of the jungle receded behind them. Any moment, he expected a monstrous shape to burst from its depths and come pounding down the transit-way. Desperate to share his unease, he opened a channel to Chalenboor.

'It could be right there… watching us…'

'What?'

'You know what,' he snapped. 'How in Cadia's name is it tracking us? God-Emperor, *why* is it tracking us? We're one tank.'

'Yeah, but we slipped it, din't we?' she replied.

'Did we? Surely it could have run us down…'

'I dunno then,' she replied, sounding irritable in her turn. 'Maybe it's playin' with us, felid with a duct rat, you know? Huntin' us with heretic wyrd-shit or whatever.'

'Or maybe it's hoping we'll lead it straight to our rally point,' Verro opined grimly.

'Or maybe it ain't there at all, yeah?' Chalenboor shot back. 'Maybe you're jumpin' at shadows, mate, 'cos we ain't actually seen anythin', have we? Not since the sprawl.'

'Do you think so?' Verro asked.

'I dunno, but I'm not inventin' danger out there just now. Not when it's already in here with us.'

'In here? What do you mean?' Chalenboor snorted into the vox. It came through like a blurt of static.

'This… like, all this mess. We've been beaten, 'alf buried, almost died 'alf a dozen times. We're lost, proper shut down. We're runnin' out of fuel, and she's only been in charge, what, three days?'

Verro was suddenly conscious that individual vox-channels were not the same as private vox-channels. The commander could listen in to any of their conversations if she had a mind to.

'Nix, Throne's sakes, think about what you're saying,' he hissed.

'I am thinkin' about it, serious. Not just thinkin'.'

Verro felt his exhaustion deepen at the thought of more trouble. 'You can't hold the commander accountable for everything that's gone wrong since we left the line. She's kept us alive this far, hasn't she?'

'Luck ain't skill, mate,' she replied, sounding uncharacteristically sombre. 'And it was us kept us alive, not her. Back on Dakturia, down in the Crawls, a weak leader meant a weak gang, and weak meant dead.'

'Nix…' he said, then found himself unsure how to continue.

'Garret, just watch your screens, yeah?' she said, not unkindly. 'Someone's got to be the lookout man, and that's you. Let me worry 'bout her.'

'What do you mean worry about her?' he replied.

Chalenboor cut the vox-channel. She ignored his repeated attempts to reopen it. Verro knew he couldn't do more without rousing suspicions. He sat, barely feet away from the friend he felt a desperate need to talk to, as cut off as though they were on different worlds. He stared miserably at his vid screens and wondered what more could go wrong.

* * *

They rolled into the dancing shadows of the hab-blocks. Understanding of the heretics' impact upon their captured territories only grew. Skulls lined windows, impaled on silver spikes. Etsul saw fetish poles jutting from upper storeys, chains and flayed skins dangling from them.

Most unsettling were the glass sculptures set incongruously amidst the rubble. She had only seen a few of them: pastel-tinted prisms warped into darkly suggestive shapes that made Etsul uncomfortable. They reminded her of heathen idols, of frenzied intercourse and ritual murder. Where the eclipse light touched them, it made them glow from within and sent warped rainbows flickering through the falling rain. She felt with grim certainty that the enemy were here, somewhere, and the sooner *Steel Tread* cleared the hab-belt, the better.

The poor visibility was fraying Etsul's nerves. She alternated between her blurred vid screens, the stuttering auspex and the periscope, whose aperture looked out above the Demolisher cannon's barrel. She considered unbuttoning, rain be damned. Up in the cupola she could get a proper look around. The thought of snipers dissuaded her.

'Trieve, are we still on course?' she asked, squinting through her periscope.

'We are, sir,' he replied. 'Depot should be less than half a mile ahead along this processional, providing we don't hit any blockages we can't cross.'

Steel Tread weaved between the blackened hulks of tanks, transports and crashed civilian vehicles. Trieve took them over barricades festooned with desiccated human remains. He used the Demolisher's bulk to shunt aside wrecked vehicles, and ground the rubble of destroyed homes beneath its tracks.

There was fire damage everywhere. Ash formed drifts about the hab-blocks, with here and there a lumen pole or skeletal tree jutting skyward. They rumbled past the entrance to a subterranean maglev station; it took Etsul a moment to discern what clogged the opening top to bottom. Her mouth twisted when she realised it was blackened bone, and she wondered what in the Emperor's name had befallen this place.

She turned to the periscope again, just in time for tainted light to leap from a nearby sculpture and fill her view. Etsul recoiled. She gagged. She tasted hot flesh and copper, smelled sea salt and vomit and perfume. There came a sensation of squirming motion on her tongue so visceral that she opened her mouth and stuck her fingers inside to check nothing had slithered in. A sigh caressed her ears. Invisible nails raked the skin of her arms almost hard enough to break the skin.

Etsul crossed her arms and scrubbed at herself, screwing her eyes shut until the sensations faded.

'Holy God-Emperor, Shepherd and Steersman, protect your faithful servants from all that is unclean.'

'Sir, Munitorum depot dead ahead. The Emperor isn't done testing us yet, though.'

Steeling herself, Etsul risked the periscope again and saw what Trieve meant. The depot was huge, a dozen storeys of utilitarian minimalism squatting at the heart of a wide plaza. Storage sheds with sagging roofs clustered about its skirts. On its western side, silos and vent-stacks marked the fuelling shrine she had hoped to see.

Between them and the building, however, was a sea of twisted metal. Etsul couldn't count how many tanks, how many armoured transports and iron-fleshed heretic engines packed the plaza. Many had been malformed by heat, fused together into hideous sculptures and coated in ash.

'How did the depot survive... this...?' asked Verro, sounding awed.

'Void shielding?' suggested Etsul. 'Some installations have generators buried in bunkers beneath their foundations.'

'Whatever it was, there are no energy signatures now,' said Vaslav.

'A miracle of the God-Emperor,' said Trieve.

'Can you get us through?' Etsul asked him.

'Sadly, sir, I can but pray to the Emperor for miracles, not work them. Skirting the plaza's edge should be possible, but I don't think...'

Etsul glanced at her screens, set her eye to the periscope. She scanned the rooftops and empty windows around the plaza and did her best to separate the memory of Yarroe Canyon from her nightmares of it. The rain poured down. Gravity pulses made rubble jitter and banners ripple. The poisoned light danced like a faulty holoprojector. No way in all this to pick out the sly movements of hidden foes.

Cadian caution, she considered, was a more appealing concept when one could remain within one's tank.

'Moretzin, what do we have left in the way of fuel cans?'

'Four, sir. The rest were crushed. So were the bigger barrels.'

'Barrels wouldn't help us anyway,' said Etsul, running rough calculations in her head. Four cans ought to suffice, barely. She had no more excuses to put this off.

'I'm taking the cans,' she said. 'I'm going to the refuelling shrine on foot to see if it's operational. Trieve, get us as close as you can without risking the tank. I need a volunteer to accompany me and carry the other two cans. The rest of you, remain at your stations, cover us as best you can. Sergeant Vaslav has command until I return.'

Etsul told herself she was doing this because the crew knew

and trusted Vaslav, and that after last night's exchange she would take the moral high ground even if she did find his attitude repugnant.

A small voice whispered in her mind – maybe Masenwe's, maybe her own. It asked if Etsul was doing this because she could no longer sit in the command chair and order others to action. Or whether, perhaps, she just sought to escape the toxic atmosphere within the tank.

She might have engaged in deeper introspection but, as Trieve took the tank along the edge of the wreckage field, Verro spoke up.

'I volunteer, sir.'

'Nah, he won't,' Chalenboor chimed in. 'My gun's broke, yeah? I'll go. You're the lookout man, remember, Garret?'

'Sir, I insist,' said Verro. 'You need a proper Cadian out there to watch your back, sir.'

Etsul's jaw clenched. Her reply was frosty.

'I will put my faith in Gunner Chalenboor's experience of urban warfare over the supposed benefits of astrographical origin, Verro.'

'Yes, sir,' he replied, sounding taken aback.

Etsul blew out a breath and reminded herself not to tar all Cadians with Vaslav's brush. Otherwise, she was no better than him.

'You are an excellent shot, Verro. You're more use to me behind a heavy bolter than lugging cans of fuel.'

'Yes, sir,' he repeated, sounding resigned. Etsul rubbed her eyes with thumb and finger.

Trieve brought *Steel Tread* to a halt, hull down behind a derelict Baneblade. The huge wreck had subsided into a crater, its right track unit and great portions of its hull peeled back or melted.

It was the work of moments for Etsul and Chalenboor to sling a lascarbine each across their backs, and to grab a couple of frag grenades apiece along with the fuel cans. On Etsul's orders, Trieve kept the engine idling, ready to leap to combat readiness in an instant. She offered her crew what she hoped was a reassuring smile before she and Chalenboor slipped from a side hatch and into the pummelling rain.

Etsul felt exposed. The stink of corruption nearly made her gag. The eclipse throbbed overhead. Gravity tugged at her, trying to throw her off balance. Filthy rain streaked her skin and ran into her eyes. Wet ash clung to her boots like mud. Snipers might be lurking in every window, and the first clue would be a las-bolt to the head.

She spat water that tasted like bile.

'Emperor, guide us through this storm,' she said then jerked her head to Chalenboor. 'Come on.'

Perhaps the Emperor heard her prayer, for they crossed the wreckage without incident. Etsul forged ahead, Chalenboor a silent presence behind her. Within minutes they had made it into the lee of the depot and were standing before the fuelling shrine. Its huge promethium tanks sprouted pipes, gauges and gantries. Etsul knew little enough about how such a place might operate, but she knew a fuel gauge when she saw one, and as a tanker she understood the rudiments of pump-stations.

The first tank she tried was bone dry. The second looked viable until Chalenboor pointed out the ragged bullet holes riddling its piping. On the third try, Etsul was rewarded with flickering green flow runes and a gauge that read more than half full.

'We're in luck,' she said. Chalenboor nodded, set down her fuel cans and unslung her lascarbine. The gunner met her gaze pointedly, then turned and started panning her gun across the empty windows around the plaza. It seemed that Etsul would be doing the fuelling.

As she unscrewed the cap on the first fuel can and primed the pumping mechanism, she considered talking to Chalenboor. The former ganger had joined this crew before her, as a non-Cadian native, an outsider. Quite possibly she had faced the same prejudice from Vaslav, and from others; if she had, how had she achieved the level of integration she now enjoyed? It was absurd to be considering conversation at a time like this, but Etsul could not shake her need to have *someone* on this crew she could trust.

She wondered if Aswold was still alive, and found a tremor running through her hands. She could not stop now.

Etsul bent to the pumping mechanism, setting the can in place and intoning the rites of operation. Behind her, she dimly heard Chalenboor chanting a prayer over her lasgun, urging it to help her purge the weak and the unworthy.

Verro tapped a foot against the deck. He shifted on his fold-out seat, readjusted his targeter. He couldn't believe that even Chalenboor would do anything stupid at a time like this. But then again, everyone was strung out, on edge, dosed with stimms. And if accidents were going to befall unpopular officers, they had a habit of doing so in no-man's-land, far from official eyes.

Chalenboor was impulsive, and when she believed something, she had the conviction of a preacher in a pulpit.

Verro asked himself again why his friend had volunteered. It wasn't as though Chalenboor wanted to watch the commander's back. Indeed, she'd probably cheer if a Spineback blew Etsul's head off. So what was she doing out there?

He wiped sweating palms on his tank suit and frowned at his feeds. Chalenboor and the commander had just reached the fuelling shrine. Grav nausea rolled in his gut.

'We would not suffer these trials were the masses not so faithless,' Trieve was saying. 'It is the fault of those who will not be humbled before His glory. It is the fault of those who believe themselves great and blameless.'

'Trieve, shut up,' grunted the sergeant. 'Just be ready to get us clear the moment I give the order.'

On his vid-feed, the rain-blurred figures of the commander and Chalenboor were flitting between the fuel tanks. They halted, the commander out of sight, Nix with her lasgun unslung.

Verro turned to look at Moretzin, who had settled into Chalenboor's station to watch the feeds. The loader returned his stare, forehead creased.

'Sergeant, I request permission to join the commander and Nix,' he said. 'They need someone out there with a gun to cover them on the way back, and I can't see a damn thing with this rain.'

He looked to Vaslav, who had turned to glare at him. The sergeant seemed to weigh his words. Verro held his breath. Vaslav shrugged.

'All right, Whiteshield, you're so eager to get drenched, go. The sooner we have that fuel on board the sooner we can leave.'

Verro sprang up from his station, snatched a lascarbine from the depleted arms locker and slid out of the side hatch.

He hoped he was wrong.

He hoped he would get there in time.

Etsul wiped stinking rain from her face. She was crouching by the control panel for the pumping mechanism, muttering curses and prayers. Again, the mechanism gave a gurgling groan. Again, the flow into the can choked off.

'Emperor, give me strength!' she snarled, and had to restrain herself from slamming a fist into the machine. Breathing out slowly Etsul pressed her thumb to the pump rune until it lurched from crimson to green. There came an awful screech, and the chugging flow of fuel began anew.

At this pace, filling four cans would take hours, and if there were enemies in the vicinity, they couldn't help but hear the racket. There was nothing else for it, though. Without the fuel there was no way to make their rendezvous.

Etsul felt a tingle on the back of her neck, some survivor's sixth sense whispering a warning. Then came a wordless shout from behind. Not Chalenboor's voice, Verro's.

Etsul was reaching for her lascarbine even as she turned. Her heart lurched as she found herself staring into the barrel of Chalenboor's gun. The sponson gunner stood bare paces away and had the weapon raised. She might simply have been panning the weapon around, and Etsul had stood up into her line of fire.

Or she might have been aiming the weapon directly at her commander.

Chalenboor, too, was looking back over her shoulder at Verro. He was scrambling over a rubble heap, waving his arms.

'What–' Etsul began.

Red light streaked across her field of vision, turning raindrops to minute rubies. Verro cried out. Blood puffed from his shoulder and he spun, tumbling out of sight on the far side of the rubble mound.

As though this were a signal, a storm of las-bolts rained down. Shots struck the fuel tanks. They sizzled from ferrocrete, scorched the depot wall. One seared by Etsul's face, so close she recoiled with a hiss of pain.

'Chalenboor, the cans!' she shouted, making a grab for the one that sat beneath the pump. Las-bolts slashed around her and she was driven back. Etsul's heart missed another beat at the thought of fuel erupting in a fireball.

She scrambled for cover and saw Chalenboor running towards the rubble heap Verro had fallen from. Empty fuel cans toppled in her wake. A las-bolt punctured one with a dull *spang*.

'Throne *dammit!*' yelled Etsul. Breaking from cover she dashed after Chalenboor, slinging her gun back over one shoulder as she ran.

'Chalenboor, get into cover!' she shouted. The sponson gunner ignored her, weaving through the slashes of las-fire at a run.

Etsul threw herself into a diving tackle and wrapped both arms around Chalenboor's legs. The gunner sprawled. Her lasgun skittered from her grip. Ruby fire sliced the air.

Over the hiss of rain and las-bolts, Etsul could hear Verro cursing from beyond the rubble heap. Chalenboor squirmed and rolled over before raking Etsul with a glare of such venom that the commander recoiled.

'Ain't you done enough? Get off me, you duct-squirmer!'

'Gunner Chalenboor, keep your damned head down or it'll get blown off,' barked Etsul in answer.

'Yeah, hide, run away, s'all you do, in't it? Leave everyone else to get fragged.' Chalenboor raised a booted foot and drove it forward. Anger and panic made the blow clumsy; it hit Etsul in the shoulder and skidded painfully from the wet material of her tank suit.

Chalenboor drove herself to her feet, only for a grav-pulse

to send her stumbling. Etsul lunged. She swept the gunner's legs from under her again. She was on top of Chalenboor in an instant, aiming to pin one arm into the small of her back. Chalenboor was fast though, and slippery. She wriggled around and jabbed a punch at Etsul's face.

Tsegoh was a hard world to grow up on. Perhaps not hive-slums hard, but Etsul had seen more than her share of brawls when fishers and agri-workers riled each other up in the dock taverns. She'd known how to fight even before the Astra Militarum trained her to. She took satisfaction seeing Chalenboor's eyes widen with surprise as Etsul swayed and took the blow on her collarbone, then slapped aside the follow up.

'Chalenboor! Think! They've got the angle on us. If we get up–'

'Rot you! Dreg coward! You ain't fit to be anyone's boss! You're goin' to get us all killed.'

Etsul's fractional pause was enough for Chalenboor to thump a knee into her ribs, winding her. The gunner lashed out again, clipping Etsul's chin with her knuckles, smashing her teeth together.

Etsul wound up and slugged Chalenboor in return, hard enough to rock her head back and bounce it off the ferro-crete. Blood squirted from the gunner's split bottom lip. She lolled drunkenly. Etsul unslung her lascarbine and, gripping it with one hand, she crab-walked into cover dragging Chalenboor with her by the scruff of her tank suit.

Etsul squinted through the rain, trying to gauge where the shooters were and how many of them they faced. Beside her, Chalenboor groaned.

'Stay down. If you ever point a weapon at me or raise a hand to me again you won't live to meet the firing squad. Clear?'

Chalenboor replied with a slur of vowels. Etsul continued. 'I am done trying to prove myself to you idiots. I have never seen a more ill-disciplined shower in all my life. If I could wind back time, Chalenboor, I would give us both back the commanders we had and be glad if I never saw another Cadian uniform again. But here we are, in the middle of this storm, and it is my job to drag you all safe to shore. And I'm going to do it, too, whether you deserve it or not, whether you help me or not, because that's my duty. Masenwe wouldn't expect any less.'

'Masenwe?' mumbled Chalenboor, pulling herself up to sit against a chunk of rusted metal.

'My old *boss*,' replied Etsul, peering out into the rain. 'Throne, but he'd have whipped you lot into shape soon enough. Since he's not here, looks like I'm stuck with the job. *Thanks*, commander…'

From the corner of her eye Etsul saw Chalenboor roll her shoulders and tense to move. She tensed in turn, ready to defend herself, but the gunner just worked her jaw ruefully with one hand.

'You punch like a gang-brute. A big one.' Etsul didn't really care what Chalenboor made of her right cross, but if this signalled a cessation of mutinous violence then it would do. She would consider the long-term implications of the gunner's actions when they weren't under fire.

'Get into a few drunken fist fights with dock haulers who think size is all that matters,' she said. 'You soon pick it up.'

Verro cursed again. Las-bolts flashed around their cover. Chalenboor tried to rise and Etsul grabbed a handful of her tank suit, pulling the gunner back down. This time, Chalenboor didn't resist.

'We can't just run out there, we'll get shot too. Then we're all dead.'

'But he's hurt, yeah? Might be dyin'.'

'I know, Chalenboor, I'm not just going to let him bleed out. We need to–'

An animal scream pierced the air; it took Etsul a moment to realise that it had come from Verro. She turned as if bidden to look back at the southern processional where they had entered the plaza. Her scalp tightened and her throat closed with fear.

'Throne,' breathed Chalenboor.

There, teetering on its grotesque needle-limbs, was the Knight.

CHAPTER TEN

THE BEAST

Once, as a child, Etsul had volunteered to help two of her parents' agri-hands in the tidal paddocks. She'd been seven, maybe eight, and she knew now the two men had been irresponsible to let her tag along. They'd been barely more than boys themselves, amused at the thought of the boss' child getting covered in brinemud and caeturid dung.

None of them had expected a bull caeturid, come early into its mating season and sure they were intruding on its territory. The huge beast had gored one agri-hand against the paddock wall then crushed the other under its bulk as he ran for the tidelock gate. Too small and frightened to help, Etsul had scrambled under the motorised crawler they had ridden to get there. She'd lain in the brine-stinking half-light as the caeturid thrashed about, hearing again the screams of the agri-hands, imagining the tusked head thrusting into her prison and dragging her out to be crushed. As the waters of the paddock rose, she'd prayed to the God-Emperor in abject terror.

It had been a close thing. Had her father and his servitors arrived even a few minutes later she would have drowned under the crawler, or else been slain by the bull caeturid.

She was viscerally reminded of that childhood terror now as she stared at the mutant Knight. Etsul wanted to burrow deep into the wreckage around her, to cower there in the hope the monster wouldn't find her.

She couldn't.

There was no one to save her. It was her responsibility. To this day, when that memory came back to her, she felt again her guilt and impotence as she heard the agri-hands dying. Logically she knew there was nothing a child could have done to save them from nine hundred pounds of angry caeturid. That knowledge hadn't spared her feelings of guilt, any more than the same truth spared her agony over Masenwe's death.

She promised herself no more ghosts.

Steel Tread didn't cower. Even without her guidance, the tank was rotating on the spot, traversing to bring the monster into its sights.

The Knight threw back its head and howled. Even as it tottered out into the plaza, its cry was echoed by human voices all around. To Etsul they sounded exultant and insane.

She looked to Chalenboor and was pleased to see the gunner wore a resolute expression.

'Fire's slacked off,' Chalenboor said. 'Reckon they're busy watchin' their monster, yeah?'

'This is our chance,' said Etsul. 'We need to grab Verro and get back to *Tread*.'

'Stick crawl-close, yeah?' Chalenboor replied, then she was off, running bent double. Etsul followed, doing her best to emulate the former ganger's stance.

Up the rubble heap they scrambled, Etsul waiting for a

las-bolt that never came. Chalenboor crested the rise and slithered out of sight. As Etsul followed, she spotted Verro below. He slumped against a heat-warped mound of metal, rain diluting the blood that pooled around him.

Etsul half scrambled, half tumbled down the rubble heap and splashed into the muck at its foot. Chalenboor glanced at her, dark fringe plastered down above hunted eyes. Together they hastened to Verro's side.

Massive footfalls caused puddles to ripple, the weight of the Knight's presence forcing Etsul into a hunted crouch even at a distance.

She heard the thump-boom of the Demolisher cannon firing, and thanked the God-Emperor that *Tread* was still alive.

There was a scorched hole in the shoulder of Verro's tank suit. His eyes were closed, and Chalenboor crouched over him, muttering.

'Is he...?'

'I'm alive, commander,' croaked Verro.

'You're a ratwit, is what you are,' said Chalenboor. Etsul heard real worry in the gunner's voice.

'I'm sorry,' Verro continued. 'Careless.'

'How bad is it?' asked Etsul.

'Las-bolt's cauterised the entry wound, but reckon it's snagged somethin' deeper in,' said Chalenboor. 'Whatever that is, it's leakin' like a sump-pipe. He needs a med.'

The Knight howled and all three of them cringed. As the echoes died away, Etsul heard bestial voices raised in answer, closer than before.

'The enemy are coming to worship their god,' said Etsul bitterly.

'What d'we do?' asked Chalenboor with a worried look at Verro.

'There's no time to do this subtly,' she told Chalenboor as she moved to Verro's side. 'We carry him between us, stay low, and make a dash for that wrecked Baneblade. There's a hole in its right track skirt about halfway along. If we can get in there, we can crawl through like we did with the Chimera and *Tread* can pick us up from the hole in its other flank.'

'If they ain't had to do a runner before we get there, yeah?'

'They'll wait for us,' said Verro.

'And that will get them killed if we don't get a move on,' said Etsul.

Verro grunted with pain as the two of them hauled him upright, but managed to get his feet under him. Blood welled from his shoulder and mingled with filthy rainwater, spattering Etsul and Chalenboor as they set off at a stumbling jog.

They stayed as low as they could, but there was no question now of crawling through cover. Every step Etsul expected a las-bolt between the shoulder blades, but the shot didn't come. She wondered briefly if the snipers had abandoned their posts to join the mob she could hear drawing closer.

Gravity pulsed. Etsul snarled with frustration as she staggered drunkenly. Verro gasped, but they kept him upright.

Etsul was soaked in blood and rainwater, caked in ash-mud. Her limbs shook with adrenaline and the threat of exhaustion. Every hot breath brought with it the stink of heretical corruption. Verro was getting heavier by the moment as his strength seeped from his shoulder wound.

She looked up and felt a surge of relief. The Baneblade was a few dozen feet away at most. The rent in its track skirts was only a little way off the ground, directly above the lip of the crater into which the vehicle had tipped.

Beyond the wreck of the Baneblade, the mutant Knight had drawn terrifyingly close. Its gruesome visage made her want to vomit. The monster swung one lance-limb high and brought it down with such savagery that she feared her tank slain for certain. A moment later though, she heard the shriek of *Steel Tread*'s lascannon firing again. Even if the crew inside were as frightened as she was in this moment, the tank was not, its machine-spirit facing the challenge with belligerent vigour.

The Knight had overcommitted with the ferocity of its blow. Its momentum bore it onward and Chalenboor yelped as one of the monster's limbs pierced the ground mere feet to their right. Its shadow passed over them. Wreckage flew and the ground shook as the monster tottered, trying to regain its balance for another lunge.

They were almost at the rent when wild cries erupted from their right. Etsul saw mutants squirming from the wreckage like maggots from rotting flesh. More spilled over the slain tanks like a cresting wave. They brandished improvised cudgels and shivs. Their eyes bulged in their deformed faces. Their fanged jaws slathered.

'Go!' she barked at her companions, pushing them ahead of her towards the wreck.

Darkness fell as the Knight swept overhead, storming back towards *Steel Tread*. It scrambled over the wrecked Baneblade as it went. Etsul heard the squeal of rending metal behind her and could only pray the Knight hadn't crushed her gunners or blocked their escape.

Its passing drove the mutants into a worshipful frenzy. Some threw themselves grovelling into the muck. Others raised their arms and ululated.

Etsul whispered heartfelt thanks to the God-Emperor, and followed Chalenboor and Verro into the Baneblade's darkened interior before the creatures remembered she existed.

She found herself scrambling up steeply tilted decking. She

saw her crewmen above her, clambering through a hatch that led deeper into the tank. She checked her lascarbine's cell and found it depleted.

Just an encumbrance, she thought. With a guilty apology to the weapon's machine-spirit, she discarded it and kept scrambling.

Etsul now found herself in the dead tank's enginarium. She couldn't help but marvel at the size of the generatoria packed in around her. Chalenboor and Verro were still ahead, halfway along the tilted gangway and heading for another hatch.

'We need to find the rent in the tank's other flank,' she gasped, following them.

'Workin' on it, chief, glim of light comin' from up 'ere,' Chalenboor called back.

Even as her crew vanished through the next hatch, Etsul turned to see mutants spilling through the one behind her.

'Drowned saints!' she cursed, fumbling for a frag as she ran. Daylight gleamed ahead. She heard rain rattling against metal.

Half turning, Etsul ripped the pin from the frag grenade and hurled it into the mob. In such close confines, it was a desperate move, but it was all she could think to do.

The blast hurled ragged corpses in all directions. It punched Etsul off her feet, lifting her and throwing her through the hatch after her crew.

Her head hit metal decking.

Blackness.

Thumping noises.

A roar like water in her ears.

She surfaced again with a whooping intake of breath. Rain-water splattered her face. Her head pounded.

'Nice throw, chief,' said Chalenboor, her voice competing with the whine in Etsul's ears. Etsul blinked, shook her head, raised a hand to her temple and brought it away bloody. They were in another compartment, she realised, and Chalenboor had managed to slam the hatch behind them. Fists thumped against it.

Etsul forced herself to her feet, grabbing Chalenboor's arm as her head reeled. Senses settling, she looked out through the rent flank of the Baneblade to see *Steel Tread* reversing fast, weaving between wrecks, giving ground as it tried to evade the stabbing blows of the Knight.

The monster looked to be toying with its prey, drawing out the kill. Etsul imagined it would tire of its sport soon enough.

'They can't wait for us any longer, we need to go to them,' she barked. Etsul drew her laspistol. She took one of Verro's arms as Chalenboor took the other, and together they heaved him upright and made the desperate leap from the flank of the Baneblade.

It was a good five-or-six-foot fall. Etsul hit wet ferrocrete and slipped, her legs almost buckling. Chalenboor skidded but stayed up. Verro yelled in pain. Then they were moving again, *Steel Tread* drawing closer with every step.

The Knight wheeled. Its fanged maws howled as it tried to gain enough distance from its quarry to angle a killing blow. *Steel Tread*'s turret was traversing, trying to track the armoured beast. Etsul had a sense that whoever landed the next hit would be the victor in this uneven fight.

There came a gibbering howl from behind her. She didn't look back, just drew her laspistol, pointed it over her shoulder and loosed off wild shots.

God-Emperor, just a little further!

They were feet from *Steel Tread* when the tank suddenly halted. The Knight drew itself up, lance-arms raised high for the killing blow. It looked exultant, a killer whose victim can run no further. The awful thought entered Etsul's head that her crew had accepted their doom.

'Vaslav, you bloody coward,' she wheezed, then the Demolisher cannon roared. The shot hit the monster full in the chest. The Knight, already teetering on the edge of balance, gave an ear-splitting shriek as it toppled backwards trailing flames.

Etsul had no time to revel in her tank's victory, and no breath to spare besides. She wheezed as a side hatch clanged open, Moretzin surging out with a lascarbine raised to fire. The loader's fusillade drew animal shrieks of pain from somewhere close behind. Etsul didn't look. She just shoved Verro and Chalenboor forward, helping first one then the other to squirm into the tank.

'You too, sir,' said Moretzin. Etsul dived into *Steel Tread*, relief flooding through her at the sight of its cramped interior. She looked back to see Moretzin backing up, swinging the butt of her lascarbine into a mutant's face.

Etsul leaned through the hatch, grabbing a fistful of the loader's tank suit and pulling her backwards.

'Moretzin, get in here,' she gasped as more hands reached out to help bundle the woman unceremoniously into the Demolisher.

A twisted face with too many eyes filled the gap. Etsul shot it.

Something grabbed the hatch and she put a las-bolt into that creature too. Then Moretzin was dragging the door closed with all her augmetic might. It clanged shut, muffling the gibbering of their pursuers.

Fists battered the hull. The muffled thump of Chalenboor's heavy bolter kicked in.

Shaking, Etsul hauled herself into her command seat. Her

lungs still burned from their mad flight. Her vid-feeds were filled with mutants swarming around the tank. Yet it was not this sight that chilled her. Amidst the wreckage, something massive was fighting to heave itself back to its feet. Etsul watched for a moment in horrified fascination, wondering how something so huge could move like that. Recognising shock trying to paralyse her mind, she tore her gaze away.

Steel Tread powered away from the felled giant. The tank shuddered as it crushed mutants under its tracks. More of the vid-feeds went dark as blood splattered them.

'Sergeant, see to Verro's wounds,' Etsul ordered as she buckled her saviour belt across her lap.

'Sir,' replied Vaslav, vanishing back into the tank.

Part of Etsul wanted to order Trieve to turn them around so they could go back and finish their enemy while it was down. She discarded the notion as gung-ho idiocy. What if the Knight regained its footing before they could slay it? Her depleted crew had performed heroics to survive its attentions as long as they had, not to mention being blessed with the Emperor's own luck. It would be unforgivable hubris to believe they could replicate the feat.

Moreover, the mutant hordes were all around them, and Spinebacks mingled in amongst their ranks. Every second they lingered was another in which their tracks might be blown, their intakes clogged. They had survived, by the grace of the Golden Throne. It would not do to push their luck.

Besides, there would be fuel to be found further along their route.

There had to be.

Verro hung on to consciousness by his fingernails. His shoulder felt like it had been packed full of crushed glass. He was dimly aware of the tank shuddering, of Moretzin hunched over his station and working his sponson gun.

A shadow passed above him, and Verro flinched before realising it was the sergeant. Vaslav pulled a med-kit from its webbing and took a knee next to him.

A hand fell on the sergeant's shoulder. He turned and met Chalenboor's eyes. She was rain-sodden and dripping, covered with muck and gore.

'Let me,' she mouthed over the engine's roar.

Vaslav glanced down at Verro then back up at Chalenboor. He clapped her on the arm and took her place on the sponson. She, meanwhile, knelt next to Verro and started unpacking medical supplies. Her expression was murderous, but if her anger was for him Verro found he was too far gone to care. He could feel his blood pooling under him. But at least he was back aboard *Tread*. There were worse places to die.

'You're goin' to be all right, mate,' Chalenboor said, leaning down and shouting to him over the roar of the power plant. Verro grabbed a fistful of her tank suit and pulled her ear to his mouth.

'No more. T-they'll shoot you, might… still.'

She scowled then leaned in to reply.

'I was wrong, you was right. That what you want to hear, yeah? Well, I was, and you was. But I don't think the chief sorts stuff out that way.' She touched a hand ruefully to her swollen lip.

Verro relaxed when the word 'chief' left her lips. In all the time he'd known Nix, he couldn't remember her ever referring to Commander Holtz that way.

'I… did enough… then?'

'Mate, all you did was get shot, yeah? She did the rest.'

CHAPTER ELEVEN

COMING UNSTUCK

Verro could hear the growl of vehicle engines. The sound dwelled in the space where consciousness blended with dream, interspersed with a faint thump and rattle that he couldn't place. He wondered why the repair shrines had started their labours early today. With that thought came the familiar stab of irritation that the Whiteshields were barracked closest to the source of the racket, and that disturbing the new recruits' sleep was a quite deliberate part of their training regime.

That wasn't right though, was it? The repair shrines had been part of his childhood. This was Kasr Haark. That din would be coming off the live-fire training ranges on the moors to the north. He groaned at the thought he'd be out there soon enough, soaked and freezing, trying to tally enough target-kills to earn his breakfast.

They'd better be proud of me, he thought, semi-coherently, and rolled over in his bunk.

A lance of pain shot through his shoulder, like someone had stuck hooks into his muscle, inflexible things that pinched cruelly and refused to move when he did. He remembered the crimson flash of a las-bolt refracting through rain, and placed the pain.

Old grief washed over him as the blessed amnesia of unconsciousness fled. The Cadian Kasrs, his squadmates... his family... Marko... All years gone. All ashes.

New memories surfaced, dumping adrenaline into his veins. Verro fought off the last tatters of sleep as though clawing his way out of a shroud.

He was propped in the corner formed by a stowage box and the depleted shell-rack. The roar he'd heard was *Steel Tread*'s power plant. With consciousness came the realisation that it was labouring.

Verro squinted, eyes tearing against brightness.

There came the thump-rattle again and he recognised bolt-fire.

He looked towards the commander's seat, which was empty but limned by daylight spilling down through the hatch above. Etsul must be on the pintle, he realised.

Verro's mouth was dust dry and his head thumped in time with his heart. Waves of nausea billowed through him, and he couldn't tell if they were the result of pain, medication or the grav-pulses of the eclipse.

He registered that Chalenboor was hunched over her station while Moretzin occupied his.

The next thing that struck him, as the power plant revved again, was that *Steel Tread* wasn't moving.

Verro took a quick self-inventory. Tender lump at his temple, which might explain why he felt so woozy. A few sore spots that experience told him were minor cuts and bruises and could be easily ignored. The main damage was in his shoulder, which he found was tightly wound in a compact of gauze-weave. Gentle prodding revealed the give of a medi-poultice underneath to pack and sterilise the wound. Chalenboor had done a good job – a thought that made him feel both guilty and grateful.

After a few steadying breaths, Verro managed to sit up straight. He could just see the backs of Trieve's and the sergeant's heads now, both bent over their stations.

'Hey,' he said.

Hopeless. Even if his voice hadn't been a dry croak, no one would have heard him through the din.

Bracing for the inevitable pain, Verro tried to stand. Pulling himself upright with a grab rail made his wound feel as though someone had jabbed their thumb into it. He hissed with pain. Sweat popped out on his forehead and slicked the back of his neck.

He persisted. He managed the two steps needed to reach his station then fell back into a crouch, leaning against the hull and waiting for his head to stop spinning. He'd caught Moretzin's attention, at least. She glanced down at him. Verro saw exhaustion and worry in her face, but there was relief there too. She gave him a brief nod, then turned her attention back to the heavy bolter's controls.

He took a breath, then another, then forced himself to move. Verro grasped the side of his sponson console with his good arm and pulled himself up.

'Throne shit and bastards!' he hissed as the pain made his vision swim. He swayed, steadied himself against a lurch that might have been a grav-pulse or might just have been in his head, then leaned in so his lips almost touched Moretzin's ear.

'What's happening?'

She looked at him, frowned a question, then tilted her head so his forehead was touching her temple. She smelled of sweat, fyceline and unguents.

'What's happening?' he asked again, managing a louder croak.

'Ambush,' she replied.

Verro focused on the vid-feeds at his station. He was alarmed by the number now blinded by filth or filled with the static of banished machine-spirits. Those still operational showed rusting industrial ruins rising around them from a sea of bile-yellow mud. Fronded creepers choked gantries and spilled from within ruptured chem-tanks whose flanks were streaked with pollutant residue. Verro saw the suggestion of a transitway ahead and behind, but it was more like shattered islands of ferrocrete jutting from the mire.

There was movement all around. Spinebacks infantry lurked on gantries, or else waded through the waist-deep filth towards the tank. These latter clutched bundles of krak-charges affixed to the now familiar butcher's hooks. He saw heretic corpses sinking into the mire, ruptured by bolt-shells.

Fumbling a spare vox headset from its cradle, Verro donned it and opened a channel.

'Chem-yards?' he asked. Moretzin nodded. 'How long was I out?'

'About three hours,' the loader replied. She thumped the firing runes then cursed as her volley of shots went wide and blew geysers of poisonous mud into the air. Spinebacks fired back from what cover they could find amidst the ruins.

'Throne, is the commander up there facing that? She'll be killed!'

'Said we needed the firepower,' Moretzin replied. 'Can't risk the Demolisher, low on shells.'

'So what? Conserving ammunition won't help us if we're overrun.'

'We need them for when that… thing… catches up,' said Moretzin.

Verro blinked.

'The Knight?'

'Appeared on the auspex again about an hour back,' said Moretzin. 'It's lurking. Commander reckons, whoever's piloting it we gave them a shock. They're biding their time, maybe hoping we'll run for home, but they're not letting the insult go.'

The ammo rune flashed red on Verro's console. Moretzin grunted. Verro mechanically crouched and pumped the release handle on the ammo hatch. He only remembered his wound when he reached in to decouple the magazine from the ammo feed. Still, he refused to be dead weight.

Wincing, puffing out pained breaths, he managed to drag the heavy magazine clear, ignoring the hot metal scalding his palms.

With gentle but inexorable strength, Moretzin took the magazine from Verro and pushed him back into a leaning position against the hull. She retrieved a fresh magazine from an alarmingly sparse ammo rack then slotted it into place, lips moving in prayer. Then she was back at the sponson controls, firing off shells that burst traitors like blood blisters.

'You're wounded, idiot,' she said, not unkindly.

'Why aren't we moving, Erika? Did they trap us? Blow the road surface?'

Moretzin creased her forehead.

'Isaac did their work for them. We tried two transitways off the silo road, but they were both too badly subsided. This was number three. Commander said no, but we're running on fumes. Trieve said he'd pray for the Emperor's intercession, that his faith would carry us across.'

'And he got us stuck in the middle of a Spinebacks ambush?'

'Emperor wasn't listening.'

'Throne's sakes,' groaned Verro. 'Has anyone suggested Trieve gets out and gives us a push?'

Moretzin smiled bleakly.

'Might come to that. Whatever happened to the power plant back in the sprawl, it's getting worse. I don't think *Tread*'s got it in her.'

Verro felt sick, and this time he knew it wasn't gravity or med-nausea. The commander in the firing line, tank stuck, low on ammo and fuel, and with that *thing* catching them up by the minute?

He wondered what they could have done to offend the God-Emperor so.

Etsul ducked behind the scant cover of the storm bolter and its pintle mount, letting las-fire splash from the metal. Searing pain shot through her ear into her jaw. She clamped a hand to the side of her head, flinching as she felt cauterised flesh around an absence where her left earlobe and a chunk of cartilage had been. It stung as though the side of her head were on fire.

'Foul, twisted bastards,' she snarled, shock turning to fury. Heedless of the incoming fire, Etsul swung the storm bolter and sent shots stitching along the gantry. Bursts of blood showed where the rounds hit home, first one, then a second ruptured Spineback tumbling into the mud below. A third figure ducked deeper into the frond-vines and took another shot at her, which spanged from the open hatch cover at Etsul's back.

Not for the first time, she resisted the urge to order Vaslav and Moretzin to ready the Demolisher cannon. It would be deeply satisfying to blast some heretics into atoms, but it would also be wasteful overkill.

Etsul glanced back down the transitway. Hazy yellow chemfumes rose from the mire, dropping visibility to less than a quarter of a mile. Each time the eclipse threw out another grav-pulse, the mists stirred and tricked Etsul into thinking she had seen movement behind them. Each time she thanked the God-Emperor when nothing emerged from the haze.

At least the rain had stopped. Etsul told herself this must mean the eclipse storm was waning, though she had scant idea whether it was true.

More shots whined from the tank's hull. The sponson guns thundered in return.

'What I wouldn't give for one platoon of infantry,' she growled.

A fresh storm of las-bolts rained around Etsul and she ducked again. New pain shot through her as a las-blast scorched a line across her shoulder. Staying crouched, she grabbed the vox handset from its mount in the cupola.

'Chalenboor, knot of them coming through those hanging creepers at four o'clock. Are they in your arc?'

'About to be, chief.'

Though it couldn't traverse, Chalenboor's weapon could still fire; the cluster of Spinebacks discovered this a moment later. Gore stained the luridly coloured mud.

'Good shooting, gunner,' said Etsul. 'Driver Trieve, why is my tank still wallowing in this bog?'

Trieve sounded frustrated and frantic.

'Doing all I can, sir. Offering all the prayers I know. At full power, *Tread* would have no problem hauling herself free. Damaged, though…' He trailed off. The tank gave another futile lurch, spraying fans of mud out behind it.

'Fuel count?' she asked.

'Problematic, sir,' replied Trieve through gritted teeth. 'If you would but allow an offering of pain for His favour.'

Etsul popped back up, squeezed her storm bolter's triggers and blew apart the final sniper on the gantry. The weapon clicked dry and she ejected its magazine before ducking down to avoid return fire.

'No, Trieve. That's final. Just do your duty.'

She crouched awkwardly and cursed whatever tech-adept had thought stirrups were better than a secondary seat. Etsul strove to free a fresh storm bolter magazine from the ammo rack inside the turret. She keyed the vox-mic again with her other hand.

'Ideas? Suggestions? We haven't been through everything we've been through only to die like this!'

She was surprised to hear Verro's voice come through the vox, weak but determined.

'Sir, I picked up a few things back on Cadia that might give *Tread*'s machine-spirit a boost. It's nothing sanctioned, just wire-wife spells, sir, but–'

'It is heresy!' Trieve's voice was shrill. He sounded glad to have found someone to direct his frustrations at.

'Isaac–' began Verro, sounding immeasurably exhausted. The driver overrode him.

'Pious men do not interfere in the forbidden mysteries of the machine. By such exchanges are man and engine alike tainted and heresy spawned!'

'Dreg me, Prayer book, now's not the time, yeah?' Chalen-boor sounded ready to put her fist into Trieve's face. Etsul sympathised.

'I will not–' began the driver, but Etsul barked over the top of him.

'Verro! You have my express permission to try whatever tricks you know.'

Still fumbling one-handed for the bulky magazine, Etsul caught movement below her. To her astonishment, she saw Trieve rise from his station with an expression of righteous outrage.

Unable to believe what she was seeing, she drew breath and thundered, 'Driver Trieve! Get back to your station!'

Vaslav half rose and his hand clamped Trieve's shoulder like a vice. The sergeant had moved away from his vox-pickup, but he was still close enough that Etsul caught his words over the howl of las-bolts and the snarl of the engines.

'Trieve, your commander just gave you a direct order. Sit back in that seat and get us out of this bog, or I swear on Cadia's sacred ashes I will drag you to a side hatch by your scrawny neck and throw you to the heretics.'

The two men stared at one another, then Trieve retreated to his station with what little dignity he could muster. Vaslav resumed his seat. Etsul blinked in surprise.

At last, she managed to work the magazine free. Etsul slapped it into place, chanting, 'Oh divine machine-spirit, take into thyself these bolts of the Emperor's wrath and with them lay low the servants of ruin.'

She hit the bolter's arming rune, then tilted the weapon down to aim at a pair of Spinebacks who had waded close. They looked up at her, eyes yellow through the grubby lenses of their rebreathers. One was already spinning a hook-bomb.

Etsul squeezed her triggers and blew the two traitors apart. She ducked back as the hook-bomb detonated, throwing a spray of toxic mud high into the air, and spattering the flank of *Steel Tread*.

More heretics were closing in from both sides. She couldn't hold them off much longer. Again, her glance flicked to movement in the mist behind them. It would be chasing them, might already have realised they were stuck. They had to get moving, or they were going to die.

'Hurry, Verro,' she muttered, then swung her weapon to bear and let fly.

Verro was on his hands and knees crawling to the power plant, each shuffle forward sending pain pulsing through his shoulder. Behind him, faintly, he heard Vaslav yelling. He tuned it out. He had his orders.

His vision greyed around the edges, then cleared again. Verro urged his limbs to move, determined to get the job done before he passed out.

He reached into the rudimentary tool rack bolted to the hull next to the power plant and plucked out a socketblade. Hands shaking, he fitted its decoupler around first one affixing bolt and then another, unscrewing them while muttering, 'Sacred machine, forgive my trespass. Sacred machine, forgive my trespass.'

Next, Verro set aside the inspection plate, thanking the God-Emperor that Trieve kept the tank's toolkit properly stocked. Mechanical repair was the sacred duty of the enginseer; humble tank crews were permitted to perform only the most rudimentary of battlefield repairs, and then only in the direst of circumstances. Less pious drivers than Trieve had quietly 'lost' their tools over time rather than risk the temptation of tampering with sacred machineries while in combat.

'You're committing tech-heresy right now,' he muttered to himself. 'God-Emperor, if you're watching, I pray you understand.'

Verro was faced with a nest of wires, a small gauge and two clear plex-glass switches, one lit red from behind, the other green. None of it meant a thing to him, but he remembered the wire-wife spell well enough.

He reversed his grip on the socketblade and jabbed its point into the palm of his faithful hand, by which, he hoped, the wire-wives meant his right. Squeezing his palm, he let three fat drops of blood well onto the blade: one for the God-Emperor, one for the Omnissiah, and the last for his heart's desire.

The tank shuddered. Something went bang outside, close enough to be heard through the hull. The commander's bolter thumped. Verro took a steadying breath and turned his attention to the wires packing the small compartment.

'Green is poison's bane, the machine to keep pure,' he recited to himself. 'Grey the wire forbidden, touch not lest darkness fall. Blue the saintswire, not for mortal hand. Red the heartsfire, thirsting for libation. That's it… right?'

Before he could second-guess his way to paralysis, Verro leaned in and reverently applied his blood to the red wire, taking care not to let it splash the others.

'Last must you toll the switching bell, that the machine-spirit can know of your offering and accept it,' he muttered. 'Sinister the switch, twice to toll, first from wrath to quiescence then again from quiescence to wrath. And… sinister means left… I think?'

Fighting the tremors in his hands, Verro reached in, pressed his finger to the red-lit switch and flicked it to quiescence while chanting, 'Oh machine-spirit, in the Omnissiah's holy name, accept the offering of my humble heart and make my strength your own.'

With his first flick, he heard the power plant's rumble drop off a notch. Fear gripped him that he had angered it with his unworthy offering, but he persisted, flicking the switch again from quiescence to wrath and repeating his prayer. Green light bloomed behind the switch and the power plant snarled. *Steel Tread* surged forward, straining as though at the leash, then settled back onto its springs with a heavy clang. The light behind the switch had turned red again.

Verro felt encouraged. *Tread* wasn't free, but surely that had worked. He glanced over his shoulder to see Chalenboor and Moretzin both staring at him in amazement. Chalenboor made a frantic 'keep going' gesture before turning back to her gun.

Head swimming from the power plant's fumes, Verro pierced his palm again. Again, he dripped blood onto the socketblade, pausing as a particularly violent grav-pulse threatened to spill him onto his side.

'Emperor... please...' he croaked, flinching as impacts hit the hull inches from his head.

Again, the libation. Again, the prayer, first one flick, then the second.

This time the green light behind the switch burned furiously bright. He couldn't help but hear the power plant's bellow as one of triumph as *Steel Tread* heaved its bulk from the mire.

Verro fell back, socketblade spilling from his hand, head spinning. He saw Chalenboor and Moretzin whooping and grinning at him, though he couldn't hear them over the renewed roar of the power plant. He managed to return a weak smile. Verro patted the power plant's housing, leaving a smear of blood from his pierced palm.

'Thank you, *Tread*,' he breathed.

203

CHAPTER TWELVE

THE LAST LEG

Hours had passed since the ambush and afternoon was giving way to early evening. The darkness obscuring Croatoas' star had finally dissipated. Etsul checked her charts and nodded to herself. *Steel Tread* had made good speed along Transitway Eight-Sixteen, which had brought them up out of the mire and now carried them above dry uplands lined with rows of overgrown warehouses.

Signs of recent battle were clear to see. Wrecked vehicles smouldered, too ravaged for Etsul to be sure which side they had belonged to. Lights danced on the eastern horizon, accompanied by the distant thunder of artillery fire. Once, a flight of aircraft passed high overhead, causing Etsul several nervous minutes before they dwindled into the distance. Still, they saw neither friend nor foe up close.

Throughout the day, something flickered at the edge of auspex range. Etsul watched the telltale return, and wondered if they had truly given the monster pause. She found herself wishing the damned thing would either pounce and be done, or else leave them be. It was impossible to shake the thought that they were leading it straight to their rendezvous point, but Etsul couldn't worry about that. Any other course was surely a death sentence for her crew. Besides, where there were more Astra Militarum forces, there was a better chance to slay the nightmare war engine and end its hunt for good.

Etsul might have felt more optimistic, despite her exhaustion, had the fuel situation not been so dire. According to Trieve, they ought to have run out half an hour earlier. She was as surprised as her crew that the tank was still going. Privately she wondered if its persistence had something to do with the libations Verro had offered. Whatever the cause, Etsul was happy to accept their apparent grace period; by her assessment they were overdue a miracle.

Through the periscope, the foothills ahead had grown from a dark smudge on the horizon to rearing uplands in the last hour. Every minute *Steel Tread* kept running took them closer to their rendezvous.

If the fuel did run dry, Etsul already had her plan. They would grab whatever gear they needed, seal the vehicle, and set out on foot. She'd take the first off-ramp she could find, or else order them to abseil down over the saviour rail if needs be. Verro would struggle, but they'd get the wounded gunner down somehow. They would gain the cover of the ruined warehouses then foot-slog all the way to the rendezvous coordinates. If they had to come back to *Tread* with an Atlas recovery tank then they would do so.

There was no way she was going to admit defeat now. The logistics would be tough, but the landscape ought to offer them enough cover to avoid the hunting Knight.

Etsul tried not to think about what might happen if it found them without *Steel Tread* to protect them, or if it fell upon the tank after they had abandoned it.

'Emperor, Steersman, if there's another way then I beseech you to show me.'

'Wrecks ahead, sir,' reported Vaslav. 'Heavy hauler, couple of escort vehicles. I'm seeing minor battle damage only.'

'Emperor be praised, He rewards our faith with the hope of fuel,' cried Trieve.

Etsul blinked in surprise. She didn't believe in last-second reprieves nor prayers answered quite so directly, but a chance was a chance. They couldn't ignore it.

'The miracle is that we're running at all,' she said. 'Trieve, bring us alongside the wrecks, close as you can. We've no fuel cans left so we'll have to use a rubber hose and a positive attitude if we're to syphon them. Sponsons, eyes peeled. Any sign of enemies, you put them down.'

'Yes, sir,' said Verro. He sounded a little steadier for sleep and rations.

'Trieve, once you're in close, shut her down. Be ready for a combat start at a moment's notice. Recite the rite of awakening in advance, just in case.'

'Respectfully, sir, with this little fuel in the tank, *Tread* may not have the breath in her lungs to move again no matter what prayers I offer.'

'Risk we have to take, driver,' replied Etsul, already checking the magazine of her sidearm. 'We can't refuel with the power plant running. Offer a few prayers to the Emperor for our success, as well. Perhaps He'll be more amenable this time.'

'I will do what I can to beg His intercession,' Trieve said stiffly.

'The rest of you, we'll need to move quickly. Moretzin,

Chalenboor, arm up. You're on fuel duty. Sing out the moment you find anything we can use. Sergeant Vaslav, man Chalenboor's gun. Eyes open for ambushers.'

Her orders were met by a chorus of 'yes, sirs' that sounded tired but resolute. Etsul wasn't sure she had ever felt so exhausted or anxious for such a sustained period, yet she was surprised to find she also felt satisfied.

And you believed earning your place in a Cadian regiment would be hard work, she thought, unable to stifle a wry snort of amusement. Then her exchange with Vaslav the night before came back to her. Her smile died.

As though he had heard the thought, the sergeant hailed her over the vox.

'What will you be doing while they're foraging for fuel, sir?'

'I shall inspect the tank, sergeant, while there's a moment to do so. Perhaps clean the filth off a few vid-feeds.'

'Permission to accompany you and to lend a hand, sir? Chalenboor's gun can't traverse and she's all but fired it dry anyway. Better to preserve the remaining ammo for Verro's sponson.'

Etsul found herself searching for grounds to refuse his request. She considered doing so just to make a point but discarded the idea as cowardly.

'Very well, sergeant. The rest of you, stay within sight and earshot. We're all tired. We're all hungry. We're all more than ready for this little voyage of ours to be over, but we're almost there. This is enemy territory. No mistakes.'

Steel Tread shuddered to a halt. Etsul tried not to hear a note of finality as its power plant cut out. Laspistol in hand, she opened the turret hatch and clambered out with Vaslav on her heels.

For the next few minutes, the two of them worked together in silence. Etsul enjoyed the cool air outside the tank, shooting glances back down the transitway as she and Vaslav scrubbed filth from armaglass vid-lenses. The sergeant clambered back into the tank and had just returned with a hand-welder when Etsul heard a jubilant shout. Leaning around the hull she saw Chalenboor waving and grinning.

'Hauler's got, like, half a tank on board!' she called. 'It's total crap, but Russ'll run on anythin'.'

'Good enough,' Etsul called back. 'We'll make our apologies to *Steel Tread*, but needs must. Is there enough to take us to the rendezvous, gunner?'

'Yeah, reckon so, chief,' came the reply.

'Emperor be praised, proceed,' said Etsul. Chalenboor grinned then turned to help Moretzin, who was running the hose into position.

Etsul turned back to find Vaslav staring at her with an unreadable expression.

'Something the matter, sergeant?' she asked warily.

Vaslav looked reflectively back along the transitway.

'You don't give up, do you, sir?' he asked.

'No,' Etsul replied.

Vaslav sighed heavily. 'I envy you that. Some days...'

Etsul saw the sergeant struggling for the right words. She stayed quiet.

'I was wrong to speak to you as I did last night, sir,' he said, each word clearly costing him. 'I was wrong to let you down when you arrived. I was wrong about you altogether.'

She was taken aback, but wasn't ready to let his previous comments pass so easily. Folding her arms, Etsul leaned back against *Steel Tread*.

'Is this an apology, sergeant?'

Vaslav sighed, nodded, dragged his palm over his face.

'It is, sir, if you'll accept it. And it's overdue.'

They both stood awkwardly for a moment.

'I appreciated your support earlier, with Trieve,' Etsul offered.

'That damned Brethian,' he said, face darkening. He must have read disapproval in her expression. His shoulders slumped. 'I know how I sound, sir. Ever since Cadia... I find myself clinging to...' Vaslav shrugged helplessly.

Etsul waited for the sergeant to approach his subject from another angle. He looked a little wild-eyed, as though he regretted ever beginning the conversation but now had to see it through.

'Lieutenant Commander Holtz, Emperor rest him, always said it wasn't a coincidence. The Rift opening, I mean, right after Cadia fell. We lost so much, sir, so many friends and loved ones. I... had a daughter...'

'I am sorry,' said Etsul.

Vaslav waved her words away, though not ungratefully.

'I don't say that to engender sympathy, sir, just trying to get this out in a straight line. I had already come to terms with the fact that like as not I'd never see her again, let alone Cadia, even before what happened. I knew what being in the Imperial Guard meant. But I always knew, whatever happened to me... Cadia would be safe. But it wasn't. We lost our home, our way of life, everyone we held dear. We lost the one fight we were charged never to lose. Look at the consequences, for our failure before Him on His Throne! Whatever wars we fight, for the rest of our numbered days, there will be no victory. There will only be penance for our failure.'

'Do all Cadians see it that way?'

'No, not all. But not just me,' he replied. 'But now the Munitorum just funnel recruits into our ranks who weren't there at the end, who never went through it... How can those people possibly be called Cadians?'

Etsul felt a stab of disappointed anger. Seeing her expression, Vaslav held up his hands to forestall her.

'I don't mean they can't live up to our standards, sir. Emperor knows I said that last night, and it's the official line for a lot of the top brass, and there's a big part of me that wishes I could believe it still. But no, sir, what I mean is... The Gate was ours to guard. How can anyone else shoulder that burden? All that loss and failure? Why should they? Throne, it doesn't matter how much outsiders try to be Cadians, they just can't feel our guilt!'

Etsul had no idea how to respond to this. Vaslav, taking her silence as acceptance, ploughed ahead.

'After the fall... I'd lost everyone, everything but the regiment. I've always had... dark moods. But after... they got worse. I needed Holtz, that bastard. I needed him to be my superior, bedrock I could build a new foundation on.'

Vaslav laughed bitterly, dragged his hand over his face again.

'He failed you,' she breathed.

'He was screwed up worse than I was,' replied Vaslav. 'My *bedrock* crumbled bit by bit. I didn't build new foundations, just shored up a collapsing ruin for as long as I could. He got me made up to sergeant, but for what? Favouritism. Part of me thinks Holtz knew how badly the bottle had hold of him, and he just wanted me as a minder.'

'And then he died,' said Etsul.

'And then he died,' echoed Vaslav. 'He died, and he left me with responsibility for an entire crew. He dropped the weight of the tank on my shoulders.'

Etsul gave a bleak chuckle. Vaslav looked at her sharply, as though searching for mockery.

'Sorry, sergeant, I just... I can relate to that last part all too well.'

He managed an anaemic smile at that. It died quickly.

'I tried, that's the worst part. I tried, sir, but that isn't me. Thank the Throne that it looks like it might be you, but it isn't me. Who am I to command? Who am I to tell anyone else how to fight, or serve, or be Cadians when I haven't lived up to that name for years?'

There was no appeal in the way he looked at her, no desire for denial or validation. There was just misery. Etsul thought hard before she replied. She shot a glance down the transit-way, then looked back and met Vaslav's bloodshot gaze.

'Sergeant Vaslav, I am sorry for the burdens you have borne. I don't pretend to understand the depth of what you've lost. But I need you to be my second, now. I need you to be the bridge between myself and the crew. I'll shoulder the burden of leadership, but I need this from you in return.'

'I'm not sure that's true, sir,' said Vaslav. 'You've been doing an admirable job without much input from me.'

'Sergeant, I have nearly been killed more times in the last three days than in the entirety of the rest of the war. It is by the blessings of the God-Emperor that we're not all dead in a ditch somewhere. Let us assume that I would benefit from your assistance going forward. Besides, you know these people better than I do.'

'It's not the Emperor's blessings that have kept us alive, sir. Throne knows the old man wouldn't even have got us as far as the sprawl, let alone all the way to here. Respectfully, lieutenant commander, you underestimate yourself.'

'I would say the same of you, sergeant,' she replied, and was pleased to see a softening of his hangdog expression.

'I might not want to give you our guilt, but by any official designation I'd say you possess all the virtues of a true Cadian,' he said.

Etsul paused again before she replied. Vaslav had reached out to her, had opened up and apologised. She didn't want to sour things now, but *honesty always* had been another of her mother's favourites and it hadn't failed her yet.

'I am Tsegohan. Now, I am also Cadian. Above all, we are human. I believe it is our deeds that define us, sergeant, not the labels we are given.'

'Sir,' said Vaslav, looking uncertain. Etsul had the sense this was not the response he had expected.

'Our enemies are out there, sergeant. Throne knows the Imperium has enough blood on its hands to drown the stars, but the heretics are worse. They have renounced their humanity altogether. They spread ruin and division for their own selfish benefit, or simply for its own sake. We can't be like them, sergeant. We can't be agents of disunity. If this crew is to succeed, we need to be at one – Cadian, Tsegohan, Brethian, Dakturian or whatever else.'

The silence stretched. She felt sympathy for Vaslav's losses, and she knew it might have been easier to just excuse his earlier outburst, to mollify him with agreement and sweep it under the treads. Part of her longed to, rather than chance further confrontation. Yet this crew had suffered rotten foundations too long. They deserved for her to build something better, and that started with honesty.

Vaslav drew breath to speak. Etsul steeled herself for another argument, but relaxed when the sergeant smiled. It was a weary expression but genuine. It took years off him.

'Build bridges, you say, sir?'

'And perhaps a new foundation, sergeant.'

'Perhaps so,' he said, nodding.

Etsul placed a hand on his shoulder.

'For what it's worth, Vaslav, on those dark days I am always here to speak to if–' She was interrupted by Moretzin's shout.

'Hostile incoming!'

Etsul's gaze flicked over Vaslav's shoulder. There it was again, made small by distance but unmistakable and as inevitable as the tides. She felt suddenly foolish, standing around talking with a monster on their trail.

'Mount up,' barked Etsul.

The Knight was closing the gap with every stride, its long limbs eating up ground and bringing it ever closer to the fleeing tank. Chalenboor and Moretzin hadn't syphoned all the fuel from the wreck, but they had enough in the tank that *Steel Tread* would reach the rendezvous under its own power.

Part of Etsul persisted in feeling guilty at the idea of drawing the monster down upon comrades in arms. The coldly strategic part of her recognised it as a worthwhile risk. If she could vox ahead, warn Imperial forces of their approach, then they could spring an ambush of their own.

Even though the hills loomed larger by the minute, however, Etsul could raise no one on the vox. Her eyes scanned the horizon, picking out the shapes of distant mountains rising through the haze while she spoke into the vox on the designated backup command channel.

'Any friendly Imperial forces around muster location Imperatus Victus Regnum… Nox… If you are receiving me, please respond. We are less than an hour from designated rally point with a heretic super-heavy asset in pursuit. Requesting support and coordination.'

Static answered her. Croatoas' star was slumping behind the mountains as though exhausted by a day every bit as torturous as Etsul's. Its golden light limned the mountain-tops and stretched glimmering fingers between their peaks. The transitway was already in shadow, though, and the hills little more than dark mounds cloaked in premature night.

Doubts assailed her. She might have got the coordinates wrong. She might be leading them into a heretic trap. Throne, she might be leading them nowhere at all.

Etsul banished her fears with a growl. What did any of that matter now? It wasn't like they could do anything but run towards the hope of safety.

She looked again at her rearward vid-feed. The Knight had grown closer. She was certain now that it had simply been toying with them all the way from the sprawl. Its pace was so much faster than anything it had demonstrated previously, its stabbing strides eating up the distance with ease.

For the first time that day, Etsul missed the greater speed of her old Leman Russ.

'Sergeant, analysis please. Can we outrun it?'

'No, sir,' Vaslav replied. 'Sensor cogitation projects contact long before we reach the hills.'

'Ideas?'

'Garret could do his trick with the engines again, yeah?' suggested Chalenboor.

Etsul winced, ready for Trieve to protest. It was Verro who spoke up instead.

'I don't think so, Nix. We've already asked *Tread*'s machine-spirit for a lot. We don't want to anger her.'

'Yeah, nah, you're right,' Chalenboor replied meditatively. 'Knowin' *Tread* she'd want to turn round 'n' fight anyway.'

Now Trieve did speak up.

'Is it not our duty to do just that? We defeated the monster once before. With the Emperor's blessings we could do so again. And if we die, then better to do so facing the foe than fleeing in terror.'

'Last time it came at us in dense terrain, we got damned lucky, and I'm far from convinced it wasn't still playing with us,' said Vaslav. 'Even then all we managed was to knock it down long enough to escape. Out on the open transitway, no cover, no room to manoeuvre? It would kill us in moments.'

'Got a point though, boss,' exclaimed Chalenboor. 'We're up on this raised transitway, big drop under us. I could rig up a traitor's surprise?'

'Do I want to know, Chalenboor?' asked Etsul.

'All the krak grens we've got in the arms locker, wire 'em together on a delayed timer. Good way of spoilin' someone's day if they come to raid your stash.'

'This is not some team of law enforcers seeking to end your perfidious criminalities,' exclaimed Trieve.

'Nah, but a bomb like that'd blow a good hole in the transitway, yeah? Might be enough that the Knight's weight would do the rest, bring the whole thing down and take it with.'

'But how long would it take you to rig, Chalenboor?' asked Vaslav.

'Yeah, maybe half an hour, tops,' said Chalenboor.

'That's too long, but you are on to something,' said Etsul, her own excitement growing. 'Moretzin, shell count?'

'Six left, sir,' answered the loader.

Etsul bit her lip. Fewer than she'd hoped. There again, even a full rack of Demolisher rounds would be no use to them if they were dead.

'Moretzin, load main gun,' Etsul ordered.

'Sir,' said Moretzin.

'We fightin', chief?' asked Chalenboor.

'In a sense, gunner,' replied Etsul. 'Trieve, full stop but keep the power plant running. Be ready for ahead-full on my order.'

'Yes, sir,' said the driver. *Steel Tread* ground to a halt. The Knight pounded closer. Etsul could feel the vibration of its footfalls now.

'Sergeant Vaslav, traverse turret one-forty left. Depress to minimum safe blast range and put a round into the transit-way.'

'Sir,' barked the sergeant. The turret revolved around Etsul's head with a whine of servomotors.

'Sir, we don't know how stable this structure is,' objected Trieve. 'Too much damage and it is liable to collapse beneath us.'

'Noted, driver, and I'm counting on you to get us clear should that look likely.'

'Yes, sir,' Trieve replied unhappily.

From below came the *clang clang clang* of Moretzin's metal fist against the hull.

'Firing main gun,' said Vaslav. Etsul opened her mouth and braced.

The Demolisher cannon roared. Exchanger shrines whirred, drowned out by the boom of the shell's detonation. *Steel Tread* rocked on its springs.

Watching her vid-feed intently, Etsul waited for the smoke of the blast to clear. It tattered away to reveal the Knight now alarmingly close. Vaslav's shot had blasted an enormous crater in the left-hand carriageway. 'Enemy super-heavy has increased pace, sir,' Vaslav reported. 'Throne, look at it move!'

Etsul stared in horrified fascination at the Knight as it pitched forward only to catch itself on its lance-limbs and continue onwards on all fours. It now resembled some appalling mechanical cross-breed between an insect and an enraged simian as it bore down on them at breathtaking speed. Its maws yawned wide in a furious howl.

'Load main gun,' Etsul ordered, voice shaking with her heartbeat. Sweat crawled down the back of her neck. 'Traverse forty degrees right and fire.'

Clang clang clang.

'Main gun firing.'

Again, the thump-kick of the Demolisher spitting its shell into the transitway. Again, the concussive boom of the impact. Etsul watched the smoke clear, gripping a grab rail as she felt an unnerving shudder run through the tank. Cracks spiderwebbed the roadway.

'Sir...' warned Trieve.

'Pray for us, Trieve. Moretzin, Vaslav, load up, traverse forty right, put one more into it. Driver, the moment Sergeant Vaslav hits his trigger rune I want us gone.'

Etsul watched the Knight charging towards them like a wild animal. The transitway smouldered, finger-width cracks leaping from one crater to the next. She clung to the rail, fighting the urge to order an immediate retreat. That way lay only death, for the monster would catch them inside of a minute.

'God-Emperor, let me not have doomed these good souls to their final voyage.'

Clang clang clang.

'Main gun firing.'

Trieve didn't even wait for the recoil dampers to kick in. *Steel Tread* leapt forward. The explosion filled Etsul's screen and she hung on grimly as the tank shook around her. To her horror, she realised that *Tread* was tilting backwards, prow rearing. The bottom dropped out of Etsul's stomach and she clenched, waiting for the inevitable plummet.

Steel Tread's power plant thundered. The tank lunged forward and suddenly they were level again, accelerating along the transitway.

Chalenboor whooped through the vox.

'Transitway in full collapse behind us. That third shell did the job, sir, almost too well,' reported Vaslav breathlessly.

'The Knight?' asked Etsul.

'Still closing.'

She could wait no longer. Etsul slammed the top hatch open and thrust her feet into the cupola stirrups. She had to see, with her own eyes, one way or another.

The wind whipped around her as she gripped the cupola ring and stared at the gaping chasm they had created. A great section of the transitway had fallen, damaged slabs of ferrocrete dragging more of the superstructure down with their weight as they fell. She was in awe of the Demolisher's destructive capabilities.

The Knight hadn't slowed at all. If anything, it was gathering pace, bellowing as it approached the gap. The mere sight of it filled Etsul with terrified nausea; the sound raked her ears. Still, she hung on and watched, powerless to affect whatever came next.

To her utter, appalled amazement she realised that the monster was going to jump the gap.

She watched, heart in her mouth, as the Knight reached the edge of the gap. With a titanic surge of fleshmetal servos it hurled itself out into space, using its momentum to propel itself across. Etsul struggled to process the sight of the two-hundred-ton war engine somehow launching itself through the air.

The Knight's lance-arms whipped up, then stabbed down into the surface of the transitway. Cracks exploded from the impacts. Ferrocrete shrapnel flew. *Steel Tread* bucked with the shock wave.

In that moment Etsul felt as though the monster's myriad eyes locked with hers. She recoiled from its hatred and madness.

The Knight heaved. It raised one needle-tipped leg and slammed it into the road surface. Sinewy pseudopods slithered from the joints between its armour plates and whipped out to dig into the transitway, stretching tight as hawsers.

Etsul could not make sense of what she was seeing. Nothing so massive had any business moving with such organic agility. The mere fact of it was obscene.

Then the crumbling lip of the transitway gave beneath the monster's titanic weight. There was a rush of falling ferrocrete, a chorus of furious howls, and the Knight was gone.

Etsul slumped back against the cupola ring. She felt tears of relief sting her eyes, then she was up in the stirrups, one hand gripping the cupola ring, the other balled into a fist and punching triumphantly into the air.

'Yes! Emperor be praised!'

She dropped back into her seat, dragging the hatch closed above her, and listened to the cheers of her crew over the vox.

'Driver, ahead-full for the rendezvous coordinates please. That was neither quiet nor subtle, so let's not wait around to see if any heretics heard it. I will continue trying to raise friendly forces. Damned fine work, all of you.'

For the next few minutes *Steel Tread* rumbled along the transitway, the crew still grinning at one another in mingled elation and relief. Etsul felt she had just composed herself sufficiently to start her vox hails again when Vaslav spoke up. His tone hovered somewhere between stoicism and apology.

'Sir, I'm reading movement behind. I think it's the super-heavy, sir.'

Etsul ground her teeth. It had been a forlorn hope that the fall might have crippled or destroyed the Knight, or that the rubble of the collapsing transitway might have entombed the damned thing. Still, she had allowed herself to hope. She closed her eyes, took a slow breath, then replied.

'Driver, continue on course. Sergeant, confirm readings.'

Tense seconds ticked past. The last gleam of daylight lit the distant mountaintops like signal fires, then was gone. Stars prickled the sky above, but their light was already being swallowed by the sickly kaleidoscopic stain of the Rift.

'Rift protocols,' she told her crew absently. They all knew by now not to look; those without the self-restraint to obey that decree had perished or gone mad months before. Still, in the current circumstances it didn't hurt to remind them.

'Readings confirmed, sir,' said Vaslav. 'It's on the move again, still on our trail. Moving slower now though, either because of the dense terrain down there or, Emperor willing, because we hurt it.'

'Our first priority was to buy time, stay ahead of it,' Etsul reassured her crew. 'We did that. You all performed with courage and skill, and I am proud of you. Will we reach our destination before it catches us, sergeant?'

'At current respective speeds, yes, sir. We won't be far ahead, Tread's not what you'd call spry, but we should win the race.'

That was if they had the coordinates right first time, thought Etsul. And assumed the rendezvous wasn't simply a heretic snare. She hated feeling hunted and alone.

She looked down at her crew then, hunched over the light of their stations, toiling on despite their exhaustion. They were not alone, and neither was she. Not any more. The thought gave Etsul the strength to put her finger to the vox and start speaking again.

'Any friendly Imperial forces around designated rally point, if you are receiving me please advise. We are...'

The last leg of their journey took them a little over an hour. Full dark fell across them like a shroud. The transitway was left behind, *Steel Tread* toiling up one overgrown dirt road after another as they climbed between copses and rocky outcroppings.

The night was cloudless. The poisoned witch light of the Great Rift danced over the landscape, shimmering green, purple and yellow, and conjuring strange auras around the undergrowth. Etsul was barely aware of it. Her focus had narrowed to just three points: the distance to the rendezvous; the distance left between them and the inexorable Knight; the obstinately silent vox.

Etsul's voice was hoarse from repeating her mantra. She didn't like the note of desperation creeping into it. Yet still there was nothing: no response, no auspex returns.

'Plotted coordinates are at the top of this hill, sir. If this is it, we should pop right up in their midst the moment we crest the rise.'

'Thank you, sergeant,' she replied. 'Eyes wide everyone, crew to high alert, rouse weapon spirits and stand to.'

She knew the order was redundant, that they'd been stood to for hours now, but it was better than saying nothing. The order might focus a few tired minds, her own included.

Etsul checked the rearward vid-feed. There it was, limping uphill behind them, its silvery armour plates reflecting the borrowed hues of the aurorae. She saw the glint of the monster's many eyes, all fixed upon them. Etsul thought that, if they somehow survived to see the dawn, she would see that monster in her darkest dreams for the rest of her days.

They surged up over the rise and onto the plateau beyond. The road ahead ran straight across an open area of grass and boulders. Some way to the right was a sheer drop, while to the left, dense jungle pressed in from the foot of a higher shoulder of land. A mile or so distant, their route dropped down into the shadow of a valley before climbing again towards the rocky shoulders of a higher ridge.

It might as well have swung right and dumped them straight off the cliff.

Before *Steel Tread* lay the devastation of a recent battle. The plateau was thick with the wrecks of armoured fighting vehicles. Dark shapes scattered over the grass suggested bodies. Etsul switched her feed to night-sight with numb fingers and saw the green glint of dozens of eyes peering from amidst the corpses. The scavengers raised their hackles then fled, low vulpine shapes racing back towards the safety of the treeline.

'Auspex, sensors, any sign of friendly forces?' asked Etsul over the roaring in her ears.

'Nothing, sir,' replied Vaslav in a hollow voice. 'Only the Knight, closing on our position. It's two minutes behind us at most.'

'Sponsons, you see anything?' Etsul knew it was a stupid question, but she had to ask it. She felt like the drowning mariner, snatching at a last spar of their ship's hull even as the great wave of Tsegohan legend crashed down upon her.

'Nothing, sir,' said Verro.

'Not a thing, chief, sorry,' added Chalenboor.

Etsul gripped the edge of her seat and reminded herself that the coordinates had been approximate. The rendezvous could be miles from here. Yet the battlefield wreckage told its own story.

'Was this the muster?' asked Moretzin.

'Could be enemy wrecks,' Verro suggested.

'No, these were surely loyal. Throne have mercy, the enemy must have come upon them as they gathered,' said Trieve. 'Another damned ambush...'

Etsul's earlier hope seemed laughably naïve. She grappled for some semblance of a plan, but nothing would come. Her mind felt like a limb worked until the muscles could no longer comply. No pain, no panic, just a numb absence.

'Orders, sir?' asked Trieve. 'Should I follow the road, or try to lose the beast amidst the undergrowth?'

Etsul didn't know.

She had no answer to give him.

ACT THREE

AURIC

CHAPTER THIRTEEN

HATRED, FAITH AND VENGEANCE

The Knight crested the hill with the inevitability of death.

Bereft of orders, Verro felt Trieve pour power into the motive systems and send *Steel Tread* roaring into the debris field. He hung on to his console, hissing as his wound flared with pain.

Verro's heart thundered. His mouth was dry, and his skin prickled with terror. His vid-feeds jolted with the motion of the tank but still he could see the monster, stalking them across the hilltop. It was hunched, walking on three limbs while dragging one leg like dead weight. Wounded the Knight might be, but still it kept its clustered eyes fixed upon them.

Its mouths gaped as it gave vent to a screech that pierced Verro like knives. One of his vid screens cracked and went black. He felt blood trickle from his ears.

He could barely think. Verro knew on some level that he was panicking, his mind cramping with fear and fatigue and dismay at the thought they'd come all this way just for it to end like this. He fumbled at his controls with the vague notion that he could fire at the monster and perhaps drive it off. He shot a look up at the commander's seat but she sat frozen. He could see the fingers of one of Etsul's hands, wrapped around the edge of her chair with a white-knuckled grip.

'Sir?' asked Moretzin. 'Commander Etsul, what do we do?'

Static hissed across the vox.

'Chief?' Chalenboor tried.

'No more running!' Sergeant Vaslav's voice was a parade-ground bark. 'Trieve, bring us around and get us hull down. Put some wrecks between us and it.'

'What use is that? The Emperor has abandoned us and–'

'Driver Trieve! You will do as you are damned well ordered!'

'Yes… yes, sergeant.'

'Moretzin, load main gun,' Vaslav ordered. 'We've got three shells left and a good half a cell for the lascannon. You see that thing limping? We hurt it. If we hurt it, then by Cadia's sacred ashes we can kill it! Who are you?'

The familiar call surprised Verro, bringing the response to his lips like muscle memory.

'Hammers!' he shouted and heard the rest of the crew do the same.

'And what do you do?'

'Crush heretics!' shouted Verro.

'Bloody right you do! Now, the commander's got us this far, we're not about to let her down, are we?'

'Dreg that,' yelled Chalenboor, sounding manic.

Despite everything, Verro felt reckless defiance surge in his breast. If they had to die, then they'd go down fighting.

'Cadia stands!' he yelled, and the thunderous response

resounded within the hull. The voice of every crew member, even the commander's, together. United.

'*Cadia stands!*'

Etsul snapped out of her stupor and roared a war cry from a dead world she'd never known. She was ashamed of her momentary despair. She was grateful to the sergeant. But most of all, she was furious at this monster that had chased them across half a damned continent as though they'd done it some personal insult. She knew it wouldn't relent until it had taken her tank, her crew and her life.

'Hatred!' she yelled, the words coming unbidden. 'Faith! Vengeance! And never fear!'

Etsul keyed her vox-panel as Trieve brought them around behind the burned-out hulk of a dead tank. The turret motors whined as Vaslav traversed the main gun.

'This is Lieutenant Commander Etsul, Hammers Eleventh Company, calling any loyalist forces on this frequency. In the Emperor's name, if you can give aid we are at coordinates Imperatus Victus Regnum Nox engaging a super-heavy heretic war engine. Say again, this is *Steel Tread* calling for aid. Cadia stands!'

Words she had never thought to utter, but which now felt as natural to her as her native Tsegohan tongue. She might not be able to feel Vaslav's guilt, but damn it, she could feel his defiance.

Trieve was praying over the vox.

'…and in the sight of the God-Emperor let us now smite that which is evil and unclean, so that it might trouble the realm of humanity no more, but instead be cast back into the abyss whence it crawled.'

From below she heard the *clang clang clang* of Moretzin's fist.

Steel Tread's power plant roared, the tank's machine-spirit eager for the fight.

The Knight limped closer, snarling and slavering. Serpent-swift, it lunged.

'Fire main gun!' Etsul barked.

'Main gun firing,' called Vaslav.

The shell hit the Knight's protective power field and detonated with a blinding flash. The force of the blast was enough to stagger the monster, driving it back. Two shells left, and no space for dead weight.

'Moretzin, load main gun,' she barked. 'Sergeant, harassing fire with the las, see if you can break that shield. Trieve, evasive manoeuvres at your discretion. Keep us out of range as long as you can. Verro, eyes open for weak spots. Don't waste ammo but if you see a chance, take it. I don't imagine even that thing would shrug off heavy bolt-shells to the face.'

'What about me, chief?' asked Chalenboor, sounding frustrated. 'Gun's loaded but unless that thing decides to step right into my line of fire, I can't do dreg all.'

'You don't have half an hour, gunner, but whatever you can throw together with krak-charges and wiring, get on it,' ordered Etsul. 'If we must, we'll get out and shoot the monster with lasguns. Throne, we'll die throwing bloody rocks.'

'Yes, chief,' replied Chalenboor. To Etsul's amazement she sounded like she was grinning.

Etsul gripped a grab rail as Trieve reversed at speed. The Knight came after them, swinging a lance-arm and smashing aside the wreck they had just been hiding behind. The ruined tank rolled three times, spewing broken metal, before finally coming to rest on its roof.

Vaslav fired the lascannon and the Knight's force field flared. He chanced another shot and this time the beam seared a deep furrow across the monster's armoured torso. Presuming an opening, Verro fired too but his shells burst like stars across the force field.

The Knight came on, emitting another nerve-shredding scream.

Clang clang clang.

'Fire main gun!' barked Etsul.

Vaslav didn't have time to reply. The monster was on top of them. The Demolisher cannon roared, and the shell whipped low to connect with the Knight's good leg. The fireball obscured the limb but Etsul had no time to see what damage they had done, for at the same moment the Knight caught their prow armour a swiping blow.

Steel Tread was spun to starboard with tremendous force. Sparks erupted from panels and screens. Etsul was flung sideways in her seat, just getting her arms up in time to protect her head. One forearm connected with the hull and she felt more than heard the meaty crunch of impact. Her cry of pain was inaudible to her over the cacophony of tortured metal. *Steel Tread* began to tip sideways, but before it could roll the tank's skid was arrested with sudden violence.

The lumens flickered. The power plant stuttered then roared, and the lights flared back to life.

Etsul's head rang. Her arm throbbed.

'Crew status report,' she gasped.

Vaslav was first to respond. 'Station amber. Main gun's operational but las and auspex are dead. Prow armour badly compromised.'

'Station amber, lost fore vid-feeds,' reported Verro. 'Nix is station crimson, sir, she hit her head when we spun.'

'Station amber, possible damage to right track assembly,' reported Trieve. 'Controls still... Sir! It's coming at us again!'

'Evasive!' urged Etsul.

Steel Tread leapt forward with a roar. Something jolted the tank from behind. Etsul's eyes flicked to the rear vid-feed, and she saw one of the Knight's lance-limbs buried in the ground just to their stern.

Trieve took them ahead-full, weaving between wrecks and emerging near the cliff edge. He wheeled *Steel Tread* and gunned the engine, awaiting orders.

The Knight followed. Etsul saw it was limping worse than ever, Vaslav's shot having torn a deep wound in the armour of its good leg. The mechanism had been blasted apart, borderline severed, but wet worms of muscle had slithered from the broken armour plates and knitted, forming a blood-slick mass that held the lance-limb together. The fleshy mass writhed like maggots in a gut-wound, and Etsul fought back bile rising in her throat.

'Throne's sakes, what do we have to do to kill you?' she gulped.

Moretzin at last delivered her station report in a wheeze. Etsul felt a pang of guilt that, in the mayhem, she had momentarily forgotten her loader.

'Station crimson, sir. One round left for the main gun. I think I broke a couple of ribs when that thing hit us, and my augmetic has seized.'

'One more shell, Moretzin. Can you do it?'

'If it means killing that monster, sir, then yes. I bore my share of heavy loads before I ended up with this hunk of metal.'

'Load main gun then, Moretzin. Verro, see to Chalenboor but for Throne's sakes brace in case that thing hits us again.'

She didn't know if Verro had heard her, didn't have time to look and see if he was already attending to his fallen friend.

The Knight was closing the gap. It half limped, half dragged itself towards them.

Below, she caught movement as Moretzin heaved the last shell into the breech by main strength. The loader's face was white, her eyes glassy with pain, but she slammed the breech and managed to clang her seized mechanical fist against the hull before sinking down, doubled over.

I'm sorry, thought Etsul. She checked her feeds and felt vertigo snatch at her as she realised the cliff edge lay just feet behind their tracks.

'Main gun, hold fire until my mark,' Etsul ordered. 'Driver, ahead-full when I give the command. Ram that wounded leg, see if you can't finish the job Sergeant Vaslav started.'

She barely heard their acknowledgements. She couldn't think about her wounded crew, the damage to her tank, the drop behind them. She had room in this moment for nothing but the approaching Knight and ensuring her timing was perfect.

'Worry what is, let the rest go,' she told herself.

The Knight lurched closer, smashing wrecks from its path with furious swipes. It roared. Dirty fluid drizzled from its wounds, glowing in the witch light.

The monster reared to strike.

'Now!'

Vaslav fired. The Knight's force field flared, but Etsul didn't have time to curse their luck as Trieve already had them surging forward. *Steel Tread* lunged beneath her opponent's guard and slammed into the Knight's wounded shin. Etsul braced, but she was flung forward in her seat all the same.

'Station crimson,' shouted Trieve. 'Right track assembly inoperable. We're immobilised, sir.'

Etsul let out a slow breath, watching in her vid-feed as the

Knight took a lurching step backwards. It didn't fall. She saw ichor spewing from mangled muscle strands where *Tread* had mashed them with its impact, but it hadn't been enough.

The Knight still stood.

Calm settled across Etsul in that moment.

'Emperor, I pray you judge us kindly and accept us into your harbour, for we did all that we could,' she whispered.

'It has been an honour to serve with you all,' she said over the vox, as the Knight raised a lance-arm high above them like an executioner's axe. Etsul was disgusted to see its mouths twisting into leers of pleasure. Its clustered eyes glinted with the stupid cruelty of a child tormenting an insect. This wasn't a machine with a pilot inside it, she realised. Not any more. Witchery had given it a sentience of its own, made it a monster in the truest sense.

She hoped their fuel tanks blew its damned legs off when they went up.

A shell hit the Knight from the side, bursting in a flare of energy against its shield and causing it to stagger. Etsul blinked stupidly as her mind tried to catch up. Another round erupted against the shield before a third passed through and detonated against the monster's shoulder guard. Torn metal and fire blossomed in the night.

Dimly, Etsul registered her vox pinging an incoming hail. She fumbled at the panel, eyes still on her vid-feeds.

'...*say again*, Steel Tread, *do you receive? Hadeya, do you live?*' Aswold.

'Receiving, *Vexation's Cure*, we're alive,' she said, relief making her voice shake. 'We're crimson across the board.'

'*Understood, lieutenant,*' said Aswold.

The Knight steadied itself. It turned on shuddering limbs and shrieked at the trio of Leman Russ tanks approaching through the wreckage field. Etsul saw infantry advancing alongside the vehicles, Cadians dropping into firing crouches and setting up heavy weapons.

Poised above *Steel Tread*, the mutant Knight wavered, torn between finishing off its quarry and going after the newly arrived prey.

Another salvo of shots hit the Knight's shield, tank shells and missiles birthing a constellation of energy bursts in the air before it. Etsul saw rounds punch through. The Knight reeled, keening and swiping as though trying to fight off stinging insects. Its lance-limbs punctured the ground like piledrivers. Etsul held her breath, willing the monster not to inadvertently impale them at the very moment of their salvation.

Suddenly, over the vox, she heard Chalenboor. The gunner's voice was hoarse with pain, but there was no mistaking her glee.

'You know when I said that thing'd have to step right into my field o' fire, yeah?'

The thump of Chalenboor's gun resounded through the hull. On Etsul's vid-feed, heavy bolt-shells punched into the bloodied meat of the monster's shin then detonated. Gore and gristle misted the air. Stressed beyond endurance, the leg finally gave way. The monster's roar shook *Steel Tread* as it tottered, toppled and slammed down on the very edge of the cliff. There came a tortured groan of metal. Etsul saw the Knight's eyes roll wildly, its limbs and pseudopods whipping back and forth.

It slid over the edge and was gone.

'Yeah...' gasped Chalenboor, sounding groggy. 'That's what you get for...' Her voice dropped off the vox.

Etsul sank back into her command chair, eyes closed.

Aswold was saying something in her ear but she could make no sense of it. A sound escaped her, something between a laugh and a sob. Her forearm throbbed with pain. She sucked in a breath. She had wounded crew. She couldn't rest yet.

Etsul took several more steadying breaths before reaching for the med-kit in the cupola webbing. It was the last unused kit they had on board.

'Well done, *Tread*,' she said, patting the hull. 'You really are a fighter, aren't you?'

Etsul unbuckled her saviour belt and half climbed, half fell down to see to her crew.

CHAPTER FOURTEEN

SABRE CAMP

Etsul woke slowly. She opened her eyes and stared up at plasti-canvas, lit from without by morning light, striped by the shadows of nodding fronds. She was lying on what felt like a fold-out camp bed in an insulated sleep-sack. She was in a tent large enough for six. There were other beds laid out, a foot-locker at the end of each, but at that moment she was the tent's only occupant. Noise and bustle intruded from outside. The air bore the smells of a military encampment: unwashed bodies, chemical latrines, sanctified engine oils. None were objectively pleasant, yet Etsul found them all infinitely reassuring.

She let out a long, slow breath, took another in. For a time, she just let herself breathe and give silent thanks to the Emperor for their deliverance. She was alive, and so were her crew, and the monster that had hunted them was no more.

She had expected a lifetime of nightmares from what she'd just endured. Instead, it was the first time in days that Etsul hadn't woken from fire and blood.

Anxiety stole upon her soon enough, of course. Her memories of the night before were blurred by fatigue and delayed shock. She remembered little after seeing to her crew – an impression of the cold night air outside her tank, a sense of being enfolded by a protective crowd, Aswold's worried face, then the dark comfort of unconsciousness.

'And… that's it,' she said to the empty tent. 'Where am I now?'

For that matter, where was *Tread* or its crew? Fleeting peace scattered in the face of Etsul's massing questions. She needed to know how her wounded were doing, and why no one had answered her vox hails the day before, and, frankly, what in the Emperor's name was going on.

Recalling again Commander Masenwe's advice, Etsul set her worries aside until she had taken inventory of herself. Only a week before his death, the commander had advised her to weigh her own burdens and acknowledge them before she sought to heft those of others, reminding her that she was no use to anyone buried.

She smiled sadly at that memory.

The smile became a wince as Etsul acknowledged the abominable ache in her right forearm. A memory surfaced, lone and bewildered as the solitary survivor of an artillery barrage. She remembered a young Cadian medicae telling her how lucky she was as he applied salves to the limb. They had been in the back of a moving vehicle, possibly.

'Nothing broken, but I warn you now, lieutenant commander, it's going to bruise up like you lost an arm-wrestling match with an ogryn.'

Etsul's head hurt also. The steady ache and faint nausea could have been the result of mild concussion, or just the cumulative effect of stimms, exhaustion and borderline dehydration.

'Why not both?' she asked herself in a tone of mock cheer.

Beyond these more obvious ills, there didn't seem to be a part of Etsul not stiff, aching or stinging. For all that, she still felt better than she had in days.

'*Sleep is good medicine.*' Another of her mother's favourites; she smiled at the memory. Then, at last, she permitted the worries for her wrecked tank and wounded crew to loom. Her smile faded.

'Get your arse out of this sack and get some answers,' she told herself.

It was a wrench to exit the sleep-sack, but Etsul made herself do it. She spotted her boots and tank suit dumped in a heap beside her footlocker, resembling little more than a mound of caked ash-mud and gore with some cloth poking through. She had no idea whether she'd removed them herself or if someone had done it for her, and didn't really care. Clad in her sweat-stained vest and undershorts, Etsul swung her legs off the bed and set bare feet to hard-packed earth. She felt the pain of her bruises anew now that she could see them.

'Ow,' she said flatly.

She recalled that she and Vaslav had been the only occupants of this tent the night before. The sergeant's bed was already neatly made. Of the man himself there was no sign.

A polite cough from the tent's entrance caught Etsul's attention. She smiled when she saw Verro hovering there. A fresh medi-compact swathed his wounded shoulder. The gunner had a clean tank suit draped over one forearm and a steaming tin mug in hand.

'Mine, Verro?'

'Yes, sir – sergeant thought you'd appreciate them.'

If it was a peace offering to seal the deal, Etsul thought, she was more than happy to accept.

'You are both lifesavers,' she said, beckoning Verro into the tent. She smelled recaff and had to force herself to take the tank suit first instead of snatching the mug from his grip.

Verro looked somewhat awkward as he said, 'Well, sir... you did a fair bit of life-saving yourself, the last couple of days.'

Wishing for a proper wash and full change, Etsul hauled on the tank suit, zipped it up to her neck and fastened its clasps. Dry socks followed, produced from one of Verro's pouches, then her boots. They weren't in as bad a condition as she'd feared, she noticed. Someone had cleaned the worst of the filth from them.

Only then did she take the mug from him and allow herself a sip.

The steaming liquid was gritty, bitter and quite possibly the best thing Etsul had ever tasted in her life. She offered fervent thanks to the God-Emperor for His benevolence.

That done, she fixed Verro with a stern stare.

'I assume you know where we are?'

'Sir. It's called Sabre Camp, sir,' Verro replied.

'And how did we come to be here, gunner?'

'Medicae Taurox, sir. Part of the rescue column that First Lieutenant Aswold led to support us last night. They hooked *Tread* up to an Atlas and brought her back here too.'

Etsul sipped recaff as she digested this.

'And where precisely *is* Sabre Camp?'

'We're in a valley, sir. Couple of miles from the rendezvous point, I think.' Verro sounded apologetic. 'I'm not absolutely certain, sir, I wasn't my sharpest when we got here.'

'That's all right, Verro, you were hardly alone in that,' Etsul reassured him. 'Any idea whose vehicle wrecks those were up on the plateau, or what's been going on here?'

'I'm sorry, sir, that's all I know.'

Etsul sipped and waved the apology away.

'Your shoulder?' she asked. Verro looked washed out. He had shadows under his eyes and a tightness to his jaw that bespoke pain.

'Better, sir. It aches, and medicae said I won't have full mobility for a while, but...' He shrugged without thinking, then winced.

'Chalenboor did a good job,' said Etsul.

'She's a tremendously capable soldier,' he said. 'An asset to the crew.' He held her gaze as he spoke, as though willing her to agree.

Etsul realised that Verro was worried that she was about to throw Chalenboor to the Commissariat. She took another slow sip of recaff, considering. Now that she had time to think about it, she was undoubtedly angry with Chalenboor for what she'd contemplated.

She certainly *should* report the sponson gunner for what she'd sought to do. Indeed, failure to do so implicated Etsul by extension. For that matter, by her estimation Trieve was due lashes for repeated insubordination, and Vaslav ought not to fare much better.

But her crew had finally started to cohere. Etsul considered herself a reasonable judge of character and couldn't deny that Chalenboor's attitude towards her had improved markedly since their altercation. The change seemed genuine. Winning the woman's respect only to throw her to the wolves seemed wasteful and short-sighted, even if it would be entirely justified.

It would also reduce the bridges she had built with the rest of her crew to ash.

Besides, she wasn't above putting another shot across her sponson gunner's jaw if the lesson ever needed reinforcing.

'I recognise Gunner Chalenboor's worth, Verro. But I also believe that there is no room in a tank crew for mistrust or ill will. You know her better than I do. Do you believe I can rely on her?'

Verro started to speak, paused, then continued in a lower tone of voice.

'After… everything that happened yesterday… sir, you've earned her loyalty in a way that I never saw Lieutenant Commander Holtz manage.'

Etsul nodded slowly, drank off the rest of the still-steaming recaff and set the mug aside.

'That's good to know, gunner. I hope that she appreciates how lucky she is to have a friend willing to speak in her favour, and how close she came to the firing squad.'

'Yes, sir,' said Verro, pale but relieved.

Distantly from outside the tent, Etsul heard engines rumbling, the hiss and crack of welders, and the tramp of booted feet.

'So, Sabre Camp,' she said. 'High time we walk the port.'

Verro frowned in confusion at the Tsegohan saying, then nodded as he caught her meaning. He followed her into daylight. Etsul found herself at the heart of a larger armed encampment than she had dared imagine. Trees crowded all around, their canopy a dense roof that turned the daylight green. Underbrush had been cleared to make paths and open space for rows of tents, but as far as Etsul could see few trees had been felled. She guessed they were more useful as cover than as lumber.

For all the density of jungle around her, she could see the camp was packed with soldiers coming and going. Etsul saw Cadians, Geskans and Maesmochans, many with bandaged wounds or haunted expressions. They exuded a sense of resolute determination all the same.

'Bring me up to speed, gunner,' she said. 'How do we come to have a camp established beneath the enemy's nose? Where's the sergeant? How are the rest of the crew? Throne, how's *Tread*?'

The two of them walked slowly and without direction, past tent after tent of walking wounded. Survivors. Etsul stretched out her back, enjoying being able to stand free and tall after hours confined to *Steel Tread*.

'As to Sabre Camp, sir, rumour is it was earmarked as a fall-back position should the last push of Operation Jotunn go awry. After the sprawl, command couldn't be sure which operational positions had been compromised so they switched the rally point to this valley. Supposedly there's some spiritual disturbance in the region, maybe in all the valleys around the foothills of Mount Auric. I'm not sure, sir, but word is auspex around here is a mess so the enemy's got less chance of spotting us.'

'This place was always part of the plan? It wasn't in my mission briefing.'

'Not sure about that, sir, but there're natural caves in the sides of the valley and word is command's been stocking them with supplies for weeks. They've certainly produced fresh ammo and fuel from *somewhere*. And there's a cleared patch north of here, near where the road runs through the valley, where they've parked up all the armour under a big natural shelf of rock. Might already have been there but...' Again, the habitual shrug, followed by a grimace of pain.

'You're going to have to stop doing that, Verro,' said Etsul.

'Yes, sir,' he replied sheepishly.

She was starting to grasp the scale of the gamble Mandriga command had taken in nominating this rally point. A concealed valley with ready supplies seemed a smart location to muster loyalist survivors for a fresh assault. Yet they were damnably close to the Temple of Saint Carthusas, right in the heart of heretic territory. If the enemy had caught wind of the loyalists' true rally point and attacked, there would have been a slaughter.

There was no sense getting angry. For all Etsul knew, Mandriga command had reams of intelligence she wasn't privy to and direct mandate from the God-Emperor Himself. Not seeing the full picture was a stark fact of life in the Astra Militarum. You worried what was, and let the rest go.

'As to the sergeant,' Verro continued, 'he went to oversee repairs on *Steel Tread*. She's coming along nicely, sir – he wanted me to tell you. Enginseers worked overnight on her. She'll fight when we need her to, though we shouldn't expect miracles.'

'I would say she's delivered a couple of those already, gunner,' said Etsul with a smile.

'She's a fine machine, sir,' agreed Verro. 'Chalenboor and Moretzin are both in the medicae tent still, but I checked on them before I came to wake you. Thought you'd want to know how they were doing, sir.'

'And?' Etsul prompted.

'Nix hit her head pretty hard, sir, but between you and me that's the toughest part of her. She'll be fine. The chirurgeons have seen to Moretzin's ribs. Not much you can do but let the Emperor heal them, apparently, but they've got her strapped up and dosed on stimms. They're just waiting on a tech-priest to work rites of hydraulic... something or other... on her augmetic brace. Supposedly that'll unbind the machine-spirit and help it to compensate for her injury until she's healed. Once they've done that, providing the machine-spirits are amenable, she'll be back on her feet and ready for duty.'

'Good news,' sighed Etsul. 'Trieve?'

'Unhurt, sir,' Verro replied, sounding a little disappointed. 'Last I saw him, he was adding his prayers to the enginseers' efforts on *Tread*. I'm not sure they appreciated his help, mind you.'

As they spoke, a squad of Cadian infantry marched past. They made the sign of the aquila to the two tankers. Somewhat nonplussed, Etsul offered it in return. Seeing her confusion, Verro grinned.

'Word of our... ah... recent exploits has gone around the camp, sir. If you can believe it, they're calling us the "Giant-killers".'

'Giant-killers,' Etsul repeated, shaking her head.

'That's what they're saying, sir.'

Etsul was unsure whether to be amused, dismayed or proud. She settled instead for focusing on the practical.

'Well, gunner, my sidearm is almost dry, I'm hungry enough to eat a gutfish, and I doubtless need to report to whatever's left of company command. First Lieutenant Aswold mentioned the captain's survival last night. I should make my report to him at once.'

'Sorry, sir, of course, that was actually the main reason the sergeant sent me to wake you.'

'Oh?' asked Etsul.

'Yes, sir. Commissary and the captain's tent are both this way. There's a plan, apparently, and we'll be the last ones to get briefed, on account of our having arrived late. I'm to take you to the captain at once.'

Etsul couldn't help a flash of irritation.

'I seem to be the only member of this crew who didn't rise at first-tide. Why am I only now catching up on events, gunner?'

Verro coughed.

'Sergeant said you'd ask that, sir. Respectfully, he told me to tell you that, as you'd let him off for sleeping late that one time, he wanted to extend you the same courtesy on account of you having saved all our lives.'

Etsul couldn't help herself. She barked a laugh and it felt good.

'The sergeant and I shall be having words, but very well, Verro, consider me mollified. All the same, we shouldn't keep the captain waiting. I hear Cadians are sticklers for punctuality.'

'So they tell me, sir,' replied Verro with a quick smile, and he led her off through the bustling camp.

Ten minutes later, Etsul was finishing a ration block and clutching a second mug of recaff as Verro led her along a tight-packed row of tents. Ahead she saw a larger plasticanvas structure erected in the shade of a nodding mass of guasa trees. Flakboard screens flanked it. The flag of 11th Company hung listless from a pole.

Etsul was surprised and relieved to see a knot of officers waiting beyond the tent's pinned-back flaps. They were gathered around a chart table, several sipping from tin mugs of their own. Horathio Aswold looked up as she approached, and they exchanged tight smiles. She also saw Olgher Jorgens of *Ogre*, who nodded respectfully to her. She returned the gesture and wondered briefly what hardships her fellow Fourth Squadron tankers had endured to catch up to the advance and join the muster.

The other five officers Etsul vaguely recognised from Mandriga command. She found herself wishing she had made more effort to put names to faces. There was a statuesque woman with Cadian eyes and an air of noble hauteur; a stocky man, dark of complexion, with a comb-over and a bionic eye; a rangy Cadian with grey mutton chops; and a short, heavyset woman with hard, green eyes and a scar down one cheek. Completing the assemblage was a surprisingly youthful-looking Cadian who wore a captain's insignia on his shoulder.

'Ah, Lieutenant Commander Etsul,' said the captain. His attention caused the rest of them to turn. Etsul found herself on the receiving end of a swift but heartfelt round of applause. She caught the words 'Giant-killers' murmured again.

She offloaded her mug to Verro and offered the sign of the aquila. Hurriedly, she ransacked her memory and dredged up a name.

'Captain Lothen. Reporting as ordered, sir.'

'Allow me to congratulate you and your crew, Lieutenant Commander Etsul, on behalf of Eleventh Company and the entire Forty-Ninth Armoured. Giant-killers indeed!'

'Thank you, sir,' Etsul replied. 'I'll be sure to pass your comments on to my crew.'

Lothen followed her gaze to the insignia on his shoulder. He sighed.

'Regrettably, Captain Brezyk was lost during the battle in the Costmarus sprawl, as indeed were so many others. I was his squadron second, and so I received brevet promotion to his post upon arriving at Sabre Camp.'

'Speaking frankly, sir, there's more of us left than I'd imagined,' said Etsul. 'We saw precious few loyalists on our journey here, and none who'd survived. And then when we saw all those wrecks on the plateau...'

'Theirs, mostly, not ours,' Aswold reassured her. 'That fight happened almost two days ago, an enemy probe misdirected by Geskans and drawn into an ambush.'

'After our hails went unanswered, seeing that wreck-field, we thought the heretics had done the ambushing.'

'Unavoidable, I'm afraid, lieutenant commander,' said Captain Lothen. 'Standing prohibition on non-essential vox communications – can't be chattering away beneath the enemy's nose, you understand. But First Lieutenant Aswold here convinced me to lead a rescue party once we heard you were incoming with that fiend on your tail.'

'He did?' she asked, eyeing Aswold.

'How did you put it to me, first lieutenant?' Lothen prompted.

'I do not recall, captain,' Aswold replied, hands clasped behind his back, eyes on the middle distance.

Lothen barked a laugh.

'The first lieutenant has carefully forgotten, it seems. His exact words were that, if I did not authorise a rescue, he would go on foot, carrying a laspistol and a sharp stick if necessary.'

Amusement rippled through the assembled officers.

'Thank you, First Lieutenant Aswold,' said Etsul with heartfelt gratitude. 'My crew and I owe you our lives.' He accepted her firm handshake awkwardly.

'I could not very well leave you to your fate, Lieutenant Etsul,' said Aswold, eyes smiling behind his formality. 'We will need every tank and skilled crew we can get if we are to pull this off.'

Etsul looked to Lothen.

'Pull what off?' she asked. 'What happened, captain? What *is* happening?'

'Yes, of course, you'll need bringing up to speed,' said Lothen. 'Very well then, gather round, soldiers of the God-Emperor. We haven't long, but let us go through this all properly.'

Etsul unholstered her sidearm and passed it to Verro.

'Gunner, see that my laspistol gets a blessing and scare some ammunition up if you can, then inform Sergeant Vaslav I want everyone assembled and *Steel Tread* ready to go as soon as the Emperor permits. Fuel, ammo and prayer-prep.'

'Yes, sir,' said Verro, managing an awkward aquila before hurrying off. Etsul joined the gathered officers around the table. She glanced at the charts, which showed the South Peninsula theatre from coast to mountains. They were heavily annotated.

'As to Lieutenant Commander Etsul's first question, the Archenemy hit us hard in the Costmarus sprawl. This much you know. We here survived the experience, and I don't doubt we've all seen enough horrors to last us a lifetime. Latest strategos estimate has us losing eighty-four per cent of our front-line forces during that conflict.'

Lothen paused to shake his head at the numbers. Nightmare images of roiling fog and slavering madmen flashed across Etsul's mind's eye.

'After the battle at Costmarus, the enemy capitalised upon their victory, but neither as methodically nor as completely as would the loyal soldiers of the God-Emperor, had our roles been reversed,' Lothen continued. He gestured to the charts as he spoke, methodically translating the scrawl that covered them. 'A sizeable strength of heretics pushed south under several of Baraghor's key lieutenants. They drove our rear-line survivors back into our support formations, and then pushed the whole parcel into a fighting retreat. The heretics' momentum carried them all the way to the Mandriga Line, and I regret to inform you that they are even now besieging Mandriga command. We've been forced to keep our vox exchanges limited for fear of discovery, but I'm assured the situation back there is serious.'

If that was the enemy failing to capitalise, Etsul didn't want to know what complete success would have looked like.

'Is that where our air support went, sah?' asked the lieutenant with the bionic eye.

'Got it in one, Baumstaph,' replied Lothen. 'I'm given to understand that the good lads and lasses of the Navis are pounding the heretic counter-attack with everything they've got. If it's any consolation, they'll be giving the traitors a beast of a headache.'

'You said that *some* of the enemy pushed south after Costmarus, sir,' observed Etsul. 'What about the rest? What about Baraghor?'

'Quite right, Etsul,' replied Lothen, gesticulating at his charts again. 'While a sizeable portion of Baraghor's forces went south, it seems that his sorcerous means of victory proved disruptive to his own troops, albeit not to the degree they did ours. A number of his warbands became mired in the sprawl doing battle with our... casualties.' He cleared his throat. Everyone looked uncomfortable.

'Emperor preserve their souls,' said Jorgens.

'Indeed, and praise Him also that the enemy pursuit was ill-disciplined,' Lothen said, rallying. 'Strategos believe that the wildest of Baraghor's followers were just waiting for the opportunity to slip the leash, and so dashed off in pursuit of our retreating forces then scattered themselves to the four winds in the process. He may have lost as much as twenty per cent of his own strength to desertion and infighting. If the boot had been on the other foot, I assure you we'd have mopped the buggers up.'

Murmurs of agreement rippled around the map table.

'As for the traitor king himself, he made one mistake when he unleashed his heretic sorcery upon us. Psykana division back at command now have a fix upon his empyric signature. I shan't pretend to understand exactly what that means, and frankly I don't want to. But we received priority intelligence yesterday evening when the disruption from the eclipse cleared. Psykana say that Baraghor has retired to the Temple of Saint Carthusas and left his underlings to continue the fight.'

'Isn't that rather out of character, sir, given our previous briefing?' asked Aswold. 'I thought the entire thrust of Operation Jotunn was that Baraghor would want to fight us in person?'

'Just so,' replied Lothen. 'However, according to psykana's divinations, he's led a portion of his most loyal followers back to base and taken with him a substantial number of our own after capturing them in the sprawl.'

Etsul grimaced. She prayed those taken had all been tainted, that they had already lost their minds before they fell into the heretics' hands. Lothen pressed on despite his officers' discomfort.

'Given typical heretic practices, strategos are theorising that he's indulging in some manner of ritual sacrifice, or else that he's going to try to interrogate what's left of our soldiers should their sorcerous madness wear off. There again, who knows the minds of heretics? One can assume, at least, that whatever Baraghor is doing, it isn't anything of which the God-Emperor would approve.'

'What now, sir?' asked Aswold. 'I will confess that I have not toured the entirety of Sabre Camp, but my impression is that we are a shadow of the strength that set out to enact Operation Jotunn, no?'

'That's a fair assessment, first lieutenant,' said Lothen. 'At last count, we've amassed approximately eight thousand infantry, mixed Geskan and Cadian plus a handful of abhumans. Armour pool stands at twenty-three Maesmochan self-propelled artillery platforms, and fifty-seven Leman Russ tanks of varied pattern. Beg pardon, fifty-*eight* now, Lieutenant Etsul.'

'That's... not a large force, sir,' said Etsul carefully. 'Are we expecting further reinforcement?'

'We are not, Etsul, no,' replied Lothen regretfully. He stabbed a finger at the map. 'You can see that here, and here, there're other Imperial holdouts. I'm informed half of Fourth Company and a few Second Company machines made it to this rally point, and over here, you see? Some Geskan senior officer has managed to round up a decent force including a number of engines from our Seventh, Ninth and Tenth companies. They've fortified the old agri-complex at Holock and filled the surrounding marshes with booby traps. Command considers both holdouts to be more useful maintaining position and making as much noise as they can about fighting back.'

'Every heretic attacking those positions is one less troubling us, or Mandriga command,' observed the rangy Cadian.

'That's the thinking, Lieutenant H'mak,' said Lothen. 'Ergo, what we have is what we have, and we make do with what the Emperor gives us.'

The aristocratic-looking Cadian glanced down her nose at the charts.

'He has given us the position of the enemy commander, and a second opportunity to complete Operation Jotunn,' she observed.

'Just so, Lieutenant Blenkney,' said Lothen with a sudden grin. Etsul couldn't help feeling this young man was rather enjoying his new captaincy. 'Orders from Mandriga command are to proceed with the elimination of Baraghor as a matter of

252

highest priority. You will all be pleased to know that our own regiment's Commander VanKalder survived the sprawl, and has operational authority here. He and his senior advisors have already drawn up a plan, and I am honoured to inform you that we of Eleventh Company feature rather centrally.'

Lothen looked around at them all as though inviting questions. They all looked back at him expectantly. The captain cleared his throat and continued.

'Even with a substantial portion of his forces either besieging Mandriga command or drawn off by our secondary musters, Baraghor is still estimated to have with him a substantial strength of infantry and some armour. They're dug into a fortified position and on their home territory.'

'Filling us with confidence here, sir,' growled the heavyset officer with the scar. She took a slug of recaff. Lothen chuckled.

'On the surface, First Lieutenant Na'Koriss, I concur this all sounds a bit dicey. By the grace of the Emperor, though, we've got one or two points in our favour. First and foremost is that back at Mandriga command, they've got a Deathstrike missile launcher bunkered down and awaiting a firing solution.'

Etsul had a sudden, vivid memory of almost getting run over by that very weapon. She'd forgotten it in the mayhem. She frowned.

'Respectfully, sir, if they have a Deathstrike and Baraghor's coordinates, why is any of this necessary? Can't they just scrub the entire temple off the map and him along with it?'

'Would that it were so straightforward, Lieutenant Etsul. Unfortunately, the Omnissiah saw fit to arm this particular missile with a Solfire-pattern plasma warhead. I'm informed that its wrath is prodigious, but its blast radius won't exceed one hundred feet. It's a precision tool designed for killing Titan-class engines, and so it falls to us to aim it.'

A mutter passed around the table.

'Now, the Emperor takes, but He also gives,' said Lothen bracingly. 'You'll already be aware that a number of Martian priests have reached this encampment amongst our muster. They fought their way through substantial enemy forces so as to see to our war machines, I'm told. Veritable fanatics. Well, one of them is a high-ranking magos. Don't ask me for specifics, but he's apparently modified a set of servo-skulls with high-gain targeting arrays. If he's able to deploy these near enough to Baraghor, they'll triangulate the heretic king's position and bring the Omnissiah's wrath right down on his head.'

Lothen thumped his fist down on the charts to reinforce his point.

'What about the enemy's sorcery, sir?' asked Blenkney. 'Given what occurred in the sprawl, what's to stop the enemy unleashing another curse upon us?'

'Command are taking steps to lessen the potential of such a disaster, lieutenant. Rather than massing our force into a single spearhead, we shall be deploying in assault groups. I have your assignments here. Plan is to hit the temple wall along its entire frontage, stay spread out and then push for the temple itself once inside the walls. Even if he does unleash more sorcery, he'll be hard-pressed to catch more than a portion of our forces with it. Also, from what the Geskans have observed, the temple complex itself is far from an impregnable fortress. Seems likely Baraghor picked the site more for its symbolic nature as a centre of Imperial faith than through any desire to exploit its strategic virtues.'

'All the same, it's his seat of power, eh, sah?' said Lieutenant Baumstaph. 'These heretic warlord types can't stand by and allow an insult like us kicking the doors in and trampling all over the shop. Leads to dissension in the ranks. He'll have to come out and fight.'

'Granted, but when he does, what precisely is the plan?' asked Etsul, directing the question to Lothen. 'More to the point, sir, what's our part in it?'

'Well, Giant-killer, you're going to love this...'

CHAPTER FIFTEEN

JOTUNN UNBOWED

Etsul strode through Sabre Camp. At her side walked Aswold and Jorgens. They passed through a whirlwind of activity. Soldiers offered final prayers, stocked ammunition bandoliers, jogged out double time by squads towards the muster at the northern edge of the camp. Priests moved amongst them, offering the Emperor's benediction while hunched acolytes swung censers and scourged themselves with flails. Somewhere ahead, engines rose in a rumbling chorus that sent avians fluttering and squawking from the canopy.

The three officers had walked in silence for several minutes before Aswold cleared his throat.

'Hadeya...'

'I know, and it's fine,' she reassured him.

'After what you and your crew went through. After what you achieved. It should be you taking command of Third Squadron.'

'We've all been through the mill,' put in Jorgens, then

shook his head and whistled. 'But really, Cadia's Gates, Etsul, a Knight?'

Etsul blew out a breath. 'I've been at the helm for a matter of days. My crew were each as responsible for slaying that monster as I was, some of them more so. As were you, come to think of it, Horathio.'

Aswold made noises of protest; Etsul spoke over them.

'Regardless of all that, there is a chain of command which armour-kills and good luck do not supersede. You and Na'Koriss are already first lieutenants. There's only enough tanks left in the company for three squadrons and even then, the other two are under size.'

Aswold raised a finger to interject. Etsul ignored it.

'This mission is going to be hard enough with someone in charge who *does* have squadron command experience. Responsibility for getting our weapon of last resort into position and then pulling the trigger? Everything potentially riding on it? Frankly, sir, I don't envy you this one.'

Aswold gave up with a rueful chuckle. 'We certainly have been assigned a daunting task, but I understand. The commander believes that Baraghor is most likely to respond to our assault by confronting and defeating the greatest concentration of our forces. When that concentration is smashing down his main gates and pushing headlong for his inner sanctum, doubtless the attraction of the lure is doubled. It makes sense that we would deploy the magos' weapon there, and as his escort we go where he goes. And with commanders like yourselves at my side, how can we fail?'

Etsul felt a familiar mix of warmth and mild exasperation towards the former Maesmochan.

'That right there is why you're in charge, first lieutenant.'

'My inspirational oratory?' asked Aswold.

'Fancy name for a good line in grox-shit, sir, but call it what you like,' said Jorgens. The three of them shared a laugh.

'Besides, this is all your fault, Lieutenant Etsul,' said Aswold. 'If you and your crew had not earned yourselves such a reputation, you might never have caught Commander VanKalder's eye for this duty. The rest of us are simply whirled in your wake like leaves upon a gale.'

Etsul snorted and tried to ignore the guilty sense that Aswold might be right. No good deed went unpunished, after all.

The jungle parted to reveal a dirt road cutting across their path. Beyond it the underbrush had been churned to mud by tanks. A shelf of rock stretched out from the valley wall to shield the marshalling ground. Its shadows were deep enough that lumen poles had been erected to guide crews down the impromptu alleys between parked vehicles.

Infantry flowed past the tankers, their officers directing them into the open hatches of waiting Chimeras and Tauroxes. Tank crews bustled about their vehicles, making way for enginseers as they worked final ministrations and chanted binharic rites. Servo-skulls skimmed overhead. Some blared hymns from laud hailers. Others trailed incense burners or thuribles, or clutched missive scrolls in metal talons.

A commissar stalked past, shouting encouragement to the embarking soldiery.

'The Emperor is watching. Men and women of Cadia, this is your moment to stand. In victory are we saved, in failure damned.'

Etsul and her companions offered aquila salutes as he passed. The commissar returned the gesture and prowled on, leaving them to hasten towards the banner poles that indicated their squadron's mustering point.

'It's a pretty desperate gamble though, isn't it?' said Jorgens.

'No reserves. No air cover. Assaulting a dug-in and forti-fied foe. No clear picture of where our target is hiding, and every chance that he's seen us coming and prepared some-thing awful.' Aswold counted the points off on his fingers. 'And let us not forget that, should the enemy attacking Man-driga command threaten to overrun the Deathstrike, its crew have orders to launch blind at the heart of the enemy posi-tion rather than miss their shot altogether. Yes, Lieutenant Jorgens, it truly is a challenging operation. I suspect it is reflective of how desperate our position has become, and I trust that if there were a better way, command would have ordered that instead.'

'We just have to kill him,' said Etsul fiercely. 'Whether we drop that warhead on him or hit him with a Demolisher shell for First Lieutenant Askerov, or someone else catches him in their crosshairs before we even see him… it doesn't matter so long as it gets done.'

'And never mind how many of us die in the process,' said Jorgens, bitterness creeping into his tone.

'Probably, but that's life in the Guard,' replied Etsul. Privately, though, she didn't consider herself or her crew expendable, and damn what command might think.

'What if he isn't there?' asked Jorgens. 'What if he sees us coming and runs?'

'Doesn't seem the type,' said Etsul. 'Besides, psykana divi-sion would know if he ran, wouldn't they?'

'One assumes,' replied Aswold.

'Our single operational priority is to get the magos in posi-tion the moment Baraghor is spotted,' she said, keeping her tone firm. 'There's no point asking other questions that we can't answer.'

'It is the soldier's lot, is it not?' said Aswold. 'We have our orders. We will do everything we can to fulfil them, no matter what heretical trickery our enemies might have in store. We have faith. We are warriors of the Emperor, and we will do our duty. Agreed?'

'Agreed,' said both Etsul and Jorgens.

As they passed another Leman Russ, Jorgens raised a hand in greeting to its commander, who was helping her crew with final loading prep. She smiled and nodded in response, then went back to hefting magazines.

'Lieutenant Velesko, Fourteenth Company,' Jorgens said. 'Good to see she made it. That woman could drink a Space Marine under the table. Seen a few engines from the Eighth, Ninth and Fifteenth about too.'

'Considering the carnage within the sprawl, I thank the Emperor that so many of our regiment made it out alive,' said Aswold. 'I wish good fortune to them all.'

'I think our fortunes will depend upon how quickly we get this attack under way,' said Etsul, quickening her step. 'Surely the enemy can't miss all this for long, not so close to their headquarters?'

'Heretics,' said Jorgens in a tone that eloquently communicated, *Who knows?*

Aswold touched two fingers to the aquila about his neck and raised his voice over the growing bellow of engines that echoed from the stone ceiling. 'Every minute they are blind to our approach is another blessing, no? Speaking of which, allow me to offer my wishes of good luck to you both before we begin this. We have already been through so much. I will not soon forget the sprawl, or fighting our way through... all of that...'

'We've lost crew. We've lost friends. But we're Cadians, we

serve the God-Emperor, and we'll do our duty to the end,' said Jorgens.

'I'm proud to fight alongside you both,' said Etsul, almost having to shout to be heard. 'When we come out the other side of this, we'll raise a glass to those we've lost, eh?'

'A fine notion, Lieutenant Etsul,' replied Aswold. 'Keep that flask of yours handy for the victory toast.'

Etsul clapped a hand to the pocket where the flask was stored, mock outraged. 'This is my last taste of Tsegoh! Respectfully, sir, get your own!'

Again, the three of them chuckled, but Etsul could hear the nervous adrenaline behind the mirth. They were all whistling past the boneyard, putting brave faces on the idea of going in unsupported against such odds.

Etsul was aware she had enjoyed far more than her fifteen hours, but that only made the thought of being sent to probable death seem crueller. She had no desire to become an Imperial martyr, not now nor ever, and she didn't wish it for her comrades either. No amount of camaraderie could take the sting out of what would come next.

'Here we are,' said Aswold. Amidst a pool of artificial light, *Steel Tread* waited alongside its fellow Demolisher, *Ogre*, and Aswold's own Russ, *Vexation's Cure*. Etsul had to catch her breath at the sight of her tank, battered but unbowed and clearly battle ready. She saw Sergeant Vaslav up in the cupola, making final checks on the storm bolter. His eyes met hers and he offered her a firm aquila before dropping down into the tank.

'And there *they* are,' said Jorgens.

Parked beside the row of Third Squadron tanks was a heavily modified Chimera painted dusty Martian red. The vehicle's silhouette was distorted by a bulky turret weapon Etsul didn't recognise, and an oversized servo-arm assembly at its rear. Where she would have expected to see rows of lasguns jutting from its troop compartment, the vehicle instead boasted additional armour layered down both flanks.

Waiting beside the vehicles were a pair of figures that Etsul recognised. The more eye-catching was the hulking servitor, eyes glinting beneath its tattered cowl. She saw that its arms had been refitted for combat duties since it had almost trampled her back at Mandriga command. One limb now boasted an ornate rotary cannon, the other a pneumatic crushing claw. Etsul's skin crawled at the sight of the grey-fleshed monster, and she focused instead on the tech-magos hunched in its shadow.

'Magos Hengh,' she said in greeting.

He fixed the three of them with his glowing green gaze. A trio of servo-skulls hovered above him on suspensor units, heavily augmented with what Etsul assumed was the crucial targeting gear.

'Interrogative: you are to lead my escort?'

'That is correct, magos,' said Aswold, his tone respectful. 'We will see you safe to your destination.'

'Advisory: I cogitate a forty-three per cent probability of that being the case, first lieutenant. It will be as the Omnissiah wills.'

Aswold frowned. 'Magos, you are in the care of three fine crews and their venerated war engines. I assure you if–'

'Clarification: I have inspected the war engines in person, first lieutenant. I have absolute faith in their machine-spirits. It is the necessity of their operation by unaugmented biological units that impacts my percentile cogitations. Rest assured, however, that I shall enact those compensatory stratagems that are within my power to ameliorate the inefficiency of your crews.'

The magos turned and swept aboard his Chimera with a creak of rubberised robes. His servitor lumbered after him, stooping and squeezing itself aboard the transport in a way that reminded Etsul of a mollusc compacting its flesh into its shell.

Aswold gaped after them.

'Preferred your pep-talk, sir,' muttered Jorgens.

'I suppose that we do not have to *like* the magos in order to successfully escort him to his destination,' said Aswold, blinking.

Etsul leaned in conspiratorially. 'Our orders didn't say anything about escorting him back *out* of danger, sir.'

The comment raised smiles, but the moment was upon them and levity could find little purchase.

'The Emperor protects,' said Aswold.

'The Emperor protects,' replied Etsul and Jorgens. The three officers turned and clambered aboard their tanks.

The attack force rolled out, leaving only a skeletal garrison of medicae personnel, vox-officers, priests and serfs in their wake. They were defended only by the walking wounded, those soldiers too gravely hurt to be anything more than a hindrance in the assault to come.

As *Steel Tread* joined the armoured column snaking its way out of the valley, the most ambulatory of the guardians limped out to offer salutes. The Demolisher rumbled past knots of men and women leaning on crutches or swathed in bandages, offering what clumsy aquilas they could manage. Etsul couldn't help feeling she was abandoning them. In theory, Commander VanKalder's forces would fall back to Sabre Camp upon successful completion of Operation Jotunn. The facility would be ready to receive wounded soldiers and damaged vehicles, and then serve as their rallying point while they awaited new orders.

Privately, Etsul suspected the camp would soon be in trouble. The enemy could hardly fail to notice the emerging mass of armoured vehicles, and if they traced the attack force back to its point of origin then Sabre Camp would be assailed soon enough. To her, the poor bastards left to oppose them didn't even look capable of holding lasguns.

'God-Emperor, if you see us, and if you have some grace to spare, watch over those brave souls,' she prayed. 'Give us safe harbour to return to. Reward their faith and courage.'

Steel Tread rumbled up the steep roadway, part of the great single-file procession of vehicles that made up the last strength of Operation Jotunn. Dozens of tanks, transports and artillery platforms packed the roadway between dense walls of undergrowth. To an inexperienced observer it might seem an unstoppable assemblage of armoured might. Etsul had been through enough battles to know better. It took more than one blow of the hammer to drive the nail home, but here they would have just a single strike.

Her crew had welcomed her aboard with smiles and salutes, and they had all bent to their stations readily enough, but the vox was quiet.

Etsul knew she should say something, but she wasn't sure what. She didn't know what words could encompass all they had been through since the Mandriga Line. Were there any that could ready them for the coming ordeal? Etsul found herself hesitant to speak, as though in doing so she would walk them all over some unseen precipice.

Steel Tread followed *Vexation's Cure* over the lip of the valley and out into rock-strewn highlands. Many of the tank's vid-feeds had been returned to life by the ministrations of the enginseers and now Etsul stared through them over a landscape far removed from the swamps of the delta. The road cut across a broad shoulder of land dotted with boulders like broken teeth. Up here on the high ground, Croatoas' ever-present jungles thinned to copses of trees that looked as though they were huddling together to whisper secrets. Thick underbrush and thorned lianas still proliferated. As the tanks of the Astra Militarum spread out into their assault groups, they churned swathes of plant life to pulp.

'Form up on the first lieutenant, escort formation.' Etsul issued the order automatically as she watched the rugged ballet of armoured vehicles playing out around her. There was a taut urgency to it. No one wanted to be caught by the foe while still nose to tail in single file.

'Yes, sir,' replied Trieve.

The vox lapsed back into its pregnant hiss.

Self-propelled guns dropped back, Basilisk crews clinging to the guard rails of their fighting platforms as tanks jockeyed past them to take the lead. Every assault group was led by at least one Leman Russ or variant, from which that group's most senior officer commanded. Captain Lothen, First Lieutenant Na'Koriss and others led their own assault groups towards the distant temple complex, fanning out as they went.

For simplicity, it had been decreed these groups would be named for their commanding officers. Thus, *Steel Tread* and *Ogre* were now part of Assault Group Aswold. Etsul saw that they were joined by six Cadian Chimeras in addition to the magos' own transport, while a battery of five Basilisks stuck close on their tails. A complement of Geskans completed Assault Group Aswold, racing along on their warquads.

Etsul watched the horizon for enemy aircraft, and the underbrush for concealed foes. She spared a brief thought for the squads of infantry seated aboard their vehicles, waiting in ruddy gloom and praying to the Emperor for their chance to fight, and to see another sunset. To either side, on her vid screens, she saw the assault groups growing farther apart. Those headed for the flanks of the offensive would soon be little more than dust trails.

She could no longer avoid it.

Etsul took a deep breath and peered through her periscope to where Mount Auric loomed ahead. The mountains formed a wall in the near distance, but Auric thrust out from amidst them like a champion stepping forward in challenge. The mountain's craggy shoulders were lost in a mantle of cloud. Its bare slopes glimmered with the veins of pyrite that gave it its name.

There, at its feet, Etsul caught her first glimpse of the Temple of Saint Carthusas. It was still a dark splotch at this distance, just an asymmetrical mass of shapes lurking dead ahead.

Her eyes flicked to her auspex screen, wondering how much closer they could possibly get before the enemy engaged. The heretics would have to be blind not to have registered their approach by now.

Another look through the periscope showed her the shapes of watchtowers and fortifications spreading out around the temple, though not as thickly as she might have feared.

Steel Tread roared onward. The tank's vibration was familiar to her now. The straining note in its power plant had gone, and its engines sang lustily as the tracks churned over the scrubland. Around them, the armoured might of the Astra Militarum bore down on the enemy stronghold, assault groups making for the temple's five gates, the famed Tower of Contemplation on the western wall, breaches torn in the eastern walls by plant life, and numerous other targets besides.

Etsul pressed her lips into a thin line.

'Crew station readiness report,' she ordered.

'Station green, sir,' Vaslav replied. 'Main gun's ready and wrathful. Cogboys couldn't save the hull las, but they've transplanted a heavy bolter from another wreck. *Tread*'s got some bite back, sir.'

'Noted, sergeant, excellent news,' replied Etsul. 'I see we also have auspex and more than half of our vid-feeds.'

'That's right, sir, heretics can't hide from us now.'

'Station green, sir,' said Trieve, sounding grudging. 'The Martians have worked the proper ministrations upon *Steel Tread*, and hopefully undone whatever taint was left by others' touch. I have full steering, though the priests warned that we shouldn't run the power plant too hard lest the tank's machine-spirit become fatigued.'

'Thank you, driver,' replied Etsul, ignoring Trieve's sour swipe at Verro. Now was not the time.

Moretzin replied next. Etsul noted she sounded a little winded.

'Station green, sir. We've nineteen rounds for the main gun, sufficient reloads for the pintle and hull weaponry, and enough fuel to get *Tread* halfway back to Mandriga command.'

'And yourself, loader?'

'Amber, sir. The priests adjusted my brace. Nothing I can't handle.'

'Alert me if that changes, Moretzin,' ordered Etsul.

'Will do, sir.'

'Station amber over here, sir,' said Verro, jumping in next. 'I've vid-cover and use of my shoulder, but both are about as limited as each other. I'll do my duty.'

Etsul smiled. 'I don't doubt it, gunner.'

'Amber here too, chief,' said Chalenboor. 'Cogboys got me

limited traverse back but there's somethin' too shot for 'em to fix outside of a forge, or somethin' like that. Besides which my head's bangin' like an absolute basta–'

'Will it affect your accuracy, gunner?'

'Nah, chief, I'll probably do my job 'bout as good as Garret does when his rig's tip-top, yeah?'

'You actually *do* something around here, Nix? Besides make a damnable racket?' Verro asked in mock surprise, eliciting a ribald cackle from his fellow sponson gunner.

'That's enough of that,' barked Vaslav. 'You're Cadians, not bloody Catachan inbreeds!'

'Sir,' replied both gunners.

'Trieve, Vaslav, eyes peeled for enemy movement,' said Etsul. 'If it was us on the ramparts, we'd have spotted this attack wave incoming, so I'm expecting trouble soon. Meantime, briefing in detail. You will all have noticed our assault group is escorting a Martian transport. It will also not have escaped your attention that we're making for the main gates.'

'Bringing righteous deliverance with us, sir,' replied Trieve.

'Hopefully so, driver. I can confirm what you may already have heard rumoured – the magos on board that Chimera holds the keys to dropping a fully armed Deathstrike missile onto Baraghor and atomising him in the Emperor's name. We just have to get our Martian comrade into position. He'll do the rest.'

'Baraghor,' said Verro.

'That's what I said, gunner. We're to be instrumental in his destruction.'

'But no air cover, sir?' asked Verro. 'Or word on exfiltration?'

'No, Gunner Verro, neither of those,' replied Etsul. 'Will that be a problem?'

'No, sir,' he replied, in a singularly unconvincing tone.

Trieve spoke up. 'Sir, while I believe the God-Emperor watches over us, what is to stop the arch-heretic from unleashing sorcery upon us as he did in the sprawl?'

Etsul kept her voice confident as she replied.

'You'll note our dispersed deployment, intended to counteract just such a threat. Besides which, psykana division have caught his scent now, Trieve. They'll curtail his witchery.'

'With witchery of their own,' grumbled Trieve.

'We're facing Cadia's Bane in there, Trieve,' Vaslav replied. 'Whatever aids us in destroying that monster has the Emperor's blessings as far as I'm concerned. Don't disparage His gifts.'

Before Trieve could reply, Chalenboor sang out over the vox.

'Muzzle bloom ahead, sir. Heretics woke up.'

'Throne help us,' said Etsul to herself beneath the snarl of the power plant. 'Here we go.'

Steel Tread shuddered as ranging shots detonated all around. Shrapnel clattered against the hull. To their rear, one of their force's Chimeras took a direct hit and came apart in a tangle of scrap metal and burning bodies.

'Throne, of all the luck...' breathed Verro.

'One last thing, all of you,' barked Etsul. 'Understand that we are on the clock. Mandriga command is under heavy enemy attack. If they believe the Deathstrike's position is threatened, and we have yet to triangulate our target, they'll aim for the centre of the enemy complex and fire, then just pray that Baraghor is at ground zero. They can't be more precise than that.'

'Would that not be the best plan anyway?' asked Moretzin.

'Not with a pinpoint plasma warhead on the missile, loader, no,' replied Etsul.

'Can't see that havin' much chance,' commented Chalenboor.

'Agreed,' replied Etsul. 'If that happens, we will have failed in our mission. And we are not going to fail in our mission, are we?'

She received a rousing chorus in the negative.

The vox flashed a priority hail. Etsul hit accept and a strident voice filled all their ear-beads.

'All Operation Jotunn forces, this is Commander VanKalder. The heretics have woken to our threat at last, but we shall not be deterred. Now is our chance to do the Emperor's bidding. Now is our moment to turn the tide of this campaign, and to lay low the degenerate animal who has caused such misery and woe to the loyal servants of the Emperor. Soldiers of Cadia, of Geska and of Maesmoch, this is our day of glory! Soldiers of the Imperium, this is our finest hour! Forward, warriors of the God-Emperor, unto victory!'

The commander's address ended. Explosions shook *Steel Tread*. The tank bucked as they crossed a stake-lined ditch. Aswold's voice took the place of VanKalder's.

'All crews to high alert, all weapon spirits roused. Be ready for anything. Tanks, ward the Chimeras where you can and shield the magos at all costs. We push straight through the gates, into the heart of the shrine, and the first one to see the arch-heretic, sing out. The Emperor protects!'

With that, they sped onward into the teeth of the enemy guns.

CHAPTER SIXTEEN

THE GATES

Verro hunched over his station as *Steel Tread* shook. Despite the enginseers' words of caution, it felt as though Trieve were goading the tank for as much speed as she could give. There was no time to waste.

He gripped a grab rail with his good hand and felt sweat beads pop out on his forehead. Verro hadn't admitted to the commander how badly his shoulder still hurt, hadn't wanted to risk her consigning him to the medicae tents. He refused to let his comrades down; wasn't just some damned White-shield, no matter what the sergeant called him.

As he rode out each fresh jolt of pain, Verro hoped he hadn't made a mistake. There was no dismounting now. He just had to hang on, and hope that in doing so he didn't cause irreversible damage to himself.

He glanced at Moretzin, hanging on ashen-faced and tight-jawed. Verro eyed her augmetic arm, the liminal collision where flesh met metal and fine cabling plunged into nerves.

He doubted he'd get anything so high-tech if he wrecked his shoulder too badly, but there was an awful lot more to the loader than her metal arm. Even unaugmented, she could outperform him in her duties nine times out of ten. Verro vowed to himself that he would follow her example if worst came to worst.

Part of him was angry with Chalenboor. It was her fault he'd been shot. Yet Verro's annoyance was eclipsed by his relief that, at last, they seemed to have peace within their tank even if all was fire and mayhem without. The crucible of the last few days had wrought changes that months of comparative safety might not have. Verro liked to think they were all a little better for them, despite everything.

Apart from Trieve, he corrected himself. The Brethian was still an arsehole.

A shriek cut through the bellow of the power plant. Something exploded close enough to make *Steel Tread* shudder. Verro tightened his knuckles around the grab rail and hissed out a breath.

He glued his attention to his vid-feeds. The enginseers had only managed to reconsecrate two for his station: one looked straight outward, and the other ahead. Through the latter, Verro could see the temple's outer wall growing larger, the glimmering mass of the mountain looming beyond it.

Between the tank and that wall lay a stretch of no-man's-land criss-crossed by trenches and razor wire. To Verro they looked bizarrely scattered, as though their layout owed more to aesthetic or ritual than defensive strategy. It was the same with the brass-and-silver watchtowers dotting the landscape apparently at random, and the half-ruined outer shrines left like slumping hulks here and there about the walls.

Beyond them lay the temple's main gates. These at least

the enemy seemed to have fortified well. A pair of heavy gun platforms flanked them. The gates themselves were tall metal slabs engraved with images of a robed figure Verro assumed to be Saint Carthusas. Their gatehouse had been reinforced with flakboard gun-nests and bristling iron spikes. Yet even here, the wall to either side of the gates seemed far less daunting than he had expected. Twenty feet high at most, the stone barrier appeared more ornament than fortification, and was in many places crumbling under the grip of coiling lianas.

'This it?' asked Chalenboor over their direct channel. She sounded personally offended by the poor condition of the enemy defences. 'Pretty gates an' that, but I thought they'd 'ave more guns.'

'You're not wrong,' agreed Verro. He could see towers and cracked domes beyond the walls, and the peaks of ziggurats thick with smaller stone structures, but these too looked only lightly fortified. 'They've spent as much time painting obscene murals as they have shoring up their walls or emplacing artillery.'

That wasn't to say the guns weren't there, nor the throngs of Spinebacks even now settling into firing positions. He busied himself running final checks and muttering prayers to his weapon spirit.

'I ain't complainin' though.'

'Makes a change.'

'Dreg you, Whiteshield,' she replied, but her heart wasn't in the insult. There was a pause then she asked, 'How's your arm?'

'Good enough,' Verro lied.

On his vid screen the gunner could see deformed figures dashing to man the ramparts.

'Still, though, what sort'a twist-brain sticks up more dreg-ugly statues than guns?' wondered Chalenboor. 'Makes me think they're goin' to pull another sprawls on us, yeah?'

Verro had been trying not to look at the twisted sculptures rising from the enemy ramparts. They reminded him of the prisms scattered through the Orphide hab-belt. Now, though, he felt his gaze drawn to them.

Refracted light danced across his vision. He saw sorcerous fog spilling towards him, madness overwhelming those it claimed. He was gripped by the fear that those vapours would rise like a wave and flow over the temple wall, coiling about *Steel Tread* like serpents. He imagined vapour filling the tank, their lungs, their minds. He saw the crew turn on one another anew, eyes bulging with madness, nails raking, teeth sinking into yielding flesh, warm blood squirting into his mouth–

Verro recoiled from his vid-feeds. He swallowed hard, and pictured the Cadian moorlands in autumn, their leaves crimson and gold. He visualised them carpeting the ground around the weather-beaten statue of some ancient lord general.

These memories no longer brought him refuge.

The fall of Cadia had poisoned all that remained of his former life. His heart settled heavy in his chest. His shoulder throbbed. Verro was relieved when the commander's voice cut through the static of the vox.

'Load main gun. Sponsons, free-target the heretics in the trenches and on the towers. Suppressing volleys. Watch your ammo counts. Don't waste more on these vermin than they merit.'

Verro punched up a targeting rune and squeezed his triggers. Spinebacks were firing from the trenches ahead. He fired back, sending tight bursts of shells into each knot of heretics he saw.

'Oh, weapon spirit, direct thy wrath, purge the unclean,' he repeated, timing his bursts to the cadence of the prayer.

Steel Tread was crossing trenches now, tracks churning air as heretics threw themselves flat to avoid decapitation. Verro was afforded brief angles of fire down on the traitors packing each trench. He made his chances count.

'We really *have* caught the heretics by surprise,' he said hopefully. 'Watch them scramble!'

'Rather watch 'em bleed,' snarled Chalenboor.

Ahead, Verro saw a bright flash as one of the heavy gun platforms vanished in a pillar of flame. Detonations marched along the rampart to the right of the gatehouse. Stone and blazing bodies flew.

Fire came back at the Imperial force. Wall guns swivelled and spat. Spinebacks popped up to launch shoulder-mounted rockets. A warhead whipped across Verro's vision. He heard a dull clang as it ricocheted off *Tread*'s front armour. One of the force's Chimeras spewed smoke. Before it vanished from Verro's sight, he saw the transport slew to a halt and its rear ramp drop. His last glimpse was of Cadian soldiers piling out, already firing into the traitor trenches.

A formation of Geskan warquads overtook *Steel Tread*, goggled riders leant low over their handlebars, pillion troopers snapping off shots at traitors on the walls. It was a stirring sight, at least until a shell slammed down in their midst.

More targeting runes, one after the next.

More thumping volleys, more jolts punching him in his wounded shoulder.

Verro was dimly aware of the wider battle. The dark masses of Imperial assault groups were engaging further along the wall. Muzzle flash blazed back and forth. Explosions blossomed. In the middle distance an ornate tower toppled, ploughing a breach into the wall.

'Gates opening,' reported the sergeant. Verro saw the huge metal slabs swinging inward. Crimson light spilled between them.

'Enemy armour!' barked the commander. 'Full counter-charge. Multiple enemy squadrons. Prepare to engage.'

'They're Leman Russ, barely,' said the sergeant, sounding revolted.

'Such abominations do not deserve that name!' spat Trieve.

'For once I agree with you,' Verro replied.

The battle tanks surging through the gates were monsters melded of metal and unclean flesh. He glimpsed a tusked tank with a brazier-like flamethrower in place of its turret gun; a horror covered in bristling black spines; an obese and fleshy Demolisher with a slobbering maw deforming its front armour. Freakish figures rode high in the cupolas of several tanks, clad in rubberised tank suits with skull helms that boasted feathery plumes or curling horns.

The traitor tanks charged headlong into battle with little apparent regard for formation or discipline. Shells and energy blasts filled the air. *Steel Tread* rocked under multiple impacts, fire billowing over Verro's feeds.

'Taking hits, damage to prow armour,' warned the sergeant.

'Ahead-full, evasive manoeuvres, driver,' ordered the commander, rune-marking an enemy structure on the vid-feeds. 'Keep that watchtower between us and the heretics until we're at optimal range. Moretzin, load main gun. Sergeant, await my word.'

Verro clung on as the rival tank formations sped towards one another. Fire filled the diminishing space between them.

The Imperial machines were outnumbered, but where they manoeuvred for flank-shots and sought to shield their damaged fellows, the renegades attacked like rabid beasts. The spined heretic tank took a direct hit and shuddered to a fiery halt. *Vexation's Cure* lost its pintle bolter in a blast of fire, then shuddered as an exploding round peppered its rear armour with shrapnel.

A gruesome vehicular mass rolled forward, two tanks fused together by flesh and bone. Its twin turrets focused their fire on *Ogre*, hitting the Demolisher with a pair of battle cannon shells at point-blank range. One of the Demolisher's sponsons was reduced to sparking scrap and a terrible gouge was torn in its prow armour.

Jorgens slowed his tank even as the enemy vehicles sought to encircle him and fire on the lighter armour to the Demolisher's rear. *Ogre* swerved then stopped hard, punching into reverse and traversing its turret. The Demolisher cannon fired at the same time as the prow-mounted lascannon. One blew apart a renegade tank crawling with eyes. The other punched through one of the conjoined traitor tanks and set it ablaze. Verro was nauseated by the sight of the vehicle's melded companion swivelling its turret madly as though seeking escape from the spreading flames. It pulled wildly to the left in an attempt to tear free but pitched sideways into a trench with its blazing twin atop it.

A blinding flash whited out his vid-feed, so bright he worried the magos' transport had taken a direct hit. As the screen tried to adjust, he realised this was no heretic weapon – the magos' own vehicle had opened fire. The Chimera's turret sent a beam of energy arcing into the midst of jostling traitor tanks, and a second violent burst of light rendered his screen useless.

When the image returned, two renegade vehicles were nothing but smoking wreckage. Another slewed to a halt, its right flank melted to slag.

Verro looked to his other vid-feed. Something odd happened as he stared into it. Colours blurred, ran together, pulsed in fascinating, arrhythmic sequence…

'Gunner Verro, situation report? Why have you stopped shooting? Do you have a malfunction? Verro, report!'

The commander's voice shook Verro from his stupor. He was shocked to find a string of spittle dangling from his lip. He grubbed it away with a forearm and squinted at his vid-feeds again. Now he saw the source of his momentary trance, rounding the enemy watchtower as it came towards them.

The enemy tank was an Executioner, bristling with potent plasma cannons. Its armour was onyx-black, polished to a mirror sheen. The weapons in its turret and sponsons pulsed with neon brightness, flickering through a kaleidoscope of colours that flowed back along ropey organic pipes that wound sinuously about the tank's hull. The effect was a hyp-notic shimmer that reflected from the Executioner's sleek armour plate.

'Throne's sakes,' Verro spat, tearing his eyes away as he felt them slipping out of focus again.

'What is…? That's…' Trieve slurred over the vox. *Steel Tread* slewed off course, emerging from behind the bulk of the enemy watchtower.

'Driver!' The commander's voice was like a whipcrack, but it came too late. The Executioner went pitch-black as it fired, venting every iota of its mesmerising starfire through its weapons.

Steel Tread bucked under the assault. Verro's port vid-feed turned to static, its machine-spirit banished. Sparks exploded from overloaded wiring. The stink of hot metal filled the air. Trieve screamed through the vox.

On his remaining feed, Verro saw the enemy watchtower toppling, a glowing bite taken out of its supports. Spinebacks fell from it, flailing wildly, to hit the hard earth.

'Damage report!' said the commander.

'Station… amber, sir,' gasped Trieve. 'They must have hit the prow armour right in front of my station. I… ah… I'm burned.'

'Can you proceed, driver?'

'Affirmative, sir,' Trieve replied, fervour suffusing his voice. 'In suffering… we show our faith!'

'Good man, then get us point-blank with that monster,' spat the commander. 'We won't let it hit us twice. Vaslav, lay on and fire at will.'

'Yes, sir!' barked the sergeant. Trieve brought them around the fallen tower and gunned headlong towards the Executioner. Verro saw the kaleidoscopic colours pulsing back into life through the tank's veins.

God-Emperor, aid us, he thought.

'Main gun firing!' said the sergeant. Verro opened his mouth as *Steel Tread* bucked again. The shell connected and Verro's last vid-feed blanked again with the fury of the explosion. Then they were rumbling through the glowing crater where the Executioner had been, burning chunks of tank rattling from their hull.

Chalenboor whooped.

'Fine shot, sergeant,' said the commander. Verro couldn't fathom how she still sounded so calm. 'Driver, bring us back into formation. Moretzin, load main gun.'

'We got bloody lucky when Commander Etsul took that chair,' Verro voxed Chalenboor on their direct channel.

'Yeah, well, you 'ad to be right about somethin' eventually, yeah?'

Etsul's heart hammered in her chest. Those dancing witch lights had so nearly stolen her wits. She didn't want to think about what would have happened if they had been a moment slower.

She gritted her teeth and checked her feeds. Burning wrecks littered the area outside the temple gates.

In their overeager charge, the heretics had taken the worst of it, but the fight had cost the loyalists, too. *Ogre* looked battered, dragging the wreckage of its right sponson behind it. *Vexation's Cure* had a deep dent in its turret. Smoke trailed from its power plant. Two Cadian Chimeras remained, flanking the magos' own vehicle, which, thankfully, appeared undamaged.

Only one of their Basilisks had survived, left far in their wake. Even now Etsul could see a firefight raging around it as Cadians and Geskans sought to defend the artillery tank from Spinebacks flooding from nearby trenches.

On their foe's side, not a single heavy gun remained operational around the gatehouse. The only Spinebacks she could see were fleeing, or sprawled dead in the dirt.

'Permission to double back and support our artillery crew,' Jorgens voxed over the command channel. Etsul wanted to second his request, but she bit her tongue.

The magos' voice crackled through the vox.

'Prohibitory: insufficient temporal latitude for acts of inefficient organic sentiment. Our requirement for haste outweighs the utility of an additional artillery platform. I am proceeding to target and require your continued escort.'

'Those are soldiers of the God-Emperor back there, part of our force. They deserve our aid!' snarled Jorgens.

'The magos is right,' said Aswold. 'There is no time and I have had no reported sighting of Baraghor. He has not been drawn out by our assailing his gates, so we must seek him within his fastness.'

Jorgens grunted. 'Emperor save us, then, let's get the job done,' he said.

'Moretzin, sergeant, open the gates,' Etsul ordered.

'Pleasure, sir,' replied the loader.

The enemy had closed the gates behind their salient. Demolisher cannons rendered it a fruitless gesture. Their fire blew the gates from their hinges and sent them flipping back into the temple grounds. With *Ogre* in the lead, the three battle tanks roared through the gatehouse with the trio of Chimeras on their tails.

Etsul tensed, eyes dancing over her vid-feeds, hunting for something barely a week ago she'd have sworn was folklore.

The Imperial tanks emerged into a wide plaza flanked by clustered stone buildings and exited by several wide processionals. Las-fire and a few heavier projectiles whipped at them from the buildings ahead.

'Purging,' snarled Jorgens over the vox. His tank's fire brought the roof down upon the enemy rearguard with decisive finality.

'Hold for orders, driver,' said Etsul. 'All guns, reload and honour weapon spirits. Chalenboor, get a med kit and see to Trieve's burns.'

Over the command channel, Aswold reported to their superiors.

'This is Assault Group Aswold. We have broken through the main temple gates. Enemy resistance slackening at this location. No sign of primary.'

'Excellent work, first lieutenant,' replied Captain Lothen over the muffled sounds of battle. 'Proceed with all speed to the *temple proper and establish a foothold. Assault groups Na'Koriss and Havlan have broken through within half a mile to either side of your position. They have orders to add their infantry assets to yours. You ought to have sufficient forces to storm the structure, and to locate Baraghor if he is within.'*

'If we locate the arch-heretic within the structure, sir, do we have your permission to extract what forces we can before calling in the strike?' asked Aswold, his tone suggesting he already knew the answer but couldn't have lived with himself if he hadn't tried.

'Negative, first lieutenant, can't risk the time delay,' Lothen replied. *'Call down the God-Emperor's wrath at once, and pray that He's feeling merciful.'*

Etsul had expected the answer, but still her heart sank at the words.

Such was life in the Astra Militarum.

'Yes, sir,' said Aswold, carefully toneless. *'Assault group, ahead-steady. All crews, high alert, take the northern processional. Sharp as cut glass if you please.'*

Framed at the end of the processional, perhaps two miles distant, Etsul could see the high dome of the temple. The structure grew out of the living rock at the mountain's foot and shared its veined pyrite lustre. She studied it with grim fascination as she relayed Aswold's orders.

Behind the outer wall lay a belt of jumbled stone structures resembling a cross between mausolea and low hab-complexes. They clung to the stepped sides of marble ziggurats. Winding stairways and narrow foot-walks cut between them. Everywhere Etsul looked, she saw signs of heretic desecration.

'Priest houses, acolyte blocks, pilgrim hostelries,' said Vaslav as they rolled forward. 'This place once teemed with the faithful. Look at it now.'

'Would that the Emperor had granted us the grace to look upon it unspoiled,' said Trieve. Etsul heard the suppressed pain in his voice. She was impressed despite herself at his ability to soldier on in the face of his burns.

'Perhaps one day, Trieve,' she said. 'We've not lost this world yet, nor shall we. For now, focus, all of you. The enemy can't have failed to notice us knocking on their door.'

Sure enough, they had travelled only a few hundred yards when a swarm of figures burst from the side streets. They wore lavender robes that billowed open to reveal black leather straps and grossly scarified flesh. Their faces were lost behind expressionless silver masks.

'Gunners!' she barked.

The sponsons and hull heavy bolter let fly, chopping through the mass of charging figures. Etsul saw no weapons amongst them larger than silver stiletto daggers and the odd pistol. The cultists hurled themselves at the Imperial tanks nonetheless, those not gunned down vanishing beneath churning treads. It took less than a minute for them all to meet their deaths.

'What in Throne's name was that?' exclaimed Vaslav.

'Such is the madness of the heretic, sergeant,' replied Trieve. 'Willingly do they flock to their own destruction!'

'The sick bastards can throw themselves under our tank all day,' Vaslav shot back, but he sounded appalled.

'Contact right!' barked Chalenboor, and her heavy bolter thumped again. Etsul saw Spinebacks dashing down the steps of a nearby ziggurat, a cloaked officer goading them with a silver whip. The heretics dropped into firing crouches and loosed volleys into the flank of the Imperial vehicles. The shots splashed from the armoured hulls of the tanks. A handful of heretics attempted to rush the assault group with hook-bombs but were gunned down. The rest were driven back by las-fire from the Chimeras, before vanishing in the armoured column's wake.

'Assessment, sergeant?' asked Etsul.

'Rushed redeployment, sir. I'd speculate we've broken their line and they don't have the reserves in place to stop us.'

Etsul checked her auspex. 'Agreed, and heartening,' she said.

'But let's not get carried away, sir?' asked Vaslav.

'Yes, sergeant. Firm tiller, steady course.'

Shells looped high over the ziggurats to the west, a desultory cascade of mortar fire detonating in the roadway. The bombardment seemed imprecise, almost panicked; the explosions rocked *Steel Tread* but did little to slow the column.

Huge shrines now rose up on either side of the processional, gothic foothills to the domed majesty of the temple. Etsul saw curtains of flayed skin fluttering in windows and doors, but no sign of enemies.

Beyond the shrines, the land opened out into what must once have been elegant prayer gardens. Croatoas' frenzied fauna had run rampant, but in places the heretics had burned it back before putting the former idyll to a new and horrible use.

'God-Emperor preserve us,' cried Trieve.

Blackened clearings marched away to either flank, ringed by androgynous statues that looked graven from still-quivering flesh. Each burned circle contained a domed silver cage several times the size of *Steel Tread*, and within lay heaps of rotting bodies. She tried not to look but it was impossible not to see the marks of ritual sacrifice upon some corpses. Others lay entangled in death, teeth sunk deep into one another's peeled flesh.

'Now we know what Baraghor did with his captives,' said Vaslav, sounding painfully weary.

Etsul shuddered and checked her auspex. Contact runes showed the shape of the battle. Firefights still raged along the walls, while other runes showed where assault groups had been slowed by ambushes in the residential belt. Others still glowed within the defiled gardens. On her vid-feeds, she could see the closest battles raging.

The enemy manoeuvred with increasing desperation. They launched scattered ambushes or fell back from one holding action to the next. Etsul felt cautious confidence as she watched the strategic picture developing. It truly looked as though Baraghor had over-extended his forces.

'Targets ahead, improvised roadblock,' said Vaslav.

'Looks like a last line of defence,' observed Verro.

Etsul saw they were fast approaching a line of broken statuary, flakboard and razor wire thrown across the processional in the shadow of the temple. Heretic stubber teams blazed away at the approaching tanks in what looked to Etsul like panic.

'Watch out, dreggers might scuff up our paint, yeah?' sneered Chalenboor.

'*Maintain pace and blast a path,*' voxed Aswold, who clearly held a similar opinion of the enemy's futile defence. '*These pitiful souls cannot slow us.*'

'Main gun, lay on and open a path,' ordered Etsul. 'Sponsons, mop up, then eyes on the temple grounds. This *can't* be everything.'

Steel Tread bucked, and blasted a rent in the enemy barricade. Bolt-shells and las-blasts scythed down the dazed survivors. The Imperial tanks tore through the roadblock without slowing.

Etsul supposed she should have felt exhilaration as they swept towards their goal. Instead, she voxed Aswold on a private channel.

'This isn't right, Aswold. If it was just traitor dregs, I might believe we'd caught them tied to the docks but... a Heretic Astartes so unprepared? It's not plausible. What if Baraghor isn't here at all? He could be leading the final push against Mandriga command even now.'

'I think it more likely that he waits to play his hand, Lieutenant Etsul. We are the proverbial thrown stone and our duty remains to trigger our enemy's trap. We shall press on and secure the temple grounds, and hope that in the process we lure the arch-heretic into the open.'

'That doesn't mean we shouldn't seek to unpick the net before we find ourselves entangled, Aswold. We have to be careful.'

'We will be ready, Hadeya,' he replied. Only the slightest tremor in Aswold's voice betrayed his reassuring tone.

The temple loomed over them, the mountain rearing at its shoulder. Etsul's nerves sang like gutwire on a fisherman's line. Her eyes flicked to the structure's windows, expecting to see figures appear there and rain fire upon them. She held her breath, waiting for a sudden storm of sorcery to sweep them away or drive them mad.

'Sponson gunners, have hand-welders ready just in case we need to pressurise,' she ordered. At this juncture, she was less concerned about spooking her crew than she was about ensuring they survived the next few minutes.

'Masks are still spent, sir,' advised Vaslav. 'No spares to be had at Sabre Camp.'

'Understood, sergeant,' Etsul replied.

She willed Baraghor to show himself, as though she could

somehow drive him into the open with hope alone. Better the storm break swiftly than continue to build.

Runes flickered suddenly to life across multiple screens. Vox exchanges paused, broke off, degenerated into panicked shouts. Even through the tank's thick hull, Etsul caught a distant cacophony of throbbing bass booms that filled her with instinctive dread.

There was a sense of prophecy fulfilled as Captain Lothen's voice burst from the vox, a study in controlled alarm.

'This is Assault Group Lothen, we have eyes on primary! Repeat, Baraghor has just entered the engagement theatre on the extreme eastern end of the outer wall. He has just emerged from one of the ruined shrines the enemy left intact outside the walls. Be advised, target is accompanied by a squad of Heretic Astartes. Can't identify, but they're wielding some manner of sonic weaponry and… ahhh!'

Etsul cut the channel as it filled with squealing feedback, only to hear more reports flooding through the vox. Crimson runes sprang to life on the auspex.

'This is Assault Group Draeko, heavy Spinebacks reserves taking up firing positions on outer wall ramparts to our rear. Where in Throne's name are they coming from? They have heavy weaponry! Engaging!'

'Assault Group Na'Koriss, we are on the edge of the shrine-gardens, be advised there are traitors exiting the mausolea and moving to surround us. Buggers must have lain up in the tunnels under the gardens. Emperor's oath, there's a lot of them.'

'…Assault Group Jardin, repeat we remain outside the walls. Under heretic assault from trench lines but we have artillery ready to lend support. Requesting fire mission coordinates.'

Then came the firm and decisive voice of Commander VanKalder, overriding all other communication.

'*Primary target has entered the combat engagement zone on our extreme eastern flank. We believe he is accompanied by Heretic Astartes, renegade battle tanks and Spinebacks shock troops. Enemy strength unclear. All assault groups, re-form the line along incoming coordinates. You have your mission, servants of the Emperor! Whatever the cost, eliminate Baraghor and confirm the kill!*'

Aswold uttered a lyrical string of curses in what Etsul assumed was Maesmochan.

'*Throne, that is a long way from us,*' said Jorgens. '*Did he know?*'

'I don't think so,' said Etsul as Trieve brought *Steel Tread* to a halt in the temple's shadow. 'This feels like a plan made up on the fly by a commander happy to spend his followers' lives.'

'*Sacrifice the temple complex and all those deployed in its defence,*' said Aswold. '*Conceal his elites in shrines and mausolea and, Throne knows, anywhere else approximating a bunker, and chance that some of them might die to shelling and structural collapse before they ever got to fight. Hit us when we are as strung out as we are likely to get.*'

'*Seems the enemy's command structure is even more callous than ours,*' Jorgens observed. '*But now what? He's a long way away.*'

'We have the gauntlet to run a second time,' said Etsul. 'And this time will be worse than the last. We might have triggered Baraghor's trap, sir, but he's outplayed us in turn.'

'*Steady, both of you,*' said Aswold. '*The primary target is in play and our mission has not changed. Assault group, rally on* Vexation's Cure *and prepare to advance on Baraghor's position. He shows his arrogance by leading this attack in person, just as command always said he would. Even now, at this bloody end* to matters, I believe that we have played just as well as he. We punched through the heretics' lines once, we can do it again. We just have to get Magos Hengh close enough to end Baraghor, and now we have the chance.'

CHAPTER SEVENTEEN

THE BREACH

'Chalenboor, targets starboard-flank.'

'I see 'em, chief.'

Etsul saw the small knot of Spinebacks blown apart by Chalenboor's salvo.

Her eyes flicked across the tank's remaining vid-feeds. The assault group had halted on the inner edge of the residential belt, stymied by a line of barricades thrown up between two of the ziggurats. A squadron of Leering Skulls tanks had drawn up behind the barricades and traded fire with the loyalists as they approached.

One of the heretic tanks had been reduced to a burning hulk, while another had suffered heavy damage from the intense, close-ranged firefight. A deft shot from *Ogre*'s gunner had blasted a sizeable breach in the barricades themselves, wide enough that Assault Group Aswold would be able to push through.

Before they could capitalise on Jorgens' success, however,

the Spinebacks had struck. Twisted heretics flooded down the steps of the ziggurats. They took up positions in fire-blackened priest houses and behind toppled statues. Many carried tank-busting weaponry, or else clutched hook-bombs in eager hands. The boldest amongst them had spilled out onto the processional, looking to encircle force Aswold entirely.

'There's something wrong with their eyes,' said Sergeant Vaslav.

'They glow with the fire of heretic stigmata!' exclaimed Trieve. 'The marks of damnation are upon them.'

Some amongst the Spinebacks were indeed manifesting a strange glow that burned from their eyes and left dancing after-images in the air behind them. Etsul wondered briefly if this were some effect of Baraghor's sorcery, or perhaps the telltale sign of an unholy blessing or perilous alchemical stimm. She discarded the line of thought as the fire pouring into the armoured column intensified. *Steel Tread*'s hull rattled under the onslaught. Something burst with a tremendous bang against the side of the turret.

'Gunners, maintain suppression fire. Moretzin, load main gun and give me an ammo count.'

'Seven shells remaining, sir, including this one.'

Clang clang clang!

Etsul switched to the assault force's command channel.

'Sir, we can't stay here. We should pull back and try another route.'

'*Emperor's eyes, we have to break through!*' snapped Jorgens. '*This is the third processional we've tried and we're no closer to that heretic bastard than we were ten minutes ago. We can do this, sir!*'

Ogre's gunner lobbed another shell into the enemy barricade, widening the breach they had already blasted.

Etsul stared into the enemy firestorm. Another gang of Spinebacks were blown apart by sponson fire and the multi-lasers of the last two Cadian Chimeras.

'Quandary: both Lieutenant Etsul and Lieutenant Jorgens appear partially correct in their conflicting assessments,' stated Magos Hengh. *'Probability is high that any attempted route of ingress through the residential belt will meet a similar level of resistance, but our temporal allowance is surely all but depleted. Logic dictates we must press forward, first lieutenant.'*

'No, we retreat,' barked Aswold angrily. *'Regroup in the square at the mouth of this processional. Let us pull our necks out of this noose and see if we cannot draw the enemy onto our guns. If we thin their numbers sufficiently, then we can attempt once again to break through. We cannot reach Baraghor, magos, if we are all dead.'*

Etsul gave the order and felt *Steel Tread* lurch into reverse. As the Imperial column pulled back, her eyes crept to the crimson rune marking Baraghor's position on the auspex. It flashed, mockingly out of reach. She saw Imperial unit designators blinking out as Baraghor's force advanced steadily upon them, gathering traitor reinforcements as it went. Etsul clenched a fist and thumped it against the inside of the turret.

A new voice came over the command channel. A Cadian sergeant, one of the survivors of their charge, and amongst the last dregs of their infantry escort. Etsul thought her name was Chasnov.

'First Lieutenant Aswold. Do you require assistance, sir?'

Etsul saw *Vexation's Cure* was lagging behind the retreat. Smoke billowed from its wounded power plant.

Aswold's voice jogged as his tank rode out a direct hit from a krak missile.

'Your concerns are appreciated, Sergeant Chasnov. Vexation's Cure is losing motive force, but my driver assures me the tank's spirit remains formidable.'

Finally reaching clear ground, Aswold's column spread out in a defensive formation with the magos' Chimera sheltered at its centre. They were surrounded on three sides by man-high grass and thorned creepers, while to their fore rose the ziggu-rats and towers of the residential belt. Columns of black smoke rose from other battles raging nearby, while a greater and darker cloud showed where Commander VanKalder fought Baraghor outside the walls.

'They've took the bait, all right,' said Chalenboor.

The Spinebacks came on in a headlong rush, glowing eyes flaring amongst them. Sponson guns thundered, stitching bloody swathes through the heretic charge. It didn't slow them.

'Those with the… glow… seem to be moving faster,' Verro observed. 'Throne, they take some killing, too!'

'Their master empowers his slaves with witchery,' said Trieve.

'You're right, Isaac,' said Verro. 'I know they're mutants, but I don't remember them being this tough.'

Spinebacks stumbled onward with limbs missing, or their guts torn from their bodies. Etsul saw one heretic, his head a burst and bloody ruin, manage to pull the pin from a krak grenade and hurl it, before at last succumbing to death.

'Requesting permission for myself and Sergeant Blonsky to deploy our squads, sir,' voxed Chasnov. *'We're more use on the firing lines than canned.'*

'Denied, sergeant,' replied Aswold. *'I understand your desire, but we require swift mobility if we are to exploit any gap we make in their lines.'*

Etsul saw more Spinebacks digging in on the slopes of

the ziggurats. Others dashed across the open ground and plunged into the tall grass.

Hastily, she scrolled her auspex map.

'There is another processional a quarter of a mile to our west. If we relocate to that position–'

'Then we'll find more heretics waiting for us,' interrupted Jorgens. 'At this rate, we'll still be trying to break through when Baraghor comes to finish us off himself.'

'If we sit here, they're going to encircle us,' snapped Etsul. 'And if we advance, we might as well pop our hatches and invite them in!'

Aswold answered firmly.

'Fire for effect. Thin their ranks. Sergeant Chasnov, Sergeant Blonsky, watch our flanks and rear. If the opportunity presents itself within the next two minutes, then we charge the breach. If not, then–'

'Imperative: Mandriga command reports situation critical. Inner compounds breached by heretic shock troops. My fellow magi cannot guarantee the continued sanctity of the holy Deathstrike. Launch rituals have commenced!' blared Magos Hengh. 'I have initiated an impact countdown chron: current time to warhead arrival now twenty-nine minutes and fifty-four seconds.'

Etsul's nails bit into her palms. She glanced through her periscope, as though she might see the missile already streaking over the horizon towards them.

'Magos, there are other units already engaging Baraghor. Can they not guide the warhead in?' she asked.

'Negative: the Deathstrike's targeting spirits are complex and haughty. They require machine choristry and will not attend the beseechment of mere flesh-voices. We can still guide the missile to its target, but I must employ my holy instruments to do so. Otherwise, the Omnissiah's gift will be squandered.'

'*Then there's no more time for debate,*' said Jorgens. '*Sir, respectfully, your tank won't keep up – bring up the rear with the transports. Etsul, are you coming?*'

Ogre's exhausts snorted smoke. The tank surged forward, trailing its sparking sponson.

'*Jorgens!*' barked Aswold. '*Lieutenant commander, hold your post!*'

Etsul clenched her teeth, then thumbed the vox.

'Sorry, sir. There's no time. We have to try. Just watch our backs, and you can set the commissars on us later.'

'*Damn the heretics for pushing us to this, you know I would not do that,*' he snapped. '*Very well, Demolishers force the breach. We'll support you. For Throne's sakes watch your flanks.*'

'I will, Horathio. You know we have to do this.'

'*I do,*' he replied. '*But you do not have my permission to embark upon your final voyage, Lieutenant Etsul. Clear?*'

'As a tide-pool, sir,' she replied, then switched to the crew channel.

'Time for some of that vaunted Cadian caution. Driver, take us in. Gunners, flank sweeping. This is going to be rough. Moretzin, load main gun. What are you?'

'*Hammers!*'

'And what do you do?'

'*Crush heretics!*'

Her crew leapt into action. As they did, so too did *Steel Tread*. *Ogre* ploughed ahead, grinding bloodily over the advancing Spinebacks, who scattered in surprise before the sudden armour charge. *Steel Tread* followed its squadmate into the meat grinder. Verro and Chalenboor mowed down those heretics who tried to charge Jorgens' tank. Missiles and grenades fell like rain, exploding against *Tread*'s hull.

Etsul willed *Steel Tread* to endure, pressing a palm against the hull. She had entrusted all their lives to the tank, and could now only hope that it would prove worthy of her trust.

The crossfire intensified until it became a roar of noise and light and impacts. *Steel Tread* smashed through squads of Spinebacks. Blood sprayed the vid-feeds. *Ogre*'s hull was ablaze, but the tank sped onward trailing fire and smoke.

Ogre's main gun spoke, and a Leering Skulls tank detonated. Another backed frantically out of the Demolisher's path, ichor welling from its cratered hull as its turret swung to bear. *Ogre*'s lascannon spat a beam of searing light and the enemy tank burst like a ruptured organ.

Fire whipped past *Steel Tread* – multi-laser salvoes and a coruscating blast from Hengh's tank. In the rear feed, Etsul saw *Vexation's Cure* lob a shell into a mass of heretics as they descended a nearby stairway. Aswold's tank might be limping, but it still had teeth.

She flinched as a missile punched through the hull of Blonsky's Chimera. The transport slewed off course and ploughed to a halt, burning fiercely.

Etsul gripped her seat, her eyes flicking across the enemy's elevated positions. Part of her expected bullet holes to pucker the turret armour, her last moment one of abject surprise as she followed Masenwe into death.

Clang clang clang!

Moretzin's signal snapped Etsul from her momentary fugue. Hull ablaze and dented, Jorgens' tank was at the breach, barging aside flaming wreckage. Etsul saw a Spinebacks officer haranguing several heavy-weapons teams on a rooftop above. They leaned out, aiming their missile launchers at *Ogre*.

'Sergeant,' she began, but the turret was already traversing. 'Main gun firing.'

The weapons teams were obliterated along with the top two floors of their priest house vantage point. The shock wave flattened more of the flimsy buildings to either side.

Etsul had time to hope vehemently that those structures had been packed with heretics, before she was alerted by a shout from Verro.

'Sir, *Ogre*'s port flank! I can't get an angle!'

Etsul saw a wounded Spineback staggering through the wreckage behind the barricade. He was brandishing a hook-bomb and making for the flank from which *Ogre* had lost its sponson gun.

'Jorgens, on your left!'

The heretic swung his weapon into *Ogre*'s churning tracks. He was dragged off his feet, still clinging to the hook he had driven into the tank's treads, then burst like a ruptured wine-skin as the krak-charges detonated.

All the same, he had done enough.

Tattered metal sprayed. *Ogre*'s track unspooled, and the tank slewed hard left before grinding to a halt just beyond the breach.

'*Supporting fire!*' barked Aswold. '*Protect* Ogre! *Hold the breach open!*'

Etsul heard Jorgens cursing over the vox. '*Throne's sakes, not again! Ghansk, flank sweep. M'baru, check–*'

Shimmering columns of energy stabbed into *Ogre*'s right flank. Time seemed to stretch as furious heat haze danced before Etsul's eyes and a white-hot glow grew from the right flank of Jorgens' tank, before the moment snapped back and the Demolisher exploded with such force the shock wave almost stalled *Tread* in the breach. Shrapnel rattled from their hull, and Etsul felt her gorge rise at the thought of her comrades' remains vaporised in amongst the shards.

'You dreggin' heretic scum!' yelled Chalenboor. Her heavy bolter thumped, riddling a band of Spinebacks armed with meltaguns. Etsul realised belatedly that the traitors must have emerged from a priest house to *Ogre*'s right while everyone was preoccupied with the threat from the left. It had taken only a single salvo from their tank-killing weapons to accomplish what platoons of heretics had failed to achieve.

'Orders, sir?' asked Vaslav.

'Load main gun. Driver, ahead-steady until we've some space around us, then wheel and halt. We'll cover the column as it comes through.'

Trieve accelerated past the blazing ruin of *Ogre*. Etsul tried to watch every feed at once.

Her rear feed glowed and she looked in time to see *Vexation's Cure* burning. Its main gun was a mangled mess.

'Horathio!'

Aswold's voice came through the hiss of his tank's fire-suppression shrine. *'We're all right. Push on, lieutenant commander. Hold that breach.'*

Etsul saw Trieve had brought them into a plaza beyond the ziggurats. Buildings pressed close all around. They reminded her of the coral reefs she had seen as a child, rising to the surface of Tsegoh's oceans. To her relief, they looked abandoned. With luck, the enemy had thrown everything they had into their blocking force.

Trieve brought *Steel Tread* about, just in time for Etsul to see a missile streak down from the window of a priest house high up on the ziggurat slopes. The warhead hit Magos Hengh's transport and burst in a fireball that momentarily blinded Etsul.

'No!' she shouted. The crimson transport rolled on through

the breach, but its turret was a twisted wreck, and it was lurching along with one flank blackened.

'Gunners, maintain fire,' she ordered. 'Their ranks are thinning. Prioritise that priest house, they've a heavy-weapons nest up there.'

'Main gun firing.'

Steel Tread bucked. More shrines and priest houses collapsed in the blast, the offending structure amongst them. Burning Spinebacks corpses rolled bonelessly down the steps.

Etsul drew breath to congratulate Vaslav, when Verro shouted again.

'Enemies left, Spinebacks with hook-bombs! Throne, my damned shoulder... I can't–'

There was a ferocious explosion. The lumens flickered to crimson. The power plant died with a choked growl.

'Damage report,' Etsul gasped into the gloom.

'Station crimson,' groaned Verro. 'They rushed us with hook-bombs. Sir, Throne, I'm sorry, I couldn't get an angle on them, my shoulder cramped up. They got our tracks, and my gun's junk.'

Trieve overrode Verro's apologies. 'Station crimson. No response from left track. Power plant's inoperative. We're running on casket, sir.'

'Trieve, do what you can to awaken main power,' ordered Etsul. 'Vaslav, Chalenboor, keep shooting.'

She might as well not have given the command. The assault that had crippled *Steel Tread* had been the last convulsive spasm of the battle. Mauled by the loyalists' armour charge, the last of the heretics were falling back, snapping off parting shots, some tumbling as bolt-shells or las-blasts found them.

Quiet descended.

Etsul's heart thumped.

Her ears rang, and her wounded forearm throbbed like a rotten tooth. She felt slightly detached from reality, numbed by the carnage of the last few minutes.

Through the hull armour, she could hear the muffled rumble of battle continuing nearby.

'*We have broken the line, but the cost was great,*' said Aswold.

Etsul cast a sorrowful look at the ruin of *Ogre*.

'I'm sorry,' she said.

'*For what?*' demanded Aswold. '*You and Jorgens were absolutely right. My hesitancy was inexcusable. The Emperor expects. Even now the Deathstrike is airborne, and we will not complete our mission dithering on the fringes of enemy territory. But now we must determine our course of action. Magos Hengh, what is your status?*'

'*Assessment: sub-optimal, first lieutenant. Heavy battle damage, and the vehicle's spirit is unsettled. I assess that it will not endure transition to the target zone without extensive repair, for which there is not time.*'

'*Nor, I fear, will* Vexation's Cure,' sighed Aswold.

'We're immobilised, running casket,' Etsul reported.

'*Sir, our Chimera is still operational,*' said Sergeant Chasnov. If she was at all shaken by everything they'd been through, Etsul couldn't hear it in her voice. '*If the magos cares to transfer his holy personage to our vehicle then we and* Ashen Pilgrim *will see him safe to the target zone.*'

'*You will be travelling alone, sergeant, but it seems our only recourse,*' said Aswold.

'One Chimera, unescorted, in this terrain?' asked Etsul.

'*If you have another option, lieutenant, I will hear it with gratitude,*' replied Aswold. '*Magos, what is the count?*'

'*Updated: twenty-one minutes, twelve seconds to warhead impact.*'

Etsul wracked her brains. Baraghor's rune had settled upon the fortified gatehouse through which they had roared what felt like hours before. A heretic battle line was forming upon his position, the battle now raging both inside and outside the walls. She was disquieted to see more loyalist runes blinking out one by one.

'I do not like this but, magos, you must transfer yourself and your skulls to Sergeant Chasnov's Chimera,' said Aswold.

'Couldn't the magos work some repairs, sir?' asked Vaslav. 'Get us rolling again?'

'I doubt there's time, sergeant,' Etsul replied. 'We've taken a lot of hits.'

'Yeah, well, not like we're a small target, is it?' commented Chalenboor.

Etsul blinked, thunderstruck.

'Gunner Chalenboor, you're a genius.'

'Doubt that, chief,' replied Chalenboor, sounding nonplussed.

Etsul thumbed her vox.

'First Lieutenant Aswold, my sponson gunner just hit upon a solution. Magos, how close do you need to be to target Baraghor?'

'Expositional: the las-targeter arrays possess an operational range of seven hundred feet, and are equipped with grav-impellers to allow for optimal self-positioning. I myself must remain within three hundred feet of at least one of the las-targeter arrays so as to facilitate their choral network.'

'And how swiftly can they guide the missile to its target?'

'Additional: the system requires unified choral fix for at least ten seconds to achieve correct triangulation.'

Etsul nodded to herself then pressed ahead.

'We go on foot. This is nightmare terrain for armour. Without escort, I wouldn't rate that Chimera's chances of making it even halfway to Baraghor. Even if it does, the engine noise will bring heretics down on them like mudflies on a beached carcass. But we're, what, ten minutes double time on foot to the gatehouse?'

'Amendment: nine minutes and thirty-seven seconds assuming an average ambulatory pace of four miles per hour, though without correcting for potentially hazardous encounters with hostile forces.'

'There's time, sir. We can slip through where the tanks can't and use this tangle to our advantage,' Etsul urged.

'To confirm, you would have the Cadians escort the magos on foot?' asked Aswold.

'Us too, sir. We have arms lockers, don't we? Leave skeleton crews with both tanks to defend them in case the foe return. They can act as bunkers to hold this intersection and guard our rear. The rest of us accompany the insertion team and see the mission through.'

'Advisory: this plan presents the highest cogitated percentile for success, of those presented,' said Hengh. Etsul quirked an eyebrow in surprise at his unexpected support.

'Very well then,' said Aswold. Etsul thought she heard him clap his palms together. 'There is little time remaining and I will not see those who we have lost sacrificed for nothing. I will lead the insertion team. Lieutenant Etsul, divide your crew as you see fit. Sergeant Chasnov, you and your soldiers will guard the magos with your lives. We depart in one minute.'

Etsul looked down. Sergeant Vaslav met her gaze.

'Sergeant, you'll look after my tank?'

'Done it before, sir. You can trust us. I've failed one watch in this lifetime and on Cadia's ashes I shan't fail another. Go. We'll keep the filth off your backs.'

Etsul smiled and Vaslav smiled crookedly back. He still

looked careworn, but his shoulders were squared and his eyes clear.

'You don't think there should be a Cadian in charge of this mission, sergeant?'

Vaslav sighed at that, then shrugged.

'Reckon you could be right about the relative importance of labels, sir, though this hardly seems the time to discuss it.'

He offered Etsul a salute. She returned it.

'I'm taking Moretzin and Chalenboor,' she said. 'One for muscle and the other for urban instincts. The two of you get armed up. Trieve, think you can load in Moretzin's place?'

'The God-Emperor will lend me the strength I require,' replied the driver, hiding his burned hands in his lap. No one mentioned that they had so few rounds left for the Demolisher cannon that it would make scant difference.

'Hold this position, the three of you. Defend *Steel Tread*. We'll see you when this is done.'

'Cadian caution, eh, sir?' said Vaslav.

'Hatred, faith and vengeance, sergeant,' she replied.

'Always, sir.'

With that, Etsul grabbed the frag grenades Chalenboor handed her, then clambered through the tank's top hatch.

Verro slumped into Nix's station, noting unhappily that the seat padding was still warm. He rolled his traitorous shoulder and managed not to moan aloud at the pain. If they ran out of time now, if they got killed en route, the others might say different but Verro knew that it would be on him and his damned pride.

He thought of Chalenboor's last nod to him, her last cocky grin.

His throat tightened.

Verro watched as the insertion team filtered up a stepped alleyway between priest houses, moving fast with their guns up. He kept his targeters fixed on their location until the last Cadian disappeared, then found himself praying for some heretics to show themselves so that he could gun them down in his friends' defence.

He jumped when a hand landed on his good shoulder.

'I can hear you kicking your own teeth in all the way from my station, Verro,' growled the sergeant. His tone wasn't unkind.

'Sorry, sir, I just...' Verro gestured his frustration at his shoulder.

'There are those in our regiment, Verro, who say that so long as a single Cadian stands then Cadia stands also. What do you think of that?'

Verro felt a surge of pride. 'They're right, sir.'

Vaslav grunted.

'Could be, Verro. Could be we all need reminding that Cadia wasn't the only planet in the Imperium worth fighting for, or the Cadians its only worthy people.'

In his surprise, Verro forgot his guilt for a moment.

'It's what Cadia represents that matters, sir. So long as there's people willing to fight for that, so long as they're standing, then Cadia stands with them.'

Vaslav grimaced.

'Good lad. Stop giving yourself a hard time for missing a shot at a charging target while you've got a crook shoulder, eh? Trust the commander. She'll get the job done.'

'She does seem to have the Emperor's blessings,' added Trieve.

The vox crackled.

'*This is Sergeant Willens of* Vexation's Cure. *You awake over there,* Steel Tread?'

'This is Sergeant Vaslav, stood to and ready, Willens.'

'*Good, because we've got incoming from the direction of the shrine-gardens. Looks as though the enemy's rallied up some reinforcements.*'

Verro checked his vid-feeds. Sure enough, there were hunched figures festooned with bone spikes, hurrying along the slopes of the ziggurats. Their eyes burned with purple light. He felt his stomach drop as he took in the enemy's numbers.

'Understood, Willens,' said Vaslav. 'Let's keep them busy for as long as we can, eh?'

'*My thoughts exactly, Vaslav. Cadia stands!*'

'Yes, she bloody well does,' said the sergeant. 'Trieve, give us a prayer and I'll help you get that loaded.'

The driver was already crouched by one of the tank's few remaining Demolisher shells, burned arms wrapped around it as he strained to lift. His face was a mask of pain.

'Wouldn't you prefer some Cadian jingoism?' he gasped. 'Perhaps a ribald jest?'

'Those are more Nix's thing, Trieve,' said Verro. 'And no, a good Brethian prayer would be just the thing, don't you think?'

Trieve gave him a long look, then nodded. As the sergeant helped him hoist the shell into its sling, and the enemy drew closer, and Verro settled into Chalenboor's station, the Brethian began his prayer.

'Oh God-Emperor, almighty Master of Mankind, though we face this day adversity and know the divine rigour of suffering, know that we offer all we have and all we are to thee, and that we ask only in return for you to bless our

endeavours and aid us in the purgation of those who would
despoil thy holy realm…'

CHAPTER EIGHTEEN

PRIMARY TARGET

The cold upland air stung Etsul's lungs. It might have been refreshing, had it not been for the reek of blood and smoke. Worse were the wafts of perfume and acrid filth that issued from within despoiled priest houses. Those made her feel dizzy and euphoric, yet somehow soiled.

Now that she had disembarked *Steel Tread*, the buildings loomed menacingly on all sides. Etsul felt exposed. The mountain seemed to watch her progress with unfriendly eyes. She thought the sky had no business being so clear and blue on a day so full of death.

Assault Group Aswold moved quickly along stepped back-streets and between higgledy-piggledy structures. The first lieutenant might be in titular command, but Etsul had no doubt this was Sergeant Chasnov's theatre. The Cadian infantry moved with crisp efficiency, flashing hand signals to one another as they flitted from one cover position to the next. They managed to cover every window, rooftop lip and side street with their lasguns. A grizzled veteran stayed on point, eyes hard above the hissing pilot light of his flamer.

Moretzin and Chalenboor stuck protectively close to Etsul, for which she was silently grateful. She, in turn, attempted to stay close to Aswold and his loader, a rangy young Cadian called Wynter whose bare forearms were all tattoos and corded muscle.

Magos Hengh strode along as though marching down the nave of some tech-cathedrum on Mars. His skulls hovered behind him. His monstrous servitor lumbered at his side, crimson targeting beams stabbing from beneath its cowl.

As they halted at an alley corner, the magos made a half-hearted attempt at taking cover. His servitor loomed protectively over him, shielding its master but clearly too bulky and inflexible to hide in its own right. Sergeant Chasnov turned to Aswold.

'If the enemy spot that servitor, they'll spot us all,' she muttered. 'Can we leave it behind?'

Overhearing Chasnov's words, Hengh offered her a green-lensed stare.

'Dismissive: this unit is my assigned saviour unit. Its combat capabilities are prodigious, its loyalty absolute. It will not be "left behind", but it will destroy itself to protect us.'

Etsul winced at the sergeant's expression.

They pressed on, up the flank of a ziggurat and along its topmost tier. As they descended the steps on its opposite side, Etsul saw the gatehouse ahead. It still looked a daunting distance away.

'Magos, how long?' she asked.

'Update: seventeen minutes and thirty-four seconds.'

Etsul exchanged a look with Aswold. He raised his eyebrows and shook his wrist-chrono. She nodded.

They hastened down a long flight of steps then halted, pressing themselves to the walls at a signal from Chasnov. Etsul's heart thumped as she listened to the echoes of clattering equipment and footfalls. She knew the sound of soldiers on the move, but it was frustratingly hard to pin down its origin in the echoing warren of streets.

She glanced at Hengh, again standing in the shadow of his hulking servitor. Etsul considered how quick and messy a firefight would be in the confines of the alley. In that moment she missed *Steel Tread* more than ever. She imagined the Deathstrike streaking through the troposphere, tilting its nose down towards them as it began its death-dive. Moretzin caught her eye, and the loader's steady gaze was somehow reassuring. Etsul let out a slow breath and waited.

The footfalls faded. Chasnov motioned them onward, the flame trooper again taking point. They continued down the winding stair.

'No danger of us losing sight of our objective, at least,' breathed Etsul, unconsciously slowing as she stared in horror at the spectacle ahead.

'In that you are undoubtedly correct,' replied Aswold, sounding nauseated.

'Dreg-dirty heresy is what it is, sir,' said Chalenboor.

Etsul couldn't disagree with her. The rampart above the gatehouse was lit by erupting flares of purple, pink and shimmering silver light. The sky churned with half-glimpsed spectres. Etsul saw suggestions of writhing tentacles and contorting humanoid forms up there. From amidst this spectral mass, bolts of energy struck at targets outside the walls.

'Is that... him? Baraghor, in the flesh?' asked Aswold.

Etsul squinted after Aswold's pointing finger and saw humanoid silhouettes picked out against the sorcerous lights.

Her blood ran cold at the sight of them. Their proportions were all wrong, hulking and distorted in a way that bespoke monstrous strength. They seemed too big, somehow, twisted beings whose inherent wrongness stirred primal fear deep down inside her. Etsul felt a sudden need to be as far away from those half-glimpsed ogres as she could, and it was all she could do to keep her faltering feet moving forward.

The wind changed. It brought with it the hammering sound of gunfire and the roar of explosions from the battle. Louder than either came a discordant cacophony of harmonics that set her teeth on edge. Etsul's head ached.

'What is that damned noise?' she croaked.

'Captain Lothen mentioned sonic weapons,' said Moretzin. Etsul shuddered, and tried not to think about how much worse it would feel as they drew closer to those unclean emanations.

Realising that their group had slowed almost to a walk, she squared her shoulders and hastened on down the alley. Stirred by her example, the others followed, then dropped into cover at another signal from Chasnov. Etsul could hear frantic voices squawking from the portable vox-set on one Cadian trooper's back. The tone told her things were not going well.

'Magos, what's the count?' whispered Aswold.

'Update: sixteen minutes and twelve seconds,' the magos replied. 'At our current pace, our chance of success is decreasing exponentially.'

'Respectfully, sir, we can move quicker,' put in Chasnov. 'If we do, we'll soon be spotted. Sounds like the dance is mostly outside the walls, but I'd not like to gamble on how many heretics are between us and the gatehouse.'

Aswold looked questioningly at Etsul.

She met his gaze steadily.

'The mission is what matters, sir,' she said. 'If it gets choppy, we'll have to fight our way through.'

'Let us move more swiftly then, sergeant,' Aswold ordered. 'There is precious little point in us making it safely to the gatehouse if the Deathstrike missile sails over our heads halfway there, no?'

'Sir,' said Chasnov.

The Cadians increased their speed, passing under an archway festooned with long-withered bunches of devotional flowers. Magos Hengh lengthened his stride to keep pace, while his servitor broke into a shambling lope. The tankers did their best to keep up, Chalenboor looking more at home amongst the backstreets than the rest of them combined. She ducked and jogged, spinning to point her lascarbine down side streets Etsul hadn't even noticed.

They reached ground level without incident and plunged into a winding network of backstreets that took them ever closer to the gatehouse. The structure looked altogether larger and more menacing now that Etsul wasn't sitting in the command seat of her Demolisher.

She tried not to keep glancing skyward.

As they flitted across a cramped and bloodstained square, the magos' servitor gave a sudden bell-like chime. It rotated at the waist and its crimson targeting optics painted a first-floor window across from them.

Servomotors screamed as its cannon barrel spun to life.

'Hostile life signatures acquired, high threat probability cogitated,' blurted Magos Hengh.

The servitor let fly and the stone façade of the priest house's first floor exploded in a storm of stone shrapnel. Etsul saw blood and spinning body parts in the mass.

'Contact, contact, contact!' barked Sergeant Chasnov, brandishing her laspistol. 'Protect the magos and keep moving. Shift your backsides, Cadians!'

Gunfire lit the windows around them. There was no cover in the confined square, but the servitor's salvo seemed to have wrong-footed some unseen enemy ambushers. Etsul saw Spinebacks spilling from priest houses still fumbling with their arming runes. Through a doorway she caught sight of large vox-consoles, operators rising from them in shock.

The element of surprise didn't last long before the air was full of las-blasts and bullets. Three Cadians fell in quick succession. Spinebacks tumbled from windows or were blasted back through open doors. The Cadians' flamer let fly with a breathy roar. The servitor's cannon screamed as it kept firing. Chasnov was shouting something inaudible, but Etsul couldn't mistake the sergeant's straight-arm point towards a nearby opening.

Moretzin grabbed Etsul and propelled her in the direction Chasnov had pointed, shielding her commander with her bulk. The two of them entered a high-ceilinged tunnel. Daylight shone at its far end. The space funnelled the sound of the gunfight into a tidal roar that beat against Etsul's ears. She passed Chalenboor on one knee at the tunnel entrance, snapping off las-rounds that sent Spinebacks tumbling.

Etsul got close behind Aswold, who was supporting his wounded loader. She grimaced at the sight of the large, burn-blackened wound in Wynter's side. Even as she reached out to help, the loader gave a wheezing gurgle and slumped. He almost pulled Aswold off his feet before Etsul grabbed an arm and helped lower the body to the ground.

'Damnation,' said Aswold, shaking his head. Etsul glanced

along the tunnel, to where firefights raged at both ends. Magos Hengh swept past them with a creak of rubberised robes. Moretzin and Chalenboor hovered urgently nearby. Etsul saw the servitor was bringing up the rear, back to them, still firing out into the square. The ghoulish thing was shuddering with bullet impacts. Flames licked at its cowl.

A vivid memory of Mandriga command came to Etsul, and she realised that the servitor might well back right over them without hesitation, so long as it continued to protect its master.

She gripped Aswold's elbow.

'Come on, sir. We'll honour him with duty.' Aswold looked at her, and it hurt her to see the strain behind his eyes.

'That we shall, Lieutenant Etsul. Magos, count?'

'Update: thirteen minutes precisely.'

'How much further to the gatehouse, magos?' asked Etsul.

'Advisory: my cerebral auspex suggests only another five hundred feet, lieutenant commander.'

'You hear that, all of you?' barked Etsul as they hastened along the tunnel. 'We're almost in range for the magos to release his skulls! Just a little further.'

Sergeant Chasnov looked back at her. 'Could be an issue, sir.'

The Cadians had bunched up at the tunnel mouth. They hugged the dubious cover of the walls and fired into the open space beyond. Etsul saw another, larger square, bisected by more enemy barricades. They faced out towards the walls and the gatehouse, but it had evidently been the work of moments for the Spinebacks to take cover along the outer face of their defence line. Still, Etsul thought wearily, a wall was a wall.

She counted at least a dozen Spinebacks, maybe more.

She leant out a little further, only to be dragged backwards by Chasnov. Stubber rounds whipped in from the flank and chewed up the ground where she had stood, peppering them with stone chips.

'There's a railed pulpit up there,' the sergeant explained. 'It's on our right, looks like there's a couple of stone stairways leading up to it. Perfect vantage point for a stubber team. I could hold off a platoon with a position like that.'

A Cadian took a round through the skull and dropped. At Etsul's back, the servitor had almost reached them, still firing, still jerking under impacts. She felt claustrophobia as she had never known inside a tank.

'Malkov, Cheng, Lumley, flank right and knock out that nest. We'll cover.'

At their sergeant's orders, three Cadians burst from cover, the veteran with the flamer taking the lead. They ran hard for the sweeping stairway. Lasguns sang as the rest of Aswold's depleted force gave covering fire. Shots scorched the barricade. Spinebacks ducked, glowing purple eyes leaving afterimages in their wake. Etsul put a round through a heretic's shoulder but saw no sign the wound even troubled him.

One of the Cadians had his legs shot out from under him halfway to the steps. He fell face first and didn't rise. Another made it to the foot of the stairs only to be smashed off her feet by stubber rounds. The flame trooper kept going, making it into range with a bellow of 'Cadia stands!'

He was hit by a fusillade of shots that threw him sideways just as he squeezed his trigger. The jet of blazing promethium went high, but not high enough to spare the stubber team as it engulfed their heads and shoulders. One heretic rose burning and screaming, beating at his skull, then toppled out of sight. The other ran madly into the pulpit railing and pitched over it. His glowing eyes left streaks in the air before he landed head first on the stone floor.

'The stubber's down. Can we rush them?' asked Etsul.

'They're still dug in tight,' said Chasnov. 'We charge that barricade, I can't guarantee any of us makes it alive.'

Etsul turned to ask Aswold for orders. She stopped at the resolute expression on his face. The first lieutenant looked her in the eye and tapped himself thrice on the chest, just above his heart. Then, before Etsul could stop him, he broke from cover and ran for the steps.

'Sir!' she shouted, then, 'Throne, cover him!'

Aswold sprinted. Autogun rounds whipped around him and struck sparks at his heels. Etsul stepped from cover, raised her lascarbine, and sprayed fire on full-auto at the barricade. A scream of mingled frustration, panic and anger ripped from her throat. Moretzin was beside her, firing too. Chalenboor joined the fusillade as the Cadians did likewise.

Shots whipped back at them. Etsul felt a hot lash across her cheek.

She glanced right to see Aswold reach the top of the stairs. He vaulted the sandbags and vanished for a moment. The first lieutenant reappeared, heaving the heavy stubber up onto the pulpit rail, its ammo belt trailing behind it.

She saw the calm expression on his face as he lowered its barrel to point at the Spinebacks.

She saw the first bullet as it tore through the side of his neck.

She saw the second hit him in the chest.

She saw him sway.

Aswold squeezed the heavy stubber's trigger and rained fire on the heretics below. Geysers of gore erupted from behind the barricade.

'Charge!' bellowed Sergeant Chasnov.

Etsul howled a wordless war cry as she ran, a sound of such hate it hardly sounded human. A Spineback rose into a firing position and she put a volley of las-bolts through his rebreather. To her left a Cadian fell, one eye a blackened crater.

Moretzin dropped her augmetic shoulder and roared as she hit the barricade. Bolts tore, metal buckled, and an entire plasteel segment fell with a resounding clang.

Chasnov bowled a frag grenade into the gap. Las-bolts flashed.

'Finish them!' roared Etsul. 'Someone get to the first lieutenant! He–'

'Incoming!' howled Chalenboor, then hit Etsul in a flying tackle and bore her to the ground. There came the shriek of shells falling. The ground shook as explosions filled the square with fire.

Verro hit his firing runes. Bolt-shells blew heretics apart. His station's ammo rune flashed crimson.

'Reload!' he shouted.

'Nothing left,' Trieve replied. 'We have exhausted the Emperor's bounty!'

'Well, that's a damned shame,' growled the sergeant. 'Considering how many dirty heretics there still are to smite. Storm bolter's still got ammo, I'll get on that.'

Verro looked at the crowd of Spinebacks outside, the purple flare of their eyes mocking the Cadians' violet.

'They're all around us, sir. You won't last a minute up there!'

'Won't last much longer if we let them stuff grenades in our intakes, or rip a hatch, either,' replied the sergeant. 'Besides, we need to lend *Vexation's Cure* a hand.'

Verro saw hulking Spinebacks clambering over the crippled Leman Russ, heavy iron hooks in their hands.

'Throne, they're going to open her up.'

Thumps came through the hull. Trieve grabbed the last lascarbine from the arms locker.

'Not just them.'

Verro swallowed a throatful of panic before asking, 'Anything else in there, Trieve?'

'Regretfully, just a couple of frags.'

'Verro, take those,' said the sergeant. 'I promised the commander I'd look after her tank. If the heretics get past me and Trieve, you turn the inside of this place into an abattoir, understand? They don't get *Steel Tread*.'

'Yes, sir,' said Verro, saluting as best he could. Vaslav offered them both a lopsided grin.

'Good lads. Now. Let's die like proper soldiers of the Emperor, eh?'

'He shall know our worth,' said Trieve, a fanatical light in his eyes. Verro nodded. His thoughts were elsewhere, with the commander. Wherever she was right now, he prayed that she would make this count.

Etsul's ears rang. She blinked away dust and grit. She coughed, spat, then managed to push herself into a sitting position. She looked around, bewildered amidst the dust and smoke. Her thoughts came like ice melting to water then suddenly into a rush of scalding steam.

The barricades. The enemy. Aswold!

A figure emerged from the murk. Etsul recognised Chalenboor as the gunner hauled her upright. Chalenboor spoke, but her words were muffled. Etsul thumped the side of her head in frustration, worked her jaw. Chalenboor, realising the problem, shouted louder.

'Sorry, chief. Are you all right?'

321

Etsul caught the words, but she didn't respond. As the air cleared, the ruined remains of the pulpit were revealed. Horathio Aswold lay broken, half buried amidst the rubble. There could be no doubt that he was dead.

Etsul gritted her teeth and turned away. She couldn't grieve now. There wasn't time.

'Readiness report?' she asked Chalenboor, her own words muffled by the ringing in her ears.

'Moretzin's hurt, chief. And the magos is messed up.'

'How long was I out?' Etsul asked with a sudden stab of panic.

'Few seconds,' replied Chalenboor, and something in Etsul's chest relaxed a fraction.

She glanced up through the dust, then aimlessly about herself.

Sorrow tried to swallow her, and she thumped a clenched fist against her thigh. If they had only known there was ordnance incoming...

Her fingers fumbled to where Aswold had tapped himself on the chest. They clanked gently against her flask of Medoch, and she understood. Etsul's jaw clenched. Her knees shook. Chalenboor braced her, shrugging off her commander's grateful look.

'Take me to Hengh,' Etsul said, aware she was probably shouting.

They picked their way through the rubble to where the magos sat propped against a wall. He turned his green-eyed gaze on Etsul as they approached. She saw to her horror that a shard of metal jutted from the side of the magos' head.

Sergeant Chasnov and two of her Cadians stood guard over the fallen tech-priest. Moretzin crouched next to him, clutching her ribs. Half her face was a mask of blood, dust sticking to it like cheap face paint. Etsul wanted to check on her loader first, but time was running out.

'Magos, what's the count?' she asked, as the whistling in her ears faded slowly.

Hengh's voice had developed an unpleasant static rasp when he replied. 'Advisory: my chron has been disrupted. Regrettably, a sizeable fragment of shrapnel has pierced my secondary crania and effected substantial damage to auxiliary cogitational systems. Remote motive actuators are inoperable.'

Etsul looked skyward again through the slowly clearing dust. She wondered whether the shellfire had been friendly or hostile, aimed or simply unfortunate. She felt absurdly like a seer, peering at the heavens in search of portents, praying she wouldn't see the Deathstrike streak uselessly over their heads.

She couldn't keep the impatience from her tone.

'Magos, slow, loud and in Low Gothic. What does that mean?'

'Additional: Unit Epsilon-Three has recovered the targeting units, but with my remote motive actuators negated they are incapable of self-powered flight.'

The magos turned his gaze to his hulking servitor. Auxiliary limbs unfolded from the pulped nightmare of raw flesh and metal that was its body. They gripped the three servo-skulls, their las-lights still glimmering but their grav-impellers clearly dead.

Etsul closed her eyes and let out a long breath.

'Will they still work?'

'Clarification: the problem lies not with the servo-skulls, but with the foreign object lodged within my cranial systems. Without my cogitational oversight, the targeter units cannot operate their gravitic impellers to self-position. The targeters will still work, but they require manual triangulation.'

Chalenboor barked a mirthless laugh.

'How do we do that?' asked Etsul.

'Instructional: three of you will have to bear the skulls physically to locations within operational range and appropriate dispersal. You must then direct the emitters towards the target's vicinity and hold them steady in concert for a slow count of ten seconds. For guaranteed efficacy, recommend two skulls deployed to elevated rooftops to the right and left of the gatehouse, and one upon the structure's external walkway, halfway up the inward face of the structure.'

'The third operator will be within the blast radius?'

'Conjectural: cogitating the height of the gatehouse and relative yield of the missile, they are likely to be within maximum effective dispersal, dependent upon angle of descent and impact.'

Sergeant Chasnov looked dejectedly at Etsul.

The commander returned a fierce glare.

She glanced down at Moretzin, placed a hand on her shoulder.

'How bad is it?'

Moretzin looked up, pain creasing the corners of her eyes. 'Bloody hurts, sir. Think the shock wave made my ribs worse, besides which something hit me in the head.'

'Better get my guess in before things get worse then, eh, soldier?'

Moretzin blinked.

'I reckon you were a dock worker,' Etsul pressed on. 'Lost that arm saving someone rich from a falling cargo container. They fixed you up as thanks.'

Moretzin gaped. Chalenboor spat.

'Do not dreggin' tell me the chief's got it on 'er first guess!'

Moretzin managed a weak chuckle. 'Better luck next time, sir.'

Chalenboor snorted with laughter. Even Etsul managed a hard smile, despite the taste of ashes in her mouth. She looked around at the Cadian infantry and felt satisfaction at their reaction. Chasnov and her troopers might not be in on the joke, but there was no way they were going to give up when a soft gang of tank-rats were still defiant.

'I'll take the right-hand rooftop, sir,' said Chasnov, standing straighter.

'Agreed, and Gunner Chalenboor will take the left,' said Etsul. 'She's fast in a tight spot. As for the gatehouse, that's mine.'

'Chief–' began Chalenboor. Etsul silenced her with a glare.

'Command prerogative, Chalenboor. We get to make stupid decisions, and you all have to live with them.'

Etsul looked at the two remaining Cadian troopers. 'You two guard the magos and my loader. You take a bullet before either of them does, yes?'

She received two aquila salutes.

'Take the skulls, point them at Baraghor, count to ten. Anything else we need to do, magos? Prayers and the like?'

'Imperative: you would not be able to utter the binharic cant necessary, lieutenant. I shall do that from here. Your only task now is to make haste.'

'Then let's end this,' said Etsul. She, Chasnov and Chalenboor grabbed a skull each and set off at a run.

Etsul navigated by the lurid glow of sorcery rising above the rooftops. She hadn't been prepared for the skull's prodigious weight, nor its bulk. She had to carry it tucked firmly under her injured arm, ignoring the way its mandibles jabbed her ribs with every step and how quickly it brought the rotten throb back to her damaged limb. She had only one hand free, in which she carried her laspistol. Etsul prayed with every step that she wouldn't drop the skull, or run into enemies, or be too late. She found herself willing the sky to remain empty for just a few more moments, then just a few more.

More shells fell upon the residential belt. Etsul braced for the killing blast, but the explosions rose somewhere off to her left. She was dimly aware of a firefight lighting up a side street as she sprinted across an intersection, Chalenboor and Chasnov at her heels. As the ringing in her ears continued to lessen, so the sonic bombardment from above increased in volume. Her head pounded with the jarring din. Her nerve endings sparked like severed wires.

An Imperial tank suddenly roared across the mouth of the alley ahead. There came a dreadful sonic spike and the vehicle shuddered, armour buckling, flame bursting from within.

Etsul realised the gatehouse square lay dead ahead. She stumbled to a halt, wincing at the growing ache in her arm. She ignored it – she couldn't shoot left-handed, and there was no way she was abandoning her laspistol this close to an active battle. Chasnov gave her a perfunctory slap on the shoulder then she was gone, cutting right down a narrow alleyway. Chalenboor leaned in and shouted, 'Good luck, chief! Don't be a dregger, yeah?'

Then she too was gone, leaving Etsul alone with a half-formed rejoinder still on her lips. She stared at the mouth of the alleyway, the flare of gunfire and explosions beyond it. She hefted the skull and hissed with pain, then checked the load on her laspistol.

Etsul looked up and froze.

There, in the clear blue sky, burned a star. It grew brighter as she stared.

'No, no, not yet,' she breathed. 'Emperor, just a little more time, please!'

Etsul's first footstep towards danger was hard. As she gained momentum, she felt adrenaline surge. There was no one left to worry about but herself. Her crew would defend *Steel Tread*, or they wouldn't. Chasnov and Chalenboor would make it to their positions in time, or not. All she could do was run, and make it to the walkway in time, then pray it all worked out.

For all the pain she was in, and all the emotional hurts she had suffered, she felt liberated.

She burst from the alleyway into pandemonium. The battle had spilled in through the ruined gates. Cadian transports burned. Geskans sped back and forth on warquads, pillion riders blazing away. Imperial and heretic tanks duelled in the open space, uncaring of those they crushed as they sought to get around one another's flanks for the kill shot. Etsul saw squads of Spinebacks and Cadians trading fire from one freshly blasted shell-crater to the next.

'Fantastic,' she hissed as she dashed into the midst of the violence. She knew better than to hug the buildings, where a stray shell could engulf her in fire or bury her in rubble. Instead, Etsul sprinted through the open. She weaved and jinked, willing the anonymity of massed battle to keep her from the enemy's notice.

A heretic tank swerved towards her and Etsul threw herself aside. Its turret came about, then burst as something armour piercing and packed with high explosive struck it, sending the tank shuddering drunkenly off course, aflame and spewing ichor that reeked like sweat.

Etsul was up again and running, not even feeling the pain of her skinned knees. A bolt of purple lightning tore down from the clouds and into the battle's midst. Blazing wreckage rained around her.

Another sonic howl made her scream, pain lancing through her chest as though her organs were about to burst. The ground behind her detonated in a shower of shattered stone. Another screech and Etsul stumbled, bile rising in her throat. A Spineback stumbled into her path. She shot him through the face then ran on.

Bullets ricocheted around Etsul. Hot pain bit her right calf and she fell into a hop-limp gait that carried her the last ten feet to an archway in the gatehouse wall. She fell shoulder first into cover, breath coming in hot rasps. Her heart thundered. Her head pounded. She didn't dare look up.

'Worry what is...'

Etsul ducked through a doorway and limped up the stairs beyond. The stonework of the gatehouse throbbed with the audial storm coming from above. Cracks leapt through it. There came a thumping throb, the beat of monstrous hearts overlapping in demented arrhythmia. Piercing feedback caused the stairwell's armaglass windows to crack. Etsul felt blood on her top lip.

The stone steps were punishingly steep. She felt as though someone were driving a knife into her right calf with every footfall. Her breath came in angry grunts. The skull's machinery was rubbing her side raw, its polished bone becoming slippery with her sweat and blood as it dragged at her wounded arm. Etsul was about to cast her pistol aside in order to switch her burden to the other arm when a brute in a rebreather appeared at the top of the stairs.

They looked at each other in frank astonishment, then

Etsul shot the heretic in the throat. The Spineback stumbled but didn't fall. He gave a muffled roar and lunged for her. She shot him twice more then fell to one side and let her assailant tumble past her down the steps.

'The Emperor protects,' Etsul spat after him, then turned to see another Spineback above her, autopistol raised.

Tortured harmonics pulsed from on high as the Heretic Astartes unleashed their grotesque sonic weapons. The stairwell shook with their power as though in the grip of an earthquake. The heretics' wildfire filled the stairwell.

A shot clipped Etsul's shoulder. Another ripped through her side and made her scream. Another still took a chunk from the meat under her left bicep. Etsul almost fell, almost lost her grip on the skull before she loosed a hail of shots into her attacker.

He collapsed backwards and didn't rise.

Etsul resumed her limping climb.

She could feel her strength draining away with her oozing blood. She was going numb. Exhaustion dragged at her as the sonic bombardment from above raged on.

'No.' She gasped the simple negation with each step she climbed, unable even to hear herself now over the whine and roar. 'No. No. No.'

Suddenly, blessedly, she was at the top of the stairs. Etsul limped out onto the walkway, soaked in sweat and gore, oblivious to the battle below. The din from all around was a hurricane and she walked within its eye. Her nerves jangled with agony.

'No,' she grunted, forcing her legs to keep working. '*No*,' she snarled as her body threatened collapse. Etsul limped along the walkway until she was dead centre beneath the gatehouse rampart. She glanced out at the nearby rooftops and felt a vicious smile creep across her face as she saw the telltale twinkle of two red lasers.

She looked up and the star blazed, closer with every breath. She couldn't see Baraghor or his retinue from this angle, but the thunder-pulse of their weapons and the infernal glow of the arch-heretic's sorcery left her in no doubt that they stood on the inner gatehouse rampart directly above.

After everything, Etsul was glad to be spared the sight of Baraghor's corrupt form.

Swaying, leaning heavily on the railing, she raised the skull and pointed the laser at her target.

'One…' she croaked. 'Two… Three…'

Below, the battle raged. Something exploded, hard enough to shake the walkway. Etsul kept her aim steady.

'Four… Five… Six… Seven…'

Something moved in her peripheral vision. She couldn't lower the skull, didn't dare look. She simply raised her las-pistol, thought *God-Emperor please*, and pulled the trigger.

A hail of las-light flashed as Etsul emptied the pistol's cell.

The shape vanished, if it had ever been there at all.

The spent pistol fell from her numb fingers and clattered off the walkway.

'Eight… Nine…'

The star resolved into a black speck trailing a tongue of flame.

'Ten…'

Still Etsul didn't lower the skull. She continued to hold it, her chest heaving with each breath. There was no indication it had worked. She wondered if they had come too late.

Then she saw the star above her flare and begin to grow rapidly as it plummeted towards the gatehouse. High above, the sorcerous energies churned and flurried, heliotrope lightning stabbing at the falling missile to no effect. It plunged onward, trailing the arcing energies like a broken spider's web.

There was no time to escape. Etsul slid down the railing and landed in a sitting position with a bump. There came the flash of a memory, her mother the night after the ork raid that had so changed Tsegoh. She recalled that typhoon of a woman reduced to a pale shadow, one burned claw reaching for her hand. She remembered the wheezing words.

'I know... you'll... make us proud.'

Etsul had volunteered for the tithe just days later. Half her world's population had done the same. Her father had been too lost in misery to stop her. And then she'd been gone. She wasn't sure, even now, if the years after that had been spent trying to fulfil her mother's dying wish, or seeking to escape it.

Knowing there was no time for anything more, Etsul wearily raised a hand to tap the flask in her pocket thrice.

'To your last voyage, Horathio Aswold,' she murmured.

From above came a blinding flash, a battering wave of heat and light and force.

Etsul felt herself tumbling as the world came apart around her.

It was enough.

EPILOGUE

Chalenboor looked down at the cards in her hand. Her expression was unreadable in the green gloom beneath the trees. Her eyes flicked up to meet his, then back down to her hand. She drew out three dog-eared cards and slapped them face up on the equipment crate.

'Saint an' Geminae,' she announced. 'An' no blamin' your shoulder for you losin' again, yeah?'

Verro stared glumly at Chalenboor's cards. The angel-winged Saint brandished her burning blade, looking improbably heroic. The lesser seraphs flanked her with their pistols drawn. He looked at his own calamitous hand and set his cards aside.

'I swear you smuggle bad cards into my hand before every game, Nix. I don't know how you do it, but...'

She answered with a feral grin. 'Nah, mate, you're just the unluckiest dregger I know. Why d'you think I play this with you so often?'

Verro pulled an expression of comic sorrow. 'But Gunner Chalenboor, my shoulder, you know...'

He ducked, laughing as Chalenboor threw her tin mug at his head. Verro bent to retrieve the drinking vessel, ignoring the stares of a Cadian squad marching past. Their glances didn't bother him, but the annoyed glare of the medicae from across the footway made him feel a little guilty. Since the survivors of Operation Jotunn had regrouped, Sabre Camp had heard plenty of vox-piped prayers, crackling lasgun drills and the howl of Valkyrie jets.

Laughter had been in short supply.

'Best of three?' he asked. Chalenboor eyed him.

'Best o' three was three games ago, mate.'

'Best of seven then? It's not like we're going anywhere.'

They both looked over to where *Steel Tread* sat encased in a repair frame. Engineers had dug the venerable tank its own earthwork behind its crew's tent, and had strung camo netting and flakboard about it to augment the protection of the thick canopy. Every machine that had survived the attack on Baraghor's stronghold had been similarly honoured, but not all of them had had Magos Hengh oversee their repairs personally.

Several of the magos' servitors were toiling around the Demolisher even now, putting the finishing touches to their work. Verro could see the honorific 'Giant-killers' stencilled in Gothic script below the turret ring. It made him smile.

'She ain't far off done now, though,' said Chalenboor. 'Lucky, considerin' the mess you ductwits made of 'er.'

Verro shuddered as he remembered heretics scrambling over the hull, the sergeant slamming the top hatch open and gunning the storm bolter, Trieve squirming up to cover his back with the last lascarbine. Verro remembered waiting in red-lit gloom to see their legs convulse as they were killed, and then to keep his promise and pull the pins on his grenades as the heretics spilled into the tank.

He would have done it. Verro had no doubt about that. But before he'd had to there had come the thunderclap of a titanic detonation away to the south. The attackers had faltered, then those amongst them with the burning purple eyes had gone wild, tearing at the traitors around them. And then had come a column of Geskans to join the fight. Verro was sure that he would feel like weeping with relief every time he heard a warquad, from now until his dying day.

He just wished *Vexation's Cure* had made it too. The last screams of its crew over the vox would haunt him for a long time, he knew.

'Garret? Mate?' Chalenboor's verbal prod brought him out of his reverie.

'You should have seen them fight, Nix. You wouldn't joke if you'd been there. Throne, even Trieve...' He shook his head and blew out a breath.

'Yeah, well, don't start writin' poems 'bout it just yet, mate. Speakin' o' Preacher.'

Verro followed her gaze and saw Trieve trudging along the dirt track between the nodding guasa trees. The driver had his prayer book tucked under one arm and his aquila hanging down the front of his tank suit. The medicae compress encasing his neck and the right side of his jaw was a match for the one wrapped around Verro's shoulder.

Verro offered Trieve a nod. The driver returned it, then winced.

'Still sufferin' for the Emperor, Preacher?' asked Chalenboor.

Trieve replied with a thin-lipped smile. 'He sees all our sacrifices, Chalenboor. Even yours.'

'What's the word?' asked Verro.

'More brothers and sisters than ever at prayer today. Several official priests joined me. Some of it is the influx from the reinforcement column, of course, but...'

'It's you, isn't it?' asked Verro. 'They're coming to see you lead the prayers.'

'Not me, Verro. Only the borrowed mantle I wear. That is hers.'

'Nah,' said Chalenboor, and Verro was surprised at the sincerity in her voice. 'None o' that, Preacher. You're a Giant-killer, same as the rest of us, yeah?'

Awkward silence settled between the three of them. Trieve cleared his throat and grimaced.

'Would you consider teaching me your game?'

Verro raised his eyebrows to Chalenboor. She returned the gesture.

'Isn't it, like, vice or whatever? Y'know, havin' fun?'

Trieve's thin smile resurfaced. 'I think the God-Emperor would understand. Besides, someone has to prevent you two from laying real wagers and landing the crew back in disrepute.'

'So, you're only doing this to *stop* us having fun?' Verro asked.

'Suffering is to a Brethian as prayer,' quoted Trieve. Chalenboor snorted with laughter. Verro gaped, unable to remember a time when Trieve had assayed an actual joke.

'Please, Preacher, fold out a stool,' he said. Trieve did so. Chalenboor began shuffling the cards.

'Any more news from the prayer circle?' asked Verro. These past days, it had become apparent that Trieve's new-found popularity as an unofficial preacher loosened the tongues of those who attended his gatherings.

'Psykana division made their report at last,' he said.

'Really?' asked Verro. 'Mandriga command's back to that level of functionality?'

'Evidently,' said Trieve.

Chalenboor rolled her eyes.

'So…?' Verro prompted. Trieve enjoyed making them work for his information.

'Nothing we could not surmise, I suppose,' said Trieve. 'Baraghor took a great risk, exposing himself as he did. His demise triggered almost instant discord amongst his lieutenants. Some fought on against us, while others turned upon one another, or simply turned tail altogether. With their casualties already so severe, and their and our ranks so intermingled, it was good Imperial faith and discipline that won the day. They fell apart just as command hoped they would.'

'An' then we got our own back on the filthy dreggers,' spat Chalenboor with relish. 'What a bloodbath.'

'We lost a lot more before they stopped fighting, though,' Verro reminded them, with another guilty glance at the medicae tents.

'The rewards of heresy are ever a bitter harvest,' said Trieve loftily.

'I just said that, just less fancy,' exclaimed Chalenboor to Verro. 'Why you always got to make it fancy, Preacher?'

'Because he thinks it makes him sound intelligent,' came Moretzin's voice. Verro looked up to see her clambering from one of *Tread*'s side hatches. The loader's tank suit was rolled down to the waist, exposing the bandages still wrapped tightly around her middle. Her skin was streaked with sweat and engine oil. She carried a large wrench in her mechanical hand as she ambled over to join them.

'It takes little enough effort to sound more intelligent

than–' started Trieve. Moretzin set her wrench down next to him with a thump, making tin mugs rattle. She checked the pot of recaff stewing over their small chem-fire.

'Be nice, Preacher,' she said. 'Deal me in, Nix. We teaching this one to play?'

Chalenboor riffled the cards. Verro smiled disarmingly at Moretzin.

'We are, but take it easy on us, eh?'

'Why? You got shot in the shoulder, not the head,' she chuckled.

'As though that would have made a difference,' muttered Trieve.

'Hoi, stop nickin' my jokes,' cried Chalenboor.

A shadow fell across their game. Verro looked up to see Sergeant Vaslav eyeing the cards disapprovingly.

'No bets, sir,' Verro reassured him. 'We're just educating Isaac.'

The sergeant's eyes flicked to the Brethian, who nodded and winced. Vaslav idly scratched the healing mass of scar tissue that was his left cheek.

'Will wonders never cease,' he harrumphed. 'Well. Enjoy your game today. Tomorrow we've got orders to get *Tread* ready to roll out.'

Verro wasn't the only one to sit up straighter at this.

'Any word on where, sir?' he asked.

'According to Captain Na'Koriss, the army group's headed north to join the push on Hive Joragh,' answered the sergeant.

'Rumours were right then. We're taking it back, sir?' asked Moretzin.

'That's the plan. The enemy in the South Peninsula theatre are still in complete disarray, apparently. Champions all at one another's throats. I suspect they've inflicted more casualties on themselves than we have these past two weeks. But for how much longer? Baraghor's death opened a window, and I reckon command are determined to move before it closes again.'

'Small wonder, then, that we have been so greatly reinforced,' Trieve observed. 'The time draws nigh to deliver the Emperor's vengeance upon the heretics.'

'Don't forget our own vengeance, Preacher,' said Verro. 'I've got scores of my own to settle with them.'

'We'll be strictly reserves for now, so don't get too excited,' said the sergeant. '*Tread* might be back on form, but it'll be a few weeks yet before her crew are.'

'Yeah, but who's sittin' in the chair, boss?' asked Chalenboor. 'Is the chief up to it?'

'That's my other reason for interrupting your little party, Chalenboor,' said Vaslav, expression stern. 'On your feet and stand to attention. Time to meet your new commander.'

Verro saw Chalenboor's face fall. His heart sank into his feet. Commander Etsul had been pulled from the wreckage of the courtyard in such bad condition that her survival had been hailed a miracle of the God-Emperor. Since then, they had heard little of their commander, despite repeated requests for information to the medicae, Captain Na'Koriss and anyone else who would tolerate them. No one had come to tell them Commander Etsul had perished from her wounds, but equally, amidst the bustle of a camp preparing for a major offensive, they hadn't been told of her recovery either. Now, it sounded as though whatever condition Etsul was in, she had not recovered sufficiently to rejoin her unit. Verro wouldn't be surprised to learn that she never would. He tried not to think of all they had been through since her arrival, and of what another unfamiliar hand at the tiller might do to shatter the fragile accord the crew had struck.

It was with a crestfallen air that they stood. Then a voice came from behind Sergeant Vaslav, and Verro gaped.

'New commander, sergeant? Whoever they are, they had best be ready to fight me for that seat.'

Vaslav turned and saluted, eyes twinkling. Etsul saw the others beyond him, offering salutes of their own and grinning unashamedly.

She limped towards them, leaning heavily on her crutches. The whine-thump of her bionic leg was going to take some getting used to, provided her body didn't reject the damned thing altogether. More difficult by far, though, was seeing through one organic eye and one crimson lens. Etsul was sure the information scrolling across her vision would come in useful eventually. For now, it confused her depth perception and reminded her quite how badly she had been hurt.

The medicae had taken great pains to elaborate more than once how lucky she had been. The walkway might not have sheared away from the structure of the gatehouse. The missile might have hit at a different angle and swallowed her in its blast-cone. The God-Emperor had blessed her, was the accepted wisdom. The thought gave Etsul a little frisson of wonder every time it came to her.

'Well, sir, I reckon we made a mess of this when you turned up the first time,' explained Vaslav. 'I thought, you know, fresh start.'

'And you wanted to see the crew's faces,' she said in a tone of mock reproof.

'And that, sir,' he said, with a lopsided grin.

'How do you feel, sir?' asked Verro.

'They only just let me out of the medicae tent,' she replied. 'I'm assured I have been technically dead twice in the past week alone, and I've got medicae compresses on what feels like most of my body. How do you suppose I feel, Gunner Verro?'

She couldn't keep a straight face for long, despite the pain she was in. As Etsul cracked a smile, she saw her crew relax by a degree.

'Good to have you back, sir,' said Moretzin. 'We weren't sure you'd make it.'

Etsul sighed heavily. 'Enough good soldiers died these past days to fill the Emperor's harbour, Moretzin. I don't think they had room left for me.'

She felt her smile fade at the memory of Horathio Aswold's last moments. She offered up a silent prayer for him to save her a seat in the dockside tavern. She would have to introduce him to Masenwe, when she finally got there. She knew they would get on.

Realising her crew's expressions had sobered with her own, Etsul tried to brighten up. She leaned on one crutch and gestured to their abandoned game.

'Well, for Throne's sakes, are you going to make me lean on these damned sticks all day? These medals they've pinned on my suit are heavy! Someone get me a seat and deal me in.'

Chalenboor laughed. Moretzin grabbed Etsul a stool and folded it out for her. She lowered her weight into it with a groan of relief, then gestured for Vaslav to join them. The sergeant hesitated.

'Sir, the Commissariat frown on excessive fraternisation.'

'We're injured war heroes, sergeant,' she said, grinning. 'Let us enjoy the perks of our fame while they last, eh? Besides, if anyone asks, I am simply having my crew instruct me in this game so that I can keep an eye out for gambling. I cannot police what I don't understand.'

'That's what Trieve said, too, sir,' observed Verro. The driver cleared his throat again with a rasp and a wince.

Still, Vaslav hovered.

'Come on, sergeant, are you worried you fine Cadians will be beaten by a Tsegohan?' she teased.

Vaslav grabbed the last of their complement of camp stools and thumped it down next to Verro. He smiled ruefully.

'I hear we're all equal in the Emperor's eyes, sir.'

'So are all who fight in His name, sergeant,' she replied. 'Cadia stands so long as we do.'

'Yeah, except Garret. God-Emperor thinks he's an idiot,' said Chalenboor, poker-faced.

Etsul laughed with the rest of them while Verro turned red. Moretzin doled out steaming mugs of recaff. They all looked to her. Their commander.

She raised her mug.

'To Horathio Aswold, and to Olgher Jorgens, and their crews, and to all of those who gave their lives for victory. They made us proud.'

Mugs clinked. A little recaff spattered the crate.

'And to Commander Holtz, may I do honour to his memory,' added Etsul. Vaslav gave her a grateful look, then they all sipped their drinks.

Chalenboor coughed and fanned her face. 'Dreg me, who toasts with boilin' hot recaff?'

'Crews with the brains not to drink still-shine on duty, Nix,' replied Verro.

'Your mother drank still-shine on duty,' she shot back at him.

Etsul laughed again, then winced. She knew the war was far from done. A victory in one theatre was hardly a world conquered. Indeed, their war would never be over. There would always be another battlefield, another planet, and their luck would run out one by one, or else all at once. That was life in the Imperial Guard.

But Etsul would fight all the same. She wouldn't do it for the memory of dead worlds, or for the ones they'd lost, or even, God-Emperor forgive her, for this cold and unforgiving thing they called an Imperium. She would fight for the living, for her comrades and her crew, and she would enjoy the good days when she got them.

It was enough for now. And in the Astra Militarum, she thought, you worried what was, and let the rest go.

ABOUT THE AUTHOR

Andy Clark has written the Warhammer
40,000 novels *Fist of the Imperium, Kingsblade,
Knightsblade* and *Shroud of Night*, as well as
the Dawn of Fire novel *The Gate of Bones* and
the novella *Crusade*. He has also written the
novels *Gloomspite* and *Blacktalon: First Mark* for
Warhammer Age of Sigmar, and the Warhammer
Quest Silver Tower novella *Labyrinth of the Lost*.
He lives in Nottingham, UK.

YOUR
NEXT READ

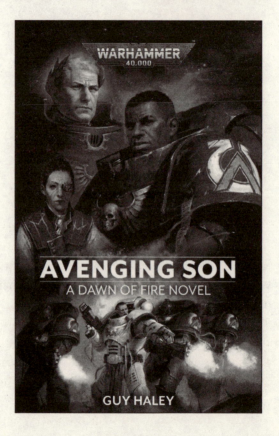

AVENGING SON
by Guy Haley

As the Indomitus Crusade spreads out across the galaxy, one battlefleet must face a dread Slaughter Host of Chaos. Their success or failure may define the very future of the crusade – and the Imperium.

An extract from
Avenging Son
by Guy Haley

'I was there at the Siege of Terra,' Vitrian Messinius would say in his later years.

'I was there…' he would add to himself, his words never meant for ears but his own. 'I was there the day the Imperium died.'

But that was yet to come.

'To the walls! To the walls! The enemy is coming!' Captain Messinius, as he was then, led his Space Marines across the Penitent's Square high up on the Lion's Gate. 'Another attack! Repel them! Send them back to the warp!'

Thousands of red-skinned monsters born of fear and sin scaled the outer ramparts, fury and murder incarnate. The mortals they faced quailed. It took the heart of a Space Marine to stand against them without fear, and the Angels of Death were in short supply.

'Another attack, move, move! To the walls!'

They came in the days after the Avenging Son returned,

emerging from nothing, eight legions strong, bringing the bulk of their numbers to bear against the chief entrance to the Imperial Palace. A decapitation strike like no other, and it came perilously close to success.

Messinius' Space Marines ran to the parapet edging the Penitent's Square. On many worlds, the square would have been a plaza fit to adorn the centre of any great city. Not on Terra. On the immensity of the Lion's Gate, it was nothing, one of hundreds of similarly huge spaces. The word 'gate' did not suit the scale of the cityscape. The Lion's Gate's bulk marched up into the sky, step by titanic step, until it rose far higher than the mountains it had supplanted. The gate had been built by the Emperor Himself, they said. Myths detailed the improbable supernatural feats required to raise it. They were lies, all of them, and belittled the true effort needed to build such an edifice. Though the Lion's Gate was made to His design and by His command, the soaring monument had been constructed by mortals, with mortal hands and mortal tools. Messinius wished that had been remembered. For men to build this was far more impressive than any godly act of creation. If men could remember that, he believed, then perhaps they would remember their own strength.

The uncanny may not have built the gate, but it threatened to bring it down. Messinius looked over the rampart lip, down to the lower levels thousands of feet below and the spread of the Anterior Barbican.

Upon the stepped fortifications of the Lion's Gate was armour of every colour and the blood of every loyal primarch. Dozens of regiments stood alongside them. Aircraft filled the sky. Guns boomed from every quarter. In the churning redness on the great roads, processional ways so huge they were akin to prairies cast in rockcrete, were flashes of gold where the Emperor's Custodian Guard battled. The might of the Imperium was gathered there, in the palace where He dwelt.

There seemed moments on that day when it might not be enough.

The outer ramparts were carpeted in red bodies that writhed and heaved, obscuring the great statues adorning the defences and covering over the guns, an invasive cancer consuming reality. The enemy were legion. There were too many foes to defeat by plan and ruse. Only guns, and will, would see the day won, but the defenders were so pitifully few.

Messinius called a wordless halt, clenched fist raised, seeking the best place to deploy his mixed company, veterans all of the Terran Crusade. Gunships and fighters sped overhead, unleashing deadly light and streams of bombs into the packed daemonic masses. There were innumerable cannons crammed onto the gate, and they all fired, rippling the structure with false earthquakes. Soon the many ships and orbital defences of Terra would add their guns, targeting the very world they were meant to guard, but the attack had come so suddenly; as yet they had had no time to react.

The noise was horrendous. Messinius' audio dampers were at maximum and still the roar of ordnance stung his ears. Those humans that survived today would be rendered deaf. But he would have welcomed more guns, and louder still, for all the defensive fury of the assailed palace could not drown out the hideous noise of the daemons – their sighing hisses, a billion serpents strong, and chittering, screaming wails. It was not only heard but sensed within the soul, the realms of spirit and of matter were so intertwined. Messinius' being would be forever stained by it.

Tactical information scrolled down his helmplate, near

environs only. He had little strategic overview of the situation. The vox-channels were choked with a hellish screaming that made communication impossible. The noosphere was disrupted by etheric backwash spilling from the immaterial rifts the daemons poured through. Messinius was used to operating on his own. Small-scale, surgical actions were the way of the Adeptus Astartes, but in a battle of this scale, a lack of central coordination would lead inevitably to defeat. This was not like the first Siege, where his kind had fought in Legions.

He called up a company-wide vox-cast and spoke to his warriors. They were not his Chapter-kin, but they would listen. The primarch himself had commanded that they do so.

'Reinforce the mortals,' he said. 'Their morale is wavering. Position yourselves every fifty yards. Cover the whole of the south-facing front. Let them see you.' He directed his warriors by chopping at the air with his left hand. His right, bearing an inactive power fist, hung heavily at his side. 'Assault Squad Antiocles, back forty yards, single firing line. Prepare to engage enemy breakthroughs only on my mark. Devastators, split to demi-squads and take up high ground, sergeant and sub-squad prime's discretion as to positioning and target. Remember our objective, heavy infliction of casualties. We kill as many as we can, we retreat, then hold at the Penitent's Arch until further notice. Command squad, with me.'

Command squad was too grand a title for the mismatched crew Messinius had gathered around himself. His own officers were light years away, if they still lived.

'Doveskamor, Tidominus,' he said to the two Aurora Marines with him. 'Take the left.'

'Yes, captain,' they voxed, and jogged away, their green armour glinting orange in the hell-light of the invasion.

The rest of his scratch squad was comprised of a communications specialist from the Death Spectres, an Omega Marine with a penchant for plasma weaponry, and a Raptor holding an ancient standard he'd taken from a dusty display.

'Why did you take that, Brother Kryvesh?' Messinius asked, as they moved forward.

'The palace is full of such relics,' said the Raptor. 'It seems only right to put them to use. No one else wanted it.'

Messinius stared at him.

'What? If the gate falls, we'll have more to worry about than my minor indiscretion. It'll be good for morale.'

The squads were splitting to join the standard humans. Such was the noise many of the men on the wall had not noticed their arrival, and a ripple of surprise went along the line as they appeared at their sides. Messinius was glad to see they seemed more firm when they turned their eyes back outwards.

'Anzigus,' he said to the Death Spectre. 'Hold back, facilitate communication within the company. Maximum signal gain. This interference will only get worse. See if you can get us patched in to wider theatre command. I'll take a hardline if you can find one.'

'Yes, captain,' said Anzigus. He bowed a helm that was bulbous with additional equipment. He already had the access flap of the bulky vox-unit on his arm open. He withdrew, the aerials on his power plant extending. He headed towards a systems nexus on the far wall of the plaza, where soaring buttresses pushed back against the immense weight bearing down upon them.

Messinius watched him go. He knew next to nothing

about Anzigus. He spoke little, and when he did, his voice was funereal. His Chapter was mysterious, but the same lack of familiarity held true for many of these warriors, thrown together by miraculous events. Over their years lost wandering in the warp, Messinius had come to see some as friends as well as comrades, others he hardly knew, and none he knew so well as his own Chapter brothers. But they would stand together. They were Space Marines. They had fought by the returned primarch's side, and in that they shared a bond. They would not stint in their duty now.

Messinius chose a spot on the wall, directing his other veterans to left and right. Kryvesh he sent to the mortal officer's side. He looked down again, out past the enemy and over the outer palace. Spires stretched away in every direction. Smoke rose from all over the landscape. Some of it was new, the work of the daemon horde, but Terra had been burning for weeks. The Astronomican had failed. The galaxy was split in two. Behind them in the sky turned the great palace gyre, its deep eye marking out the throne room of the Emperor Himself.

'Sir!' A member of the Palatine Guard shouted over the din. He pointed downwards, to the left. Messinius followed his wavering finger. Three hundred feet below, daemons were climbing. They came upwards in a triangle tipped by a brute with a double rack of horns. It clambered hand over hand, far faster than should be possible, flying upwards, as if it touched the side of the towering gate only as a concession to reality. A Space Marine with claw locks could not have climbed that fast.

'Soldiers of the Imperium! The enemy is upon us!'